LONER

HARLOE RAE

Editing: Librum Arts Editorial Services
Cover Artist: BookCoverKingdom (www.bookcoverkingdom.com)
Photographer: Rafa G. Catalá
Cover Model: Christian Perez
Interior Design: Champagne Book Design

NOVELS BY
HARLOE RAE

Reclusive Standalones

Redefining Us

Forget You Not

#BitterSweetHeat Standalones

Gent

Miss

Lass

Watch Me Follow

Ask Me Why

Breaker

Keeper

Loner

This book is dedicated to all those fighting for a better tomorrow.
To remaining optimistic during the hardest of times.
To sticking together when crumbling is easier.
To being positive and uplifting.
To patience and compassion.
To lending a helping hand.
To brighter days.
To community.
To you.

PLAYLIST

"Stay Awake" by Dean Lewis

"Free Spirit" by Khalid

"Conversations in the Dark" by John Lennon

"Don't Let It Break Your Heart" by Louis Tomlinson

"Falling" by Harry Styles

"Put A Little Love On Me" by Niall Horan

"Best Part of Me" by Ed Sheeran and Yebba

"Lover (Remix)" by Taylor Swift

"Somebody to Love" by One Republic

"You Can't Stop the Girl" by Bebe Rexha

"Rescue Me" by One Republic

"Just Friends" by JORDY

"Hate Me" by Ellie Goulding

"I'm a Mess" by Bebe Rexha

"I Found You" by Andy Grammar

"Good Stuff" by Griff

"I'm a firm believer that hugging is underrated. Such a simple gesture, that might begin as nothing more than a quick greeting, can change an entire outlook. Offer the healing of an embrace and see."

—Keegan Daniels

"Everyone deserves a chance to be rescued."

That's the mantra I'm repeating when a well-equipped biker pulls over to save me. One glance at the scowl Crawford Doxe is wearing proves he isn't impressed with the task. My efforts to change his mind deflate faster than the shredded tire at our feet. But disgruntled or not, my so-called hero still agrees to fix my flat.

I don't expect to see Crawford again, but he's suddenly very visible in our small town. Avoiding him would be my preference. That's not how this story goes. For whatever reason, my daughter finds an ally in the broody mechanic. Denying her is something I do my best to avoid. I can only hope Crawford's shine wears off before he tarnishes what little trust still exists.

As if the odds are ever on my side.

Commitments are a foreign concept to him. He doesn't make any promises to try. That should've been enough for me to steer clear. It most certainly isn't.

What follows can only be described as a disastrous clash of epic proportions.

But one indisputable fact remains. That lone soul has no plans of opening his heart.

PROLOGUE

Keegan

Healing Hug #1: The instant rush of comfort that's bonded between mother and daughter.

A SHADOW DANCES ACROSS THE FLOOR AS I PUSH THE DOOR OPEN. *Within seconds, passionate moans assault my ears. The stench of lust-fueled sweat reeks of infidelity and hangs in the air. Skin slaps to an erotic rhythm that singes my cheeks. What remains of my trust shatters at the sight of two bodies joining, neither of them mine.*

The memory sizzles from my mind with a searing burn.

I rip another shirt off a hanger and toss it over my shoulder. It's a surprise I can control my hands with the amount of trembling anger rattling through me. This bubbling fury is unlike anything I've ever experienced. Sure, I've been mad in the past. Pissed to the extreme at certain points. But this? A whole new level of rage is shooting to the surface, hot enough to scald my skin.

How dare he? After everything I've put up with, he's the one to throw down the gauntlet. Why did he bother keeping me around this long? How could I let so many transgressions slip by me? Where are we supposed to go now? The questions only succeed in boiling my blood hotter. I'm digging for my favorite pair of jeans when a thick cloud of Kirk's cedar cologne chokes me. The shock of his scent squeezes my lungs and another burst of fire flares. Nausea swirls in my gut, but I force the bile down.

Because of my chronic habit of choosing the worst men, we're being forced to uproot our lives once again. The haste to do so twitches my fingers as I reach for more clothes. The one silver lining to Kirk's rigid rules is we don't have a lot of personal belongings to pack. This pitiful pile in front of me is the extent of my wardrobe. Millie's toys are already in storage crates for easy organization. We can be gone without a trace in less than thirty minutes.

I scan the room, a fresh wave of unwanted tears blurring my vision. The luxurious condo has always been a bit ostentatious for my taste. Kirk required every pristine inch to remain spotless no matter what. Endless white walls and carpet aren't kid-friendly. Fingerprints and smudges weren't tolerated. It was a daily challenge to ensure this place stayed in immaculate condition. But with an entire wall of windows facing the lake, I didn't complain too hard. I overlooked a lot of things because of that rose-tinted view he offered, and the false promises made.

A tidal wave of guilt crashes over me. We should've left at the first signs of this being a restrictive situation. How did I allow this to continue? My daughter has been in this stifling environment for almost a year. Millie's continued refusal to communicate with Kirk should have been all the proof I needed. She's never been a chatty child, quite the opposite if I'm being honest, but total silence from her isn't the norm. It probably didn't help matters that he never attempted to form a relationship with her, even in the most basic sense. That just goes to show how blind I've been.

How could I get involved with a man so callous and selfish? Does loyalty mean nothing? I know the answer. To a man like Kirk, the value is less than zero. He didn't even have the decency to look guilty when I caught him balls deep in that busty redhead. Turns out he's been cheating on me with her for months. Such an arrogant asshole.

At this moment, albeit far too late, there's a glaring fact

I can no longer deny: all of this is my fault. Kirk offered a flimsy sense of security and financial comfort I couldn't afford otherwise. I wanted to believe so badly that he could be the one. Memories of my parents, forever meant to be together, kept the faith of true love alive. Reality is a much larger pill to choke down when all evidence pointed to the contrary.

Being on my own since eighteen had me growing up faster than most. I wasn't granted the luxury of a cushy introduction to adulthood with opportunities at every turn. The road has been far from smooth. Since Millie was born, I've tried my damndest to create a better life for us. I'm ashamed of myself and the weakness I've shown.

But that all changes today.

"Mama?" The soft voice is laced with hesitancy.

I immediately pause my mechanical efforts and glance behind me. My daughter stands in the doorway, her lips tugging low into a deep frown. The shirts in my grip drop to the floor as I turn toward her. I kneel and beckon her into my open arms. "Come here, baby girl."

Millie's stride toward me is slow and cautious, her hesitancy a knife to my heart. Once she folds against my chest, I rub her back in soothing circles, humming a quiet tune she enjoys at bedtime.

This innocent girl has already seen too much hardship in her six short years. I should've done better by her from the beginning. I clearly needed a wake-up call in the form of him seeking pleasure between another woman's thighs. Maybe I should be thanking Kirk for his infidelity.

After a few moments, Millie lifts her head and blinks at me. "Are we leaving?"

"Yes, sweetie."

"Why?"

"We need to find our own place."

Long lashes fan her cheeks. "Okay."

"Would you rather stay?" I swallow the ball of fire in my throat.

"No." One word has never held so much unwavering certainty.

I put a finger under Millie's chin, lifting until she's looking at me. "This was never a true home for us, huh?"

"Not really." Her voice is barely a whisper.

A breezy chill creeps along my spine, and I try not to shiver. This apartment has always been cold. And unwelcoming. "I'm very sorry, Millie."

She bobs a slim shoulder, offering me a jerky shrug. "It's fine."

Another fissure splits me apart. "It's really not, but I'm gonna make it up to you."

"How?"

I tighten my arms around her tiny form, wrapping us in a warm embrace. "Hugging is a good start."

"It heals the hurt," she murmurs against my chest.

I kiss the top of her forehead. "Exactly, baby girl. We stick together and all else will follow."

"Where are we going?"

"We're moving to an adorable small town where everyone is super nice. It's called Silo Springs. Isn't that a fun name?"

"Uh-huh. I like it."

"So do I. My friend lives there and will help us settle in. They have great schools, too. You'll meet a bunch of kids in class this fall. We'll start fresh. Does that sound good?"

"Yes, Mama. Can we go right away?"

"Sure can, sweetie."

"Can Bearly come with?"

The mention of her beloved stuffed animal makes me grin. "Of course. He's part of the family."

"And we protect our family." The amount of conviction she puts behind her words makes my pride swell three sizes.

I squeeze her a bit closer. "That's right, baby girl. I love you so much."

"Too much, Mama," she wheezes extra loud, adding a wiggle for show.

With a groan, I release her from my hold. "Never grow up, okay?"

"Why do you always say that?"

"Because I mean it. Being an adult isn't all cupcakes and rainbows." *That's the understatement of this century.*

"All right, Mama. I'll be your little girl forever."

"Cross your heart?"

"Uh-huh, yeah." She clears her throat. "Mama?"

"Yes, sweet girl?"

"Can we get a puppy?"

My heart clenches at her meek question. I swallow the growing lump in my dry throat. "M–maybe?"

"Maybe really means no." Her deepening frown threatens to break me.

I blow out a stream of air rather than release more flimsy excuses. She's right to call me out—I've been putting off getting her a pet for years. The timing never seems right, but who's to say it ever will be? I brush my thumb down her splotchy cheek. "Let's get settled into our new home first. Then we'll talk about getting a dog, okay?"

"Promise you'll really think about it?"

"I promise."

"All right, I'll wait a little longer." She gets quiet after that, more so than usual with me.

"What's wrong, Millie?"

She tucks some hair behind her ear. The shade of golden sunshine matches mine. "What if the kids in the Silo town don't wanna be friends with me?"

I furrow my brow and try to smooth the lines away from hers. "Why would you ever think a silly thing like that?"

Her eyes skitter off my face. "That's how it is here. They never ask me to play tag or go on the swings."

The children around these parts are a bunch of rich snobs. I don't tell her that, though. "Millie, you'll be the most popular. Everyone will want to hang out with you. Wanna know why?"

She nods. "Uh-huh."

I kiss her button nose. "Because you're smart and beautiful and kind and good. So very good." Right down to her marrow. She's the most genuine soul and wouldn't hurt the fuzz on a fly.

Her cheeks dent with deep dimples as she curls the corners of her lips. "M'kay, Mama. I hope you're right."

"This will be a good move for us. You'll see." I stand and begin picking up my mess of laundry. "All right, enough serious talk. Let's get on the road."

"We get to meet our new house now?"

"Yes, sweetie. But first, let's get some ice cream."

The megawatt smile she grants me is all the assurance I need. The strain knotting my stomach eases with another long exhale. Our lives are changing for the better, starting today.

CHAPTER ONE

Keegan

Healing Hug #2: Exchanging simple comfort without needing a side of fluffy words.

"IT'S ABOUT TIME YOU START DATING AGAIN."

I choke on my sip of coffee. A very unladylike stream of brown liquid spews from my mouth. To add further insult, stray droplets dribble down my chin. I wrinkle my nose at the frothy mess. What a waste of much-needed caffeine. After getting my mess under control, I glare at my best friend. "Pretty sure I misunderstood you. Care to rephrase that?"

Josey narrows her dark eyes at me. "Oh, come on. It's been over a year since the Kirk debacle. That might as well be ancient history at this point."

"I disagree." I allow my thoughts to wander while gazing outside through the front window of Steeped. There are moments when it feels like yesterday. I fled with Millie from Kirk's hoity-toity high-rise to the sleepy town of Silo Springs and didn't bother glancing in the rearview mirror. Best decision I ever made. This community welcomed us with open arms and never let go. And aside from her random bouts of meddling, Josey is the greatest reason to remain rooted in place for years to come. "I just finalized my mortgage. How about we celebrate that rather than bring up old skeletons from my disastrous history with men?"

She swats the air. "You would so go there."

"Without a doubt. And I'm glad that's settled." I roll my gaze to the wooden beams lining the ceiling. "Can I return to enjoying my morning in peace now?"

The light tapping of her nails against the table is answer enough. "I'm just getting started, lady. This has been brewing inside of me, and I'm ready to let it out."

"Is that so?" I purse my lips while offering her an unflinching stare. This isn't the first round we've battled on this topic. I'm not naive enough to believe it's the last. Deterring Josey is usually easy enough, but there's an unfamiliar spark in her eyes today. She's got something sneaky up her chiffon sleeve. A laundry list of possibilities begins forming while my heart picks up a faster beat. This conversation could lead in far too many directions. The silence stretches taut enough to snap. Taking the scenic route and letting this interrogation cool is the best route to avoid collision. I reach for my mug as if nothing is out of sorts.

"I never took you for a vegetarian, Keke."

"You're losing me again."

Her lips curl into a wicked grin. "Reintroducing meat into your diet is long overdue. You're a young woman in her prime with needs that extend beyond the reach of a battery-operated boyfriend." She lifts her chin at me, the angle more than haughty.

She's just lucky I didn't have another mouthful of coffee, otherwise I'd have doused the front of her shirt. All I can manage is a basic gape—lips parted and jaw hanging. I should've predicted she'd aim straight for the gutter. Heck, I certainly know better. With a flurry of rapid blinks, I collect my composure and sit upright. "I can take care of myself, thank you very much."

Her snort is loud enough to hear in the crowded café. "Right, right. Your BOB must be losing steam, though. Give that bad boy a rest. A real man has tricks of the trade."

Routine grinding from an espresso machine kicks up in the background. The grating whir is a pleasant distraction, especially from Josey's firing squad. But when the distinctive sound cuts off, my friend is still staring at me expectantly. I huff, sending a few strands of blonde off my forehead. "Can we drop it? Dating isn't on my radar, Joe."

"Why not?"

"I have more important things to focus on."

She makes a circular motion with her hand. "Such as?"

"My daughter, first and foremost."

Her brows lower. "Millie is preoccupied with being a first grader."

I frown at her easy explanation. "She needs my full attention."

"Are you worried about her?"

"Always," I respond without hesitation.

"Why? Isn't she enjoying school?"

I lift a single shoulder. "She seems to be adjusting well. Her teacher has sent me a few emails, though. Millie's lack of communication is raising some red flags. Several staff members have noticed. She's resistant to speaking with just about everyone, even the girls she's friends with."

Deep grooves cut across her forehead. "Ah, shoot. I'm sorry, Keegan. Is there something we can do?"

My exhale is long, drawn out on purpose. I'm stalling. This topic is always difficult to breach. "There are special services she might qualify for. She would have to go through an evaluation. I'm not ready to cross that bridge yet."

Josey nods. "You were a shy kid, right?"

I laugh, as if the opposite could be true. "Uh, yeah. It's safe to say she inherited the quiet traits from me."

She rests a palm over my fidgeting hand. "Then don't fret yet. Millie will find her stride and blossom."

The tension pulsing in my temple eases slightly. "That's what I keep hoping for."

"Great. In the meantime, you can cut loose a bit." She winks at me. "A little static between the sheets."

I rub my temples. "No. Just no, Joe."

"What's your next excuse?"

She earns another glare for this relentless badgering. "The last thing I need is another careless man to stomp all over my newly erected life. I made a promise to myself, and Millie, that I wouldn't make careless choices again. When I'm ready to try again, it will be for serious."

She garbles out a laugh. I cock a brow, waiting for the joke. Her jaw pops open. "Oh, wow. You've been out of the game too long. Come on, girl. You said erected."

I give her an eye roll that any diva princess would envy. "How old are you again?"

"Where'd my fun-loving friend disappear to? I want her to speak up. She would laugh with me about stupid innuendos."

"She's been kicked one too many times, I'm afraid." An all-too-familiar ache spreads through my chest. I don't bother trying to rub the sting away.

Josey sits forward. "I'm sorry, I truly am. But meeting up for a casual meal or night out won't hurt. Keke needs her groove back."

Another round of churning twists my belly. "Honestly, I'm fine."

"That isn't good enough."

I'm three seconds away from banging my head on the table. Just before I take action, a lightbulb moment flickers on in my brain. "Before I even entertain the idea of dating, Millie needs a dog."

My friend crosses her arms and assesses me with an all-knowing look. "Are you really comparing finding a decent man to getting a family pet?"

"The responsibility of it all? Yes."

"It's official. You're being ridiculous."

"Me? This is all your doing."

"Because I care about you and the cobwebs sprouting down below."

The laugh bubbling out of me shakes my entire frame. "You're taking things to a whole new level."

"Extreme measures are necessary at this point, Keke. There's nothing wrong with bumping a few uglies to soothe an ache. Or scratch that hard-to-reach itch. Even the best vibrator can't stroke all those hidden spots."

A burst of heat singes up my neck. I glance around the bustling bistro. The patrons of Steeped are getting quite the earful, thanks to my nosy bestie. "Will you turn the inappropriate badgering down a notch?"

Her eyes dart from one wall to another. "No one cares about your vibrator, Keke. And if they do, it's only because they're in the same boat."

I hold up a palm, halting her never-ending line of suggestions. "Why the desperate need to pair me off all of a sudden?"

Ruby splotches stain her freckled cheeks. Thanks to a pale complexion, my bestie can't tell a lie. I refer to this blatant tell as her Pinocchio bluff. "I met a guy who's perfect for you."

I bury my face between my palms. "And the plot thickens."

"He's really sweet and hard working. I checked into his status—totally single and ready to mingle."

"Thanks for the report, but I'm not interested."

"How about looking at his picture? He's so dreamy."

"This guy sounds perfect."

"That's what I was getting at," she sings.

"Why don't you focus this energy on making him *your* Mr. Happily Ever After?" I wince, immediately realizing that I'm an inch away from striking a nerve. A knot forms in my chest while I reach for her hand. "Sorry, Joe."

She shrugs, averting her gaze. "It's okay."

I shake my head. "But it's not. That was very insensitive of me."

"Don't worry about it. I'm happy to have all of the attention on you at the moment." Her smile droops, and I want to dump this entire conversation into the trash. Josey has struggled with finding the beauty within herself since middle school. As a teenager battling with her weight, she fell into the arms of too many bad choices. One asshole after another threatened to tarnish her sparkle. Thank the good Lord she chose to use their mean-spirited targeting to build herself up. After embracing her curvaceous figure, the true Josey was able to emerge and prosper. She's more confident and boldly aware of her assets these days, but the right man still hasn't snatched her up.

Regardless of what happened in the past, my friend remains optimistic. Bless her hopeless, romantic heart for always finding a silver lining. She's the sounding board for true love and happily ever after. It's too bad she can't find her own fairy tale. If that were the case, her relentless interest in my dating life could catch a break.

After another tense beat, her smile returns tenfold. "Maybe I should start a dating app for single folks in Wyoming."

"There are already plenty of those available."

She wiggles her eyebrows. "Been looking?"

I scoff. "Not at all."

"Hey, you can tell me. No judgment."

"Trust me, you'd be the first to know."

Her mouth forms a flat line. "You're no fun."

"I prefer being safe and boring."

"That's not going on your dating profile."

"Mostly because I won't have one."

"Not if I have anything to do with it."

"Starting an account without my permission? Pretty sure that's against the rules."

Josey cackles. "This will be my site. I'll be the one making rules."

Going on about some fake creation is exactly why we're friends. I give her a genuine smile. "You're one heck of a spokesperson for online dating, that's for sure."

"And you're being sarcastic."

"Not sure how else to be in a situation like this."

"Feisty is better than indifference. I accept your sass."

I quirk a brow. "Not sure you have a choice."

"Even better. Keep going."

"You're a distraction. We're supposed to be working." I jostle my mouse to wake up the computer screen.

"Oh, please. Our jobs aren't going anywhere."

"For now, and only because we've been busting our humps."

Josey snorts. "Demand for freelance graphic design is booming, babe. And the glory of being our own bosses is we set the schedule. We can pick up projects whenever and stay remote. Did your office hours suddenly change?"

"No, everything is falling into place. There's a stability in our life that we haven't had. Business is steady. We finally have our own house. And I'll be able to buy a new car this year. All is going according to my re-do plan."

"Aside from soothing your womanly cravings," she mutters.

"We've been over this. I'm ready to talk about something—anything—else."

"Just tell me you'll think about it."

Cue internal eye roll. "Okay, sure. I'll consider your outrageous suggestion."

"That's all I ask." She opens her laptop and immediately begins typing.

I squint at her. That was far too easy after the last thirty minutes of intense pressure. "You're suddenly ready to be productive?"

"I'm satisfied." Her smile grows. "For now."

A low groan escapes me. "I need backup."

"Oh, you'll need a lot more than that."

CHAPTER TWO

Crawford

Healing Hug #3: To stop the rage that seems to never quit.

THE SETTING SUN GLINTS OFF THE HARLEY'S CHROME FENDER in front of me. This is a mighty fine chopper, and even better after my custom modifications. I give a final twist to set the bolt, spinning the tire to triple-check alignment. Not a wobble in sight. A burst of warmth rushes over my skin that has nothing to do with the lingering heat.

The owner will cruise away from Iron Throttle as a happy customer. But Decker always does. Erik and Grady, too. We all grew up together in this small town, but can barely be considered acquaintances. If I was more socially inclined, we could probably be friends. I rarely leave my compound unless duty calls in one form or another. People call me reclusive, a loner, and they're right. I've always kept to myself and prefer to be on my own. That didn't stop Decker from being one of the first to take a chance on my garage. He's been dropping off his hog for years without second guessing. Trusting another man with your bike is an honor that I don't take lightly.

This is precisely why a job done well isn't good enough. Everything has to be perfect.

I've spent years building a brand for myself that brings in consistent business. There isn't much in my life that I can take pride in. This shop, my motorcycles, and the endless dedication I pour into every project are the foundation that I stand on. Not that I rely on a lot to keep me upright. Or have anything, for that matter. Fortunately, the general public of Silo Springs appreciates hard work and reliable service. My hands are never idle for long.

Gasoline and burning rubber saturate the air without fail. The aroma is a trademark for any garage worth its reputation. That scent clings to me deeper than the motor oil beneath my nails. A slight twitch teases the corners of my lips. I wouldn't trade this for anything.

I spend a few extra moments polishing the already glossy paint. Black and silver gleam at me, the machine's version of a salute. I'm sure Decker will grant me his version of the same for what I've done, but the satisfaction flows both ways. Not even a swanky corner office with the biggest window in Wyoming could replace this feeling. A balloon of pride swells inside of my chest for all that I've accomplished. Not many people are running their own successful business by the ripe age of twenty-six.

The sound of tires crunching over gravel has my gaze automatically lifting. A familiar red BMW pulls into my lot, popping that expanding bout of honor faster than a straight pin. Sludge fills my veins as I watch my father steer his beloved possession toward the garage. It's been months since he's paid me a visit, but I could've survived the rest of my days without a drop-in from the old man.

As if sensing my unease, Patch growls from her cushion in the corner. Malamutes are typically a docile, albeit anxious, breed. Really not much of a watch hound. But mine is more protective than the fiercest junkyard dog. If anyone dared to cross that invisible line, her canines would be hitting bone before they threw a punch.

Edward Doxe is a man with a mission, and today is no different. The slam of his car door crashes into the comforting sounds of clinking metal and classic rock that normally surround me here. I can almost see a storm swirling around his broad frame. He takes extra care to avoid the land mines of greasy puddles and scattered tools. Heaven forbid his spotless loafers get a scuff. I feel my muscles bunch in preparation for a fight, but getting physical has never been my dad's style. Cutting me down with words is his specialty. There's been a target on my forehead since I suffered from a temporary studder in kindergarten. I've always been a bit different from other kids. Being too quiet and withdrawn made me the bane of his otherwise impeccable existence. Over the years, I've learned to slam down a wall of steel to avoid the blows. My armor isn't bulletproof, though.

Patch rises in a protective stance, her eyes watching him like a hawk tracks a rabbit. A rumble of warning vibrates from her bulky form as she waits for my command. I give her a shrill whistle, swatting the air until she relents. She gives me a frustrated whine, but collapses into her bed.

"It's disappointing to see you're keeping that mangy mutt around." He lifts a brow at my companion. She curls her upper lip, showing off a set of impressive weapons.

I rescued Patch from a kill shelter. Her reality was worse than grim when I found her. Feral and considered aggressive, she had never experienced kindness until I brought her home. Not much different from my own story. We're kindred spirits, of sorts. "I'm grateful she tolerates me."

My father crosses his arms. "She's filthy, and probably has fleas."

I don't bother wasting energy responding to that. "Something I can help you with?"

"Sharron would like you to join us for dinner on Sunday."

"And you couldn't just call with the invite?"

"As if you'd answer," he spits.

"For good reason," I retort.

He stomps forward, narrowly missing a blob of grease on the concrete. I'm a little disappointed. "You're such a little shit."

I make a show of appraising my body. Nothing about me is small. Maybe I have him to thank for that. But my father will never hear me give him an ounce of credit. "Then why does your girlfriend want me around?"

"She's trying to make us a family again."

My responding chuckle is sharp enough to sting. "Good luck with that."

"You need to show her respect. I'm planning to marry that woman."

"Yeah? You're a lucky man." She's after his money, no doubt. Why else would a bombshell thirty-something go after a man in his late fifties? Digging for gold.

"I'm glad you can be bothered to notice. She's making me a better man." He puffs out his barrel chest, as if that's going to impress me.

"Highly doubtful," I mutter.

His nostrils flare wide, the vision of a teapot billowing steam. "Remember who you're talking to, son."

"Gonna put me in my place?" I haven't been intimidated by him since I hit puberty, and he knows it.

"Are you trying to force my hand?" My father paces in the far stall. His stride is stiff with the beginning stages of arthritis and pent-up aggression. He's smart to remain a safe distance away from Patch. I won't call her off a second time.

"Nah, I think we're done." I add an extra grunt, turning my glare toward the kaleidoscope of colors blasting across the horizon. Nothing beats the sunset from up here. A selling point for this plot of land—in addition to being off the beaten path—is the unobstructed view to the west. If I squint hard enough, a faint outline from the distant Rockies can be seen.

"You can't get rid of me that easily."

"No?" I pick up an oil-drenched socket set and begin scrubbing at the grime. A slither of glee tickles my spine when he glowers at me.

"Is being a grease monkey all that you aspire to be?"

I shrug off his thinly-veiled disgust. Opening Iron Throttle is the best decision I've made by a long shot. This place has kept me out of more trouble than I can count. I created this company from nothing but a pile of dusty ground Silo Springs is known for. But this man will never accept my choice of profession. "I'm not going anywhere, least of all the corporate world."

"Your brother wised up and left this line of work. I'm waiting for you to do the same."

His mention of Grant is a purposeful blow. I almost stagger from the impact. Thinking about my brother in this context is the equivalent to drilling a hole through my heart. We were thick as thieves, quite literally, as kids and teens. He watched out for me when my self-preservation scraped bottom. I wasn't ambitious enough to achieve more. Making friends and creating aspirations wasn't something I forced myself into. Goals were a waste of effort. All that mattered was ditching the punishing dictatorship of my father. But Grant cared enough for both of us. Until the day it all crashed down.

After a near-fatal accident his senior year of high school, everything blew up in a pile of disintegrated dreams. Grant gave up his grease rag for a five-piece suit and dear old dad couldn't be happier.

Fuck him for throwing that painful piece of history at me. I narrow my gaze, pinning him with the fire burning inside of me. "Heard from my mom lately?"

My father curls his hands into fists. "How dare you bring her up."

That's rich, coming from him. My mother is his biggest failure, and greatest point of weakness. Maybe the only one he's somewhat willing to admit exists. I'd almost sympathize if he didn't continue tossing Grant in my face. She's the main reason his hate for me boils so hot. I rock back on my heels. "Seems only fair."

"There's zero comparison."

He earns a low snort for that. "Mom cheated on you. Grant abandoned me. Pretty damn close, if you ask me."

My dad points a blunt finger in my direction. "I sure as shit wasn't looking for your opinion when I drove all the way to this sinkhole. You're going nowhere fast, Crawford."

A pit opens up in my gut, churning until acid burns my tongue. His words hit a bit too hard. "Because you're a prime example of how to be? Stay at the office more nights than not. Never bothering to be present except for barking demands. It's no wonder mom left you."

His waxy skin explodes with a mottled red hue, exposing his rage with bursting capillaries. "Take a look in the fucking mirror, Crawford."

"I've come to terms with my reflection. Not sure I can say the same for you."

"Well, go fucking figure. Turning this back on me."

I pat my chest. "Learned from the best, pops."

A muscle twitches in his jaw. "We're nothing alike. You've always been alone, son. No one wants to be around you. That's why you built this tin shed on the edge of town."

I stride backward, more than done with this conversation. "Thanks for the trip down memory lane. It's much appreciated."

My father begins following me. "This isn't over."

I grip onto the door leading to my office. The metal creaks under my unforgiving hold. "It most certainly is. Always a pleasure catching up with you, Dad. Feel free to fuck off and show yourself out."

The resounding bang of the metal barrier now separating us is the most gratifying farewell this moment can offer.

CHAPTER THREE

Keegan

Healing Hug #4: A saving grace reaching forward
in the darkest moments.

A SMOOTH BEAT CROONS THROUGH THE SPEAKERS, SINGING about finding love after all else is lost. I tap my foot on the floorboard while humming along to the swoony tune. The chorus belts out a line about giving him a second glance. I almost roll my eyes at the irony. But hell, it's a catchy song. Maybe Josey's outrageous suggestion isn't that farfetched.

Before I can give those thoughts more air time, a deafening pop bursts my serene bubble. The vehicle jolts and swerves at a sharp diagonal to the left. A yelp trips off my lips as warning sensors begin beeping at me. I clutch onto the wheel with a shaky grip, fighting to regain control while veering back into my lane. Thankfully, no one else is on the road. A band of bass drums boom against my ribcage, the potential of full-blown panic looming near.

"What's wrong, Mama?"

I swallow down a silent scream, smoothing my features for Millie's sake. "Not sure, sweetie. Probably a flat tire."

As if on cue, the slap of loose rubber echoes against the asphalt. Burning tar stings my nostrils, providing me with another alert I didn't need. *This can't be happening.* But it most definitely is.

Dammit. Shit. Fuck.

I bite back the string of curses. This is what I get for letting men enter my mind. While attempting to maintain some level of finesse, I slowly pull over onto the shoulder. My car bumps across the gravel, rocking to a stop. I swear the old sedan moans with relief. There's no denying the uneven tilt, favoring the front passenger side. After switching on the flashers, I bump my head against the seat and groan.

"Are we stuck?" Millie's voice has a quivering edge that rips at my crumbling facade.

I peer at my daughter through the rearview mirror. With great effort, I muster a wobbly smile. "We'll be okay, baby girl."

"Is the car broken?"

"Only a little ouch."

Her head tilts to the side. "But a Band-Aid won't fit."

I laugh. "You're right about that. Good observation."

"Who's gonna save us?" Her gaze is focused out the window. Endless Wyoming prairie land expands in each direction. The concern in her voice might be warranted, but I'm not ready to wave a white flag.

"We don't need rescuing, Mills. There's a spare in the trunk." Fingers freaking crossed. "Just sit tight and I'll get the supplies. Then you can help me, okay?"

Her lips twist to the side as she studies my reflection. "I guess so."

"Girl power, right? We can handle this on our own." And if not, I'll call a tow truck.

Millie doesn't look convinced, not that I blame her. As I shove open my door, a whoosh of hot, dry air greets me. I shiver, my skin prickling from the shock. It's still May, but the temperature is more suitable for the peak summer season. At least the car didn't crap out completely, so Millie can relax comfortably in the air conditioning.

After rounding the hood, I get a look at the damage. The

tire is nearly shredded. There's no way we're going anywhere without changing it out. I slump against the bumper, wishing my dad was still around to berate me for not listening to his lessons on fixing a flat. The thought sends throbbing splinters through my chest. But now isn't the time for wallowing.

The afternoon sun is punishing, beating down on me with unfiltered rays. Beads of sweat are already forming at my nape. More trickle down my spine, causing the fabric of my tank to cling tighter. Getting this task over with quickly will benefit all parties involved. Unfortunately, my knowledge of emergency equipment is sparse. I'm aware of the spare hidden between the rear wheels. Everything else I need should be stashed somewhere in the back. I pop open the trunk and get digging. The rear compartment, where I'm certain a jack and repair kit are stored, is empty. My stomach drops harder than a bag of bricks. This is my luck, of course.

I give myself a moment to have a mini-temper tantrum. After repeating every expletive twice, I comb through my hair and suck in a deep breath. The heat takes away most of the comforting cleanse, but I don't have the means to be picky.

While considering my options, a list of regrets begins to build. At the very top is my refusal to splurge on roadside assistance. Coming in a really close second place is not checking to make sure the necessary tools are available. I mean, seriously. Of all the foolish mistakes, this one earns a blue ribbon. I'll never live this failure down once Josey gets wind of it.

I stride to Millie's door and knock on the glass. She lowers the window, squinting at the bright light streaming in. Her thick lashes lower, shielding her eyes from the sun.

"Hey, pretty lady." I boop her chin, and she giggles.

"Hi, Mama. Can we leave now?" I have to lean closer to catch her whispered words. My sweet child. She's so quiet and meek.

"Almost. I have to find someone to help us. Hopefully it

won't be much longer." I won't admit defeat, but we do need assistance.

"All right," she murmurs.

"Are you doing okay?"

Millie nods. "Uh-huh."

"Do you need anything?" Not that I can offer much.

She shakes her head. Even though it's hotter than a jalapeño mating with a chili pepper, she remains buckled and proper in the backseat. I can only assume she's comfortable with the cool air blasting on high. Either that or she doesn't want to be a bother. A pinch twists in my chest that it could be the latter.

"Don't worry, sweetie. We'll be home soon."

Her chest rises and falls with a heavy breath. "M'kay, Mama."

I drop a loud smooch on her smooth cheek. "Love you, kiddo."

She wrinkles her nose, wiping away the evidence of my kiss. "Love you, too."

After she's tucked back inside, I lean against my closed door and do a quick search for nearby mechanics. My thumb is poised over the best option, but a distant humming makes me pause. I peer into the distance toward the fast-approaching rumble of an engine. The sound of roaring pipes is getting louder by the second. I straighten and prepare to flag the driver down. Before I can lift my arm, a gleaming motorcycle pulls over in front of us.

The rider whips off his helmet in a fluid motion. Inky, midnight hair catches the sun, matching the shiny paint of his bike. Well, well. Looks like a dashing knight has arrived to save the day. My pulse kicks up another notch. So much for my girl power speech. This guy can swoop in and save my distressed butt any day.

He dismounts his motorcycle, the shocks giving a pleasant bounce at the loss of his weight. His shoulders are broad, with a wide chest to match. Even through his shirt, I can tell he's not hurting in the muscle department.

When he turns toward me, the ground beneath my feet tips, and I nearly stumble. My belly flips and twirls, landing in a curtsy. I fan my face to chase off the flames. This cloying heat isn't doing me any favors. But there's no way this guy is hot enough to give me heart palpitations. Those ridiculous flutters have been dead since the aftermath with Millie's sperm donor. I've never been much for denying the obvious, though.

The stranger's outward appearance is more than appealing, but his scowl is enough to cool my feverish mood. The expression he's shooting at me vibrates animosity. Geesh, he needs to take it down a notch or ten. I don't focus on his demeanor for long as he stalks toward me. The rest of him is too distracting.

His hair is on the longish side, shaggy ends of black strands brushing the lobes of his ears. It's difficult to tell if the length is due to not giving a shit or trying to fit the biker vibe. Most likely the former, based on everything else he's oozing.

The rest of his features are also dark, popping against his tan complexion. Thick slashes of ebony over burnt hazel eyes. A thick dusting of stubble covers his square jaw. I imagine the rasp that coarse scruff leaves behind is positively decadent. He's quite mesmerizing, and I'm definitely staring.

My thighs clench beyond my control. I'm suddenly very aware of how long my so-called cobwebs have been collecting. That must be the reason for my extreme reaction. Josey put these wild ideas in my mind. She's going to get more than an earful from me once I manage to get through this spectacle.

I shuffle forward to meet him between our vehicles. Motor oil, sweat, musk, and gasoline stick to him like a second skin. He smells like a bad boy wrapped in a double dose of trouble and danger. Instinct and attraction have failed me enough that I know to keep my distance.

He gives my car an assessing glance. "Got a flat?"

I sigh at the grizzly grate of his voice. Good grief. "Yeah."

"How about the tools to fix it?"

"That's a negative." I tack on a smile to lighten the static zapping between us. If anything, the electric charge cranks higher. He makes no show of interest one way or another. Am I alone in these feelings?

He crosses his arms, biceps flexing with the shift. Is that for my benefit? "Did you call someone?"

"Not yet." I spy the familiar style of his shirt. "Are you a mechanic?"

"Yeah."

I wait for him to add more. He doesn't. Cool. "At a shop in town?"

"I own it."

"Would I know the place?"

He scoffs. "Doubt it."

"Why's that?"

"I don't do cars."

I blink at him. "Excuse me?"

"Bikes only."

I give him a slow once-over, trying not to judge. There's no harm in having a bit of fun. "As in bicycles?"

His expression turns more frosty. "Motorcycles."

A grin curves my lips. "Ah, gotcha. Do you have a name?"

"Sure do."

What is it with this guy? Calling him resistant is being generous. "Care to share?"

"Not really."

"And why is that? Introductions are polite."

"Never been known for my manners."

"Well, I'm Keegan." I offer him a hand to shake.

He just stares at my open palm, letting another grunt loose.

Stomping my foot feels like an appropriate reaction to his childish behavior. "Oh my Lord. Tell me your name."

"What's it matter?"

"Because."

He rakes through his hair. "Crawford. Most call me Ford."

I roll the word on my tongue. It fits the package, and I appraise him under a new scope. "Like the truck?"

"No, like short for Crawford."

A sting sizzles up my neck. "Sorry I asked."

"Likewise."

I wait a beat, for what I'm not entirely sure. Maybe his friendly alter ego will show up. "Well, thanks for stopping. Can you lend a hand?"

"Maybe."

It's becoming quite clear calling a local garage might be faster. I reach into my pocket, ready to continue where I left off.

A shadow looms over my screen. "In a hurry?"

I peek up at Crawford from under my lashes. "Are you trying to keep me around?"

His laugh is drier than the grasslands in July. "Hardly."

Crawford's special brand of surliness is so heavy that a fog descends around us. I'm well aware he's trying to repel me with his nasty ass attitude. This man is full to the top with piss and vinegar. Lucky for me, I'm fluent in decoding the asshole dialect. Kill 'em with kindness? Been there, definitely done that. I fling some loose hair over my shoulder and offer him a beaming smile. "If I didn't know better, I'd assume you're putting up a front to chase me off. But," I add with a saucy wink, "your type is more common than ketchup on the dinner table. Don't worry about me falling for you, Ford. I've had enough bullshit in my life to open a buffet, but the all-you-can-eat line isn't for me."

His hazel eyes roll to the dusty ground. "You done yapping? I got places to be."

If steam could physically billow out of my ears, I'd resemble a chimney. Instead, I give him the narrowest glare on this side of town. "If my daughter wasn't with me, you'd be on the receiving end of a blue streak so wide we'd never find our way out."

He sobers at that. "You got a kid?"

"Yep."

Crawford scrubs the back of his neck. "Shit, I shouldn't have been so crass."

I slap a palm to my chest. "Because I'm a mother?"

But he's not listening. His gaze is locked at a point over my shoulder. I follow his line of focus, finding Millie hanging out of her window. She's staring, her green eyes blown open wide. I spin around, striding toward her.

"What's wrong, baby girl?"

A crinkle forms between her brows. "Nothing. Who's that man?"

I hitch a thumb at Crawford. "He's going to fix the flat tire so we can leave."

Millie quietly watches him for a moment. Her button nose twitches, as if smelling the overpowering stench of wasted chemistry and bubbling aggravation. "Okay, Mama."

And with that she retreats back inside, the soft buzz of the window closing following behind. With a smile, I return to my position in front of Crawford. I find myself waiting for his reaction, once again. He doesn't give me more than his undivided concentration.

"That's Millie. She was just checking on our progress." I scratch at my arm, the sweat drying into an uncomfortable layer.

He just studies me. I almost squirm under his intense scrutiny.

"Okay, then. You wouldn't happen to have a, um…" I make a circular motion with my finger. The term I'm looking for has escaped me. Heat infuses my cheeks as I continue gesturing. "Uh, that one tool."

A single brow quirks. "Tire iron?"

I snap my fingers. "Yes, a tire iron."

"I don't."

A fresh round of choice words flood my brain. I tip my face up, glaring at the cloudless sky. *So much wasted effort. Why is this happening to me?*

Crawford grunts, probably enjoying my pity party for one. "A wrench will work."

"Well, do you have one of those?"

"You bet."

Before I can ask, he's walking away. He grabs a few things from a set of bags hanging off his bike. I watch with a slack jaw as he gets to work without another word. A few measured cranks and precise twists are all it takes. He's efficient, this one. It takes Crawford less than five minutes to swap the tires and get his tools packed up. My brain finally catches up, and I gape at his retreating form.

Wait, that's it?

I continue standing in one place, tension coating my limbs. "All right, well, uh, thanks?"

"Don't mention it." After a sharp jerk of his chin, he slips on his helmet and straddles the bike. His motorcycle roars to life with a swift flick of his wrist. In the next moment, he speeds off and disappears from sight.

A lingering cloud of dust is all that remains. I could almost convince myself this entire ordeal was the product of my mind after suffering from heatstroke. Almost. The thrumming in my veins speaks the truth. But Crawford gave me plenty of his own.

That dark knight isn't interested in this jaded damsel.

CHAPTER FOUR

Crawford

Healing Hug #5: For a pillar of another's strength
waging against the storm.

ONCE AGAIN, I'M SURROUNDED BY GREEN. THE SEEMINGLY simple shade has been chasing me for weeks. My only reprieve from fantasies of a certain emerald hue is the muted palette of Iron Throttle. But remaining trapped inside of those concrete walls nonstop is a punishment I refuse to endure. That is precisely why this dose of rustic escape is very much necessary, and on purpose.

I kick at a few stray pebbles littering the trail. Vibrant shades of glittering gold and green bathe the landscape. Sunlight filters through the trees overhead, casting a sparkling glow across the dirt floor. The woods surrounding my property are dense and lush. The natural protection is another perk I appreciate. Patch couldn't agree more. The isolated area allows her to run off leash, wreaking havoc on any wildlife who dare cross into her territory.

A bush shakes beside us, and Patch is immediately on the prowl. She takes off at a dead run, lacking her usual stealth. Her stark white fur is a streak of lightning across the shadows. It's clear she's tired of being outsmarted by the smaller and faster critters. Squirrels and rabbits have been dodging her efforts thus far. If she's lucky, there's a turkey playing possum, and this will be her massive payday.

I don't bother following her erratic movements. Patch will either return with a reward, or get bored and prepare to try again. I allow the quiet to wash over me, a rare calm cooling the thunder in my pulse. Nature gives me a peace I can find nowhere else. How my father and brother could prefer city living is beyond any conceivable thought. Lofty pines and aspens claim this land, their presence more stable than any person who has crossed this path. Flowers and blooms of all colors dot the ground. The bright bouquets decorate the already stunning backdrop. This space can turn the hardest man into a damn poet. I release a loud snort at the thought. Birds flap in the distance, disturbed by my intrusion. The punch of sound is too intense for this scenic serenity.

We're nearing a break in the trees on our way to the creek when I hear faint notes of muffled sobbing. The cry is quiet, as if the person is trying to mute their sorrow. Patch abandons her current hunt and dashes toward the warbling noise. She resembles a destructive moose crashing through the barrier of brush in search of a fresh discovery. Whoever is lingering on the other side gets a decent warning from her. That doesn't stop me from being hot on her heels, my boots pounding into the earth with a stretching stride. The fate of whoever waits beyond the forest wall pushes me faster.

When I enter the open area, Patch is sitting on her haunches and looking toward an aspen several yards away, where a small, feminine form is huddling at the base of the tree. Either the girl didn't hear Patch barrel into the clearing, or she chose to remain curled in on herself for protection. Another barely audible sob shakes a pair of bony shoulders. Stick-thin arms are tightly wound around knobby knees, hiding her identity.

"Hey, there." I announce my presence in the most soothing voice possible. Offering sympathy and comfort isn't typically on my roster, but kids are kids.

A pair of blonde braids swing outward when the little girl snaps upright to face me. Bottomless green eyes freeze me on the spot—the exact shade that's been haunting my thoughts for weeks. And the similarities don't end there. This child is a spitting image of her mother. Damn, that woman is fucking with me even now. But her miniature replica is who I need to focus on at this moment.

There's no doubt she's frightened. But how do I approach this kid without causing more terror? If only I had a clue about what might calm her fears. At the very least, it probably helps that I'm not a total stranger to her. If she remembers me. I force myself to release the strain brewing inside of me, blowing out a long stream of pressure while I debate my options.

Patch takes the initiative, jogging up to the girl and licking her face. I sputter out a harsh exhale at my dog's uncharacteristic behavior. All I can do is gawk as Patch continues lavishing her with slobbery kisses. The kid giggles and reaches out to hug my dog, her fright temporarily forgotten. My breathing stalls, heart racing too fast, while waiting for Patch to react. The oversized malamute just doubles her efforts on giving the girl a mood boost and a good cleaning.

And what am I doing? Staring like a weirdo. I scratch at my jaw while taking a moment to process. How do I handle this rescue mission? It's a lot more complicated than fixing a flat tire. One thing is certain, though—standing at the perimeter isn't going to solve anything. She needs help, more than Patch can offer.

I have to try communicating again, but my words are a jumble. What's her name again? Rather than dig myself into a hole, I search for a way out. "Hey, do you remember me?"

Her gaze flicks to mine before returning to Patch. She gives me a sharp nod. That's progress.

"Not gonna talk?"

This time I earn a shrug.

I remain a safe distance away, crouching down to her level. "All right, that's just fine. You don't have to say a peep." I almost grin at that. "Not a single peep."

A groove forms between her brows.

"Have you heard that before?"

She lifts a brow, adding a slow shake of her head.

"It's a tiny little noise that a baby chick makes. Peep, peep." I flap my folded elbows for good measure, earning me a grin.

The girl grins at my attempt to put on a good show.

"You like that word?"

She nods.

"All right. So, I'll call you Peep? It does have a nice ring to it."

Another bob of her head.

"That's settled then." I slap a smile on my face, hoping it doesn't look too much like a grimace. "Are you hurt?"

A quick shake in the negative.

The ball in my chest deflates ever so slightly. "Should I have someone come get you? Maybe a friendly police officer?" Did those even exist? I wasn't one to prove that theory.

She visibly recoils, shrinking back against the tree. Her lower lip trembles, and tears glisten in her eyes. Shit. The last thing I want to do is make her cry again.

"Okay, wrong suggestion. Can you tell me your name?"

Her throat moves with a heavy swallow. I'm almost certain she's not going to answer me. She tucks a long braid behind her ear, blinking up at me. "I'm Amelia, or Millie for short."

A lightbulb flickers on in my brain. "Millie, of course. My name is Crawford."

"Ford for short?" Her expectant gaze holds mine.

"Yep, you're right." I jut my chin at the guard dog turned teddy bear that's sprawled in her lap. "And that is Patch."

Her answering smile is brighter than the mid-morning sun. "My teacher tells me that I have a good memory."

"I bet you do. Shouldn't you be in school today?"

She clamps her jaw shut for a moment. "Uh, yeah."

"So, what're you doing in the woods?"

Her small fingers stroke through Patch's fur. The motion appears to soothe them both. My dog is practically asleep on top of Millie. "They took all of us for a walk to enjoy the nice weather."

That sounds like a regurgitated phrase. "How did you end up alone?"

A dimple dents her freckled cheek. "I followed a bunny this way."

I'm far too familiar with that. "Did you catch it?"

"Nope." She doesn't add more. This girl could battle with me for fewest words spoken.

"Why didn't you go back to your class?"

Millie wrinkles her nose. "I couldn't find them."

"Did you call out for help?"

Her chin quivers and a fresh threat of tears glisten in her eyes. Millie shakes her head.

"Why not?"

"I don't talk to them."

If anyone can understand that logic, it's me. "But you're speaking to me."

She squints against the blinding sun. A cloud must've parted. "You're not scary."

"Well, uh, thanks." That might be the kindest compliment I've received. I cough to cover the pressure in my throat. "So, they didn't look for you?"

A tiny shrug. "I dunno."

"Were they saying your name?"

She bobs her head. "I think so."

"And you didn't answer?"

"No." A harsh shake of her head follows.

Right, no talking. "Have you been gone long?"

Millie hums. "I don't think so."

And this line of questioning is only causing delay. Keegan will be in a fit of fury if she discovers that her daughter is lost in the woods. Thinking about her fired up and fuming gets my blood pumping faster. But those thoughts are wildly inappropriate, considering the situation. A splash of frigid reality smacks me in the face.

There's no way Keegan is single. That's the indisputable fact I keep returning to. The last thing I should be doing is obsessing over a woman who's probably attached to another. Within moments of meeting her, she threatened to steal the stale air in my lungs. She's easily the most beautiful knockout I've had the pleasure of ogling. Giving her a second thought, and countless more, is the cruelest form of torture. I could never be enough for someone of her caliber. Self-loathing pep talk aside, I can't seem to help myself.

"Should we call your mom? Or dad?"

Millie's face scrunches up as if she smells a foul odor. "It's just my mom. She's raising me all by herself." The pride radiating through her voice makes my own chest puff up.

A tight coil I didn't previously notice loosens from my stomach. I flex my muscles, shoving the misguided relief away. A deeper truth snags my attention for a moment: if only I could've been raised by a sole parent. Life would be a very different story. "A mom is all you need."

"Yep, she's the best." She moves to stand, and Patch whines. Millie strokes her head. "Don't worry. I'm not leaving, Patchy."

My dog licks her arm. I grunt at her newfound display of affection. "She really likes you."

"Good, because I love her." She squeezes her neck before walking toward me. Patch follows close behind, refusing to leave more than a foot between them. Patch is loyal to those she finds worthy.

I dig my phone out and unlock the screen. "Do you have her number memorized?" I'm banking on the faith that she does, because our options are pretty slim otherwise.

"Yep!" Millie snags my cell and starts tapping away without hesitation. Kids and technology these days.

I can barely detect ringing from the other end. But when the call connects, her face lights up.

"Hello?" Keegan's silky greeting almost makes me shiver. What the fuck?

"Hi, Mama."

"Millie? What's wrong?"

She begins chewing on her lower lip. "Uh, well...I got separated from Ms. Ross."

"Separated? Where are you? What are you doing? Whose phone are you on?" The airy caress of her voice vanishes, replaced by a much higher pitched staccato.

"Don't worry, Mama. The nice man who fixed our tire found me in the woods. He has a really pretty dog. Her name is Patch."

And cue the predatory emergency alert. It's no surprise that a loud screech from Keegan immediately follows Millie's response. I can't hear much more than the teetering edge of hysteria slicing into her ranting. I almost plug my ears. A quick glance at Patch tells me I'm not the only one suffering—my dog is backing away from Millie, choosing to investigate an uncharted clump of dirt.

Keegan is still firing out nonsense. Her curt tone is precisely what I envisioned earlier, misplaced fantasy or not. The heat in my veins returns with a vengeance. I'll be replaying her lyrical tirade for many lonely nights to come. For now, she's going to require further explanation. Do I step in?

Millie tugs the phone away from her ear, touching the screen until Keegan's voice is on speaker. "Mama, you're being too loud. Ford can hear you, too."

"Well, what do you expect?" A loud huff blows from her end. "How did this happen, Millie?"

She twirls a braid around her finger. "My class was going on a nature hike, and I got lost."

"Does your teacher know?"

"I think so." Millie tips her head side to side.

"Is she still looking for you?"

"Maybe?"

"Amelia Marie! She's probably worried sick. And if she isn't…well, either way, I'll be having a few words with her."

The little girl winces. "Sorry, Mama. There was a cute bunny and I followed its cute cotton tail."

Keegan's exhale is rough. "Where are you now?"

Millie rolls her eyes. "I already told you. In the woods with Ford. We're all alone, except for Patch."

Because that doesn't sound creepy as fuck. I swallow a groan. A fierce cramp stabs into my gut. I wouldn't blame Keegan if she called the cops.

Millie continues, blissfully unaware of my distress. "I like him. It doesn't scare me to talk to him. Isn't that cool? And I really like petting Patch. Can we get a dog, Mama?"

"We have bigger issues at the moment, Millie. Let me talk to Crawford."

"I'm here," I answer.

"Take me off speaker. Please," she grinds out.

Millie hands me the phone. "I think you're in trouble. She's using her mad voice."

"Amelia!" Keegan cuts in. "I need to speak with Ford in private."

She giggles, clapping a hand over her mouth. Her eyes sparkle with humor. "You're gonna get yelled at," she whispers through her fingers.

I lift my chin toward Patch. "How about you toss her a stick while I chat with your mom?"

"'Kay!" She bounces off with extra pep in her step.

I clear my throat. "All right, she's stepped away."

A loud sniff rattles through the line. "Thank you for finding her. I had no idea she was missing."

"It's no problem. I don't think she's been gone very long."

"I would assume not since they didn't alert me. I'll let them know once we hang up."

"Sounds good." I pause for a beat. "What should I do with Millie?"

"I'm already in the car to come get her. Is there a landmark nearby you can point out? Maybe text me your location?"

"Uh, well, that's kinda complicated." I glance around at the thick barricade of trees and foliage. "I wouldn't know where to start with directions."

"Okay, no problem. Never mind about that. Is there a spot close that will be easier to find? Just please bring her somewhere safe."

"We'll go to my shop." I rattle off the address for her.

"Perfect. I'll be there in fifteen minutes." She hangs up without fanfare.

I'm still staring down at the blank screen when Millie slams to a halt in front of me. "Is my mom coming to get me?"

"Yeah. We're meeting her at my garage."

"Is it far away?"

"Nah, just a five-minute walk." I hitch a thumb over my shoulder.

"That's super close. My mom will like that. Did she yell at you?"

"No, but she's definitely not happy." I let my frown dip lower.

Millie scoffs. The soft sound is meant to be oppositional, but I almost laugh. "My mama is super sweet. She doesn't stay angry for long. It's against her nature. That's what Josey says, at least."

She's turning into quite a chatterbox. Maybe I should take that as another compliment. But a grunt escapes me at the thought. I'm the last person anyone should find comforting. "Who's Josey?"

"My auntie. Well, kinda."

"Ah, that's, um…fun." Family dynamics tend to confuse me on the best days. "We should get going, Millie."

She pouts at me. "I prefer Peep."

I'd already forgotten about that. Kids use silly nicknames, right? Aren't they always calling each other something random? Shit, usually nothing nice. Words have the power to cut deep. But Millie is still beaming. That's the best sign I'll receive. "You really like that?"

"Uh-huh, yep." Her posture straightens, as if she has something to prove.

Now I do laugh. The low notes are gruff, out of practice. Even to my own ears the tune is rusty and disjointed. When was the last time I laughed for the sake of humor? Probably not since I had a conversation of this length. And I'm talking to a child, go fucking figure.

"I think Peep fits because I prefer to be quiet," Millie adds.

Solid argument, once again. "Well, all right."

"High-five?" She lifts her palm.

I don't leave her hanging, slapping our hands together. "You're a cool kid, Peep."

"You really think so?"

"Absolutely. Why wouldn't I?"

She digs the toe of her shoe into the ground. "I dunno. Nobody ever wants to play with me."

Well, shit. I'm all too aware of how mean kids can be. People in general, for that matter. "Don't worry about them. I'll be your friend. Patch, too. Plus, your mommy and Josey."

"Okay." I'm no kid expert, but her easy acceptance has me a little worried. I'll let her mother handle that.

"Come on, Peep. I'll show you how to replace a spark plug."

Millie hurries to catch up when I begin walking. "A what?"

Another chuckle rolls out of me. Damn, this kid is easy to be around. "Precisely my point. You've got a lot to learn."

CHAPTER FIVE

Keegan

Healing Hug #6: When emotion steals words.
But maybe nothing else needs saying.

THE TRAFFIC LIGHT CHANGES TO RED AND I EASE OFF THE accelerator. This is the third one in a row. I'm beginning to believe the universe is attempting to delay me on purpose, forcing me to waste precious moments sitting at these intersections. Millie needs me, and I can't reach her with all these damn roadblocks. I'm still shaking over the fact that she went missing at all.

When I called Ms. Ross, she was flabbergasted that this sort of thing could have happened. I can't believe it either, especially that they hadn't counted her missing yet. Their class is still out on their nature walk, none the wiser. Even after several apologies and promises to never let this happen again, my nerves are fraying to flimsy strands. That level of fear is a very palpable being that I've fortunately never experienced until now. A burn flares under my skin, prickling me to move faster. If only Main Street could cooperate.

I check the map again, hoping for a different response. Nope, the directions are still taking me to some address off the grid. Well, that might be extreme. But my destination, Iron Throttle, appears to be in the middle of nothing. It's safe to assume that's why Crawford was trekking through the woods. And thank whoever is watching from above that he did. A slow pulse ripples through me while I allow my concentration to center on him.

He's building quite the exemplary track record as a white knight. It's some damn good fortune that he's been nearby during these recent mishaps. This marks a second rescue. I can only hope there isn't need for a third. Would he be offended if I made him a shirt with *Good Samaritan Extraordinaire* printed across the front? Perhaps. Not sure Crawford is ready for my level of humor, though he seems to be handling Millie well enough.

My daughter takes a starring role in my thoughts as I make the final left turn and begin crawling up a gravel drive. She seemed unusually calm and serene on the phone, considering her predicament. Maybe the fact that Crawford saved us before made her more comfortable in this situation. Whatever it is, the fact she wasn't a sobbing mess gives me a slight sense of ease.

A lone concrete building finally comes into view within a clearing up ahead. The utilitarian structure sticks out worse than an abomination in the otherwise natural setting. It's safe to say Crawford set up his shop out here on purpose because nothing else is around for miles. Word of mouth must be great to get people out here in the sticks for a garage.

As I approach, two hunched figures are busy inspecting a motorcycle in one of the stalls. The crunch of tires rolling over rock shatters the quiet serenity. Crawford lifts his head to catch my puttering entrance. His gaze tracks my arrival, yet he makes no further move to greet me. With a tap to her shoulder, he alerts Millie of my presence. Braided pigtails swing as she faces me with a wide smile and a wave, but that's all I get from her. She remains firmly planted beside Crawford, her attention returning to the bike in front of them. Well, then. Clearly I've been missed.

I huff at their half-baked welcome while shifting my car

into park. Taking a moment to calmly breathe is necessary in this moment. With several slow passes, I release the strain from my limbs. Crawford and Millie are still perched on the dirty floor, appearing content and comfortable. Watching them is a useful distraction. He's animated in his demonstration, one big hand gripping a wrench and pointing at this and that while he talks. Millie eats up the attention. Her smile is infectious, and my mood quickly brightens, the tingle of irritation drifting away.

Millie told me that she wasn't afraid to speak with Crawford. This ovary-fluttering display proves her words. I try not to get emotional, but my nose is already stinging. My introverted daughter doesn't talk to just anyone. Her circle of trusted individuals is tiny. It took Josey months before my daughter would grant her with more than a few single-syllable answers. But Crawford? It looks like he's getting a front-row seat to a one-sided gabfest.

I clutch at my chest, uncertainty keeping me strapped to the seat. Is it weird that I'm jealous? Of what, I'm not entirely sure. As if sensing my growing green monster, Millie twists toward me. She gives me a double thumbs-up. Before I can question the gesture, she's bending Crawford's ear again. I almost feel bad for him, but this occurrence is so rare that I'm completely willing to throw him under the bus. And I don't want to sit on the curb for this.

My sandals smack against the compacted dirt when I step out onto the otherwise empty lot. Before I can walk two feet, a massive beast trots over to me, stopping several feet away with eyes locked on my form. I freeze at the sight of this wolfish breed stalking near. Dogs have never frightened me, but I'm the intruder in this scenario. All bodily functioning goes into lockdown as this threatening creature eases closer. When the canine's cool snout brushes my hand, I hold back a whimper. If only I could recall how to handle this abrupt introduction without losing my marbles.

It's all I can do to remain still. I swear Crawford sucks in a harsh breath as his dog gives me another sniff. A plea to call off the pooch patrol is ripping up my throat. The beginning notes are ready to tremble out of me when the unmistakable warmth of a sloppy lick traces across my arm. A furry muzzle bumps into my spread palm. That's a good sign, right?

I allow my eyes to lift, waiting for further instruction from Crawford. His eyes bounce from me to his loyal companion, a thunderous scowl tightening his features. I'm not being torn to shreds, so why does he look disappointed? His lips twitch with mutterings I can't hear, but Millie does.

"The female race is conspiring against you?" A familiar dent knits her brow. "What did Patch do wrong?" The dog in question whines, and I give her a cautious pat. After a few strokes through her thick fur, she retreats back to the garage and flops on a large cushion.

Crawford frowns at Millie. "You weren't supposed to be listening."

"But you told me to pay very close attention to everything you said."

"That was while we were fixing the bike."

"You're confusing," she mumbles.

Crawford's shoulders bounce with a booming chuckle. "And you catch on quick."

Even with the generous distance separating us, his appeal reaches me. Unfortunately, or maybe not, the weeks since I last saw him haven't dulled my instant attraction. I'd been able to blame those feelings on a long-neglected biological need—the cobwebs, if you will. It had been easy enough to explain those feelings away. But standing in front of him again has me questioning logic. Damn, maybe I should let Josey take me dancing. Scratch this seemingly insatiable itch, as of late. She'll be so pleased to hear my change of heart is due to a man.

I inch further into the garage without a word, giving my daughter a chance to wrap up whatever it is she's doing. They continue to ignore my presence while I keep pretending their indifference doesn't sting. I'm happy Millie is enjoying herself, but this is a tad extreme. The last thing she needs is some misguided hero worship, even if Crawford is responsible for saving the day again.

With that in mind, I hustle to erase the gap between us. I wait a few beats for either one of them to acknowledge me. When that doesn't happen, I clear the remaining pressure from my throat.

"Hey, you two. What's hogging all of your concentration?"

Millie looks at me over her shoulder. "Hi, Mama. I need to remain focused. Ford is teaching me how to replace a spark plug."

"Uh, okay. That's interesting. Thanks for entertaining her. Sorry it took so long for me to get here." What should've been fifteen minutes dragged out to twenty. They don't seem to be bothered by my delay.

Crawford barely spares me a glance, immediately resuming his work on the machine. "No problem."

The vibe he's exuding is cold enough to make my teeth chatter. He'd been relatively pleasant over the phone, but maybe the panic is fogging my memory. Crawford doesn't appear to be interested in exchanging pleasantries, much like our first stilted conversation. Not that I blame his aloof behavior—I'm some random woman whose child went missing, and I didn't even know.

Shaking the jitters from my hands, I try again. "Can I talk to you for a moment, Ford?"

Millie is the one who pipes up. "But Mama, he's busy teaching me. And I'm not ready to leave yet. We're almost done, okay?"

Damn, she's sassy. I had no idea that my shy daughter

is capable of wheeling and dealing. I'd protest harder if this sort of dismissal for my rules was typical. But still. "Sweetie, I doubt Ford—"

"She's doing just fine here," he interrupts. Crawford's posture can only be described as rigid. He doesn't move for several moments, remaining stiff and detached. When the tension finally eases from his frame, he begins cranking at the bike as if I hadn't addressed him.

Cold. Detached. Indifferent.

Asshole.

During our initial interaction, Crawford was callous and blunt. He kept his expression flat, devoid of any clear reactions. That didn't stop him from changing my flat tire. This guy? I don't even know where to begin when he won't acknowledge me.

"Great. Okay," I force out. Crawford grunts at my pitchy tone. Millie gifts me with an adorable giggle. I could never refuse her, especially when she's voluntarily interacting with someone who's not already integrated into our miniscule squad. Not wanting to intrude further, I turn my sights elsewhere.

The garage is a standard setup, at least from a surface glance. Rows of tools are arranged in neat clusters along the wall. Tubes and hoses and tires and other rubber objects are piled in the far corner. Gasoline and hard labor permeate the air. Faded stains color the floor, badges of honor from jobs long gone. There are a few fresh splotches, too. Crawford remains busy, and his place of business is showing off.

The abrasive scrape of metal drags my gaze to the conspiring duo. Millie fiddles with a screwdriver, pointing the flat end at the engine. "Is that all? Did we finish the job?"

He hums, shifting to get a better look inside the guts. "Sure did. This hog is good as new."

My daughter pumps the air. "Yay! That was fun."

"Glad you think so. You'd make a great mechanic."

"Really?"

"Not being afraid to get your hands dirty is most important."

Millie lifts her filthy fingers, wiggling them for emphasis. "No problem."

"Next time, I'll show you how to do an oil change." The barest hint of a grin curls his mouth.

Her gasp echoes off the stone walls. "I can come back?"

And this is the point I step in. "We'll have to see about that. Millie, sit tight for a few minutes while I talk to Ford." If he whips up another excuse to evade me, I'll be forced to drag my daughter away kicking and screaming. Bad manners, such as very rudely ignoring one's existence, isn't something she should be further exposed to. A whoosh escapes me when the broody jerk stands. I'd forgotten how tall and broad he was.

"I'm gonna talk to your mom for a bit, Peep."

"Peep?" I swing my gaze between them, settling on my daughter.

Millie blinks at me, completely unfazed. "That's Crawford's nickname for me."

"Why Peep?"

She wrinkles her nose, those freckles winking at me. "Because I don't talk a lot, just little peeps. You know that, Mama."

And Crawford is observant enough to notice. That traitorous organ in my chest begins beating wildly. I will not swoon. Will not. Absolutely not going to happen. But the way she's preening is impossible to ignore. He's going to be a tough bump to dodge.

"You good with me calling her that?"

I almost startle at Crawford's question. Did he actually initiate a conversation? I shove away the urge to fan my face. "Uh, yep. It's really sweet."

"Good. Take this, Peep." He passes Millie a clean rag.

"Polish the fender for me, okay?" Crawford gestures to the already spotless section of chrome.

She beams at him and gets scrubbing. I send up a silent wish that this man doesn't fracture her heart. Regardless of how he's been treating me, my priorities will always favor her.

When Crawford finally turns to me, all traces of joy vanish from his expression. All I get is a bland neutrality, as if he's slipped on a mask. That shouldn't sting; he's barely more than a stranger. So, why is there an ache spreading through my chest?

"Let's get this over with," he mutters.

The warm affection that had been spreading through me fizzles out with a hiss. I cross my arms and return his glare. "Is there a reason you're being so…grumpy with me?" Yes, I'm a mom and proud of it.

"Nope." Back to one word responses. Awesome.

I'm more than capable of taking the reins. Talking to him was my idea, after all. But where to start? I tuck some hair behind my ear and go with simple. "All right, I'll get to the point."

"'Bout damn time." He towers over me, but I don't let his bulk intimidate.

"Listen, asshat. I'm trying to play nice for the sake of my daughter, who's monitoring us very closely. The least you can do is fake it for her." My snarled words are some-what contained through clenched teeth. Millie doesn't need to see me fighting with her new buddy. Inside, I'm a seething momma bear more than ready to rip this moron to shreds.

A muscle in his jaw tics. "Fine, let's talk."

"I'm so grateful you found Millie. This is twice you've gotten us out of a bind. How can I repay you?" Not sure what the hell I have to offer him that he'll willingly accept, but I need to make the attempt.

"We're all set." His frosty tone is beginning to irk me.

"I disagree. She took up your time."

A limp shrug. "I was on a break. No big deal."

I cock out my hip, getting a slight thrill when his gaze tracks the movement. "You certainly have a knack for saving others."

"It's not intentional." Shadows cloud his gaze. He's so damn guarded, and I find myself wondering why. But that's a dangerous road to travel down.

"But natural?"

His eyes narrow. "I don't go looking."

"Imagine what could happen if you did."

"Not sure what you're insinuating, but I'll leave that for the real heroes."

I furrow my brow at his clear dismissal of the subject. "Is that why your garage is nestled between the middle of nowhere and the boonies? You're really separated from society."

"That's how I prefer it."

"Why?" I tack on the fakest grin to reflect the mirth in my voice.

Crawford's scowl deepens, and my attempt falls flat. "I'm not much of a people person. At all."

I do my best not to flinch. Yikes, okay. "You seem to be getting along with Millie well enough."

"She's an innocent kid. Big difference."

I force my smile to remain plastered on, brittle as it might be. What the hell does that make me? An insufferable hag? Talk about insinuations. I'm sure he's expecting a reaction, which is precisely why I take extra measures to school my expression. A deep inhale through my flaring nostrils provides me with a lungful of stale oxygen. The punch of oil and grease provide an unnecessary reminder of where I am. This is Crawford's space, and I'm toeing the line. I smooth the already flat fabric of my shirt.

"I'm glad she isn't hurt, or too scared." I study Millie for a moment. She's anything but traumatized. "You've turned this into a great day for her. Thank you for that."

"She's easy to be around." That might be the kindest thing he could say.

The grin I offer is genuine. "Thanks for saying that."

"Wasn't for your benefit." Ruining warm-fuzzies must be one of his hobbies.

I force myself to swallow a scream. "Of course not."

"We about done with this charade?" Crawford's gaze bounces around the room, never landing on me for longer than a second. He can't stand to look at me. Am I that re-pulsive to him? His rejection lodges in my throat, a pill of thorns meant to barb.

"Definitely." Patience is a trait I rely on. But being a doormat? Absolutely not. "Thanks for humoring me. I'm getting the hint that this"—I motion between us—"isn't your gig."

His snort is crude. "What was your first clue?"

My tolerance for his shitty attitude wears thin. Sour acid churns in my stomach, and I want to ask what I did to offend him. Wracking my brain takes less than a minute, and I'm still at a loss. A tug at the hem of my shirt has me looking down.

Millie thrusts a fistful of slightly wilted wildflowers into my hand. "Here, Mama."

"These colors are so pretty, baby girl." I touch the soft petals.

"Ford thought you'd like a bouquet."

I let my eyebrows arc, aiming the disbelief his way. He's staring at Millie, utter horror draining the color in his cheeks. "Is that so?" I coo, enjoying the moment.

A garbled choke trips off his chest. "She picked them on the way back for you."

Millie sticks her tongue out at him. "You're supposed to play along. My mama never gets flowers."

He scrubs at the back of his neck. "Well, lucky for her, you grabbed some."

Her displeasure dives deeper with a pout. "But that's not romantic."

Another sharp noise escapes him. "Trust me, Peep. Nothing your mother receives from me will be romantic."

CHAPTER SIX

Crawford

Healing Hug #7: For reassurance that tomorrow will be better.

SWEAT TRICKLES DOWN MY TEMPLE IN RELENTLESS RIVERS. The soggy bandana tied around my head quit stemming the flow an hour ago. At this rate, I'll be drenched, yet dehydrated, by noon. June is already punishing me within the first week. Air conditioning in the shop isn't feasible, given the high ceilings and hydraulics. It would cost a small fortune to keep the space cool. All I have at my disposal are fans and natural draft, which is failing me at the moment.

As if hearing my complaints, a rustle in the branches offers a slight breeze. The hot puff can barely be considered a gust, but I'll take whatever the wind is willing to give. The rising heat isn't doing any favors for my plummeting mood. I've been more foul since…nope, not heading in that direction again. I set down the pliers and reach for a fresh rag. After mopping my forehead, I wipe a glob of grease from my hand. Such a filthy mess. That last thought kick starts another battle in this seemingly endless war against myself.

I glare at my grungy surroundings. This is me—who I am and where I belong. There's no room for sunny dispositions and irresistible beauty. I blindly toss the rag over my shoulder, similar to how I pushed away a certain blonde. Shutting Keegan down is the only option. Dick move? Absolutely. I learned from the best. My father is the worst type of asshole. He has a specialized degree in treating women like trash. A growl erupts from deep within my gut. Comparing myself to him is low, even for me. I deserve it after the way I treated Keegan, though.

That woman hot wires all of my circuits. My ability to behave as a normal person misfires more than usual in her presence. I'm not sure what's possessing me to be an intolerable brute. Maybe that's my customary response. All systems jam, grind to a rusty halt, and destruction ensues.

She makes me want to be a different person, more friendly and capable and suave.

I despise her for forcing such ideas into my brain. My life is mine alone, and that's always been adequate. Existing without experiencing life to the fullest. What a damn waste. Getting out more probably wouldn't hurt, but I've been satisfied with my isolated routine. Now? Nothing fits quite right.

Patch whines from her shady spot along the far wall.

"Are you hot, girl?" There's an industrial-sized fan mere feet away, aiming directly at her. The force is powerful enough to send a constant flutter through her fur. I nod toward the direct line of sun currently scorching me in flames. "Want to trade?"

She releases a soft *woof.*

"I'll take that as a no." After checking that her water bowl is still brimming, I deduce that she's just bored and hot. "We can go to the stream in a bit, okay?"

Her ears perk up, tongue lolling out with loud pants.

"Just the two of us. We won't be seeing Keegan or Millie again," I add for no reason other than extra accountability on my part. It's not as if my dog knows what I'm talking about. Taking a swim on a hot day is good no matter who's tagging along.

Patch blinks at me, remaining oddly still. After another moment of staring, she yawns and slowly rises to her feet. A long stretch follows. She trots off toward the woods without another huff or bark.

"Figures you'd take her side," I mutter.

And here I am, talking to a dog. Maybe this weird desire to change my ways is from a lack of human interaction in general. Keegan is the first person I've wanted to have a conversation with that wasn't related to motorcycles or work. I'm too chicken shit to admit the truth—I enjoy Keegan's company, along with Millie. But I have a hard time believing anyone would balk at having that little girl nearby. Maybe the pint-size kiddo will take me up on my offer to come back. That will give me an excuse to see Keegan again. Getting her to come back causes an erotic beat to pulse through my veins. Heat travels south faster than I can groan. I adjust the bulge in my jeans. What the fuck am I doing, giving shape to these fantasies? It will only lead to disappointment and blue balls.

I should go for a ride and clear this shit out of my head. The wind against me will be a damn nice reprieve, too. Even on days hotter than Hades, speeding across county lines is a relief. Lord knows the open road will settle the fight vibrating in my bones. Relying on anything other than my bike and business is pointless. The past has taught me that well enough. But having people around doesn't have to be an undertaking. I've been an antisocial loner for most of my life. It's easier for everyone if I keep to myself. The separation never bothered me. I've always preferred my privacy, until that fateful afternoon. This recent shift is crawling beneath my skin. The sudden urge prods at me without an avenue for escape.

Once again, as if compelled, Keegan's stunning face pops into my mind, hypnotic green eyes glittering like the rarest emeralds. Tan skin smooth enough to taunt the most stubborn soul. Fair features to match my darkest. She has me craving more...proximity. Not from just anyone, only a very certain blonde with a saucy bite to her tone will soothe the ache. Does Keegan reserve her fire just for me? Millie told me that her mother is sweet and kind. She doesn't seem inclined to be overly friendly toward me. My abrasive personality has a lot to do with that, I'm sure.

Extinguishing the flames she feeds is necessary for my sanity. I'm in no position to pursue her, and that's not going to change. Keegan has enough responsibility raising a daughter on her own. She doesn't need the type of trouble I'd add to her plate. Staying away from her is the only solution, and that shouldn't be too hard considering I've been avoiding people my entire life.

All of these dead-end desires are distracting me from what's truly important. I drag over a socket set and get back to work. There's a group of bikers from the outskirts of town who gather for monthly treks. These runs take a toll on their rides, really hardcore. I don't complain about the influx of business. The damage they bring in is enough to pad my pockets for a season. Everything needs maintenance, from brake line to exhaust pipe, and all the parts in between.

I'm in the process of breaking down a flooded engine when the rumble of motors ripples through the woods. Another customer? I don't have anyone on the books, and it's not like they're just passing by. Two vehicles roar up the drive, a familiar black and chrome Harley guides the way, followed closely by a red coupe. I wipe off my palms and stride toward the open garage entrance. This pair will provide a great distraction from my current clusterfuck.

Decker Fredric swings a leg off his bike, offering me a wave. "Hey, Ford."

I lift my chin in greeting. "Deck."

His fiancée steps out of her car. Delaney's red hair sparkles in the baking sun. It's still weird as fuck that she doesn't remember anything prior to a year ago. But that's none of my concern. She smiles my way. "Hi, Crawford."

"Just Ford," I remind her.

A ruby flush zips up her neck. "Gah, fine. Force me to be informal."

I want to tell her we knew each other well enough once upon a time. Delaney has already heard enough of that, though. Instead, I motion them further into my oil-stained domain. "What brings you by?"

"Need an upgrade." He signals to his custom chopper that most men would drool over.

I do my best not to recoil. "You just had it in a few weeks ago. Did I fuck something up?"

"Nah, not at all. My baby gives me nothing but smooth rides. She practically glides across the pavement."

"Not this again," Delaney huffs.

Decker leans into her. "Don't be jealous, Dell. I love you most."

She frowns, but there's a twitch in her lips. "Sure about that?"

His arms band around her waist, hauling her into him. Their mouths clash into a seamless fusion of passion. Her hands claw at his hair. Decker's palm splays across Delaney's ass. And I feel like a fucking creeper for still standing here.

The heel of my boot slides on a puddle of oil, alerting the entangled couple of my attempted getaway. Decker clears this throat, and Delaney turns an even deeper shade of red.

"Sorry about that," he mutters. "Can't seem to help myself."

I wouldn't know the first thing about that feeling. "No problem."

Decker scratches at his beard. "Speaking of, I heard you've been playing the hero lately. Good for you, man."

Delaney gets a interested sparkle in her eye. "What's going on?"

"Nothing," I mutter.

"Not sure about that. Our buddy came to the rescue for a woman and her daughter. Twice." He holds up two fingers to avoid confusion, waggling his brows.

If we were friends, I'd laugh off his assumption. As it stands, I let a glower shadow my expression. "It was no big deal."

Delaney's eyes ping-pong between us, eventually settling

on Decker. "Why are you keeping juicy gossip to yourself? Who's the lucky damsel?"

"Keegan Daniels," he supplies.

"Oh my goodness, Keke is the sweetest. And her daughter is such a doll. Too bad she's so quiet. Although, I'm such a chatterbox…maybe we level each other out. I won't rest until Millie talks to me, at least once." Her wide smile proves the strength behind those words.

Decker tugs on her belt loop. "Dell, she's shy. Leave that little girl alone."

"But she's so cute. I want to braid her hair and make all the crafts together."

I'm stunned silent, more than normal. A storm is rapidly thrashing in my chest. Millie mentioned not talking to people at school, but Delaney is probably a family friend, at least somewhat. I can't keep the question from spilling out. "Do you know her well?"

Delaney tips her hand side to side. "Keegan? Eh, sorta. She designed a few covers for an author Sutton works with. Her graphics always stand out on social media. She's really talented."

Huh. Maybe we have something in common. Drawing freehand is one of my hobbies, when I get a chance. A portfolio comes in handy when customers request custom art on their bikes. But it's mostly just for fun.

"Why do you ask? Digging for dirt, Ford?" Delaney wags her brows.

"Nope. Just curious."

"Right, I almost believe you. When's your first date with Keegan?"

I choke on my saliva. "Whoa, none of that."

Delaney tips her head back and laughs. "That's what all the good ones say."

I quirk a brow at Decker. "Speaking from experience?"

He shrugs. "Don't bother denying the inevitable, man. Sitting around, waiting for a third opportunity to arise is a waste of resources. Put yourself out there. Keegan and Millie landed in your direct path for a reason. Why not explore what that might be?"

Since when are these two in my corner with rooting rags? "You make it sound so simple."

"Isn't it?"

"Nah, not at all." I don't do relationships. I won't even sign up for a gym membership, I'm so commitment phobic. The idea has never appealed to me. Still doesn't. But having Keegan's thighs wrapping around me while perching on the back of my bike is tempting as fuck. But that's a dream for a very different day. "Let's focus on the reason you're here."

Decker claps. "Fuck, yes. I almost forgot."

Delaney bumps her hip into his. "That's my job."

"My queen requires a bigger throne."

Delaney rolls her eyes, poking him in the arm. "The seat is tiny. My butt requires extra padding. Don't make me sound like a spoiled brat."

"Well," he trails off. "If the glass slipper fits or whatever."

"You'd be the one to know just how well *it* fits," she purrs.

I was wrong. Being near Decker and Delaney is crossing into enemy lines, surrendering to those primal impulses. These two are only highlighting what I'm missing out on. Finding that special someone to love? Must be nice.

Their easy banter sends a stab of fiery longing into my gut. I've never had that type of effortless flow with a woman. Any attempts I make are disjointed and sloppy. I trap the bellow bubbling up and avert my gaze. The call to get out on the open highway has never screamed so loud. This conversation cannot wrap up fast enough so I can follow my impulses.

"More space for the lady. Got it." Maybe I should take the hint and make room for a certain someone, too.

CHAPTER SEVEN

Keegan

Healing Hug #8: For when the sparkle and shine wear off.

YANK AT THE HEM OF MY DRESS, BUT THE STRETCHY MATERIAL immediately bounces back to indecent territory. The fabric ends mid-thigh and leaves me far too exposed. How did I let Josey talk me into this? An unladylike snort burns my nose. It's my fault for setting loose guidelines, if any at all. I fell into her trap after mere moments inside Meadow Kisses. The chic boutique is a favorite of mine, but I'm questioning my taste as of late. Josey snagged this sparkly sequined abomination off the hanger faster than a set of Taylor Swift tickets.

She saw. She shopped. She conquered.

And here I stand, dressed for an occasion of bad decisions.

A chill slithers down my spine while I turn toward the mirror. Blonde hair spills over my bare shoulders in loose waves. My eyes are smoky thanks to a heavy layer of dark shadow. Lashes curled and coated. Smooth complexion with optimal highlighting. Rosy cheeks that blush can take partial responsibility for. I pucker up at my reflection, bright red gloss staining my lips. Considering my usual makeup routine consists of little more than applying mascara, the finished product isn't half bad. This ridiculous ensemble I stuffed my body into is another story, though.

A high-pitch hum snags my attention. "Mama, you look so pretty."

I do a twirl, one thousand percent for Millie's benefit. "Thanks, baby girl."

"You're a very pretty princess," she coos.

"And flattery will get you far, baby girl." I stroke her silky cheek.

She smiles at me. "I'm glad you're going out with Josey to have fun."

"Did she tell you to say that?"

As if hearing her name, my bestie sways into the room as if a sultry tune is playing. The house is silent, aside from the rapid pounding of my heart. Once again, a heavy dose of doubt seeps into me. This is a horrible idea. I clear my throat, preparing to voice the list of reasons why we should stay home.

But when Josey sets her sights on me, a squeal peels off her lips. "Oh my stars, Keke. You're a knockout. Did I tell you that dress would be a killer or what?"

"You certainly did. And I'm the lucky duck reaping the… benefits." I give another useless tug to the hem.

She lets another squeak loose. "I'm so jealous of your figure. Check out your mama's curves, Mills. She's gonna drive the men wild."

And it's my turn to release a sharp screech. "Josephine! Don't talk like that in front of her." I turn toward Millie. "We're just going out for dinner. No guys allowed."

Her bottom lip pokes out. "Not even Ford?"

I snort out a laugh. "No way. Definitely not him."

She cranks the pouting up a notch. "But Mama, he likes you."

Is she serious? The suggestion alone baffles me. I squint at my daughter. "Honey, no. He doesn't. And that's okay. We're thankful he helped us and that's enough, right?"

Millie narrows her eyes in return. "But he teased you and was super grouchy. I thought that means he likes you? That's what you always tell me when I cry about mean boys at school."

Well, she has me there. My daughter is very clever, I'll give her that. At least she's been paying attention to me. But this is quite the predicament she's put me in. I boop her nose. "Adults are different, sweetie."

Josey snorts. "Yeah, right. Good one."

I glare at her. "Hush. You've done enough already."

"Such as find you the hottest outfit ever?"

"Exactly." I slap on a Cheshire grin.

"It deserves repeating. You are so darn fine, Keke. I mean, wow." She touches my arm, snatching her finger away as if I burned her.

I roll my eyes at her theatrics. "I'm a life-size disco ball."

"And there's nothing wrong with that. All eyes will be on you."

"That's not what I had planned when this night was discussed."

She waves off my concern. "Plans are meant to get bent."

"I don't think that's a thing."

"It is now. We're partying college-girl style. No regrets!"

"Several years too late, my friend. I'm a mom and already exhausted. Squeezing myself into this getup expended all of my spare energy."

She frowns and points at me. "This is happening."

I hold up my palms. "Yes, okay. I wouldn't dream of canceling."

Josey bounces her eyebrows. "Because you want to meet someone special."

"Ford will drool over you." Millie claps a palm over her mouth, stifling a giggle.

"Ha, very funny. He won't be anywhere close enough to slobber on me. And I thought we were done discussing him?" I cross my fingers for her to see.

"But I want to visit his shop again," she whines.

I've been avoiding her request to see Crawford like last week's trash. Nothing good can come out of either. Just when I think she's dropped the idea for good, his name pops up. I'm one request away from getting her a dog to keep the distraction going. Little does she know, the idea of having a pooch to snuggle with has grown on me. It has nothing to do with that wolfhound at Iron Throttle. Not at all.

The doorbell chimes, saving me from another round of Ford inquisition. Millie launches off the bed and takes off toward the foyer. "I'll get it," she calls belatedly.

I laugh while following her retreating form. For such a shy child, she's bold with those deemed worthy. When I arrive at the entryway, one of those few trusted individuals is crouching down at her level. I smile, giving our new arrival a wave. Alice stands and wraps me in a hug, much like she did with Millie moments ago. I met her on the first day we arrived in Silo Springs. She welcomed us to town with a broad grin and personal tour. I like to believe she pseudo-adopted us in that moment.

Shortly after, Alice introduced me to her daughter. Sutton Bowen lines me up with book cover design jobs and has become a close friend. The list of how helpful the Olsen clan is could go on and on. Their entire family is a true blessing to us in all the best ways.

Alice squeezes me tighter, reminding me of a mother's embrace. "Hello, Keegan. I'm so pleased you called. We've been really looking forward to spending time with Millie."

This woman reminds me so much of my mom. I swallow the ball of emotion that's threatening tears. "Are you kidding? I'm the grateful one. It's very kind of you to keep Millie until the morning."

"Why not make it afternoon? Then you can sleep in." She releases me, getting a good look at my outfit. "Oh, my. You're certainly dressed to impress."

"Right?" Josey approaches from behind, slinging an arm around my shoulder. "She's so darn foxy."

"My mama is gonna get a boyfriend." Millie whispers the

words to Alice, but her hushed tone is loud enough for all to hear.

I cough to cover a choking fit. "Ah, not likely. We're just going to Bronco Buck for a few dances."

Josey pinches my arm and I wince. "What she means is we'll be shaking our booties until the sun rises."

I nudge my friend away. "Quit it. Alice doesn't want to hear about your sordid plans."

"Our," Josey corrects.

"You two are a hoot. There's no doubt you'll attract plenty of suitors." Alice winks at us.

"And on that note, we should get things rolling." Josey swivels her hips.

I kneel down and grip Millie's shoulders, giving her a direct stare. "You'll be okay staying with Mrs. Olsen overnight?"

My daughter barely bats an eyelash. "Uh-huh. I get to help feed the horses."

I peek up at Alice. "That's a huge selling point."

She bobs her head. "It's a struggle getting her to leave the barn. She's so good with the animals. A real natural."

"Mama says we're getting a dog soon." Millie's slight frame is practically vibrating in my hold.

Alice widens her eyes. "Really? That's wonderful."

I shrug. "It's an old promise I need to follow through on. I've been looking at shelters. There are a few family-friendly dogs at the Gulligan Haven location."

"That will make Millie very happy, I'm sure."

My daughter nods. "Yes, so happy."

"It's not happening tomorrow, baby girl. Don't get too excited."

"In the meantime, you can come over to our farm and visit with Gus."

At the mention of the Olsen's goldendoodle, Millie begins bouncing around in erratic circles. "Yay, yay! Let's go. I can't wait to see him."

"Give me a hug, Mills." I beckon her into my chest.

She leaps toward me, throwing her arms around my waist. "Love you, Mama. Remember to have fun."

"I love you the most, sweetie. Be good for Alice and Barry."

She breaks from my embrace and reaches for Alice's hand. "I always am."

"Millie is always on her best behavior," the older woman agrees.

"Thanks again for letting her stay with you."

She scoffs at me as she lets Millie lead her away. "It's my pleasure, Keegan. Enjoy yourself. An evening out with other adults is much deserved."

"Thank you," I repeat.

I wave at them as they pile into Alice's car and drive away. Josey is at my side, sending them off with me. A sharp lash rips at my insides, causing me to suck in a harsh breath. I can count on one hand the number of nights Millie has spent away from me. Gulping down the knob in my throat is a feat, but muted sniffles shortly follow.

Josey pokes my side. "All right, mama bear. Chin up. We're going to have fun."

I muster a smile.

"Starting now." Josey produces a bottle of champagne from who knows where and drags me into the kitchen. She pours bubbly into two flutes sitting on the counter and hands me one. "Cheers!"

I clink our glasses together. "Salute!"

After she enjoys a few sips, her eyes laser in on me. "So, you're really passing on Ford?"

I groan, long and low. "Not him again."

"But why not him?"

"Seriously, Jo? He's too intense and unpredictable. Feral. I need someone reliable and level-headed."

"That's a little judgy, don't you think?"

"That man deserves my judgment after how he treated me." I cross my arms, the low neckline of my dress showing off more of me with the shift. I'm leaving little to the imagination. Not that Josey is checking out my rack. But I do have nice boobs, if I say so myself. I shake off the random train of thought. "He's arrogant and beyond rude and seems to hate me."

She shrugs, inspecting her manicure. "Maybe it's a front."

I blow out a puff of air. "If he's trying to chase off the entire female race above the age of seven, mission accomplished."

"Millie loves him."

"Precisely my point."

"You should take her opinion into consideration." She guzzles the last of her champagne and refills her flute, topping mine off as well.

"And yours, apparently. Since when are you all gung-ho about Ford?"

Josey perks at me over the rim of her glass. "He's a wild card. I think he deserves another chance."

I roll my eyes. "Not interested."

"Liar."

"Call me what you want. It won't change how I feel." I glance at the setting sun through the bay window. "Should we be going?"

"I thought you'd never ask." She shoves a pair of sky-high heels at my chest. "Here, wear these. They match your dress."

I inspect a bedazzled stiletto. To her credit, the shoes compliment my glittery attire extremely well. "I don't know why I'm ever surprised at what you pull out of thin air."

"Me, either. I'm going all in for this. We're painting the town scarlet red tonight."

"That's a very specific shade." I slip on the heels, giving myself a lazy appraisal in the hallway mirror. "Not bad. Okay, let's get this over with."

She grips my elbow, halting my retreat. "Hey."

"What's up, JoJo?"

"Promise me you'll try."

I purse my glossy lips. "I'll do my best."

"That's not good enough."

She pops out her hip, diva mode activated. "Will you just keep an open mind?"

"Not heart?" I quirk a brow.

"I don't want my expectations to be too lofty. Your heart should already be leading the charge."

"Always the romantic," I fake-coo.

"One of us has to be. The faith lives on—true love exists." She shakes her fist in the air.

"You make me sound unreasonable. I'll admit to being jaded. I just don't see the point in setting myself up for disappointment. We've both had our hearts broken so many times. I'm envious of your ability to move forward with so much hope."

Josey sighs, her smile lopsided. "I have to."

"Why?"

"Because if I don't, then what? I end up single and alone forever, with a pack of cats."

I shake my head with a laugh. "You'll find Prince Charming. I have faith in that."

"And so will you." Her no-nonsense tone has me tamping down another retort.

She'll have to believe for both of us.

CHAPTER EIGHT

Crawford

Healing Hug #9: To hold off from doing something
far more reckless.

OWNTOWN IS MOSTLY DESERTED AT THIS HOUR. ONLY A FEW places remain open past eight or nine o'clock. Stalking along Main Street isn't part of my preferred weekend routine. Usually I'd rather be elbow-deep in the vintage Harley tucked away in my shop. Restoring that beauty has been vital in chasing the numb indifference of boredom away. But I couldn't concentrate on that project for another silent second. I could tinker with shit from dusk until dawn. My focus never breaks, even to take a piss.

Being cooped up in my garage is how I'd usually choose to spend a Saturday evening. All I felt tonight was confinement. There's an itch under my skin, a coiling tension that needs release. I considered going for a ride, but I've done that a lot lately. Going hunting in the woods piqued my interest. The weight of a rifle in my hand centers me with nature, calling to my primitive instincts. In the end, those options weren't appealing. Only providing further isolation and distance from the underlying trouble. Stomping beyond the borders of my monotony is the solution I sought.

Decker's advice has been rattling against my skull for days. Blending with society for a bit won't cripple me. I'm convinced that leaving the comforting, yet restrictive, limits of my compound will ease the knots that are twisting me up inside. An almost obsessive drive propels me to prove I'm not the worthless recluse my father claims me to be. In reality, the one who truly needs to believe that is me.

The street lamp casts shadows across the sidewalk in front of me. My trek continues without pause. I don't have a destination in mind. Sludge bubbles through my veins, but I ignore it. There's nothing to guide me, or anyone to notice my efforts. Not that I want them to. Storefronts are pitch black and traffic is nonexistent. Aimless wandering through the dark is more of my style, better intentions be damned, so this suits me fine.

I reach the next block and find a crack in the sleepy ruse. Pounding bass and flashing strobe lights spill out into the languid tranquility I've been appreciating. Without moving another step forward, I know the establishment responsible for causing a disturbance of that magnitude. Bronco Buck is one of the few bars in Silo Springs and by far the most popular. This place caters to the partying lifestyle, especially with women. I'll never understand the interest or desire to stumble through those brightly painted doors.

There's no hesitation in my stride as I pass in front of the rowdy establishment. That plan is solid until something glints off the window, nearly blinding me. Against my better judgment, I squint and peer into the chaos. What I find almost drops me to my knees. Keegan is inside, smack dab in the center of my waking nightmare.

Regardless of my previous resistance, I remain motionless in front of this awful club, caught in her web. If she's a flame, I'll gladly sacrifice myself as a moth. Her arms lift while she spins in rapid circles, full of energy and zero inhibitions. Has she been drinking? Or is she always so carefree? The demand to find out flexes every muscle in my body, pumping white-hot lust through each throbbing vessel.

When she twirls again, a kaleidoscope of rainbow

reflections sparkle off her. Her outfit is gaudy as fuck. If she's trying to gain attention wearing that, her purpose can be deemed successful. Gawkers are gathering at an inhumane rate, proving I'm not the only one noticing Keegan's bold display. An animalistic roar drums into my ears. All rational thought is captured by the sight of her, sweeping away with the wind. Untapped need so potent crashes into me, leaving only the desire to claim standing.

Damn, I guess hunting is on tonight's menu after all.

I give my outfit a rushed appraisal. Faded jeans and a plain, white T-shirt are my standard. No visible stains in sight. It was appropriate for this venture, until now. Will I stick out worse than usual? Do I care? Not even a single shit. I tug the brim of my hat down lower and storm toward the entrance.

The door nearly rips off its hinges with my brute force. I prowl into the belly of blatant cravings and yearning. The urge to flee threatens to deflate my surge of courage, but burning hunger pushes me harder. A putrid cloud of sweat and artificial smoke greets me. Bronco Buck is the definition of hell for me. The space is flooded with an extra dose of everything I hate. But I long to be near Keegan more than I want to be comfortable.

This place has to be pushing maximum capacity. The actual bar is crowded with drunk assholes tossing out money for another round. Hip-hop music is cranked so loud the booming beat vibrates off my ribs. I assume the speakers will blow any minute. Stale heat clings in the dry air, giving my skin an immediate sheen. A dizzying array of flashing lights streak across the ceiling and walls. Gyrating bodies pack the dance floor, but I'm only drawn to one.

My boots are already covering the distance separating us before I can comprehend striding across the sticky ground. There's too much noise, but I can see the outline of her glittering curves just fine, her rhythm so liquid a wave should be jealous. Swaying hips that follow a far more sensual beat than the song playing. This woman is enchanting, and I'm cast under her hex. I erase the remaining feet that dare to keep us apart. Coconut, fresh flowers, and ocean breeze assault my senses—my very own strip of tropical paradise right here in Silo Springs. The temperature spikes, sending tendrils of fire straight to my groin. I reach out and clasp her hip in a bold grip, guiding her to the edge of the fray. Keegan startles against me, whipping around to see who's man-handling her.

"Ford?" Her eyes blow wide open.

I lean down, my mouth to her ear. "You look surprised to see me."

"Because I am." Her lips brush the stubble on my cheek. "But even more shocked you're voluntarily talking to me."

"It didn't feel like a choice." I squeeze her waist, relinquish my hold, and straighten so we're facing one another. In this position, we're forced to over-enunciate and shout. Two more reasons why Bronco Buck is the worst.

Keegan scrunches her forehead. "Am I supposed to know what that means?"

That I'm being a fucking weirdo? Probably not. "Just seemed necessary."

"Okay? That's…cryptic." Flashing lights paint her face, bathing her in neon hues. "What's up, Ford? This doesn't seem like your scene."

"It's not. How about you?"

"Not that it's any of your business, but it isn't my favorite. Anymore," she adds as an almost afterthought.

"Why now?" I rub at the dryness spreading in my throat. Between the smoke and having to nearly shout, I'll be hoarse tomorrow.

"Girls' night out."

"With who?"

Keegan points over my shoulder. I turn to see a familiar face watching us with laser focus. Josey grew up in this town, just like me. A big difference is she continues to be part of normal civilization. I haven't seen her since we graduated high school. She waves at me, and I give a nod in return.

Like a magnet, my gaze swings back to Keegan. That pull won't quit, thrumming from the very core of me. I can't draw a decent breath with her this close. All I want is to drag her into me so we can get lost together.

"Of course, you know Josey." She fans her face, oblivious to my internal struggle.

I focus on what's important. "Hot?"

"Sweltering," she corrects.

Hauling her out of here would easily solve that problem. I curl my hands into fists to remove temptation. Flames lick my body, but for an entirely different reason. Is she feeling this torture?

"Why are you staring at me?"

Because I want to be buried eight inches deep inside of her. Fuck, what I wouldn't give to have her molten center clenching around me. And now I'm harder than steel. My dick twitches, more than willing to show off for Keegan. Dammit. She brings out the worst in me, or maybe it's the best. I blink, clearing the fog from my mind. "Uh, what?"

She wrinkles her nose. "Are you drunk?"

"Completely sober. You?" I want to cup her cheek, tipping up until our lips meet. Would she let me?

She rocks a hand back and forth. "Eh, I've had a few. But I'm perfectly coherent. Don't go thinking you can take advantage."

"Wouldn't dream of it." I swallow, trying to soothe the ache. "Can we go somewhere quiet? Between the yelling and sorry excuse for music, my brain is ringing."

"Why would we do that?" Her smile is coy.

"To talk."

"About?"

I suck air through my teeth. "Whatever we want."

She toys with a lock of golden hair. I imagine weaving

those blonde strands through my fingers, pinning her against me while I sink to the hilt. "I have a few ideas."

Her suggestion drips with seduction, and I'm far enough under to drown. "There's a trash room out back."

Keegan sputters. "That's the first place you think of to take me?"

I hook my thumb in a belt loop. "I'm sure it'll be private."

She's still gaping at me. "Only because no one wants to be in there longer than necessary. I'm sure it smells worse than rotting ass. Gross, Ford."

I grind my teeth. I'm so bad at this. "And where would you prefer to go?"

She scoffs. "Oh, I don't know. How about the alley in general?"

"People might see us."

Her eyes narrow into slits. "Are you ashamed to be seen with me?"

I swipe at the brim of my hat. "Nah, quite the opposite. I'm sure you don't want rumors spread around town that we're alone in a dark alcove."

She swats at the air. "Let them gossip."

I swing an arm toward the rear exit. "After you, lady."

Keegan pokes a finger at my chest. "You better mean that in a genuine way."

"Can that be considered an insult?"

"You'd be surprised," she says and starts walking.

I follow behind, a loyal hound snarling at any guy who risks a glance at Keegan's ass. Not that I can blame them. My gaze has barely strayed from those twin globes since she set off toward the door. But what claim do I really have? Or want, for that matter. This conversation could swirl the drain faster than I can suggest anything pleasurable. I have no idea what I'm doing here. She begins accentuating the swing of her hips, the colorful array of rhinestones winking at me, and I push my questions aside. I'll worry about fucking up when the time comes.

We enter the alley with a clang of metal against brick. The cool air is an instant relief, whispering along my balmy skin like a siren song. My reprieve from the heat has a very short shelf life. Keegan spins on me, that same finger jabbing at me again.

"I almost forgot," she quips. "I'm mad at you."

"Why? What the hell did I do?"

She crosses her arms, giving me a generous visual of ample cleavage. "What didn't you do?"

That's fair. My list of crimes is quite long from the few instances we've previously clashed. But there's no sense giving her all of that ammunition. "Tell me why you're pissed."

Another stab to my chest. "You're turning my daughter against me. All she wants to do is visit your garage. I can't get a moment's peace."

"Really? Huh. That's cute." The ice around my heart chips ever so slightly. I rub at the sting.

"Sure is, except we"—she motions between us—"don't get along."

"Maybe we can change that."

She huffs out an indignant exhale. "I was willing to be nice. You weren't."

There's no way I can argue that. I lift my cap, adjusting it to rest higher. Keegan should see how fucking serious I am. "I don't want to fight."

"Oh? Since when?"

I move forward, towering into her personal space. "Now."

Her breath hitches. Yeah, she's with me. "You're very chatty all of a sudden."

I scowl. "Talking isn't my issue. It's the people I don't like."

"Yet you stomped into a packed bar without issue."

"Fuck that. There are plenty of problems with this situation. You don't happen to be one of them."

An easy grin softens her features. "Wow, that's almost nice."

I glare at the brick wall behind her. "Don't get used to it."

She tenses, squaring her shoulders. "All right, Ford. So, you randomly appeared. Again. What are you saving me from this time?"

I sigh. "Me."

"That's a contradiction."

"Tell me how." We're close enough to touch. Every impulse I have bellows at me to reach out. But she needs to be the one. I'm not willing to push that far.

"You're a different man tonight," she muses. "Very… engaging."

"Do you mean annoying? Appalling? Awful?"

Keegan laughs. "No, more like interesting. In a good way."

That sounds promising, but unbelievable. "You'd be the only one who thinks so."

She hums. "Well, good thing we aren't worrying about others."

Is she for real? If she's yanking my chain, I'll be an easy target. I let my gaze trail along her enticing figure. "That dress was made for you."

"Are you being sarcastic?"

"Nope. It's very…tempting. Like dessert after a full meal."

"Did you already eat?"

I shake my head. "I'm famished."

"And sexy. It's a good look for you," she blurts. Her eyes flare with that admission.

"Glad this isn't one-sided." I allow one corner of my mouth to hitch. She'll get a whole smile if this goes well.

Her eyes blaze, an inferno set to scorch the very concrete I stand on. Sparks crackle between us and launch into the midnight sky. I see the struggle in Keegan's taut expression, mirrored in my own. Surrender or fight. One of us has to make the choice.

Her exhale is a harsh stutter. "You're bad news."

"Am I?"

"The worst kind."

The truth gnaws at my gut. Damn, we'd been heading in the right direction. "Well, shit. I don't have a chance then?"

Keegan walks her fingers up my torso. "Don't pout, Ford. That's not what I meant. I just so happen to be in a rare mood for getting filthy."

I take my own liberties, cinching an arm around her waist. "Now you're speaking my language."

Her eyelids get heavy, hooding those twinkling emerald gems. "I was working so hard to stay away from you."

"What happened to your resolve?"

"You showed up and stomped all over it." She ghosts her mouth over mine, our laboring breaths swirling together with each exhale. Keegan pulls away before I can eliminate that sliver of space. Little tease.

"So, what happens now?"

She holds up a finger. "I'm not looking for anything serious."

I want to suck that pesky digit into my mouth. A low rumble rises off my chest instead. "Lucky for you, I'm the furthest thing from."

"A little fun, between two consenting adults?"

"I'm game." This plan couldn't be better if I concocted the entire thing in my head.

She holds up another finger. "And Millie can't know about this. Ever." Her stare is unflinching, searing straight into my fucked-up soul. She's likely to leave a brand if this lasts another moment.

I grunt. "I'm not in the habit of sharing my sexual conquests with anyone. Much less a kid."

"Is that all I am? A challenge?"

"What answer will get you naked faster?"

"Either one. I'm already all in."

"Thank fuck for that. No regrets in the morning?"

I barely get the words out before she replies. "Zilch."

"Do I need to stop for condoms?" There's no doubt the unopened pack in my nightstand has long since expired.

"Are you clean?"

"Fucking squeaky."

Her eyes bounce between mine, searching for something she likely won't find. A quick shake of her head follows. "I have a birth control implant. No whoopsies for me."

"Thank Christ for that."

"Glad that's taken care of. So, your place or mine?"

"Where's Millie?"

"Not home until tomorrow."

In that case, it's a no-brainer. "Tell me where you live."

Keegan sticks out a palm, signaling for my phone. I pass the device over and she enters an address into the map app. "Meet me there in twenty minutes."

I glance at the directions. She's not far from Main Street. "It'll only take me ten."

Her answering grin is dangerous, getting me harder than an iron pipe. "Even better."

CHAPTER NINE

Crawford

Healing Hug #9: When the boom of thunder
crashes too loud.

THIS IS THE LONGEST FIVE MILES IN HISTORY. ASSUMING Keegan's house is near the center of town was a massive miscalculation. The dark road seems endless, with no light in sight. I twist the throttle, forcing my bike into a faster gear. With a ground-quaking roar that's sure to wake the neighbors, I speed through the pitch black in search of nirvana.

With each passing block, my need intensifies. I'm strung so damn tight that my vision is spinning into a tunnel set on one specific point. I should be concerned about the impact Keegan holds over me. What is it about this woman that's driving me to alter my ways? I never put this much effort into getting laid, or the opposite sex in general. But there's something about her that burrows under all the bullshit I've been using as a shield.

My pulse is erratic, reckless like the influx of toxic thoughts on constant assault. If I don't hurry the fuck up, Keegan is going to wise up and change her mind. Why wouldn't she? I'm a poor choice on the best day—an asshole with nothing to offer besides a decent fuck. Her rejection would be detrimental to what little respect for others I have left.

Just as my thoughts get more grim, a vibration from the app alerts me that the destination is near. Thank fuck for small miracles. The moment couldn't have come sooner. Those gloom and doom clouds were far too close. As I barrel down the shadowed lane toward my target, the questions are replaced with a dense fog. The moments to wallow are far behind me.

I whip into the narrow driveway and cut the engine. A blast of heat rushes over my already scalding skin at the sight of Keegan's car in the open garage. That's a clear invitation to enter if I've ever seen one. My boots are a blur as I aim for the door.

Once I cross the threshold, she's on me, leaping into my arms and cinching her legs snug around me. Her mouth slams onto mine with a purr. The velvet of her tongue clashes with mine, a frantic desperation we fight to soothe. I snarl against her, the low thrum passing between us in a consuming crash. Keegan nips at me, the sting shooting straight to the strain in my jeans. I return the favor, devouring the breathy gasp she gives. The tornado of our arousal makes me dizzy, and I almost lose my footing.

"Take me to bed," she murmurs into our barely severed connection.

"Which way?"

Keegan points up a set of winding stairs. I take off, bounding up the steps without finesse. She bounces in my hold, gripping tighter until I wheeze. A giggle trickles out of her. The lyrical tune caresses the hardest part of me, which needs no further encouragement. My dick is more than ready to meet the treasure she's grinding against me. Keegan nibbles my earlobe, drawing the flesh between her teeth. This chick is a biter, and that knowledge stirs a frenzy in my blood. As if hearing my pleasure, she sinks her nails into my shoulders until the skin threatens to break. The pinch of pain she gives spurs me on faster.

I cover the remaining distance to her room in three extended strides. Keegan shifts against me, peeling herself away in the slowest downward slide. Fuck, my body is burning up. I won't last two pumps at this rate. She stares at me with an expectancy I can read. Taking control, having her bend to my will, sends another burst of raw lust through me.

"You need to be naked." My voice grinds out of me.

She quirks a brow, lifting her arms. "By all means."

I don't hesitate, reaching for the sequined-covered hem. Her dress is stretchy, but tight as fuck. The fabric clings to her as a second skin, and I fumble in my attempts to remove this cockblocker.

Keegan stills my clumsy hands. "There's a zipper." With a slow spin, she exposes the key to my access.

"Thank fuck." I nearly rip the seams with my haste. The material gapes and pools at her feet. Only a tiny satin barrier hides her from me, the black thong a stark contrast against tan skin. A low growl escapes me as I trace a line up her naked back. "No bra?"

Goosebumps erupt on her skin, and she shivers. "Not necessary."

I slide my palms forward and cup her bare tits, the weight spilling out of my grip. Keegan collapses against me with a moan. She arches her spine, jutting those perky mounds further into my hold. I pluck at her nipples and she shudders. "Get your sexy ass up on the bed. Now," I rasp against the curve of her neck.

Keegan gives another tremble, following my command on wobbling legs. My fingers itch to knead the lush shape of her ass. She scrambles onto the mattress and settles in the center, one arm resting behind her head. She gestures at my fully-clothed form, taut and ready to pounce. "Your turn."

I'm ripping the shirt over my head before the second word escapes. My boots and jeans are next, wrenched off without concern for shredding leather or denim. I stalk forward until my knees hit the silky comforter. Keegan squirms, her toes curling into the blanket. I point at her panties. "Ditch the scrap."

She tilts her chin. "You first."

"I believe ladies always have that privilege."

She huffs and rolls her eyes, but doesn't argue. I catch the sorry—albeit hot as fuck—excuse for underwear when she tosses them at me. A spark flashes in her emerald gaze when I tuck the dainty lace into my waistband. I toy with one of the strings. "A little memento."

"Does that mean I get to keep yours?"

I shrug. "Sure."

"Great. Give me my present."

I palm my aching cock. "Unwrap your gift?"

"Whatever gets you to lose the shorts."

I drop my briefs with one fluid move. My length bobs free, the tip smacking against my lower abs. Excitement for what's to come already glistens from the slit. I bite my lip, focusing solely on the restless woman in front of me. The sight of her naked, for me, is enough to reach the highest peak without a single touch. But where's the fun in that?

Her rapt focus is set solely on me. That unwavering attention makes me bold, wanting to shove more limits out of our way. With a thumb, I spread the moisture around the most sensitive part of me. A groan rolls off my tongue when Keegan's breath hitches.

"It's been awhile for me." She slams her knees together, gaze zeroed in on my erection.

I give myself a lazy stroke. "Don't get shy on me now."

She lifts her chin, fixing me with a fuck-hot glare. "I'm not, but when did you become Mr. Suave Confidence?"

"Wouldn't go that far. But about this?" Another slow upward glide. "Always."

A rosy flush spreads across the valley of her breasts. "Do you know how to use that impressive piece of equipment?"

"I'll let you be the judge of that."

She unlocks her thighs, exposing my newfound fantasy. "By all means. Show me what you've got."

The bed dips when I kneel onto the edge. "I can't claim to tolerate, let alone enjoy, many shared activities with others. But this, with you, will be revolutionary."

That seductive tongue peeks out, wetting her bottom lip. "Another compliment? I'm beginning to get spoiled, Ford."

"Just wait for the orgasms."

A strangled noise bobbles in her throat. "Plural?"

"Afraid you can't handle me?"

With that taunt, Keegan tips her head back and laughs. "Big boy with a huge ego. Show me what you've got."

A snarl rips out of me, and I crawl over her. "With pleasure."

My dick kisses her entrance, seeking a welcome only she can offer. Keegan is a priceless beauty—the rarest find. A woman who needs to be taken with tenderness and care. She deserves only the softest hands from the most thorough lovers. That has never been my style. For her, I can play along. I want to worship every inch, lavish her silky skin with the affection she deserves. But the hold on my control is unraveling.

As if her insistent need matches mine, Keegan bucks her hips against me. "No foreplay necessary. I'm more than prepared. Just get inside me." Her punchy statements are paired with panting exhales. "We can explore more during round two."

She's already planning a second. I'll never argue. The night is just beginning, and we have hours until the sun will interrupt.

"Fuck, you're incredible." The confession spills out beyond my limits. But there's no going back.

I wade into the green pool of her eyes, succumbing to the trance she has over me. With a single stroke, I slide inside of her snug warmth. The error in my ways hits me seconds too late, a sledgehammer to my fraying restraint. I'm not prepared for the onslaught of spine-tingling euphoria that pours over me.

Keegan's eyes roll back, lashes fluttering. She parts her lips with a silent scream. That soundless cry is louder than any call, urging me onward to hear the muted tune again. Her hands clutch onto my shoulders as I set a steady pace. She loops her legs around me, crossing her ankles against my lower back. The change in angle allows me to sink deeper as I glide in and out.

"Holy shit, that's so good," Keegan gasps against my jaw.

I groan in agreement as another shower of heat rains down on me. "So damn good."

We collide to a smooth rhythm accompanied by our panting exhales. I slant my mouth over hers, our ragged breathing flowing between us. She swipes her tongue along mine. I suck her bottom lip between my teeth. When she nips at me, static fills my brain. My mind goes blank, thoughts spinning wildly, as I allow the consuming pleasure to rule over all else.

Our bodies rock together to become one. I thrust in and she rolls her pelvis to meet mine, joining us to the hilt with each slap of connecting skin. Our movements are frantic, both of us chasing the promise of release with equal vigor. A flash of white flickers in front of me when her nails rake down the damp expanse of my back. That zap of pain only heightens the crackling sensations coursing through me. I grope her breast, lacking any concern for being gentle. She clenches around me at my rough treatment, inflicting more torture of her own. I lick a path along her jaw while flicking her stiff nipple with my thumb.

"You're gonna wreck me," Keegan wails into the base of my throat.

I grin against her cheek. "Now who's the one tossing out compliments?"

"Shut up and keep going."

"I don't plan on stopping until you pass out." And that's the truth. This woman can milk me dry and I'll still be up for more.

The headboard smacks into the wall, rattling the bottles on her nightstand. On my next thrust, several items roll and tumble off the edge of the table. The unmistakable crash of glass shattering follows.

"Shit," I mutter, not stopping.

Keegan hooks her ankles tighter against my ass. "Hazards of rough sex."

"I broke your shit."

"You're gonna bust a lot more than that before we're through." Spots dance in my vision when she swivels her hips.

"Fuck, you're hot."

She grabs a fistful of my hair, giving the strands a solid yank. "Finish the job, bad boy."

A shudder twitches my muscles, but I don't pause the smooth stride. I push harder and find a faster gear, delivering a shot of pure ecstasy. Keegan whimpers when I hit a certain spot, and she latches onto me tighter. A ripple of molten lava surges through me, curling at the base of my spine. The tingles intensify and spread. A dizzying rush shortly follows. "You close?" I grit.

Her head thrashes against the pillow. "Uh-huh, yes. So close. Keep going."

Keegan tilts her hips, and I drive in with brutal force. I'm pumping forward with abandon, lost to the motions that will take us higher. An eruption of quakes begins in her limbs, squeezing me until I see stars. I lose all composure, my movements becoming irregular and disjointed. Her core clamps around me, and I lose the battle. My climax hits with a roar.

A ripple of fire blazes across my back. Blistering heat has never been pleasant until this moment. Just as the flames threaten to incinerate me, all that I am fades to black. Inky nothingness steals my sight, sending me into a state of numb bliss.

I surface from the abyss with a moan. "Fuck, I might be broken."

Keegan slaps my ass and I jolt, still buried inside of her. "I'll give you ten minutes to recover."

A rare chuckle scrapes out of me. "I only need five."

CHAPTER TEN

Keegan

Healing Hug #11: Pairs well with a good, long cry.

I WAKE WITH A GASP, MY EYELIDS REFUSING TO OPEN MORE THAN a crack. Every muscle screams at me to stay still and I'm groggy enough to listen. With a slow blink, the fuzzy edges of sleep attempt to drag me back under. That promise of serene unawareness is more than tempting. But there's a prodding somewhere deep down that demands attention.

While gathering my bearings, the events from last night flood into me faster than my sluggish brain can comprehend. I take a deep breath and focus on the essentials. I'm in my bed, very much naked, with a man snoring beside me. My eyes pop wide open as that last fact solidifies.

Crawford is still here. He slept over. We had sex. So. Much. Sex.

My rolodex of blush-worthy fantasies is a scoop of plain vanilla in comparison. Never in my craziest, most erotic dreams did I imagine getting that…freaky. A fiery blush attacks my face just recalling how creative we got. Sweat and musk cling to every fiber in this room. If these walls could talk, I would have to move. He brings out this…kinky side of me. I've never been a biter, but taking a chunk out of him was a huge turn on. Same with licking, pinching, spanking… the sordid list seems endless in the light of dawn, and gets my body thrumming all over again.

There's a dull ache between my thighs, proving I didn't conjure up all those filthy positions. I'm deliciously sore in all the best places. Each twinge and cramp are a badge of honor. Patches of tender skin speckle the expanse of my chest, torso, and lower belly. The polka dot pattern is almost a brand, evidence left behind from my lover's stubble as he had his very thorough way with me. Crawford didn't miss an opportunity to explore his conquest. That word stings, even after I've had time to let it simmer and sink in. All I am is a quick roll in the sack. But that's all I expected from him. I can't be upset.

Crawford and I had agreed on one night only. We sure as hell made the evening count. His insatiable need matched mine with the type of natural flow that envy breeds on. The memories currently playing on repeat will keep me company once he leaves. There's enough material to keep me satisfied for the drought that's sure to follow. I wasn't joking about him wrecking me. That confession wasn't a flippant fib carelessly spewed while in the throes of passion.

I've always been a tame, albeit open-minded, sexual partner. The man snoozing next to me has altered that in a permanent manner. He makes me feel like the sexiest woman in existence, and that knowledge is crazy powerful to my self-esteem. I'm usually far more resistant to showing off all my dents and jiggle. Since Millie was born, I prefer under the covers with the lights off sex. Stripping naked in front of a practical stranger is a no-go. But Crawford didn't give me a chance to be self-conscious. The way his eyes hooded while roaming over my body was a serious boost to my bruised ego. After that, I bloomed under his undivided attention and released all of my reservations. I took advantage of what he offered without a single ounce of guilt.

The rising sun attempts to streak in through the curtains, urging me to get a move on. I turn to glance at the clock, a sigh slouching my shoulders. It's barely eight. Alice made me promise not to pick up Millie until at least eleven. They're taking her out for breakfast to get blueberry pancakes with sprinkles. My stomach lets a loud rumble loose at the thought of breakfast.

A yawn fit for a lion has me whipping around. The bedframe groans from my erratic motions. It's a shock the antique wood is still holding strong. Crawford rouses with a stretch, showing off slabs of chiseled muscle and temptation. The sheet tents when he rolls to his back. Much to his credit, that defined ridge delivered more orgasms than I care to count. A spasm twitches in my thighs, and I swallow a moan. Such a pity this won't go further. I shift onto my side, the movement jostling him again.

Crawford pins me with a heavy-lidded stare. "Dammit, woman. Why is your mattress so bouncy?"

That's one way to start a conversation. I huff at him, tacking on an eye roll for good measure. "Didn't hear any complaining when those springs were working in your favor."

"No, you definitely couldn't over all that screaming." A low growl rolls out of him. "Kinda surprised your voice isn't shot to shit."

I feel my face go up in flames and fight the instinct to burrow under the covers. "It takes a lot more than that." In reality, my vocal cords are rubbed raw and scratchy.

His brows shoot up. "I find that hard to believe."

"You would."

"Without a doubt." Crawford rolls toward me, the comforter shifting to give me a peek I didn't need.

The gleam in his greenish brown eyes reflects immense satisfaction. I'm sure mine mirror the same. He's sleep rumpled, yet more attractive than any man should be. His hair is disheveled, much like the rest of him. Lines from the pillow crisscross his cheek, adding to the already angular edges of his scruffy jaw. Just gawking at him gets my engine purring again. Good grief, I should be more than sated. I've had more sex in the last eight hours than the past three years combined.

He gives me a lazy perusal, those hazel depths scorching a path along my body. I tremble as the embers of lust spark in my lower belly. In that moment, and not a second sooner, I become all too aware of my nakedness. With a yelp, I tug the sheet up to my neck.

A devious chuckle drips off his lips. "I've seen it all, wildcat. No reason to hide."

I quirk a brow at the nickname, not entirely sure it's warranted. The bite mark where his shoulder meets his neck says otherwise. Guess I'm not the only one with lingering evidence. "It's morning."

He glances at the window, catching the glowing outline that's framing the blinds. "So it is."

I tuck some tangled hair behind my ear. "I'm surprised you stayed."

"You wore me out. No way was I getting on my bike after all that." His soft expression oozes charm I'm certain he's not aware makes him exactly my type. I could easily fall for him and reap the inevitable consequence for being reckless. Getting attached isn't an option. I drop my gaze from the enchanting possibilities. My heart can't withstand another fracture.

"I need to shower."

"That almost sounds like an invitation," he purrs.

"It's not."

He lets another rusty chuckle loose. The gritty sound tickles my exposed nerves. I curl my toes into the blanket so I don't do something reckless, like straddle his face.

"Damn, are you always this snarky?"

I bristle at his implication. "No, this is only reserved for those deserving."

He grunts. "I feel special."

"You shouldn't."

He straightens, fixing me with a glare meant to intimidate. "Fuck, Keegan. What's your deal?"

I grind my molars. "Nothing. I'm fine."

Crawford shakes his head. "Try again. Even I know 'fine' does not mean fine."

I open my mouth with a snappy retort, but think better of it. This is going nowhere, just as planned. "All right, whatever. Thanks for the, uh…"

"Sex?"

"Mh-hmm, exactly. It was great."

He hooks a brow up at me. "Maybe we'll do this again sometime."

"It's probably best if we don't."

A furrow lines his forehead. "Oh?"

"This was…fun. But it's over, and we can't let it happen again. I don't want to give Millie another reason to get attached."

"Ouch, Kee."

I twist my lips to one side. "Now I'm Kee?"

A single shoulder lifts. "I'm good at dishing out nicknames. Who knew?"

"Not me, but that's not surprising."

"What's that supposed to mean?" His tone clangs with the echo of going on the defense, but I ignore it.

"You're one rung above a total stranger. I know next to nothing about you."

"Why give anything away when I get nothing in return?"

I toss my hands up. "And that's fine. I didn't ask for details. We aren't dating."

"Thank fuck for that."

A scream tickles the back of my throat. "But you're still lying in my bed."

"You're kicking me out?" His expression is stony, cut marble and granite.

"This is my house."

"Didn't realize my welcome was worn out."

I repeat my mantra. Remaining indifferent is vital. "One night, remember?"

"Trust me, I didn't forget."

"So, what's the issue?"

"You're trying to get rid of me." He slaps a palm to his chest.

"Because this is what we agreed to. I can't do a casual fling, Ford."

"Never mentioned that."

"Fine, hooking up, whatever you want to call it. I'm not looking to get involved with anyone, especially for random sex. I have Millie to think about. Things get messy."

"I'm a sloppy loose end?"

"No, that's why we tie it up right now."

"Right, got it." He rolls out of bed, stalking to his lump of clothes.

I swing my legs out from under the covers. "Am I the bad guy here?"

He widens his stance, naked and totally unashamed. "Nah, we're square. Give and take. We can share the blame."

A frosty chill zips through me when my feet land on the cold floor. "I'm confused. Why are you mad? I thought we had—"

"And that's your problem. Assumptions ruin the best of intentions."

"Do you regret this?" I motion between us.

He barely spares me a glance. "I do now."

Within seconds, I can feel my self-preservation kick in. Fight or flight? I stand and snatch a discarded shirt, wrenching it over my head. The thin material does little to hide my modesty but anything is better than standing completely nude. Woodsy smoke and pine swirl around me, but the heady aroma is chased away by a cloud of red. "Nice to see you again, asshole. I was beginning to wonder when those true colors would bleed through."

Crawford mocks a wince and clutches one of his ridiculously toned pecs. "Oh, fuck. That would hurt if I cared."

Mere hours ago, this man was responsible for my

endless loop of pleasure. How did we flip upside down so fast? The memories I was planning to use are already tarnishing. Those smudges spread the steeper his scowl dips. I should've known, of course. This is a lesson I've learned enough to truly sink in. What goes up must always come crashing down. "No wonder you live alone in the woods, Ford. Pushing people away must be your specialty."

The sound that rips out of him is bitter. "At least I don't bother hiding it. You have imaginary walls built so high no one stands a chance at climbing over."

I sputter. "Me? That's ludicrous."

"Is it?"

Isn't it? I part my lips to say just that, only to snap them shut a second later. There's no way Crawford could know how close his words slice to the truth. "I should've stayed the hell away from you." The words are spat at him, but the reminder is all mine.

"No regrets, yeah?" The bastard winks at me.

The desire to throw something at his head flexes my biceps. I curl my fingers into trembling fists instead. Why did I sleep with him?

The answer is simple and standing three feet in front of me. Arrogant prick he might be, but our chemistry is combustible. My wits haven't reached their end, but those flimsy strands are splintering beyond recognition. The ability to think rationally is following close behind. Fuck second guessing. Caution doesn't exist in this equation.

Crawford yanks on his jeans, not bothering with briefs. The denim bulges over his hard length. How he's still aroused is beyond me. Well, that's not entirely true. I'm getting turned on by this standoff. An electrical current zaps over my skin as I match his fierce glower with one of my own. His exhales are ragged, puffing into the stagnant room. I watch the veins in his neck pulse. There's so much anger thrumming just below the surface. Is all of that hostility because of me? And why does the potential of that get me so...*hot*?

He tears his gaze away to search for his shirt. I gasp at the loss, sucking much-needed air into my lungs. Had I been holding my breath? Everything slows down for two sluggish blinks. After that, a burst of vibrant awareness widens my eyes. Crawford has narrowed the space separating us, hovering on the edge of my bubble. His proximity sends a bolt of electricity through me. I smash my mouth shut to trap a squeak. His lip curls in a silent snarl.

"Taking a souvenir?"

I cross my arms. The question is a puzzle, but I'm not willing to admit defeat. "That won't be necessary."

He's staring at my breasts, pebbled nipples and all. "Sure about that?"

"Such a gentleman," I mutter.

Crawford prowls closer, fury swirling in his eyes. I remain rooted in place, but my stomach is doing somersaults. "A nice guy is the last thing you want right now."

I scoff at that. "Because you know me so well."

The remaining space keeping him from me crackles with too much tension. "Claim ignorance toward me, but I studied every inch of you last night. Your body is betraying those lies spilling out of you."

My chest is rising and falling too fast. "Don't start something you don't have the balls to finish."

His expression is thunderous. "Are you giving me permission?"

As if he needs it. I tip my chin even higher. "Didn't I already?"

Crawford is on me in the next beat of my thundering heart. His pants sag with the motion, putting him on display. He doesn't give me a chance to register how this situation is affecting him. We crash together in a turbulent avalanche. The force is powerful enough to crumble the most solid structures into dust.

His massive palms grip my thighs and haul me up against the wall. I grapple against him for some fake sense of stability.

This position has me spread and exposed and his for the fucking. Crawford takes full advantage of my pinned form, not wasting a moment.

He slams into me with one savage thrust, the air whooshing from my lungs from the force. The energy passing between us is super-charged. I could almost reach out and grab the rope tethering him to me. But concentrating on anything other than this man and the riot of desire flooding my veins is impossible.

Within two pumps, speckles skip along the edge of my vision. I'm going to come embarrassingly fast. My body is too primed, already nearing the cliff of what will be utter humiliation. Every piece of me is humming for release. He will no doubt use the pleasure against me, but fringes of climax tickle my spine. I squeeze my eyes shut, shoving off the tingling plea for oblivion. Not yet. I refuse to surrender.

He rams into me with a particularly vicious shove. My bones chatter from the impact and a shudder wracks through me. I manage to keep the keening glee on lockdown.

"Where's your sass, huh? That bold woman from last night had a lot to say."

I jut out my jaw at a defiant angle. "That was different."

The brown in his eyes darkens. "Give me your wrath, wildcat."

The angry purple stain on his neck mocks me, reminding me of my wanton behavior. I latch my lips on the mark, bruising him further.

Crawford hisses as he pounds into me. "Oh, it's like that?"

I release his skin with a pop. A smile I can only hope looks wicked curves my mouth. "Absolutely."

"All right, then." His fingers dig into my ass and hips, hard enough to leave another set of reminders. "I'm not letting you wash me off that easily."

The hint of pain has me bucking against him. Not to dislodge, only for encouragement. There's nothing nice about what's happening between us. He's fucking me so hard we might crack the drywall. A flurry of emotions bombard me, all of them conflicting. How should I feel about this?

Crawford's thrusts are punishing, meant to make a statement and leave a lasting impression. I'm sure that's his intention. At this rate, it's a guarantee that I'll be feeling him for days after. There's no question this jerk is highly skilled and extremely well-equipped.

Each punch of his hips borders on the right side of hurting. I'm tender and sensitive, but the burn keeps me connected to reality. His motions are a mix of wild frenzy and rough corners, never settling into a smooth rhythm. This is very much how I experienced him yesterday. He's making good on my judgment, poor taste or not, and I'll ride this wave until we crash. A rush of endorphins has me crossing my eyes. This is too much, yet I need more.

He grabs the collar of my tee, twisting the material in his fist. The cotton doesn't stand a chance against his brute strength. With a single yank, the shirt shreds and rips down the middle.

The sound I make is pure outrage. "You ruined—"

"My shirt," he finishes for me.

I gape down at the ruined garment to discover he's right. Dammit. "Guess you're driving home without a shirt."

His teeth clamp onto the cap of my shoulder. "You'll be more bothered by that than me."

A scoff parts my lips. "Don't flatter yourself."

"Just the facts, Kee."

I don't get the opportunity to lash out because he strikes that secret spot buried deep. With a wail, I drag my nails down his arms. We sure as hell can be equal in this barbaric act.

"Stubborn woman. Just admit you love this." He punctuates his meaning with a harsh grind into me.

I suffocate the moan attempting to crawl out of me. "Never again."

"Should I stop?" He glides into me with a harsh upward jab. There's no trapping my whimper. "No?"

My body is currently ruling above all else and refuses to let a slew of lies loose. I settle for, "Just finish the job."

And he does.

Crawford doubles his efforts, hammering into me with abandon. Static fizzles in my ears as everything except him fades away. The grand finale arrives with an roar I can't contain. My orgasm is fast and ruthless, shutting down all normal functioning. A wave of heat washes over me, bathing me in flames. I don't bother silencing a scream as my skin prickles. A booming blast of fireworks explodes in my vision. With my next labored breath, a sea of black whisks me away.

When the tremors ease and I regain sensation in my limbs, reality crashes down. I wiggle my hips in a silent signal for him to put me down. Immediately.

Crawford drops me to my feet and backs away, zipping up as he goes. "You're welcome."

His mood is foul. Too bad mine is beyond rotten. "I can't imagine what for."

"The farewell fuck."

I'm about to burst a capillary from glaring so hard. "Yeah? Well, fuck you right back."

"Too late. You already did." His voice is devoid of emotion. I do my best not to shiver.

"I'll consider myself lucky if we never see each other again."

He pauses his hasty retreat to throw me another wink. "I couldn't agree more, wildcat. But, unfortunately for you, luck has never been on my side."

CHAPTER ELEVEN

Crawford

Healing Hug #12: To stop the cracks from splintering.

I PULL UP ALONG THE CURB IN FRONT OF A MODEST RAMBLER. Getting the fuck out of Silo Springs, at every opportunity, has been necessary for what little sanity I have left. Once I kill the engine, the silence is so complete it feels like a cocoon. For a brief moment, nothing is chasing me. The infinite loop of provocative images, and the corresponding catastrophe of errors, aren't pounding into my skull. But the reprieve smashes apart with a pair of furious green eyes, luscious curves on full display, and tangles of blonde hair wrapping around my fist. A breeze picks up, delivering hints of coconut and fresh flowers. There's no doubt the scent of tropical paradise is in my imagination, for an added dose of torture.

The mess with Keegan has been plaguing me this entire week. The only upside is I naturally avoid town, so the risk of running into her is slim. The war between my mind and body gains momentum with each passing second. There are several undeniable traits about her that create this internal feud. I find myself wanting another altercation with the snarky wildcat. A shaky vision alone is enough to spike my need, shooting too much heat below the belt. I shift in the seat as denim strains over my persistent arousal. The clinging desperation is ripping me in half. I haven't been that hard since discovering porn during puberty. Maybe that makes me fucked up. I've never claimed to be normal, though.

These are the moments I almost regret not having any true friends. One-sided conversations with Patch aren't productive, or very comforting. Nothing screams reclusive loser quite like talking to a dog about a woman. Being blackout wasted with a drinking buddy would come in handy right about now. I'm sure Decker or Grady would have some decent advice to pass along, especially over a bottle of Johnny Walker.

The feeling is fleeting, sweeping off with the wind after I consider the repercussions. I'm not built to have meaningful relationships, of any sort. The bloody massacre with Keegan is proof of that—a sure thing that ended in complete failure. I managed to fuck up the greatest one-night stand in the history of fantasies and wet dreams combined. Only I'm capable of such a colossal waste.

Was my behavior justified? Perhaps, but not to that extent. Now that my blood has cooled, I can admit my temper spun out of control. But she pushed my damn buttons too hard. Getting angry and playing the asshole card is my default. Squashing any possibility for more, regardless of the bullshit Keegan limits slapped down, needed to happen. This way, there is zero potential of us hooking up again. She hates me, and I despise how easily and quickly she wrote me off. Win, win.

Any crumbs leading to her would allow me to go sniffing around again. She doesn't want that. Eventually, once this misguided lust dissipates, I won't either. It's best for me to forget about her altogether.

And here I go, spinning my tires bald again.

A car creeps by me, probably wondering why I've been straddling my parked bike for ten minutes. No, I'm not a stalker. This is what the unraveling of a man's mental health looks like. I give them a choppy wave and they drive along.

This situation is dire enough to force me to make the hour-long trek to Gulligan Haven. My mother moved to a cozy suburb of Cheyenne after my dad discovered her infidelity. I dismount my bike and stride up the driveway. The woman waiting beyond these walls is my best, and only, bet to clear my conscience—not that I'll tell my mom why I'm seeking retribution. Those fine-print details aren't important.

The door swings open almost immediately after I knock. The woman responsible for raising me stands in the foyer, wearing a paint-splattered dress to match her crooked smile. "I was starting to wonder how long it would take for you to get up here."

I scrub over my mouth, hiding a grin. "You knew I was here?"

"Only from the moment you pulled up." Her laugh spreads warmth through my chest.

Of course she did. My mom is nothing if not observant. It probably works in her favor that no one in this cul-de-sac drives a motorcycle. "I was just enjoying the scenery."

She peeks outside from over my shoulder. "Anything interesting?"

"Your lawn looks good." I'd noticed the manicured grass during my so-called period of reflection.

The lightest shade of pink dots her cheeks. "A friend handles those chores for me."

I snort at her choice of label. Friend, my ass. Kellie Carver has always caught more than her fair share of male attention. Unfaithful to her worthless ex-husband or not, my mom is a bombshell. Maybe I should hold some resentment toward her for breaking apart our family, but all festering hostility is reserved for father dearest. I can't really blame her for escaping him. "Is that all he's doing?"

My mom parks a hand on her hip. "Are you going to continue questioning me or finally come inside?"

A loose chuckle rumbles out of me as I step over the

threshold. A pungent fog of varnish and primer greet me, the mix of strong odors burning my nose. My mom must be kicking off a new project. "Are you in the middle of something?"

"A few oil canvases. Nothing that can't wait a bit." Any artistic talent I have is because of this woman.

"Commissioned or for you?"

My mother glances at me while I follow her into the kitchen. "Both, actually. Looking to buy a piece?"

She earns another laugh for that. The walls of my micro loft are already decorated with her pictures. Aside from appreciating her talent, it's another way to fuck with my father. Whenever he stalks into my apartment, always uninvited, a colorful gallery from his greatest loss meets him. That's the biggest middle finger if I've ever seen one.

"Even if I wanted more, I don't have the surface space."

"You are my best customer," she muses. "Take a seat. Have you had lunch?"

My ass hits a chair before the words are out of her mouth. "I could eat."

"As always." There's humor in her voice as she turns to the fridge. "So, what brings you by?"

I drum my thumbs on the table. "I was out for a ride. Ended up nearby, so I figured why not? The oil in your car is about due for a change, right?"

My mom moves to the counter with an armful of sandwich supplies. "An hour away from home?"

"Barely opened up the throttle." I study her while she begins slicing a cucumber. "Do you need help?"

My mom tsks at me. "Let me take care of you since no one else does. You're always driving all over this state alone without a companion."

"You act as if that's unusual."

She makes another sharp noise. "I wish you'd find others to roll with. The road isn't always a friendly place."

As the mother of two diehard machinists, she has first-hand knowledge of that. Well, only one of us still is. But Grant taught her that lesson. The familiar sting lashes across my torso. It takes all of my willpower to school my expression. Maybe it's a good thing she doesn't have to think about him out on the open road anymore.

Listening to her speech, it's almost difficult to remember that she's responsible for our motorcycle craze. During the summers while I was growing up, we spent almost every weekend at the motocross track or a biker event of some kind. Sturgis is still my favorite rally.

We were garage junkies and couldn't wait to have a ride of our own. I saved every cent in a piggy bank until I could open an actual bank account. It was an ongoing joke that my dad would eventually wise up and crush our dreams. But that never happened. He was always too busy with work, and didn't care enough anyway. When Grant turned sixteen, he got his license and bought a bike the same afternoon. I still remember the envy that tingled in my gut. Two years later, we were coasting down the highway together.

Those were the best damn months of my life. Nothing that great can last, though. Grant dropped off the broken parts of his once-beloved hog without batting an eyelash. I haven't had the strength to touch that pile of rusting wreckage since he dropped it. One moment can change several lives.

I wade out of those dark memories and glare at a water stain on the ceiling. My mother's "friend" needs to improve his game. I'm about to tell her so when she plops a plate in front of me. The juicy aroma of smoked turkey and toasted bread tempts my taste buds. I wait for her to sit down before taking the biggest bite my jaw will allow.

"Good?" She watches while I chew. I'd be creeped out if she wasn't related to me.

"Mh-hmm, this is great." I chomp into the middle,

nearly groaning when a burst of my mom's homemade honey mustard hits my tongue.

She grins and bites down on a carrot, crunching happily as if the vegetable is made out of chocolate. "What else are you doing with your life, Ford?"

I furrow my brow at her weird phrasing. "Besides working my ass off? Hiking and hunting. Drinking the occasional beer." No need to make her worry about something else.

"How about going out with friends?"

Prickles attack the base of my neck and I try not to slouch. Why do I feel like that awkward teenager again? "Don't need 'em. I have Patch, and my customers."

"But you do need others. People to depend on when things get rough, and spend time with for fun."

Am I ashamed to admit that my mom is the only person I can rely on? Not even a little bit. But I can't make this too easy on her. She'll use the smallest scraps to piece together the entire story without me realizing it. "I'm fine on my own, Mom."

She huffs and crosses her arms. "You're not getting any younger."

"I'm only twenty-six."

"How about finding a good woman?"

"Not interested," I grunt.

"Don't you want kids someday?"

These questions from her almost bowl me over. The idea of getting married, or having a committed relationship in general, is enough to shrivel my balls. To add insult to that painful injury, visions of snotty children running amuck sends a chill across my skin. No fucking thanks. Although, not all of my experiences with little tykes are bad. A quiet little girl helping me replace spark plugs comes to mind.

Keegan mentioned that I'm turning Millie against her. The meaning behind that is still a mystery to me. I only spoke to her that one morning when she was lost. Keegan didn't give us the chance to make plans, not that I want any sort of connection to them. I did invite Millie to visit my shop again, though. Maybe that was a mistake. But it's been weeks and there's been no sign of those blonde pigtails. I swallow the lump in my throat. It's for the best, on all accounts. Even if Millie spoke to me when she rarely talks to others. That doesn't make me special. Keegan has plenty to bark about in regard to that. An involuntary thrill shoots through me. Damn wildcat.

My mother drums her nails on the table. "Choosing to ignore me? Why ever might that be, Ford?"

I reel in the whipping sails of my thoughts. This is not the place to be recalling Keegan or Millie or anything slightly positive in regards to the female population. If my mom catches me smiling, I'm done for. I lean down to dig into my toolbox and toss her a wrench. "Are you giving Grant this lecture?"

She frowns, the expression dimming the sparkle in her eyes. Unlike me, my brother blames her for every wrongdoing since his accident. Talking about him is about as pleasant as swallowing staples, but it beats the birds and bees chat. "No, he's a different story."

"And why is that?"

"Your brother made it clear the bachelor life is for him."

I grunt at that bullshit excuse. "That's real rich."

She smooths a palm down her stained outfit. "Isn't it? He takes after a certain someone in that regard."

"And many others," I mutter.

My mother reaches for my hand. "Be better than him."

She doesn't have to specify further. I'm well aware of who she's referring to. "I'm nothing like him."

Her smile droops at the corners. "You're not, that's true. I think that's what upsets him most."

"If only Grant would see the truth." I force down the ball of fire rising in my gut. "He's the better one. Older and wiser. More likely to get hitched and spawn a bunch of hellions."

My mom averts her gaze. "I highly doubt that. He's changed so much that I barely recognize him. All he cares about is work."

I scrub over my forehead. "Wasn't that the first thing on my list?"

She waves me off. "You're different, always have been. It's just going to take the right woman and you'll be a goner."

A strangled noise rips out of me before I can conceal it. I leap up and make a mad dash for the fridge and swipe a beer. "Not a chance. Ever."

She quirks a pencil-thin brow at me. "Why the snippy attitude? Is my son finally dealing with lady trouble? That would explain the random stop to see me."

I choke on my sip of the foamy brew. Damn, she truly is perceptive. I should've known. "Hardly," I mutter.

My mom flattens her lips, still studying me far too closely. "Yeah, that's not your style. Something wrong at the shop?"

"Why does there have to be a problem? Can't I just check in on my mom?" And make random sounds that resemble a struggle. Nothing to see here—move along.

"You can, but you don't." She taps her chin.

"Have to change your oil," I remind her.

She scoffs nice and loud. "Don't bullshit me. I can see right through you, kiddo."

I guzzle another swig of beer. "Just having a rough week."

"Money issues? Are you gambling? I warned you about that."

I groan. "No, mother. It's not important. She's not interested and neither am I."

Her gasp toes the line with a fatal blow to my resolve. I can almost feel my walls crumbling from the impact. "So, it is a woman. Who is she?"

A slew of curses slam into me and my loose lips. Dammit, there's no easy way out of this trap I set for myself. "No one. I didn't mean anything by that. There's nothing more to say."

My mom looks far too pleased with herself. The sly grin curling the edges of her mouth make my knees bounce. "You don't have to tell me more, son. Mother's intuition. I'll be here when you're ready. In the meantime, I can give you some advice. My current beau is very talented—"

I clap my hands over my ears like a scandalized child. "Please don't."

Her laugh is over the top. "You are many things, but a prude isn't one of them."

I'm certain my eyes are blown wide. "I don't want to hear about my mom's private affairs."

A palm flutters to her chest. "Oh, Ford. You make me sound so classy. I like that. But listen, if you take the time to really get—"

And that's my cue to get the fuck out of this nightmare. I stand, almost toppling the chair over in my haste. "Nope, nah, not doing this."

"Wimp," she mutters.

I bend and place a quick kiss on the crown of her head. "Call me whatever you want. I'm outta here."

"I expect more details and soon." Her giggle follows me to the door.

"Good luck with that. There's no woman and never will be."

"Oh, Ford. Don't bother lying to me. I'm certain you've already met her."

I stumble over the rug, narrowly missing a full-on face-plant. Once again, her suspicions are spot on. How the hell do I prove her wrong when she's exactly right?

CHAPTER TWELVE

Keegan

Healing Hug #13: When a shoulder to lean
on isn't quite enough.

I EASE OFF THE BRAKE SO MY CAR CAN CRAWL FORWARD A FEW inches in the drop-off line. These unstructured bouts of time used to be a blessing—a slice of quiet before the chaos is every parent's dream. But now, as I sit and wait to reach the unloading zone, my idle mind ambles into enemy territory.

There aren't enough days in a week to move past the destruction known as Crawford Doxe. Each second that ticks by is a curse I can't escape. My body has become a traitor, demanding actions I refuse to take. Regret has been consuming me, swirling in my belly on a constant basis. But more potent than that is the burning desire for a repeat performance. The latter is what takes all of my energy to stave off.

My good intentions don't stand a chance against the cravings for Crawford's wicked smirk and sinful moves. Why does he have to be so incredible in the sack? And stupid-hot? The type of good looks that make women lose touch with reality, their integrity, and common sense. Yeah, he's beyond a menace. What's worse than a blob of putty melting in his palm? Whatever it is, that's me. And I need to stop obsessing over this.

"Mama?"

The twinkling tune knocks me out of my intrusive musings. Crap, I'm busted. These wandering thoughts need to quit. I adjust the rearview mirror to get a full glimpse of Millie. "Yeah, sweetie?"

"You're frowning again." She's wearing one of her own.

I shove the rest of the murky distractions away, pasting on the widest grin and feeling guilty I've worried her. "I'm always sad for you to leave me."

My daughter wrinkles her nose. "There's something else bothering you."

No secret there. Double crap. She isn't aware of my additional *interactions* with Crawford, obviously, and that's how this secret scandal shall remain. It would probably break her heart to discover the not-so-shiny knight could hurt her mama's feelings. I refuse to be the one who reveals his true nature. That doesn't mean I need to encourage the obsession, though. I'm banking on Crawford fading into the distant past soon enough.

To be fair, finding out her mother is responsible for half of the blame won't bode well either. When she asked about my night out, I glossed over the hours spent away from her. She pestered me a bit, mostly about a certain mechanic, but let the topic drop when I kept my lips sealed. I'll be adding that evening to the list of debauchery she'll never be aware of. Distraction is the key to my well-meaning ploy. The rapidly approaching summer break is a great trick, too.

"Do your teachers have anything fun planned for the final week?" I discreetly cross my fingers that another nature walk isn't on the list. Losing my daughter in the woods should be enough to veto that field trip in the foreseeable future.

"There's a talent show tomorrow," Millie whispers.

I let my jaw hang loose. "What? Why didn't you tell me sooner?"

"Because."

"Did you try out? Is there something I need to sign? Do you need a costume?" I tick off the questions with my fingers.

"No, Mom." Her tone bangs against the back of my seat, vibrating the cushion.

I wince. "Whoa, Miss Priss. What's the deal?"

"Being on stage in front of everyone is my worst nightmare." Sometimes she sounds ten years beyond her seven. My sweet little girl.

"Okay, Mills. That's just fine. Are you okay?"

Her gaze is pointed out the window. "I'll be better once school is out."

"Is someone bothering you?"

She traces an imaginary pattern on the glass. "Just the usual."

Her muted voice scratches at the softest, most delicate parts of me. The anxiety and stress she is feeling stacks on my shoulders in wide bricks. I don't want to prod too hard when the topic has been discussed at length. My daughter isn't a social butterfly, and that's perfectly fine. "You'll tell me if it's something serious?"

"Uh-huh, sure. Are you working with Josey today?"

I let her off the hook. If anything extreme is going on, I'm counting on her teacher to tell me. "Yup, sure am. I'm meeting her at Steeped once you scurry that cute little bootie inside."

Millie groans. "Mom, don't be embarrassing."

The gasp I release is mock to the extreme. "Me? Never. Plus, you're still young enough to believe I'm the coolest person ever. We can review that concept once you're thirteen and truly think I'm ridiculous."

"You're being silly," she murmurs.

And my baby is growing up too fast. This grumpy goof is going to need ice cream later. Or that other surprise I've been holding out on. "You cannot start the pre-teen drama yet. Not happening."

"I'm not." She totally is.

"If you say so."

"I do." Millie smiles, wide and genuine. "I'll always be your little girl, Mama."

"Much better. I love you, sweetie."

"Love you lots."

"What else—"

"We're in front of the school, Mama."

I whip a fast glance out the windshield for confirmation. How did we arrive so fast? Must have been my lack of concentration. Again. "All right, well, run along. Have fun getting your learn on. Mama has a lot to do."

She manages to stretch her grin wider. "Like see Ford?"

Would it be too telling if I bang my head against the steering wheel? "He's not on the list." As in ever again. "Nice try, though."

Her bottom lip sticks out a mile wide. "I wish he would be."

"Okay, bye! Have an excellent great day, Millie."

My daughter blows me a kiss before hopping out onto the sidewalk. With her head down and shoulders slumped, no one spares my little girl a glance. I can only hope this is a phase. Once she gains more confidence, others will see what I do so clearly. Those days are just beyond the horizon.

As I pull out of the parking lot, a popular, fast-paced pop song croons from the radio. I recall shaking my ass to this tune at Bronco Buck. Muscle memory kicks in, and I begin shimmying to the catchy beat. Along with my smooth moves, sneaky reflections filter into the cracks.

The air conditioning is blasting, but a tingle of heat begins crawling under my skin. Certain moments rise to the surface faster than others. Crawford's parting blow has been plaguing me since he stormed out of my house. Farewell fuck? Who says that? He should've just left before I woke up, dignity intact and great memories to keep us warm. But then we wouldn't have shared that mind-melting, extremely erotic—

Dammit, there I go again. I inwardly curse myself. This nonsense reminiscing needs to quit. While turning onto Main Street, I shove all thoughts of Crawford and what we did to the darkest recesses of my mind. I've been avoiding Josey almost as much as the stupid asshole responsible for this fiasco. She's been texting me nonstop about him since we left the bar together. Appeasing her with tiny morsels has postponed the inevitable, and I've stayed away from our typical meeting spots to avoid confrontation of the spilling-juicy-details variety. One look at me and she'll be able to tell exactly what's on my filthy mind. So many dirty images.

Avoiding her forever isn't an option, though. Which is exactly why I'm parallel parking in front of our favorite coffee shop. While smoothing down my hair, I repeat a few proactive mentality boosters.

This is just another day in my office.

Josey will never suspect a thing is out of place.

I'm a boss bitch.

If all goes to shit, I'll hide in the bathroom until she relents.

I slide into that mindset and strut into Steeped. Josey is waiting for me at our regular table along the far wall in the corner. A steamy cup of what I assume is hazelnut vanilla latte is waiting in front of an open chair. Either she's buttering me up or feels guilty for hounding me. A slight ache pinches my chest. I should be the one treating her after all the ghosting this week. She follows my slinking stride as I move toward her.

"Hey, you. Thanks for ordering." I plop my butt into the cushioned seat, pick up the mug, and inhale a greedy whiff. "Smells like heaven."

Josey gives me a lopsided smile. "Figured you'd need it after spending days hiding."

I try not to flinch. "I deserve that."

"You do, but I get it. We all recover at different speeds."

She pauses, probably waiting for me to fill in the blanks. I don't take the bait. "How's Millie?"

"Good, I think. She misses you."

"I miss her more. Is she ready for summer?"

"Big time. I think she's done being in first grade."

My friend laughs. "Doesn't surprise me. She's always been ahead of the curve."

"That's what I keep telling myself."

Josey shrugs. "Don't stress, mama hen. Your little chick will spread her wings soon enough."

"Chickens don't fly."

"So? They still need to leave the nest."

"Good point."

"Anyway, I'm glad you finally showed."

"Being cooped up at home isn't quite the same." I start unpacking all of the daily essentials. Once my laptop is flipped open and the screen flashes on, I feel prepared to face any hurdles heading for me. My shield is locked and loaded.

"Sitting at a café by yourself isn't that great either," she mutters.

I don't bother hiding my wince. "I'm sorry, Joe."

She scoffs. "It's fine. We're all good."

My nod is slow. Based on the knot twisting my belly into a solid mass, I'm not entirely sure she means that. But the tension between us wanes with each passing beat. I blow out a long exhale and begin scrolling through my email.

So far, all seems normal. We get settled into our routines with little fanfare. But the calm is almost deceptive. We're busy working, focusing on our respective devices, but there's a tension in the coffee-scented air.

Josey squirms in her seat, nearly tipping a plate off the table. I quirk a brow, but otherwise manage to ignore her movements. She taps a pen on her mouse, the clacking going straight to my temple. Humming is her next choice of irritant. Is she doing this on purpose? Maybe this is how she's been adapting in my extended absence. Drawing attention will only open the door to more questions. I narrow my eyes on a detailed list from my client, but the words are blurring.

A loud huff breaks our terse silence. "So! Ford Doxe."

I can't help but grin while checking the clock. It only took three minutes. "What about him?"

She tips her chin and quirks a brow, giving me that disgruntled look I know so well. "As if I wasn't going to bring him up. Count your blessings that I gave you this long of a reprieve."

I let my smile spread. "I appreciate your patience and discretion."

"Don't even try pretending that we're not discussing Saturday night, and probably Sunday morning, at great length." She holds up both hands, putting a few feet of space between them. I release a loud snort at her humorous generosity. Yeah, in his dreams.

I twirl a curled tendril of hair around my finger. "Um, nice try."

"Give me the dirt or I'll march my ass to Iron Throttle. Getting the truth from the other guilty party shouldn't be too difficult."

Her bluff rolls off my bouncing shoulders. "As if you would."

She crosses her arms. "Is that a dare?"

I hold my breath while studying the fierce lines of her expression. There's no flush or twitching nose in sight. Shit. "There's no way Crawford will spill the beans. He's antisocial and broody on a good day."

For once, I'm glad he's separated himself from society. My salacious acts can be buried in a restful peace with him out there. A frown tugs on my lips. I might miss that hussy.

A sparkling gleam shines in Josey's eyes. "Ah, I knew it! You totally bumped uglies."

I cross my arms. "What part of that speech alluded to sex?"

"Oh, please. This isn't ninth-grade gossip. You went home with him. I'd have to be pretty gullible to believe that you only invited him inside to watch the evening news."

"If it's written on the ceiling…" I trail off.

She huffs. "It's not, and I'm not going to double check until you leave."

"It was a really great film."

"Of your own making."

I feel my cheeks go up in flames. "Definitely not."

"Yeah, I can't see Ford doing that either."

That reminds me of something. "Why didn't I know that you grew up with him?"

She circles the rim of her cup. "Figured it was obvious."

"Not to me."

Josey winks. "Is the big city girl still acclimating to small-town living? My high school had three hundred kids total. It's safe to assume I'm well acquainted with anyone our age."

I cluck my tongue. "Noted."

"All right, no more diversions. How was Ford in the sack?" She bobs her eyebrows.

I glance behind me, scanning the surrounding area for eavesdroppers. "Josephine! I'm resisting telling even you. Do you think that means I want all of Silo Springs to hear?"

She makes a show of checking for bending ears. "I doubt anyone is listening."

"That's what you always say. Then, during my next spree at Springs Market, the entire rumor mill is whispering and pointing. The gaggle gals don't play." I point at her, infusing as much accusation into my finger as possible.

Josey leans forward and bites at me. "You're paranoid. And if they're talking about you, take it as a compliment. You're spicy news, especially after a romp with the town's re-clusive bad boy."

I groan. "No. No, no, no. The last thing I want is for a bunch of strangers to be making assumptions about my personal business. This is precisely why I didn't want to go out dancing in the first place."

"You had fun. Don't bother denying it."

I let my eyes slide shut, inhaling the rich aroma of freshly ground beans and melting chocolate mixed with spun sugar. A shiver runs through me from the scent alone. After clearing my vision, physically and emotionally, I stare at my best friend. This woman is the closest thing I have to a sister. Other than Millie, she's my only family. "Okay, I surrender. That night is going down as one of the best in all of history."

Josey squeaks. "Oh. My. Gah! I totally called it. In my mind, of course. Tell me everything. Right this moment. I need to live vicariously."

"He, uh, brought out this animal inside of me. We stayed up until four o'clock in the morning. It was freaking wild." A familiar buzz tickles across my limbs. I cross my legs, only to let them fall open a moment later.

She scoots closer, edging toward me to whisper. "Did you love it?"

I feel the blush bloom in my cheeks. "Um, maybe?"

"Don't be shy, Keke."

"Okay, yes. I've been replaying every filthy moment since he left."

Josey motions me on, spinning her wrist in rapid circles. "I need more. Talk dirty to me, Keke."

And I do. I spill all the spine-tingling, toe-curling details. Well, only to the extent that keeps my dignity intact. She doesn't really want to hear about me being bent over in half while taking a very solid eight inches from behind.

Josey smacks the table. "Holy shit. My bestie likes it rough. You're a crazy sex fiend. I love it."

I'm certain my face is redder than a ripe tomato. The burn has me tilting my chin down. "Shhh, keep your voice down. And this was completely spontaneous and out of my comfort zone. I just needed to get that experience out of my system. I'm done and regulated and back to plain vanilla now. No more insane sexcapades."

"Yeah, okay. I'm more likely to believe you just held hands while playing Scrabble."

"For real, Joe. One and done. I'm a mother and need to be responsible."

"You're also a woman. Just because you have a daughter doesn't mean your needs vanish. Don't be ashamed of your sexual appetite or preferences. Sounds like Crawford opened your eyes."

"Did he ever," I mumble.

She claps a hand over her gaping mouth. "You naughty girl."

"Oh, hush. It's nothing *that* bad."

"Yet," she adds.

I shake my head. "We won't be having a repeat."

She scoffs. "There's no way you can ignore this sort of ravishing chemistry."

"Yes, I mostly certainly can. We agreed. But even if we didn't, Ford turned into a massive dick after his balls were empty. I don't need his kind of attitude."

"The ridiculously great in bed kind? Knock your socks off each night? Delivering fantasies at your command?"

"Ah, not exactly. More like he doesn't get his way and acts out worse than a spoiled toddler."

"So, what did he want that you didn't give?"

"I don't even know anymore. We had a big fight. I'm moving past it."

"Did you erect a wall without giving him a fighting chance?"

"No." I roll my eyes toward the wall.

Her lips form a thin line. "Not even a smile at my clever choice of words? You've definitely been self-sabotaging."

"Have not," I retort.

"He needs more from you."

I furrow my brow. "Absolutely not. He made that clear."

Josey blows a puff of air through her pursed lips. "You can help each other."

"With orgasms, maybe."

"Now you're thinking."

"Right, but that's the extent."

"No way. You're both in need of healing. Very different varieties, but that will work for your benefit. He seems to have a knack for rescuing you, right?"

Here she goes again. My romantic bestie is up on her soapbox. She has her chin resting on an open palm, a dreamy glint in her gaze. More than anything, I want her to find someone. No one deserves a happily ever after more than her. I hate to disappoint her, especially when she's nearly bubbling over with glee.

It would be easy enough to offer myself on a silver platter to the brash asshole for another round. The fire still racing through my veins couldn't agree more. But the possibility of temporary pleasure isn't worth the risk of my heart or my pride. "It's not going further with Ford. He's too surly with an extra scoop of jaded." I release a sharp exhale. "Guess we have that in common."

Josey whistles. "You haven't met his brother. Hot damn."

She earns an exaggerated eye roll for that. "I can't imagine anyone being sexier than Ford."

"To you, maybe. Grant is just…yum. I'm just sad he left Silo Springs."

"Why did he?"

"There's some family drama." She buttons her lips. "That's not my story to tell."

There's almost nothing worse than getting teased with the idea of getting the inside intel, only to have it snatched away. But what do I want that information for? I stow any hint of interest from my expression. "I'm all too familiar with that."

Josey's grin trembles ever so slightly at the corners. "Life is messy, Keke. That doesn't make it any less beautiful."

"No truer words, bae."

"Speaking is the truth." The sparkle returns to her eyes. "Does Millie know about your adult slumber party?"

I lift the mug to my lips, very thankful I hadn't taken a sip. "You better be joking with that question."

"Don't fault me for trying to lighten the mood."

"Wouldn't dream of it." I giggle and resume my attempts at getting work done. "Keep the entertainment coming. Unlike a certain someone, I enjoy the company of others."

CHAPTER THIRTEEN

Crawford

Healing Hug #14: A little self-love goes at least halfway.

THE PRODDING IN MY SKULL DOESN'T GIVE ME A MOMENT'S rest. Blonde hair. Green eyes. Snarky wit that gets me harder than steel. But to be fair, everything about Keegan makes my dick twitch. Her bewitching spell is precisely why I find myself parking in a rear lot off Main Street.

The slap of my boots bounces off the brick walls as I stride through the shadowed alley. A streak of sun pours across my back, the unrelenting rays finding me regardless of where I try to hide. It seems the elements of nature, along with a few select individuals, are also conspiring against me to lighten up.

I straighten my shoulders and continue stalking forward, shoving those idiotic thoughts away. The weather is warm and bright. My mood just happens to be the polar opposite. What else is fucking new? This is a regular afternoon in June. No one is forcing me to change my ways or be more visible in town. These decisions are my own. I'm allowed to drop into a bar for a beer. That's a normal thing to do. But who the hell am I trying to convince?

The desire to be better is driving me faster than before. These needs are chasing me, hounding me with relentless efforts. The familiar path I'm on led me to a very different place two weeks ago. I reach the sidewalk and hang a right. The opposite direction offers a collection of memories that I've been trying to erase from existence. That's an impossible task, especially when a coil tightens in my gut just being in close proximity.

I'm staying the fuck away from Bronco Buck indefinitely, but there's another bar on this same street that calls to me. It's a safe spot where I'm guaranteed to be left alone, for the most part. The patrons at Howlers aren't known for idle chatter or being overly social. I can blend in with the throng without trying. Misfits and outcasts. Bikers and guys from the worst side of the tracks. They find solace in the rundown tavern. I couldn't ask for a better establishment to escape in.

The thrum of midday traffic vibrates the ground beneath my feet. I dodge a puddle on the cobbled concrete, a sure sign that Wyoming isn't just blue skies and rainbows. A thick sigh whizzes off my lips when a neon sign flashes at me from the end of this block. That familiar beacon hauls me in, offering a sense of security I would never admit to wanting.

Being isolated at home for days on end remains more grueling as of late. The limited options I've managed to entertain myself with in the past have fallen flat. I've been leaving more often, for whatever excuses I can create that don't risk an encounter with a particular breed of wildcat. Running into Keegan would be catastrophic to any semblance of progress I've made. A few more weeks, or months, and that woman will be out of my system. I don't care how fast my heart races at the mere idea of seeing her. Or that my body is strung so damn tight with rampant arousal. There's no doubt I'm being punished.

I jerk my head in a sharp nod. That's fitting, and all the more reason to stay on the safe side of town. No way will I risk running into that busty blonde. This afternoon, I'm only looking to enjoy a drink that I don't have to pour myself. That whole concept of getting shitfaced with a friend circles back to me at this moment. I could definitely see that happening at Howlers.

Am I craving some sort of camaraderie on top of everything else racing through my brain? Maybe. Being a loner is a box I folded myself into. I can blame my father or Grant or any number of people who played a role, but the choice has always been mine. Alone. Much like this sudden shift in my demeanor. Apparently, all I had been missing was the perfect motivational cocktail to kick my ass into public. Fingers fucking crossed this outing doesn't fail as epically as the last one.

Without further delay, I wrench open the heavy wooden door. The aroma of stale beer and burned pizza welcomes me as I cross over the threshold. There are only a few people littered around the dimly lit space. A lungful of hot air I didn't realize was trapped rushes out of me. Erik Rhodes waves at me from behind the bar. I haven't seen him since spring, but that's because he hasn't been by my shop. His bike requires little maintenance, and there's no other reason for him to visit Iron Throttle.

"Well, well, well. Crawford fucking Doxe. I'd be likely to believe this is a hallucination if I wasn't stone-cold sober."

"You fantasize about me often, Rhodes? Maybe I was wrong about this place."

He rubs his nose with a middle finger. "Fuck you for calling me out. Take a load off and let me add to my spank bank."

An empty stool near the wall is calling my name. Everyone else seems to be congregating on the other end. Perfect. I settle onto the ripped leather cushion and the seat groans under my weight. "Thanks for the five-star greeting."

He pastes on a fake-ass grin that I'm sure grants him extra tips. "We aim to impress around here. I'm sure you've heard."

I take a glance at the array of outdated decor, peeling paint, and stained tile. A renovation is decades overdue, but probably won't happen for another ten years. "Why do you think I chose Howlers above all else?"

"Because the options are slim. Doesn't hurt that this place is a dive and no one will bother you."

I point at him. "Exactly."

"It's my loyal bartender duty to know these things. Speaking of, pick your poison." Erik gestures to the rows of liquor behind him.

"Whiskey. Make it a double."

He grabs a bottle of Windsor and fills a short tumbler to the rim. "Ice?"

I wave him off. "Nah, this is great."

Erik leans against the counter while I take a hearty gulp. "You look like shit, bro."

Smoky heat flares along my tongue. The booze burns a trail of fire down my throat. "Fuck you very much."

He strokes his chin. "Lady trouble?"

"Why does everyone keep assuming that?" I swallow another mouthful of whiskey. A telltale blaze is already coating my stomach.

"Because it's fairly obvious." He motions to my face.

I swirl the remaining liquor in my glass, using the waves to change directions. "Decker and Delaney stopped by a few weeks ago. They gave me some shit to think about."

Erik snorts. "Yeah, they're good at that. I hear them waxing poetic to customers at every turn. Not to mention inducing nausea with their sickly-sweet performances."

"Something like that."

He shrugs. "They mean well, at least. Whether or not those efforts make others puke is another story."

"Love, right?"

"Apparently," he drawls.

"Good for them." I blink the spots of green from my vision.

A smirk curls his lips. "Jealous?"

An image of Keegan materializes in the forefront of my fogging thoughts. Go fucking figure. The picture of emerald depths and golden curls twists my gut into an unrecognizable mass of knots. I glance down, focusing on a large gouge in the wood. "Nope. That's not for me."

His snort screams of bullshit. "Ah, that's what they all say."

"But I mean it." Why does my voice sound scratchy?

"For now," he retorts.

"I'm beginning to remember why this isn't my scene," I mutter.

Erik chuckles. "Don't be so sensitive. We grew up together. That means I get to give you shit."

"Wasn't aware that's part of your job description."

"Show up more often and you'll get used to it."

Those words prod at me, a tingle spreading through my limbs. I narrow my eyes at him. "Why didn't we ever become friends?"

"Damn, dude." He scrubs the back of his neck. "Is that a serious question?"

"I wouldn't bother asking if it wasn't."

Erik averts his eyes. "Well, you're not the easiest guy to get along with. I know shit really went south when your parents split and Grant left. You also never seemed interested in hanging out."

I drain the rest of my drink. "I'm an insufferable asshole. You can tell me the truth."

His laugh is a sharp bark. "I wouldn't go to that extreme, but you definitely stick to yourself. What's up with putting me on the spot?"

"Just curious. I've had an epiphany of sorts." Heat spreads through my veins, a kiss from the inebriating liquid.

He spins his finger in a circle. "Don't keep me in suspense. Are you getting hitched? Did you knock someone up? Do you need bail money?"

"Fuck all of that. I've just been thinking about the future. Contemplating my goals. Being insightful and shit. The whiskey is helping."

"Shit, that's deep. Didn't take you for the sentimental type."

"Because I'm not, or didn't used to be." I tap the bar next to my empty glass. "Another."

"Think this occasion calls for the bottle."

"You'll never hear me disagree."

He grabs the Windsor and gets pouring. "You should talk to Grady." Erik nods toward a table in the front corner. "He went through some mind-melting shit when Sutton came home from college. That's your best bet."

Grady Bowen is sitting with his wife, only inches separating them. She's preparing to straddle him and he thrusts at the air with a laugh. They're wearing matching smiles, the kind screaming of secrets and dirty promises. Erik is right. That's not the guy I grew up with. But I already knew that. "He looks plenty happy."

"With her, yeah. That's what I mean. Think back to high school. I'm surprised you two didn't have a club or some shit."

The whiskey is doing its job, loosening my tongue and opening the doors to the usually hidden alcoves inside of me. "Nah, he's always been better with people than me."

"Not necessarily. If he is, it's because of that girl sitting on his lap. You choose to shut others out."

He's not wrong. I'm an antisocial mess mixed with bitterness. That fact is becoming more fuzzy the longer I sit on this stool. "I'm not really sure when that started. Being around people has never been my favorite. Biker rallies were one thing, but social situations in general make me itchy. My asshole of a father certainly doesn't help. Why do you think I'm such a loner, Rhodes?"

"Great question, but you're asking the wrong guy."

I spread my arms out. My limbs feel heavier than normal. "I don't see a better one."

"Only because you're not bothering to look."

"This"—I motion between us—"isn't really my thing. I don't handle idle chit-chat well."

"You don't say?" He chuckles. "Just trying to point you in a more useful direction. If it's dick jokes and crude stories you're after, I'm your man."

I return my gaze to Grady. If possible, his grin has stretched wider as he gropes Sutton and whispers in her ear. What would I say to him? I usually have nothing to say to him beyond talk at the shop. In reality, we're all relative strangers. "He doesn't serve booze."

Erik shakes his head. "No, but he can build you a house."

"Already got one of those."

"What the fuck do you need advice for? Sounds like you're all set."

I swipe a hand over my mouth. "You got a girl?"

"Yeah, sure. Don't we all?"

"A serious one, I mean."

He gets a suspicious gleam in his eyes. "Seems that way. How about you?"

I let the barest hint of a grin touch my mouth. "You didn't hear?"

"Rumors are shit."

"That's the truth." I grunt and motion for more whiskey.

"If you've got something to tell me, I'm all ears."

I have no doubt that Erik has met Keegan. He's always been the one to have a triple scoop of info on everyone's business. Like one of those old ladies swarming the market, but younger and with a shitload of tattoos. I'm sure word has spread about my possessive display with Keegan in and outside of Bronco. What else can I confess? Nothing good. "It was a wild night."

His brows bounce. "I can only imagine. That happens

quite often around these parts. Might as well cause a bit of trouble. Nothing else to do, right?"

"Damn small towns," I grumble. That's one reason why keeping to myself has always been appealing. Lonely at times, but safe in a fortress of my own making.

He crosses his inked arms. "As if you'd live anywhere else."

"I'll drink to that." And I do.

"What's next?" He knocks on the bar.

"Turning over a new leaf, or whatever the fuck this is."

"For a woman?"

Lush curves and cutting remarks try to break through the blockage of alcohol. "Maybe she started it, but this is for me."

"As it should be."

"I'm learning that," I mutter.

Erik juts his chin at me. "You got anywhere else to be?"

I let another grunt loose. "You're looking at it."

"Well, this calls for a toast." He pours himself a drink.

"What are we celebrating?"

He hikes up his brow. "You."

I roll my eyes. "That's another new one."

"Get used to it, yeah? A fresh awareness goes a long way." Erik lifts his glass.

Eh, why the hell not? I raise mine with a salute, clinking against his. "Here, here."

He slaps his hands together. "With that settled, tell me all about Keegan Daniels."

CHAPTER FOURTEEN

Keegan

Healing Hug #15: For long-awaited wishes being granted.

"WHERE ARE WE GOING, MAMA?"

Over the span of thirty minutes, I've lost track of how often that question has popped out of Millie's mouth. A giggle trickles off my lips while I try to count, fruitless as it might be. My daughter is nothing if not persistent, especially when it comes to surprises. I wonder where she gets it. A thrill skates down my arms at what we have waiting for us in a few short miles. I grip the steering wheel tighter in an attempt to focus my tension elsewhere. Just a bit longer and the news can fly free.

"Please tell me." Millie's pout becomes more pronounced with each second I delay.

I shake my head, blonde hair fanning out against the seat. "It's a secret, sweetie."

"But we've been driving forever." Her last word ends on a whine and I stifle another giggle. The young mind warps distance in such a dramatic way.

"We'll be there soon, baby girl." I change the radio to a station she likes, but the commercial that's playing isn't helpful to my cause.

Millie kicks her legs against the floor. "Mama, I have to pee."

I quirk a brow at the rearview mirror. "Do you really?"

She huffs. "Yes."

"How bad?"

An exaggerated potty dance begins. Her movements are limited by the padded booster straps, but she's getting the point across. "Really bad. My bladder is full."

I gnaw on the inside of my cheek. "Can you hold it for five more minutes?"

Millie's ploy of sneaky intentions reveals itself with a satisfactory grin. "Uh-huh. That's not very long."

I stick my tongue out at her. "Little turkey."

"You got played, Mama." She dusts her small hands off.

I laugh at her antics. "Did Josey teach you to be sneaky?"

"Maybe." Her smile gets bigger. "I mostly learned from you."

"No way," I sputter. "I'm always telling you to behave like a lady."

Millie crosses her skinny arms. "Because I act out so often in front of others."

My little diva princess is making another appearance. But she's right. I never have anything to worry about when it comes to her behavior. "Okay, fine. You bottle up all that sass for me."

"And spilling secrets," she adds.

I scrunch my forehead, unsure where she's going with this. "We don't spread people's private stuff, Mills."

"Mama, you're the worst at that. You also don't like it when others won't share something with you. I can't believe you didn't tell me where we're going by now."

A sigh deflates my stiff posture. It's always fun having my daughter call me out. To be fair, I spent a large portion of my life without anyone to trust. Once I paired up with Josey again, all of the delicious gossip poured out of me. Not in front of Millie, of course. She's just all too aware that I enjoy social hours. There are far worse traits.

I cluck my tongue at her. "This will be more fun as a surprise, baby girl. I promise."

"You already said that." Her gaze drifts out the window

just in time to see the first fringes of Gulligan Haven. The bold welcome sign can't be missed, a glorious sight for the most impatient set of eyes. Millie reads the name aloud, her gasp vibrating the steel and glass encasing us.

"Mama! Does this mean what I think?"

"Maybe…" I let the implication hang as we drive across the center drag of town.

"Are we finally getting a dog?" She's not taking any chances, apparently.

"If we find one that wants to come home with us."

Millie squeals and doubles her efforts with rattling the car. "This is the best day ever!"

Her excitement is infectious, and my belly swoops with every giddy sound. I turn into the shelter's parking lot, my foot pressing a little harder on the accelerator. Millie is bouncing in place as I find a spot near the entrance.

A tainted memory tries to worm into this moment. When I was only a bit older than Millie, my parents brought me to the pound to pick out a dog. What began as a highly anticipated occasion of my childhood quickly crashed into smithereens. We left with an empty kennel and heavy spirits. I cried the entire ride home and refused to entertain the idea of another try. "Don't get too attached to this idea yet, okay? They might not have the perfect fit for us."

She's already shaking her head before I finish my speech. "Our perfect pet is here. I can feel it." Millie presses a little palm to her chest.

My heart threatens to burst from the sight. I cross one finger over another and send up a silent prayer that this pans out. Stealing my daughter's smile isn't on the daily agenda.

Millie leaps into my arms when I open her door. I clasp her hand in mine while we walk inside. The precaution is for safety, and in the unlikely case she needs to be reined in. She skips along beside me, tolerating my helicoptering while her mind is preoccupied with visions of puppies.

A woman at the front desk stands as we approach. "Hello there. Welcome to Rover & Meow. How can I help you?"

"Hello," I greet. "We have an appointment with Kellie."

"Ah, yes. She's waiting for you in one of the indoor group spaces—Room Two. Just head down the hall and you'll see it on the left."

"Perfect, thank you." I guide Millie in that direction with a hand on her back. My daughter is practically vibrating with too many emotions, all rooting for control and snagging her voice.

"You okay, baby girl?"

"Uh-huh, yep."

I offer a soft squeeze to her shoulder. She's twisting her fingers so tight that the skin is white. "Are you sure?"

"Positive. I'm just super ready and nervous and freaking out because this is crazy amazing."

I laugh and brush a kiss to the top of her head. "Love you, kiddo."

"I love you, Mama. Thanks for bringing me here." Her shoes squeak on the glossy floor.

"It's about time, right?"

"I'm glad it's happening at all." Her smile lights up the plain white walls with splashes of vibrant color.

My sweet little angel has been begging for this, and I've been dragging my feet. My insecurities and concerns hang me up, but those are mine to deal with. Reflecting them onto Millie is plain wrong. Assuming history will repeat is a crippling way to live. It's my duty to provide a normal life for her.

Millie bumps into me with a giggling snort. She can brighten the darkest hour. This isn't a freaking doom festival. I twist my neck side to side, forcing my tense muscles to release. The responsibility of this decision will rest on us, but I'll carry any burden.

We reach the room and I exhale a deep breath. Millie is the one who reaches for me now, giving my hand a much-needed hug with hers. I knock, fidgeting with the hem of my shirt. The door opens an inch before the woman swings it wider.

"Keegan?" Her hazel eyes are warm, creasing at the corners with a growing grin.

"That's me," I say with a little wave.

The woman's gaze swings lower, focusing on the little girl clutching to me. "And this must be Millie."

My daughter doesn't give a verbal response. Her eyes are fixed behind the lady, to all the yips and yaps spilling out to us. She begins nodding so fast I worry her neck will hurt tomorrow. They exchange a friendly smile that eases the remaining swirling in my belly.

"Well, good morning. I'm Kellie, one of the volunteers. Come on in. These pups are ready to meet you."

"Thanks for setting this up for us."

"That's my job," Kellie sings. "Getting these babies a forever home is what it's all about."

"Millie couldn't be more excited. Right, baby girl?" I give a light tug to one of her pigtails. She's still nodding, her wide eyes trying to take in every section of the space as we step inside. Energetic enthusiasm floods the room with each tiny movement.

The acrid odor of rubber and bleach burns my nostrils. A symphony of whines, panting, and soft barks carry over to us. Three dogs are zipping around the rectangular play area. They're all medium sized, as I requested. That's one of the few specifications I gave. I wanted this experience to be at least somewhat organic for my little girl. Letting her into the main room with dozens of cages would be too much. Maybe more so for me.

Millie is rooted to a spot near the wall. Her gaze ping-pongs between the playful trio. She's smiling, so wide all of her front teeth show, but doesn't make a move otherwise. I can feel happiness rolling off her in waves. The same thrumming joy rushes through my veins.

When the door clicks shut behind us, the light brown pup notices our arrival and races closer. The other two barely spare us a glance, but I find myself giving them the same lack of attention.

The curious canine sits down a few feet away, tongue lolling out and tail thumping against the mat. A quick glance at her belly leads me to believe she's a girl. A large white splotch covers half of her face. More random spots paint her side and paws. I don't have the slightest clue what breed she could be, but that doesn't matter. Whatever background she's from blends into an adorable mutt.

The way she inspects us reminds me of an interview. Under her intense scrutiny, I feel my pulse climb several notches. Will she like us? Is that a silly thing to wonder? No, this is important. This process needs to be approved from both sides to be truly successful. I find myself silently sending every positive vibe through our stare down. Her dark eyes dart from Millie to me, finally settling on the one who will ultimately choose.

My daughter presses a finger over her lips, trapping a squeal. I can make a decent guess about what that noise means. Is there such a thing as insta-love with pets? With this pup, I find zero doubt.

Kellie moves to my side. "What are your initial impressions?"

I glance down to Millie, finding her gaze already locked on me. "Well, I think it's safe to say there's a front runner." I point to the pretty girl scooching on her butt to get near us. "What's her name?"

"Ah, that's very good to hear." She signals to the brown dog, who's brought herself almost within reach. "This is Elsa."

Another loud squeak bubbles out of Millie. If her mind wasn't already made up, that about seals the deal. My daughter yanks on my arm until I bend down.

"She's a princess, Mama."

Her soft voice tickles my ear. "She sure is. Do you like her?"

"Uh-huh. Can we pet her?"

I look to Kellie, who's grinning at us. "Absolutely. Just place a hand out in front of you so she can sniff."

We do as instructed and Elsa immediately responds, erasing the sliver of distance between us. Our palms take turns getting slobbery kisses and lavish licks. Elsa nudges Millie, who giggles and scratches the pooch behind her ears.

"Oh, she loves you," Kellie coos. "Is it safe to assume the other two can go? I'll take them outside for a walk."

I glance at Millie, but she only has eyes for Elsa. The two of them are forming a wriggling pile of laughter and unbreakable bonds. I blink at the heat pooling in my eyes. What a perfect pair. A lump forms in my throat, and I swallow roughly.

"My daughter seems hooked on this beautiful lady. Do you have her information card or file?"

Kellie nods. "Absolutely. I can give you some time alone with Elsa. Get to know each other a bit more, see how y'all get along. I'll take the others for a stroll and return shortly."

I rub the sting in my nose. "Thanks again for this. I really appreciate everything this shelter does for animals and the families looking to fill that special void."

She squeezes my arm gently. "No, thank you. To see this level of happiness brought to a child means so much. And you're potentially saving that animal from a much crueler fate. This is the type of connection we all strive for."

I return my eyes to Millie and Elsa. "It truly is. I couldn't have asked for a better introduction."

Kellie leans closer. "She's probably not letting you leave here without that dog. You know that, right?"

A laugh cracks through the emotion sticking to my tongue. "I sure do, and that's what we planned for."

She studies me for a moment. There's a certain sparkle in her eye that makes me want to squirm. "This probably isn't appropriate for me to say, but everyone knows that I don't have a filter."

"Ah, okay?" A sharp inhale gets trapped in my lungs as I wait for more.

"Not sure if you're attached to a fella or not. It doesn't really matter. I'm bummed that my son is hellbent on staying single for all of eternity. I think you two would hit it off."

I force out the breath with a whoosh. "Oh, that's so sweet of you. I'm not really looking for a relationship."

"Isn't that what we always say? It just takes the right one. Much like Elsa and your daughter. Match made." She snaps her fingers.

"You sound like my friend."

Kellie takes a step toward the door. "I bet she's very wise."

"Josey would appreciate hearing that."

"I give you permission to tell her. Especially if a gorgeous woman such as yourself is attempting to ward off men." She winks at me, and I find myself laughing again. This woman is a riot.

"Um, thanks? I think."

Kellie picks two leashes off a hook. "I'll get these boys handled and grab Elsa's file for you. Then we'll see where we're at."

I'd almost forgotten the other dogs were in here. When I turn to search for them, they're chasing a ball along the far wall. "Will they be okay?"

She waves me off while walking toward the rambunctious pair. "They're young purebreds. Don't worry too much about them."

"Oh, that reminds me. Do you happen to know what

Elsa's pedigree is? Not that breed matters at all. We just need a good personality." I know enough to determine she's a combo platter. My parents used to say that a mix is always a safe choice. Turns out, at least in this instance, they're right.

Kellie taps her temple. "I just went over her paperwork. Elsa is almost a year old. I'll have to double check her exact age. She's a blend of retriever and Australian shepherd. Maybe a bit of Labrador thrown in, too."

"Can't go wrong with any of those. They're all great for being around kids."

She nods. "Definitely. I remember she spent several months with a foster family who had young children. Elsa has always been socialized with other pets. She's never shown any sign of aggression."

"How long has she been here?"

"A little less than a month. She's had several serious inquiries, but none have taken to her quite like your daughter."

I glance over at the newly acquainted best friends. Elsa swipes her massive tongue along Millie's cheek. My daughter giggles and wipes off the slobber. She's a goner. I know that giddy expression quite well, and there will be no dulling of that shine if I can control it. A sigh whisks any drop of tension from my posture. "Well, Kellie. Unless there's anything major in her file, I believe we're set."

Her light eyes twinkle in the harsh overhead lamps. "Yeah?"

"Absolutely. I can't tear them apart. It might hurt me more than my little girl to do so."

"I can empathize. We don't want to cause any pain, that's for certain. This is a big decision," Kellie reminds.

"We aren't making it lightly."

"It's settled then. I'll bring the care instructions and adoption agreement with me. Give me five minutes."

"Sounds great."

Once Kellie is gone, I kneel beside Millie and Elsa. Our

dog—calling her that might take some getting used to—grants me a sloppy smooch before returning her affections to Millie. "I can see you two are getting along."

My daughter beams at me. "We get to take her home, right? Mama, I love her. Please tell me she can be our dog."

That title again. It warms every fractured piece inside of me. "If everything checks out, she can leave with us today."

"Yay!" Millie pumps her little fist in the air. "She's the best pup ever."

I give Elsa a pat of my own. "It seems that way."

"Thank you, Mama. This is the best present ever. I'm going to take the best care of her." She buries her nose in Elsa's fur.

"Seeing you this happy makes me extremely happy, too."

"Now we're a bigger family," she mumbles against Elsa's cheek. I swear the dog tilts lower to accept more hugs.

I wipe under my eyes, more moisture gathering from the display. Before this day is done, I'll be wrung dry. "You two are adorable. Let me take a picture."

Millie's smile is huge as she poses for the camera. Elsa is naturally photogenic, as well, and the image they create is enough to melt me into a sentimental puddle of tears. I snap a few shots before tucking my phone away. "We'll have to stop at the store for supplies."

"Oh, yes. Like a pink bling collar so we can take her on walks."

I laugh at her priorities. "Among other necessities. She might like to eat, too."

A dreamy look crosses her face. "Do you think she'll get along with Patch?"

I went all morning without thinking about Crawford. Over four hours of blissful peace are whisked away with a single question. It takes herculean effort to keep my smile from slipping. "Maybe? I'm not sure they'll meet each other, sweetie."

"Why not? They can play together in the woods."

I have every intention of staying away from that section of forest. Indefinitely. "We can discuss that later."

Her lips form a flat line. "That means no."

"Why does our dog have to be friends with Patch?"

"Then we can see Ford."

I swallow a scream, mostly for my crumbling pride. "Why do you like Ford so much, Mills?"

"He gets it."

"Can you tell me what that is?"

She shrugs. "He understands why I don't like talking to people."

And I'm officially the worst mom ever. I feel my eyes get hot again and blink at the quickly forming tears. "Oh, baby girl. I'm so sorry. I had no idea you felt that way."

"It's okay." From her flat tone, I can tell it's most certainly not.

And just like that, my own defenses take a brutal hit. My daughter is a terrible influence on me when it comes to that man. How can I stay away from Crawford when Millie is his number one fan? If she knew what a temptation he is to me, there would be no avoiding another seemingly chance encounter. "Maybe we'll bump into Ford and Patch soon."

Millie's mouth twitches with the first signs of a happy comeback. "Can you call him?"

I choke down my immediate response. That doesn't mean I have to form a lie. "I don't have his number, sweetie."

"Should we look it up? Or we can just stop by his shop."

How do I respond to that? Simple. Focus on the positive. "How about we celebrate finding our perfect dog and worry about Ford later?"

She narrows her eyes on me, and I brace for another retort. The strain in my neck eases when Millie relaxes against Elsa. "Okay, Mama. I'll accept that answer." I'm about to begin a mental victory dance when she quietly tacks on, "But only until tomorrow."

CHAPTER FIFTEEN

Crawford

Healing Hug #16: A last resort when all else fails.

I SINK DEEPER INTO THE CAMPING CHAIR, COMMANDING MY BODY to unravel and accept a lazy state of relaxation. This is the same task that I've been attempting for almost an hour. Deep breathing and beer be damned, my muscles won't quit twitching. I've been wired all afternoon without the slightest inkling as to what's behind the sudden influx of distress. Silence and serenity are no longer my friends.

Sure, I've been out of sorts and battling with myself. No fight is an easy win while I push at borders of my own making. My level of normal has been subjected to a serious overhaul, and I know adjusting to new habits takes longer than a week or two. I'm not expecting miracles. Being calm and collected has never been part of my skill set. But dammit, I'm more than capable of adapting to minor changes.

Thinking is far easier than executing.

Patch dives into a pile of needles and leaves, scaring the shit out of a flock of birds in a neighboring tree. A chorus of flapping and squawking blasts through the woods. My dog circles the massive pine, barking and clawing at the trunk. The ruckus isn't helping this fake-ass Zen I'm going for. I tug my hat down lower and try to think about peaceful things. A dull throb hammers into my temple with the waste of effort. It backfires much the same as everything else I've tried.

I'm about to raise a white flag on this entire venture when the crack of a twig snapping halts my retreat. The intrusive sound has me whipping around so fast that I nearly topple out of my chair in the process. With the next thudding beat of my heart, three figures move into the clearing I've been using for a hideout. Time slows until a single exhale drags on without ending. Shining blonde hair, the golden color of my fantasies, paints the bland surroundings with a vibrant glow.

With my sights tunneling on Keegan, I fail to notice the addition to their typical duo. A dog dutifully trots beside Millie. The neon pink collar clues me in that the pup is a girl. She appears to be a very well-mannered companion for the little girl. Patch doesn't miss the new family member, of course, bounding over in graceful leaps. I jump from the chair with a bellow, knowing I can't get there to stop what might happen. But once again, I'm proven idiotic for showing concern.

Patch greets the newcomer with a few meaningful sniffs, no sign of territorial defense or agitation in her bouncy gait. Millie kneels on the grass, petting both dogs with equal enthusiasm. The theory of girls sticking together has never been quite this clear. I continue to stand motionless with my jaw hanging in the wind. After the females complete their initial introductions, Millie is the one who knocks me out of my frozen trance. Her gaze lifts to mine, and she aims a brilliant smile at me.

"Hi, Ford!"

"Hey, Peep."

She settles cross-legged onto the ground, making herself at home. "We've been looking everywhere for you."

Her sunny mood is infectious, lifting the brick resting on my chest. "Is that so?"

"Uh-huh." She nods, turning to her mom. "Mama, aren't you glad we finally found him?"

"Just thrilled." Keegan crosses her arms, slamming a wall

down between us that's meant to lock me out. Too bad that's not happening, but I can appreciate her efforts.

"Well, this is definitely an interesting surprise. Wasn't sure I'd see you two again. And who's this?" I nod to the wiggling brown and white dog pressing against the little girl's side. Patch is all too willing to play the fourth wheel, sprawling out in front of them.

"She's our new dog. Her name is Elsa." Millie's blinding grin outshines her mother's scowl by one hundred watts.

"That's a pretty name."

"She's a princess."

"I can, uh, see that." I motion to the collection of sparkly, pink embellishments she has on. And are her nails painted? The mutt doesn't seem to care one bit that she's being subjected to dress-up. Patch barely lets me attach a leash on her most tolerant days.

"Are you like Prince Eric?"

"Who?"

Millie blinks at me. "From *The Little Mermaid*."

Ah, she's talking fairy tales. Those are the furthest thing from my wheelhouse. "I've always been more of a beast type."

She giggles. "My mom doesn't mind."

I shift my gaze to the lady in question. "No?"

Keegan remains silent, fuming in the privacy of her own bubble. Shit, why does she have to look so fucking tempting? The surge of current sizzling against my skin is enough to set this entire forest on fire. This woman is a living, breathing centerfold sent to test my restraint. Those measly fibers are already threadbare. With her in reach, I'm ready to snap.

It doesn't matter what clothes she has on. I'm intimately aware of every curve she's not bothering to hide very well. My imagination gladly runs rampant and peels off every layer. The athletic shorts she's wearing barely cover the globes of her ass. Her breasts and waist are somewhat concealed by a white tank top. I widen my stance to conceal just how hard she makes me. A dizzy spell is imminent if I don't get a handle on this lack of blood flow to my brain. The pressure is enough to bring me to my knees. Will she always have this effect on me? She probably earns a great deal of satisfaction from torturing me.

I rip my ravenous gaze away from the mouthwatering display Keegan is serving. Focusing on safer sights is necessary to survive this standoff. I cut my eyes back to Millie and find her eyes bouncing between her mother and me. A smile I can only describe as sly curves her lips. The little girl leaps to her feet and tugs on Elsa's leash.

"I'm gonna take the poochies for a walk. They'll keep me safe, and we won't go far. You two stay here." She makes a pointing gesture from us to the ground.

Keegan's lips part, probably to refuse being told what to do by a child. Her own daughter, for that matter. But in the end, she snaps her mouth shut. Millie skips away with Elsa and Patch flanking her. Her absence gives us privacy—alone in the middle of nowhere. How convenient.

I rock on my heels, taking a minute to figure out how to kick this off. "So, you got a dog."

A groan almost wrenches out of me. *Great job, moron. Way to state the obvious.*

Keegan quirks a brow. "We did."

"From where?"

She huffs. "Not sure why you care, but Rover & Meow in Gulligan Haven."

I stroke a hand over my jaw. "That's where I picked up Patch."

"They have a great facility."

"Sure do." This superficial conversation scrapes at my skin worse than a rash. That's really saying something, considering my general lack of giving a shit whenever talking is involved. "And you just so happen to be walking her in my woods?"

Keegan pins me with a fierce glare. "Your woods?"

I hold my arms out to the side. "Do you see anyone else wandering in these parts?"

She rolls her eyes. "Millie is especially attached to this piece of property. Why might that be?"

I take a glance around at the endless rows of trees, streaks of sunlight breaking through the leaves. "It's a beautiful spot."

"You almost sound sentimental," she mutters.

That dull tone twists a knife in my gut. "Even I care about some shit."

"Shocking."

This is going slightly better than a botched root canal. I lift my hat, fiddle with the brim, and yank it back on. "You, uh, look good."

She tilts her head, sending a cascade of shimmering waves over her shoulder. "Is that painful to admit?"

"Yes." I bore my gaze into her, shooting every drop of sexual frustration into the static sparking between us. What the fuck am I doing? My intentions are murky, even to me. "It is when there's nothing I can do about it."

Keegan gives my appearance a lazy perusal. My torso flexes, muscles straining to be under her microscope. Her lashes flutter as she treats herself to another once-over. I want to believe she's picturing me naked, much as I was doing to her moments ago. Or is she repeating the last words we exchanged? Perhaps the knockout punch I foolishly delivered to myself? Based on the severe frown tightening her expression, Keegan hasn't forgotten my parting blow—not that I expect her to forgive me. But why the fuck do I care so much if she does?

Because this is the woman who's responsible for my demise. Not that it's been all bad. If Keegan hadn't blown a hole in my reclusive existence, I wouldn't be standing here right now. Does she know the hell I've been in? What are the chances she feels the same? Pretty fucking low, considering how I treated her. I wouldn't fault her for slapping me across the face. That's the least I deserve. Maybe I'll offer up the option if she's willing to hand over something in return.

I set this chain of shitastic events in motion. Does that mean it's my job to stitch the rips? "You've been giving me a lot to think about."

"I could say the same for you." Her tone is husky, dropping several octaves.

"We're very compatible in the ways that count." What am I trying to accomplish by leading us down this winding trail?

Keegan licks her bottom lip, pulling the plump flesh between her teeth. "What's rolling around in that dirty mind of yours?"

"That's a great fucking question. Is it freaking you out?"

"A little."

"Why?"

"I'm the one doing the asking," she deadpans. "Why are you looking at me like that?"

"Maybe I'm reminiscing."

Her cheeks burst into a blood-red hue. "Don't you dare."

I offer a lame shrug. "You can't stop me."

Keegan waves an erratic finger into the still forest. "My daughter is feet away. She can hear you."

"Don't search for an excuse."

She scoffs. "We're not doing this now, or ever. That possibility is a dead-end."

As if they're hiding in the bushes listening to us, Millie and her loyal guardians pop into the clearing. I flare my nostrils, releasing a stream of hot air for being interrupted. But maybe it's for the best. Who knows where our battle of words would lead us?

Millie tugs on my shirt. "Are you friends now?"

The laugh that bursts out of me is brittle. "Not sure about that, Peep."

"But you're talking and smiling. My mom has that look on her face that means she's happy. She doesn't smile like that for just anyone."

I can't stop my gaze from trailing to Keegan. "Is that so?"

Millie nods. "Uh-huh. You're special. I've been trying to tell her that. She doesn't like to listen, even though she always tells *me* to be a good listener."

Keegan begins coughing. "All right, sweetie. That's enough."

She frowns at her mom. "Why? We shouldn't keep secrets. Unless it's about a super cute puppy. That's a good surprise. Ford should know that we like him."

There's a real smile splitting my face. The expression is wide enough to lift my cheeks. "That's nice to hear, Peep. I like you, too."

"What about my mom?"

I scratch at the stubble on my chin. "If she likes me, I will like her back."

Millie stomps her foot, narrowed gaze set on Keegan. "See? It needs to be mu–tu–al." The way she pronounces the last words makes me believe it's her first time using it. That works in my favor.

"I couldn't agree more, kid. That's how the closest friendships build." What the fuck do I know? But it sounds good.

"Yep, uh-huh. That's how I'm going to make friends in second grade."

"It's a guaranteed success."

"Okay." Keegan claps her hands. "This has been fun. I think we should leave Ford alone now."

That's actually the last thing I want. The truth rattles against my ribs. Watching them walk away might shadow the sun and allow thunder to strike. But admitting any of that is a step too far right now.

Once again, Millie steps in to save my pansy ass. "But I don't want to go yet."

I peer up at the forest ceiling, watching the branches dance in a light breeze. "I don't mind the company."

Keegan cocks out a hip, taking a fighting stance. "From her, maybe."

How can I argue with that? "You're part of the package."

"Because you don't want to make Millie sad."

I grind my molars. This is heading in the wrong direction. "Seeing that little girl upset would hurt you more than me."

"If I cry, can we stay?" Millie sniffs for good measure.

Oh, she's good. I know some women who could learn a few tricks from this one. "Please don't do that."

Keegan struts over to her daughter. "She won't. Right, Mills? That would be misleading and naughty."

Millie's bottom lip wobbles, and I wince. "Okay, Mama."

"You're not in trouble, baby girl. Just turn the sass down a couple notches." I snort at the irony. There's no question where she learned it from. Keegan whips a glare at me. "Do you have something to add?"

I hold up my hands. "Nope."

Millie remains rooted in place, her gaze set on me. "Can we hang out again soon?"

Keegan lays a gentle palm on her daughter's back. "I'm sure he's a busy man, sweetie."

"Didn't we already cover this once?"

"I'm trying to help you out, Ford."

"I don't need rescuing." Especially when I'm already heading straight for hell.

"If you open this door, she won't close it."

"Will you?"

Her eyebrows soar into her hairline. "What are you getting at?"

"There's no harm meeting me in a few agreed-upon locations, right?"

"I can't even begin to imagine where those might be."

"There are several parks and trails nearby. I've been taking Patch out into public more. Socialization and all that."

"Oh, that's rich, coming from you." A scoff packed with disbelief tumbles out of her. "Millie will be relentless now."

"Not always a bad quality, if it's aimed in the right direction."

Keegan stares at me, fiery emeralds blazing into my blackened core. "Lucky for me, I tend to search the left first."

CHAPTER SIXTEEN

Keegan

Healing Hug #17: Offering support is never a weakness.

AGAINST MY BETTER JUDGMENT, AND EVERY SINGLE GUT instinct compelling me to bust a U-turn, I pull into a gravel lot that marks our final destination. I glance out the windshield to get a lay of the unfamiliar land. This is another expansive piece of Silo Springs that's been left untouched, for the most part. The huge grassy field, sprawling far and wide, is sectioned off with chain-link fencing. A large board plastered with multiple columns of rules is visible from where I sit, huddling in the safety of my car.

The twisting clench in my belly increases. "Maybe this isn't such a great idea."

"You're such a chicken." Josey snorts from her spot beside me.

Millie gasps from the backseat, and I glare at my best friend. "Calling people names isn't very nice, Josephine."

"She's right, JoJo. You should apologize." Millie's scold has the power to make grown men weep.

I cross my arms, giving Josey the smuggest grin on history. "I also accept chocolate and lattes."

"Getting backed up by a seven-year-old. You must be so proud." She flicks some hair over her shoulder with a flourish.

I turn off the ignition and turn to face my accuser.

"I certainly am. She follows the rules and never gets into trouble."

"Uh-huh, I'm a good listener. My mama is, too. That's why we're meeting Ford. He asked us to, and we don't want to make him sad." Millie unbuckles her straps, wiggling in the slightly raised booster. Elsa perks up from the commotion and stares out the window. Her tail begins whipping against the door when she catches sight of where we are.

"We shouldn't leave him waiting." Josey motions to the entrance gate.

"You're coming with me," I grumble.

"Obviously. Why else would I tag along?"

"For a good show?"

"True. You're providing the entertainment today."

"I'm beginning to regret inviting you."

"Make up your mind, woman. No wonder you're driving Ford crazy."

It's my turn to gasp. "That's not true. We did each other wrong."

Josey waves me off. "Mutual fault is boring. I prefer to pretend you have all the ass kissing to do."

Millie releases another squeak of outrage. "JoJo said a bad word!"

My friend flinches. "Crud, I'm sorry."

"I'll be expecting your dollar in the swear jar by sundown."

She wrinkles her nose. "Such a stickler."

"Just wait until you have kids. The last thing I want is one of her teachers calling me to say she's using potty talk."

"Oh, that's too cute." She winks at Millie.

I pinch her arm. "Don't be a bad influence. I can't even deal with you right now."

"It's only going to get worse once we catch up with your lover boy." Josey smacks her lips.

An exaggerated groan vibrates my chest. "Please don't embarrass me."

"I make no promises." And with that, she hops out of the car.

I scramble to follow her lead, grabbing Millie and Elsa along the way. My daughter giggles when her new best friend spins circles around us. Someone is definitely ready to play. My pulse crashes louder with each hurried step. Crawford better show or he'll be the unfortunate recipient of my mama wrath. I pray that this isn't the biggest mistake I'll ever make.

We make it five feet inside of the gate when Millie takes off running. I'm about to call for her to wait when I see who she's racing toward. Crawford is sitting on a lone bench, looking hot enough to give me acid reflux. I'm certain the green shirt he's wearing brings out the color in his eyes. How doomed I am to already be imagining that belly-fluttering view?

My stride turns into more of a stomp as we cover the remaining distance.

Josey tips her head back and laughs. "You're so screwed."

I wish.

Instead of letting the truth slip, I shoot her a glare. "Oh, hush. I'm just frustrated in general."

"I can see why." She nods in Crawford's direction. "How in the world do you resist that walking orgasm?"

I allow my gaze to follow her rapt focus. What I find has the breath stalling in my lungs, setting a fire inside the very center of me.

Millie is jumping up and down, flailing her arms in animated circles, while talking so fast it sounds like gibberish. Crawford is just watching and listening, giving her the softest smile. Just like that, my ovaries go into hyperdrive.

"Oh, dear Lord." I reach out, wildly gripping onto my friend's elbow.

She giggles. "Yep. Super screwed."

"You're not helping," I spit. A string of the most foul expletives tickle my tongue.

"Be patient." Josey pastes on the most obnoxious smile I've had the displeasure of seeing. If Crawford didn't hear us talking about him, her megawatt grin is certain to clue him in.

His keen eyes zero in on me in particular, the hazel shade flaring at whatever he discovers. A slight lift of his chin pairs with the scorching stare. "Afternoon, ladies."

My temperature spikes from two insignificant words. The deep rasp of his voice glides across my balmy skin. How will I manage to maintain my cool if he lets more loose? A shudder I refuse to acknowledge sends a spasm through my muscles.

"Hi, Ford." Josey gives him a little wave.

He barely spares her a glance, choosing to pinpoint his intensity on me. I'm trapped in his fog. There's no exit route from this type of unavoidable disaster.

My friend makes a noise of agreement in her throat, walking toward Millie and the pups. I blink and return to my senses. After clearing my overly parched throat, I shuffle forward to be part of the group.

"Hey. Thanks for telling us about this spot." I flick my gaze to the side, down to a patch of dirt, looking anywhere but at Crawford.

He grunts. "Yeah, it's all right. Midday isn't too busy. But in a few hours, the place will be swarming."

"I didn't know there was a roam free park in Silo Springs."

"No reason to unless you've got a dog."

I kick at the ground. "Right, duh. That makes sense."

"Wowza," Josey wheezes. "It sure is steamy. I can practically feel the sticky heat clinging to me. Can you sense that… tension in the air?"

"Don't start." I glare at her.

She presses a hand to her forehead. "I've behaved. How long do you expect me to stay quiet?"

I roll my eyes back to Crawford. "So, how does this work?" Patch is at his hip, still attached to a leash.

He crosses his arms, sinewy biceps bulging under his shirt. "Didn't you read the rules?"

"Uh, no." Flames burst across my cheeks. "I guess we were in a hurry."

"Should I take that as a compliment?" The corner of his mouth tics.

"If you must," I mutter.

"And on that note—" Josey tugs at the collar of her shirt. "It's clear you two have some unfinished business. We'll just be over there, letting the dogs sniff butts or whatever they do."

Before I can interject, she loops an arm around Millie and grabs Patch's leash from Crawford. Josey leads their quad-pod toward a hill without a backward glance. I tuck my chin and expel a long breath.

"We need to quit meeting like this."

"You invited me." As if he needs the reminder.

Another torch ignites in his smoky eyes. "That I did."

I feel exposed under his seductive watch. "Do you, uh, come here often?"

If my face wasn't already the shade of a tomato, that comment would finish the job.

Crawford adjusts the ballcap on his head. "More so lately, whenever the mood strikes. I want to come more often."

That earns him a snort. "I bet you do."

"Maybe you can assist in those efforts."

"I thought we decided not to discuss that again."

He scrubs a finger over his brow. "I never agreed to keep it clean."

Good grief this man can turn the filth on and off faster than a switch. The way he acts with Millie, gentle and almost polite, is a drastic difference to how he treats me. I could admit the same about myself. Josey was right—this man brings out an untamed side of me. All I want to do at this moment is climb him like one of the ancient pine trees surrounding us.

I narrow the gap separating us until only a foot remains.

The need to reach out to touch him singes my palm. "What're you proposing?"

"We can be...friends." The suggestion sounds like the last thing he wants. Not that I blame him. The idea of being strictly platonic with him is less than appetizing.

Why not add a little flavor to spice this platter up? "Not gonna tack on any benefits?"

He growls into his fist. "Watch yourself, Kee."

That nickname again. I wasn't sure he'd bother with it after the way we left off. I settle a palm flat on his chest. "What's in it for me?"

"Your daughter's happiness, apparently."

I glare at him, my blood beginning to boil. "You'd use her as leverage?"

"Nah, I'm not that big of an asshole. But if she wants us all to be together, what's gonna stop you from making it happen? And conveniently, Elsa fits into the dynamic."

He's got me there, and I bet my taut expression shows it. I'm on his hook without any leverage. Why did I agree to this again? Cue an internal eye roll. Millie's pleading has no bounds, an endless stream of whining until I can't hear anything else. I wasn't joking about her being relentless. "Using the dogs and Millie against me is a low blow. Even for you."

"I'm a motivated man."

"Since when?"

Crawford towers over me. "Snap judgments are beneath you, Keegan."

I wrench my gaze away, cursing myself in the process. "What are you trying to prove, Ford?"

"Not sure what you mean."

"You're done with me. I got mine, so we're set. Nothing else needs to happen. That much was clear with your remarkable farewell."

He stands, bringing our bodies into startling alignment. "Tell me that I'm not the only one still thinking about it."

His hot breath trickles down my neck, burning a path straight to my core. I try not to shiver. "You're crazy."

"Maybe. You didn't seem to mind before."

"That was different."

"How?"

"You were a stranger. Just some random guy I ran into a couple times. When you showed up at Bronco Buck, the pieces fell into place. And for one night, that worked for us. Now? It doesn't make sense. Everything is more complicated."

"You want to know more about me?"

"Not necessarily, but I won't stop you if sharing makes you feel better."

Crawford takes a tiny step back. I'm grateful for the sliver of space so my breasts don't brush against him with every exhale. "It's no damn secret that I'm a loner. I've been this way for years. Meeting you and Millie lit a fire under my ass. Maybe I don't wanna be stuck out in the woods all alone anymore."

Thunder rumbles in my ears. "What're you saying?"

"Exactly what I already told you. I never wanted to be around others more than required to survive. My friendships are nonexistent. I decided that needs to change. We seem to get along well enough. So, tell me we can meet up once a week or whenever you have a free afternoon. Not for dates or anything romantic. Millie comes along. Invite Josey if that makes you more comfortable."

I shake my head, trying to process what he's saying. After several moments, his meaning still doesn't compute. "I don't get it. Why me?"

"Why not you?"

"Just answer the question, Ford."

His throat bobs with a thick swallow. "You're good for me."

"How?"

"Why are you making this so hard?" Crawford yanks on his hat again. "I can't explain it very well. You just make me feel...happy."

My heart is beating too fast. I can't catch a decent breath. This man is showering me with compliments to the best of his ability. Yet my broken spirit refuses to believe the sincere quality. "This seems like a trick."

His hazel eyes skewer me to a nearby tree. "What do I have to gain from scamming you?"

"Sex."

A twitch leaps in his jaw. "I already got that."

"And you don't want a repeat?"

"Another question." A snort flares his nostrils. "If I did, lying and being dishonest is far too much wasted effort. I don't need to be shady and resort to deception. How bad do you think I am?"

"That depends on what version of personality you're using."

"Are you going to deny me compassion either way?"

I shake my head, strands of blonde sticking to the stubble along his jaw. Light blending with dark, the meaning not lost on me. I release a shaky exhale. "No."

"Does that mean yes to everything else?"

Is this another future regret? Only tomorrow will tell. "Sure. We can give this friendship thing a test run."

The shimmer in Crawford's gaze speaks of victory, but what he won is yet to be determined. I refuse to let Millie be a casualty of a failed experiment. My heart, on the other hand, is a bargaining chip I'm more prepared to lose.

His lips brush the shell of my ear. "You won't be sorry."

Clarity seeps in with another impulsive assurance from him. "Don't make promises that are meant to be broken."

The smirk touching his mouth caresses my most intimate bits. Yeah, I'm completely screwed. "Only if you stop assuming the worst of me."

I don't shy away, tilting my chin to put us on even ground. "Prove me wrong, Ford."

CHAPTER SEVENTEEN

Crawford

Healing Hug #18: Given to those who aren't
brave enough to ask.

FOR THE SAKE OF ESTABLISHING EQUALITY IN THIS CRAZY-ASS experiment, Keegan gets to decide where we're meeting this morning. Switching off is reasonable since I'm the one who's orchestrating a change. If I want new challenges, this is a guaranteed way to get them. Her lack of trust isn't surprising in the least. I deserve the clouds she's casting over me. If she jumped in without questioning my integrity, I'd wonder about her genuine investment. But of course, Keegan bailed and bucked at my plans. Thankfully, in the end, she bent when it really counted.

We share stakes in this arrangement. Mine just happened to be a greater risk, at least in my opinion. There's no denying she's still interested in me. How deep that attraction flows is another story. Does the potential of sleeping with her again appeal to me? Abso-fucking-lutely. I can get hard in a moment's notice with her nearby. We can both benefit from solidifying a relationship, platonic or purely physical.

I glance at Keegan's last text while waiting for the light to change. Her location of choice is in the heart of downtown Silo Springs. The options become less appealing with each block I pass on Main Street. Patch is acclimating to our widening horizons far better than me. She's almost friendly with everyone that walks by, offering them a whipping wag of her tail.

When I approach the address, my stomach drops straight to the sidewalk. The regret for concocting this harebrained scheme is settling in real deep right about now. Keegan sent me to a fucking coffee house. This is what I get for not researching the site first. Going in blind to keep the suspense alive was a foolish mistake.

Once I'm standing in front of Steeped, there's no doubt in my mind that Keegan chose this spot to torture me. Upon initial glance, this bistro is only marginally better than Bronco Buck in regard to my preferred ratio of people to space. The interior is crawling with patrons searching for an open table or waiting in line or standing against the wall while talking to others. This is a great example of socializing to the extreme. I'm about to be one of the guppies swimming in a sea of idiocy. But, to be fair, there's a patio where dogs are allowed.

Patch drops her nose to the ground and leads us around the building. At least one of us knows where to go. Idle chatter floats over from around the corner, offering further proof I don't need. The outdoor seating area is less crowded, but there are still more bodies than I care to count. There are so many damn people in this area. If I wanted real solitude, I'd have to move a lot farther than the woods on the outskirts of town.

Millie looks up when I clang the metal gate open. She waves, pigtail braids flapping with the erratic motions. That little girl has the ability to knock some good sense into me without batting an eyelash. The other woman at the table gives me pause for another reason entirely.

Keegan's glossy, blonde mane shimmers in the direct sunlight beating down. She twists in her chair to face me, a coy grin hiking up those ruby-stained lips. If Millie is candy-coated sprinkles, her mother is a double slice of creamy cheesecake with strawberries and whipped cream. My fucking favorite. A shot of pure adrenaline gets injected into my veins, and I barely manage to stifle a groan.

Without further delay, I stride into the fray with my gaze set dead ahead. Keegan's eyes are covered by a pair of oversized sunglasses, but I want to believe she's tracking my every move. When I near the empty seat, it becomes clear she's looking at Patch. Well, damn. Talk about deflating a man's ego.

"Want this up?" I gesture to a folded shade umbrella in the corner.

She puckers that red pout at me. "If you can. I tried, but the darn thing wouldn't budge."

In one smooth motion, I slide the center mechanism up and lock the pin in place. A wide shadow immediately curtains the table, providing much-needed relief from the sky-rocketing heat.

"Better?"

Keegan doesn't answer. She seems transfixed by something on my shirt. I glance down to see what's caught her attention. My hem lifted with the movement, exposing a slice of my lower abs. I hum and allow a smirk to tilt my mouth. Now that's more like it.

"Find something of interest?" I don't bother masking the humor in my voice.

"Hmmm?" She licks her bottom lip, feeding my already overflowing spank bank. My cock jerks in approval, which is highly inappropriate considering the quantity and nature of the company surrounding us. I force images of wrinkly grandpa asses into my mind to dial me back.

"Just appreciating you enjoying the view," I drawl.

That snaps her out of the trance. Keegan shoves her shades to the top of her head with a huff. "Don't flatter yourself."

"Don't need to. You're doing a mighty fine job of it."

A rosy hue blossoms on her cheeks. "Whatever."

"Getting busted in the act looks great on you, Kee." I plop my ass down on the seat, getting comfortable under her blazing fury. Even the fresh air and overpowering scent of much-needed caffeine can't mask her pineapple paradise aroma.

"Continuing to rub my face in it makes you look like a… meanie."

Millie has been silently sitting on the sidelines until this moment. Her adorable face pinches tight. "Uh-oh, you're gonna get in trouble. Don't be naughty, Ford."

Vindication splatters across Keegan's terse expression. "Yeah, be nice."

"What did I do? You're the one ogling me like I'm a piece of—"

"Do not finish that sentence," she scolds.

I narrow my eyes on her. Mama Bear is showing up to battle. "This isn't over."

"Far from it." Keegan's eyes gleam in a way that almost makes me avert my gaze.

"Is that why you picked this spot? You almost had me running scared."

"That'd be a fun sight, but no. This is my favorite café. I spend most of my weekdays here working with Josey. Figured I'd introduce you to good coffee." She nudges a large mug in my direction.

I peek at the dark brown liquid, steam rising off the top. "You ordered for me?"

"Are you offended?"

"Not at all. I like it when you take care of me." I treat myself to a tentative sip. The rich brew bursts on my tongue. Damn, that's delicious. She'll never hear me admit that, though.

Keegan tosses her hands up. "Here we go again."

"You make it so easy for me."

"Too bad I can't say the same for you."

I wince with a hiss. "Oooh, ouch."

"We're off to a fantastic start." She glances down at the pups lying under Millie's chair. The little girl is pleasantly distracted by her fierce protectors. "I wasn't sure you'd bring Patch."

I study the slender column of her throat, moving with a thick swallow, as she watches them. "Why not?"

Keegan's gaze returns to mine. "She doesn't fit on your bike."

"Which is why I didn't drive."

"You walked all the way from…uh, where do you live?"

I hitch a thumb over my shoulder, pointing in the direction we came from. "Above the garage. Figured you knew that."

"I'm trying to curb my assumptions. That's a far hike, Ford."

"It's only seven miles."

She sputters and her eyes bulge. "That must have taken you hours."

I give her a flick of my wrist. "Only a little over one. It's nothing we haven't done before. We go for a run every morning. This wasn't a big deal."

Keegan nods. "Wow, yeah, I guess not for you. That's really inspiring."

I enjoy another swig of coffee. "It's good to know that I can impress you."

"Weren't you aware already?" She circles the rim of her cup with a fingertip.

A quick glance shows me that Millie is still occupied with Elsa and Patch. "No harm hearing it directly from the source."

"I could learn a thing or two from you," she murmurs.

My pulse leaps at her words. Such simple context from this woman gets a huge reaction. "Is that so?"

Keegan taps my arm. "Get your mind out of the gutter. I just meant being more physically active."

I wipe over my mouth, hiding a smarmy grin. "I'm the one being dirty? Plenty about that topic can be misconstrued."

She presses a hand to the flush racing up her neck. "So, anyway. You just hoof it everywhere if Patch comes along?"

"What else am I gonna do?"

"Get a car?" She clamps her lips shut, looking like there's more she wants to add.

I wait for another beat, but she remains quiet. "Nah. I can get anywhere we need to go with what I've got. Why waste more money on another vehicle?"

"What if you want to take someone out?"

"My bike seats two."

"How about a little someone?" She gives Millie a pointed look.

I almost snort. As if this woman would ever trust me alone with her kid, on purpose. "That's never going to happen."

"Why not?"

"I don't anticipate the situation presenting itself."

"Humor me." The tone she uses has a seductive twinkle on the end. That silky note fuses a spark under my skin.

My molars clack together. "I'm sure walking would be a viable option."

"And if it's too far?"

"Then we'll stay in."

Keegan taps her chin. "See? These are things you have to think about."

"Yeah, for you as a parent. Those concerns don't apply to me."

"For now."

"And the foreseeable future."

She frowns at me. "You don't want children?"

"Didn't say that. I've very recently decided to start making friends. Opening myself to the possibility of more is intimidating as fu—fun. Kids are a long way down the road after that."

Keegan seems to ponder that, allowing the silence to

stretch between us until I'm ready to fill the gaps. She finally puts me out of my misery with a tempered, "I see. That makes sense. So, isn't this weird?"

I scan the bustling space, but the rush of voices doesn't penetrate our bubble. "Only at first. I'm getting used to all the traffic."

"No, I meant hanging out with Millie and me."

"Why would this be weird? I'm very comfortable with you two."

"There has to be better options for a single guy such as yourself."

"Quit selling yourself short. I'm where I want to be. Millie is an extension of your best qualities. We both know I like you, perhaps more parts than others. But that's only because I've been properly acquainted." I run a hungry gaze along the low-cut neckline of her shirt. "Maybe intimately is a better word choice."

Keegan buries her face in a curled palm. "Please watch your language. You're worse than Josey."

"What did I say?"

"You know exactly what's being implied."

I nod at Millie. "But does she?"

She glances at her daughter, who's busy telling our dogs a story. Patch and Elsa are taking turns getting brushed, one stroke each, with a pink brush Millie pulled from her little purse. Not the most efficient grooming method, but I don't see anyone complaining. Keegan twists her lips to the side. "I just don't get it."

"That's your problem to solve. I'm having a great morning. You're the one who needs to relax."

"Me?" Her voice rises with outrage. "I'm fine."

I grunt into my nearly drained mug. "I think we already established that I know fine does not mean fine."

Millie pops out from under the table. "Mama, I already told you. Ford gets it."

I furrow my brow at the little girl. "Did I miss something?"

Keegan flutters a hand toward Millie, cupping her cheek in a comforting gesture. "She says you understand why she doesn't talk to most people. She stands up for you at every turn."

A shooting pain slices into the center of my chest. I suck in a sharp breath, choking on the ball in my throat. People have always let me down. Everyone except these two. "Thank you."

Millie beams at me. "You're welcome. We gotta stick together, right?"

I blow out a heavy exhale, loosening the tangle in my gut. "Absolutely."

Keegan points at my empty cup. "Had enough?"

That's a loaded question. I rub my temple as thoughts swirl into a complex jumble. "Yeah, I'm done."

She smiles at me, soft and warm and melting the bitter cold buried inside of me. "Let us give you a ride home."

"Nah, that's not necessary. My shop is out of your way. I don't want to impose."

"How very thoughtful of you." A tinkling laugh bounces out of her. "Since when?"

I motion between us. "This is voluntary."

Her shoulders shake as she reels in the humor. "I'm well aware. So is my offer to drive you."

"You'd be forced into spending more time with me."

"Don't read so much into a simple gesture." Keegan winks at me.

"You're confusing."

"And you'd be doing me favor. Thinking of you running another seven miles today is bad for my health."

"Well, in that case—" I give her a wink of my own. "I'll call shotgun."

CHAPTER EIGHTEEN

Keegan

Healing Hug #19: A cure for when the chill is bone-deep.

THE CRUNCH OF FALLEN LEAVES CRACKLES UNDERNEATH MY flimsy flip-flops. Millie tightens her grip on my hand as Crawford guides us deeper into the woods. That's what I'm assuming, at least. My eyesight is currently compromised by a massive palm. With permission, of course. Even so, this situation is the perfect opening scene for a horror movie. I can picture the photo caption in bold, blazing letters.

A very trusting, albeit idiotic, woman allows a broody guy to steer her and an innocent child into the dark forest. While blindfolded.

Yep, this is stolen straight out of a scary film script.

I take another shaky step forward on wobbling legs. When a twig snaps, I nearly leap out of my skin. The bastard behind me chuckles.

"So jumpy," he murmurs.

"You would be too if the roles were reversed."

"The next location is your pick. I'll follow along blindly, wherever you lead."

"You say that now." The possibilities begin to formulate in my jittery brain. Beating this supposed treat should be a cinch.

"I believe you'll steer me in the right direction."

"Ah, using the guilt factor. Well done."

Another raspy noise scrapes out of his throat. "I'll do whatever it takes to get more days like this."

I smash my lips together to silence the embarrassing sigh desperate to climb out. The sound dances on my tongue until I gulp the gooey sentiment down. We're just friends out having fun. Sure, we slept together. Those escapades might as well be ancient history, though. Our connection is fleeting. When it's time to move on, we'll go our separate ways. He'll keep in touch for Millie's sake, until she abandons the hero worship.

But it's difficult to remember the arrangement when Crawford dishes out the sweet and swoony. He makes me question the strength of our restrictions. I could easily fall for his charm, but I won't. A chaste relationship is precisely my speed. My resolve rattles through me with each shallow breath.

Crawford directs us to the left, knocking me from my reverie. "Are your eyes still closed, Peep?"

"Uh-huh," she squeaks.

He nudges me. "How about you, Kee?"

I roll the sockets behind my sealed lids. "Yes, sir."

"Oh, I like that." A rumble rolls off his chest.

I scoff into the blank unknown. "Don't get used to it."

"You two are so funny." Millie giggles, enjoying his little game far more than me. I suppose that makes sense, since this stunt is definitely for her benefit.

Creepy prickling sensation aside, my belly is in a flurry of flutters. Crawford is spending extra energy being creative with his presentation, and those actions are very much noted. He earns brownie points for upping the anticipation factor with each passing moment. My little girl is practically squealing with delight. Millie's laughter triggers my own, and soon we're lost in hysterics.

"Not sure we're that funny," Crawford mutters.

"We're wandering in the middle of nowhere with you

as our guide. The fact I'm still going along with this strange trust exercise speaks to my dedication for the cause." Could I peek through his fingers and ruin the surprise? Well, duh. But I find myself wanting to go along with whatever he's planning.

"Your faith in me is remarkable. I can hardly handle the weight of that responsibility." His tone is drier than the dead foliage littering the ground.

"Not sure what more you want from me." It might be my imagination, but I'm certain he presses his hips into me. I only feel the evidence of him for a moment before he's backing off. It's plenty to give me a hint of exactly what he's interested in.

"Don't fret, Kee. It's worth the wait."

Not even thirty seconds later, the sound of flowing water hits my ears, and I slam on the brakes. "I swear on everything holy, if you're about to dump us in—"

He squeezes my shoulder. "Relax. This is the finish line." His hand disappears from my face. "Open and see."

I follow his orders instantly, shielding my eyes to block the harsh light. A loud gasp immediately follows as the breathtaking view spans out in front of me. The wide creek commands first notice. Deep blue and rippling, the surface glistens in the sun. I follow the glittering pattern along the weaving stream until the lazy current disappears from view. A thick wall of trees lines both sides, protecting this slice of wonder from the harsh reality looming just beyond the forest edge.

When I glance at Millie, her gaze is darting from one surface to the next. She can't seem to decide where to focus her attention first. I can empathize.

Crawford moves to stand beside me, joining in the staring contest. "What do you think?"

I return my sights to the gleaming river. "Definitely worth the build-up."

"It's so beautiful," Millie adds.

Static erupts across every porous inch of me. "I've never been here before. You're showing us all the best secrets in Silo Springs."

He squints at me against the bright reflections off the water. "Ah, it's kinda off the beaten path."

"That makes it more special. A secret," I muse.

"Not many even know how to reach this part of the shore."

My daughter wrinkles her freckled nose at him. "Is that why there was no peeking? I wanted to take just a little look so bad."

He chuckles at Millie. "No. That was just to add some flash to the big reveal. Did it work?"

"Uh-huh, yeah. I'm super surprised."

Crawford nods toward the sandy bank. "You can go straight in. It's not very deep in this section. Your knees might get splashed a bit if you wade into the very center."

She whips her gaze to mine, pleading with every sparkle in those green irises. "I wanna swim now. Please, Mama?"

I glance at Crawford. "Millie is a mermaid, as I'm sure you're aware, but she has a floaty if needed. It's safe without?"

"Very much so. There are no rapids or sink holes. Sitting in the low depths is the best compromise of hot and cold." He points between the cloudless sky and inviting brook. "The better spot for swimming is upstream a few miles. But that's overrated. This area is the true gem of the river."

The way he speaks about this place makes me want to listen. It's clear he's sentimental and personally invested in this private grove. There's a lot of history buried beneath the sand, no doubt.

"Speaking from experience." It really took all of my detective skills to dig up that obvious tidbit. I internally roll my eyes.

He nods. "I've been coming here since I was a kid."

Millie spins around to face us, quick feet kicking up drop-lets. "Like me?"

Crawford sends her a grin. "Yeah, right around your age."

"Wow, that's cool. Maybe I'll still be visiting this creek when I'm old." Her grin is more radiant than the midday sun.

Crawford hangs his head, but he's still smiling. "I hope for that, too."

A loud peal of laughter has me refocusing on Millie. She's hopping in a circle, pointing at the glassy surface. "There's a fish!"

"You'll see a lot of them in there," Crawford informs.

"How many is a lot?" I do my best to peer into the river from a safe distance. My efforts are not very successful. All I catch are rocks and a few patches of weeds. I must be making a sour expression because he quirks an eyebrow at me.

"What's wrong?"

A shudder rocks through me. "The vision of fish nibbling on my skin has always made me squeamish."

Crawford snorts out a chuckle. "Don't be ridiculous. They're totally harmless."

"Hey!" I poke his stupidly chiseled pec. "How about you don't ridicule me? I'm well aware that it's a silly fear, but that's my issue."

He holds up his palms. "Fair enough. I'll be nearby to save you if the fish form a mob and stage an organized attack."

"So gallant," I mutter.

He winks. "Glad to be at your service."

"Don't be scared, Mama. I'll catch all the fishies." Millie returns her admiration to the stream, sloshing and laughing and soaring high on jubilation. Her pigtails twirl with each bubbling motion. She lifts my spirits right along with hers.

I allow the moment to loop around me until my body is absorbing nothing except warmth and fresh air. Birds sing a tune from their perches. The languid tide at the riverbend babbles along the shore. Everything else is quiet and calm, peaceful to the very roots we stand on.

"This seems like a safe choice for you, Ford." What I don't reveal is how fast my pulse is racing or how being this close to him scrambles me all up inside. The thing that stands out most is how thankful I am that he's shared this haven with us. I'm already reconsidering where we'll go next. My earlier assumption crumbled into powdery dust the second I stared into the crystal-clear creek. Topping a pristine natural paradise will be tough to accomplish.

"Look deeper," he murmurs close to my ear. I follow his gaze as he studies my thin cover-up.

"What should I be searching for?"

"A solution to my growing problem." The strain in his voice prods at me.

I take an obvious glimpse around at the woodland escape we're swaddled in. "How could there be anything wrong when you're in this environment?"

"Just one major flaw," Crawford grunts. "Nothing about spending the afternoon with you in a bathing suit is a simple decision to make."

"Am I that repulsive?" I mean to sound serious, but a flirty undertone sneaks through the cracks.

His eyes flit up to mine, narrowing into slits. "Quite the opposite, and you know it."

I toy with a stretchy strap that's crossing over my collarbone. "Do I?"

"Don't test me, woman. Your daughter is nearby. I can only hope you took pity on me and chose something that fully covers your perky ass." In an unprecedented show of affection, Crawford rubs his thumb across my nape.

A thrill zips through me, and I curl my toes into the sandy embankment. "Substantial swimwear isn't my preference."

He bites the knuckle on his clenching fist. "Now you're just being cruel."

"Does that mean you don't want to see what I'm keeping covered?" I tug at the fabric straining over my bust.

Crawford takes a sudden interest in a tall aspen next to us. "I have a vivid imagination."

I hum a sound of agreement. "You certainly do."

He squeezes his eyes shut. "It's your intention to torture me."

I blink at him, batting my lashes with extra oomph. "This was your idea."

"Maybe you should keep the dress on. Indefinitely."

I reach for the hem skimming my mid-thigh. "Never."

"My regret is expanding faster than other parts, which is amazing on its own. Choosing an activity that requires you to wear a bikini was a grave mistake." He straightens his fingers, stretching the flexed knuckles, only to curl them into fists again. "I'm already testing every ounce of my control."

I choose to focus on a specific part of his speech. A sneaky idea follows close behind. "Who told you I have a bikini on?"

Crawford's brow makes an inquisitive leap upward. "Did you take pity on me and choose a one-piece?"

"Should we find out?" In one fell swoop, I remove the garment and toss it at him. The sun kisses my skin, much like I wish his lips would. I shove that nonsense away with a harsh exhale. What am I thinking?

Crawford's eyes dip to my mouth, trailing down until settling on the modest cups covering my breasts. The underwire and push-up features emphasize my already ample cleavage. Based on the heat flaring in his hazel pools, he's appreciating the added boost. My skin pebbles under his fiery gaze. I shiver against the onslaught of warring emotions ripping me apart.

"I take it all back. This was a fantastic plan." In the next beat, Crawford whips off his white tee, revealing bronze skin and a well-toned physique. Black board shorts hang low on his waist, almost revealing the entire happy trail that leads to so much more. I'm well aware of what he's packing behind that thin layer of nylon. If I stare hard enough, the outline of his impressive ridge is visible to my desperate searching.

"That's what I was thinking." My body is too hot, sizzling from more than the direct rays beating down over us. I turn in front of him, close enough to touch, but begin walking backward before our boundaries are breached. The cool stream laps at my ankles, and a rush of relief washes over me. I bend and flick water at him. The spray hits him in the chest, trickling down to the waistband of his shorts. I've never been more jealous of liquid. "Well, don't just stand there looking pretty. Come and get me."

CHAPTER NINETEEN

Crawford

Healing Hug #20: The silent moments are most powerful.
It doesn't have to be for comfort.

I DRUM MY FINGERS TO A CROONING COUNTRY BEAT THAT'S serenading me through the speakers. The romantic lyrics aren't lost on me, but I tune out the singer's suggestions all the same. I don't need another reason to think about love and commitment and losing my damn mind. Sitting mere feet from a certain captivating blonde is more than enough to make me wax poetic. Keegan is tapping her thumb against the steering wheel, enjoying the wistful tune. Her ruby lips are mouthing the words, and I find myself sucked into the chorus all over again. She catches me staring, lifting a brow in my direction.

"Find something of interest?"

Damn straight I have. I nudge my aviators down until an unobstructed view of her face filters in. "Other than the rows of wheat and tumbleweeds?"

"Spoken like a true native of Wyoming."

I knock on the glass beside my head. "Born and raised. Glad my roots are showing."

She nods. "Seems we have that in common."

"Where'd you grow up?"

"In Cheyenne, mostly." Keegan's smile wilts at the corners. "I moved around a lot during my college years."

"On purpose?"

She shrugs. "Out of necessity. I had a baby to feed and very few rental options in an affordable price range."

"Damn, that sounds rough." I grip my thigh, holding off from saying more.

"Eh, it all worked out." Keegan glances in the rearview mirror with a rejuvenating grin.

"Cheers to that." I lift my chin at her. "Nothing beats a rich history and valuable life experiences."

She squints into the distance. "And a boundless future. Do you ever plan to travel the world?"

I chuckle into my palm. "Whoa, slow down. I haven't lived beyond the limits of Silo Springs. Any trips I've taken lately tend to be within a one-hundred-mile radius."

"Interesting," she murmurs.

"Maybe I should venture further. Doesn't matter how often I pass these fields. They all look the same blending together like this."

Keegan remains tight-lipped about where she's taking us. Based on the absolute silence filtering in from the backseat, Millie and Josey are still batting for her team. The ordinary landscape has offered zero hints as we travel along the interstate. Nothing but rolling meadows and grassy fields greet my gaze as I look out the window.

"There's beauty to be found in simplicity."

When I return my eyes to her, she's focusing on the flat road in front of us. I smirk at her stoic expression. "Spoken like a true believer."

"Good thing I am one."

"That's why I'm keeping you around."

"Among other things," she trails off.

I stroke the stubble coating my jaw. "Ah, I suppose. There's more to come."

Another quirk of her brow. "For both of us?"

"Good grief, you two." Josey's head suddenly appears

between our seats. "Why don't you take a trip to the hardware store and get it over with?"

Keegan's face scrunches up. "Huh?"

Josey flicks her arm. "Hammer and nails, Keke. Maybe some screws and caulking, too."

She sputters. "Please don't tell me you're implying—"

"Without pause. Like you two should be doing."

"Millie is sitting right next to you," Keegan scolds.

Her daughter takes the provided entrance. "Mama?"

"Yes, baby girl?"

"JoJo isn't wearing her seat belt. She's gonna get hurt."

Keegan glares at her friend. "Quit being a bad influence and sit back."

"One day, you'll thank me." Josey points between them. "And I'll get to gloat."

"So, a typical Saturday?"

"Such a sass-pot." With that parting barb, Josey settles into her seat. The click of her belt releases some of the tension that's lifting Keegan's shoulder.

"At least she provides entertaining commentary for the drive."

I flick a look at the woman behind me. Josey shrugs and offers Millie a high-five. These three are conspiring against me. Again. "Any chance either of you wanna share where we're going?"

"Not my secret to tell," Josey chides.

Millie nods. "Don't spoil the surprise, Ford."

I slouch against my seat, resigned to sit tight a bit longer. After another song fades to black, I'm still very much out of the loop. I'd stopped trying to guess our destination once we got twenty minutes outside of Silo Springs. By this point, the unknown is making me itchy.

"Are you taking me to Denver?" I bounce my knee against the dashboard.

Keegan scoffs. "On this route? Highly unlikely."

"Why else would we be heading south for this long?"

"The wait will be worth it." That sounds all too familiar.

"Very funny."

"I thought so."

"Not even a hint?"

Keegan clucks her tongue at me. "You're worse than Millie."

A mock frown droops my expression. "I'd take offense, but she's pretty bad as—"

"Asp," Keegan finishes with a glare. Josey snorts, and she shoots her a look that makes me want to wither away.

"Uh, right. One of those wicked vipers that's powerful enough to expel the evil queen."

Millie gasps. "Like detention? Wow, that's so cool. I totally wanna be an asp."

Keegan groans while I laugh. "It's better than the alternative."

"I'm just so thankful it's summer break. She has months to scrub her mind of all this bad language."

The instinct to reach over and grab her hand clenches in my gut. I resist the urge, threading my fingers together and squeezing too hard. "She's a really good kid, Kee. You've done an incredible job raising her. I have no doubt she will grow up to be a very conscientious and honorable person. That's because of you."

She sniffs and wiggles her nose. "Thank you, Ford. That means a lot."

"Speaking the truth is no skin off my back." I avert my eyes and notice the endless expanse of undeveloped land is broken apart by sporadic houses. Another two miles delivers more frequent buildings and condensing traffic—the outskirts of a city appear in the rapidly approaching distance. I recognize the name on a few signs, but can't remember the significance.

It only takes three turns off the highway for more clarity to sweep in. The outline of a Ferris wheel and a shitload of parked cars begin to take shape. My muscles strain and flex against the offense charging at me. I draw in a sharp breath, picturing a flood of people gathering in lines, pressing into me as they walk past. Fuck, that's not a pretty sight. I rub my temples against the sudden pulsing.

"You're taking me to a county fair?"

"Close," Keegan sings.

"Can I tell him, Mama?" Excitement vibrates from Millie's tone.

"Sure, sweetie. Go ahead."

"We're going to a rodeo," she blurts. "There will be horses and cows and sheep and clowns. I might be able to get a pony ride. Isn't that so cool?" Millie's skinny legs are kicking in wild disarray when I glance at her over my shoulder.

The clump of spikes lodged in my chest disintegrates with her announcement. "Wow, Peep. That's awesome. I can't wait."

"You're so good with her," Keegan murmurs. This isn't the first time she's mentioned something along those lines.

"Yeah? It just comes natural."

"That's not the case for everyone. Take the other adult in this car, for example."

"Oh, please," Josey scoffs. "I'm the best fake auntie ever."

"It's fun to rile her up." Keegan winks at me.

I chuckle. "Yeah, things were getting a bit too serious for a minute there."

"Oh, oh. Look! We're here." If she was a bit bigger, Millie would be shaking the entire vehicle with her bouncing.

I follow her erratic pointing to find a large fairground spanning across the concave valley in front of us. Most of the land is dominated by a massive arena, equipped with a variety of pens and corrals on each end. American pride is painted across every available surface. Banners and flags hang from light poles and fence posts. Even with the windows shut, I can hear country music blasting from the mounted speakers.

Keegan pulls into the designated gravel lot and finds an available space in the center row. We all pile out, heading for the open gates. She passes four tickets over to a man collecting stubs near the entrance.

I still her movements. "Let me pay."

"Too late. Advance passes were cheaper. It's already taken care of."

"I'll have to treat you next time."

Her smile is a warm blast to my frosty armor. "You've got a deal."

We stride through a canopy tent, entering our names in a drawing of some sort along the way. Fresh-cut grass and hay waft over with a lazy breeze. Moments from my past flicker in and out of my vision. This feels familiar, a comforting hug after spending too many cold nights alone. Aisles of vendors, fried food, and bleacher seats. All that's missing is the roar of engines. The thundering of hooves is a decent substitute. I walk a little lighter with each forward step.

Millie gasps and begins flaying her arm toward a colorful booth. "Mama, can I get my face painted first? Please, please?"

Keegan glances at me. "Do you mind waiting for a couple of minutes? This usually doesn't take long."

I motion to the available artist. "By all means."

Josey sidles up beside me. "Yeah, don't worry about Ford. I'll keep him company."

"Oh, great," Keegan groans and turns away. "I can hardly wait to hear what comes of that conversation."

Josey chuffs me on the arm. "Welcome to the club. You're one of the gals now, Ford."

I let my brows dip. "Uh, thanks?"

She tilts her head back and belts out a laugh. "Just messing around. We all know you two can't keep up this no-sex charade forever. I give it two weeks, at the max."

I grunt. "If I'm lucky."

"Care to place a wager?" She sticks out a palm in invitation.

"On sleeping with Keegan? That has disaster written all over it."

"Eh, you're right. Why bet on a sure thing." She nudges me again. "But as an added favor, I'll keep Millie occupied so Keegan can be all yours. Go get her, tiger."

I blink at Josey, letting her words rattle in my thick skull, before busting out a chuckle of my own. "I appreciate you tipping the scale in my favor. You're really something else."

She polishes off her nails. "Glad you're finally noticing. Make sure to pass that along to all of your single friends."

"If I see any, I'll be sure to let them know."

Just as Josey opens her mouth to speak, Keegan and Millie join us along the main path. The little girl's entire left cheek has been transformed into a sparkling dog that slightly resembles Elsa.

"Isn't it so pretty?" She races up to me with the design front and center.

I tip her chin to get a better look. "Absolutely perfect."

"Do you want them to paint your cheek?"

I do my best not to recoil. "Uh, well, I'm not so sure."

"You could get a motorcycle or a bull. They can draw whatever you want." Millie clasps her little hands in a pleading gesture.

Shit, am I really going to do this? I look to Keegan for assistance only to find her and Josey whispering at a rapid pace. When she notices me staring, Keegan's skin takes on a splotchy red hue. Yeah, she's totally busted. I lift my brows and wait.

Keegan struts over, shoulders rolled back and head held high. "I'm sure Ford would love a picture on his face, but we should get seats. All of the best spots fill up fast. Plus, you'll want to get cotton candy and popcorn first."

Millie ponders that for a moment. I'm holding my breath

while wishing for a sliver of mercy. When the little girl smiles at me, all of the air rushes from my lungs. "Okay, let's go. I'm hungry and wanna see the horses."

The three of us follow close behind as she skips toward the food stand. We order way too many snacks and sodas to wash it all down. Weaving our way to the benches is a tad more challenging with our arms full. Crowds of people are growing in numbers by the minute and closing in on us. Keegan wasn't lying about the seating situation. Over half of the bleachers are already full. We manage to score an empty row near the top and slide our asses onto the hard metal.

The view from this vantage point allows me to see all of the pregame acts and warmups. "Damn, this is quite a turnout."

Keegan glances around. "It sure is for this location. Hayek isn't considered a large rodeo. Sutton Bowen told me all about the inner circuits for this stuff. There are a ton of smaller regional events that qualify for the real money makers. Have you heard of Frontier Days?"

"Sounds familiar. Is that the huge festival in Cheyenne?"

"Yep, ten days of celebrating Wild West awesomeness. My parents took me every year while I was growing up." A long sigh breezes past her lips.

"You don't go with them anymore?"

Keegan's features pinch. "No, it's been years since we've been there. They, uh, died, when I was a senior in high school."

I hiss, feeling her loss strike me with a direct hit to my stomach. "Shit, Kee. I'm so sorry. That's awful."

She's nodding too fast, mostly likely teetering on the edge of losing her cool. "It happened so long ago. I can usually talk about them without going into hysterics, but yeah, it really sucks."

I place a hand on her knee, giving her a gentle squeeze. "I can't even imagine going through that. You don't have any siblings?"

"Nope. I'm an only child. They left me all alone, but it

wasn't their fault." Keegan draws in a shuddering breath. "My parents weren't the vacationing type. They never splurged on fancy trips or extravagant destinations. But their twenty-fifth anniversary was a reason to go all-out. They flew to Hawaii for a week and stayed in an all-inclusive resort. All of the bells and whistles, with a cherry on top. I remember looking at pictures after they booked the hotel and being super jealous. That guilt still stings."

Another shallow exhale wheezes out of her. "After they'd been gone for three days, I got a call from the hospital out there. My parents had been in a boating accident. All of the passengers died on impact. Thankfully I was eighteen, or the situation would've been worse."

I drag my fingers through my hair, tugging on the ends. "Damn, I don't even know what to say. I'm just really fucking sorry."

Keegan fans her face. "Ugh, sorry to rain on the fun. I didn't mean to get all mopey."

"Don't apologize for that. You have every right to grieve." I give her leg another reassuring squeeze.

She rubs at her red nose. "Thanks. It's good for me to talk about sometimes."

"That's good because I have two ears and strong shoulders. You can lean on me all you want."

Her humming agreement is more garbled than usual. "Be careful or I might get attached."

I pause, waiting for a pool of dread to bubble in my gut. No signs of sludge or acid appear. In fact, her suggestion leaves me with a sense of calm that I only get after a long cruise down the freeway. My reaction steals the snarky remark I might've tossed back at her. Instead, I focus on the fast pace action in front of me. A quick glimpse over reveals that Josey and Millie are doing the same. As we all should be, apparently. Two men are riding on horseback, chasing a cow, with lassos spinning in large loops over their heads.

"Woo, okay." Keegan wipes under her eyes. "I'm cleansed and all better. Let's enjoy the show."

Silence settles between us as a new event begins. Each participant is attempting to twist a steer's neck in order to wrestle the beast on the ground. It seems fairly aggressive with a bunch of kids in the audience, but what the fuck do I know. "This almost reminds me of a bike rally, just with animals and country music."

"Do you go to those often?" Keegan dips a fry in ketchup, biting the end off with vigor. Talk about being aggressive.

"Not anymore. Growing up, we went all the time. I swear, my mom loved going more than my brother and me. Those are good memories."

"Did you lose interest, or what happened?" She chomps away on another fry, her eyes going wide. "Am I prying? Feel free to ignore me."

Grant is a topic I prefer to avoid. I glare off into nothingness, seeing my brother as he was then versus now. Bringing those skeletons into the light of day is not what I want to do. But I suppose it's only fair since she spilled about her loss. "My family is a sore subject, especially my brother. Grant was my best friend until he got into a bad wreck with his motorcycle. He ditched his bike and started working for my dad. I barely speak to him anymore."

Keegan slaps a palm to her forehead. "Gah, I'm really stepping in the cow manure today. I seriously didn't plan on turning this conversation into confessional."

I chuckle at her creative non-swearing. "It's fine. I'm having a good time."

She quirks a brow. "For real?"

"Yeah, the rodeo is kickass."

"Better than biker rallies?"

I think about that for a moment, an idea sprouting and taking root. "Maybe we can start the old traditions again. Make them our own."

Keegan pushes her sunglasses up, staring at me with a ferocity that strikes down to my bones. "Don't make promises to me, Ford."

"I only will if I intend to keep them."

"Think about what you're saying."

I gulp down a long swallow of soda. "That's all I've been able to think about lately."

"What does that mean exactly?"

"You, Millie, all of this. I wasn't expecting much when I came up with this unconventional scheme, but it's really working out for me."

Keegan lets her gaze skitter off mine. "Please don't break her heart."

My pulse hammers a furious rhythm, nearly stealing my breath. "What about yours?"

"I'm not worried about me. Mine already has a few dents and dings. A couple more cracks won't hurt."

"Doesn't seem right." I want to cup her jaw, force her to look at me.

She keeps her eyes averted. "That's the way it has to be."

I want to correct her, confess to wanting...more. But what do I really have to offer? Warming one side of the bed for a few nights? This woman belongs with a man far better than me. Even so, I can't leave her hanging. "Not sure I'll ever agree with that."

Keegan smiles, but the expression is forced. "By the way, thanks again for what you said about Millie."

"Honestly, that was nothing. You deserve far more than a few simple words, Kee."

"They sounded really complex to me."

"I can do better."

A brief pause almost opens the door for regret. Until Keegan peeks up at me from under her lowered lashes. "Sometimes you're almost sweet."

"Don't go spreading that around."

"Do you have a reputation to uphold?"

"Nah, not really. I'm a mystery to most folks. But if they think I'm a teddy bear, the town will probably burst into flames."

"That's a little extreme."

"Same with you calling me sweet."

"I said almost," she corrects.

"Not sure it matters."

"Just take the compliment, Ford."

"All right, if that'll make you happy." I take a liberty, small as if might be. When I wipe specks of food from the corner of her mouth, Keegan gasps.

"I'd be tickled pink."

Pretty sure she already is. "That's an innuendo waiting to be discovered."

"Not everything has to be dirty."

I point to our surroundings, specifically the plums of dust clouds in every direction. "I can fake being a filthy country boy with the best of them."

Her lips twitch. "Oh? Do you have a Stetson and some Wranglers stashed away?"

I dip down until my mouth caresses the pierced lobe of her ear. "Would it turn you on if I did?"

Since she ditched her shades, I can see the change in her vibrant green eyes. The idea definitely appeals to her. "Yes," she whispers.

"How about asking Josey to watch Millie while we take our next…adventure?"

"What're you suggesting?"

"Maybe some of those benefits you initially implied."

Keegan tucks some golden hair behind her ear. "Thought we'd been there and done that?"

"Who's to say we can't circle back for another quick pass?"

"Just once?"

I shrug. "Maybe twice."

She pulls the glossy pout of her bottom lip between her teeth. "I could probably get on board with that."

"Is next Saturday good for you?"

She nods, her hair brushing across my neck. "Pretty sure I'm wide open."

"Not yet, but you will be soon."

CHAPTER TWENTY

Keegan

Healing Hug #21: Two broken pieces sliding
into place for a perfect fit.

THE ZIPPER ON MY KNEE-HIGH BOOTS GLIDES UP WITHOUT A hitch. I straighten and dust imaginary lint off my clothes. Once again, I'm appraising my appearance for an evening of unknowns. I've ditched the sparkle explosion dress for ripped black jeans and a long-sleeved shirt. My wavy hair is knit in a messy braid. A light dusting of makeup highlights my best features. Simple and chic.

Crawford didn't give me much guidance on what to wear, or our plan in general. It doesn't take a genius to assume he's picking me up on his bike. A quick downward glance confirms I'm prepared for the ride. On the surface, at least.

Mentally, I'm not a shining example of confidence. My mind is more conflicted than opposing sides in an epic battle. Warring thoughts aren't my only problem. Twists the size of a jumbo pretzel are knotting my stomach—but not with hesitation. The thought of having Crawford's rough hands all over my body, bending me into indecent positions, is enough to incinerate any uncertainty. These damn flutters speak the truth. The flapping wings in my belly will be the end of me.

I check the clock and my heart spasms. All of my attempts at distraction were too successful. I've wasted over an hour contemplating the possible outcomes. Crawford will arrive any minute now. Specifics of our non-date might be questionable, but the broad goal is set in cement. Am I really going through with this? Again? Now or never. I slick another layer of gloss on my lips and pucker up, but the reflection in the mirror is deceiving all the same.

Just as I'm about to second guess everything for the fourth time, a catcall whistle comes from behind me. "You're looking foxy."

I turn to Josey with a smile. "Really?"

She bites the tip of her finger, giving me a lazy perusal any man should be jealous of. "I mean, heck yeah. You're the epitome of dressed to impress a certain broody biker. But you know it's like eighty degrees outside."

"End of June or not, Crawford told me to cover up." I tug at my pants.

Josey snorts. "That seems counterproductive."

I shove her shoulder. "Oh, shush. This isn't about sex."

She bends over, cackling laughter shaking her frame. "That's a good one. You're hilarious."

"Okay, fine. It's a little about that."

"At least you're able to admit it."

"Do I actually look okay?" I study my wardrobe once more.

Josey winks at me. "You're smoking, babe. He won't be able to resist. I hope he goes all macho alpha on you again."

"Oh, that was hot." A zing zips up my spine at the thought of Crawford's reaction. Prickles skitter along my skin as if sensing him nearby. "Thanks again for watching Mills. I really appreciate it."

"My pleasure, and yours." She bounces her brows.

Millie shuffles into the hallway with a killer frown marring her beautiful face. "You look really pretty, Mama."

I kneel down to her level, bumping our foreheads together. "Hey, don't be sad. I won't be gone long."

Her bottom lip sticks out further. "But I wanna hang out with Ford, too."

"I know, sweetie. We'll all spend time together again really soon." I stroke my thumb down her porcelain jaw.

"Why not tonight?"

Josey sweeps in and ruffles her hair. "Because we have plans, Mills. You and I are doing all of the crafting. We'll take Elsa to the park. I'll make my famous homemade macaroni and cheese. You'll beat me at UNO. I bet you'll barely notice she's gone."

My daughter peeks up at her. "Yeah, I guess."

I rub her shoulders. "You two will have a blast."

Millie sighs, her shoulders curling in. "I know, mama. It's important for you to be best friends with Ford. Then he'll never leave us. I just like it when we're all together."

A cramp attacks my stomach, but I shove the ache away. Worrying is for tomorrow. For now, I boop her button nose. "Sometimes adults hangout alone, right? Just like kids. But I'll make it up to you with extra dessert tomorrow. Deal?"

A loud knock interrupts us, sending Elsa into a fit of barks and spins. Millie's eyes pop open wide and she races to the door. With a whoosh, Crawford is revealed on the stoop in all his leather jacket glory. A haze of his woodsy musk wafts over to me, and I do my best to suppress a shiver.

"Hi, Ford!" She practically tackles him, wrapping her arms right around his legs. Oh, boy. We're all going down in this sinking ship.

He gives her a few pats on the back. "Hey, Peep."

They make a rapid gesture of quick movements between them. I belatedly realize they're doing some secret handshake. My blink is weighed down with disbelief. I nearly tumble into the wall while melting into a puddle of swoon.

Hear that? It's what's left of my resistance, crumbling into rubble all around me. This guy is giving me no choice. Options are overrated anyway.

Millie ends their special bonding display with a regular high-five. "Be nice to my mama, okay?"

Crawford's hazel eyes lift to mine. "I always try my best."

I quirk a brow at that. He could probably up his game. I'm open to suggesting a few essential areas of improvement. "Nice to see you, Ford."

"The sentiment is very much mutual. You look"—his throat bobs with a thick swallow—"perfect."

From anyone else this would be a cliché, but from him it's heart-stopping. "Hopefully what I'm wearing is good enough for what you have planned."

"Like I said—perfect. I have a helmet and jacket for you on my bike."

Millie squeaks by his side. "Can I go for a ride, too?"

"Absolutely not," I blurt before he can argue otherwise.

My daughter pouts at me. "Why not?"

Crawford nudges her shoulder. "It's dangerous until you're older. I wasn't allowed to ride on a cruiser until I turned sixteen."

I send him a silent bout of gratitude for stepping in. Being the only bad guy to dish out rules gets old. "And guess what, sweetie? I've never been on a motorcycle."

Millie scrunches her forehead. "You're so old. Why'd you wait so long?"

"Little turkey." I give her cheek a light pinch. "I never had a friend who owned one until now."

Her little mouth forms a circle. "That's why you wanna go with Ford alone. I get it now."

I begin nodding slowly. "Uh, yeah. That sounds about right."

She peers up at Crawford. "Take care of my mama, okay? It's her first time. She doesn't know what to do."

When I look at Crawford, his lips are pressed tight together. The gleaming humor bleeds through his eyes, though. "And on that note, shall we?"

"I'm ready if you are."

Josey pops up beside me with a coy grin to match the sparkle in her eye. "Make sure to keep her out way past curfew."

He gives her a salute. "No problem."

I trap Millie and Josey in a group hug, squeezing until my daughter starts to fuss. "Have fun without me."

"We will," my bestie coos.

With a shake of my head, I meet Crawford on the path leading to my driveway. He grips my hip, the action so subtle I barely notice. "Are you excited? Or nervous?"

"Both? I'm not much of a scaredy-cat"—I glare at him when he grunts—"except when it comes to swimming with fish in large bodies of water."

"If you say so."

I poke him in his chiseled side, almost breaking a nail. "Don't worry about me. I won't even scream."

"That sounds like a challenge."

"Only if you want this to be my first and last ride."

"I won't be reckless, Kee. You can trust me."

And I do. Probably more than I should. The opportunity to ponder why that might be disappears as we reach his black and chrome iron steed. The Harley is impressive, even to a novice who knows nothing about the machines. The spot reserved for a passenger halts my appraisal.

"I can see you get a lot of company." The grit in my voice is unmistakable. I shake off the green monster, gluing a perky grin on my lips.

A lopsided smirk tips his lips. "Do I detect a hint of jealousy in your tone?"

I scoff and cross my arms. "Absolutely not." The lie is so vivid it's a surprise my pants aren't on fire.

"You can be possessive of me. I don't mind."

I toss my braid off my shoulder. "I'm not delusional. We have no claim on each other, Ford."

He stalks into my personal space, lifting my chin until we're locked in an electric standoff. "The idea of you fucking another guy drives me to the brink of madness. There's no denying that you have a hold on me. You're the only woman I want. And for the record, I added that rear seat specifically for you."

Well, that's one way to shut me up. Does that mean he actually cares about me? It's hard to tell when he's usually operating on pure piss and vinegar. I take a much-needed backward stumble. "Uh, wow. Wasn't expecting that."

His nostrils flare with a snort. "Get used to it."

Static buzzes in my ears. I part my lips, closing them a second later. Formulating a response to that isn't happening—all I see is an endless sea of white. "I'm not sure what you mean. Is that why you wanted me all to yourself?"

"Among the other reasons I told you about."

At least he doesn't bother denying it. If I'm being honest, his declaration floods me with a familiar molten heat. It's official. If this guy keeps playing his cards right, he's totally getting laid. Does that make me easy? Most likely. Even if it does, I'm already teetering off the ledge of caring. But where does this path lead to after a few overdue orgasms? I add that to my worry list for tomorrow.

"In any case, this is an impressive cushion." I give the elevated backseat a pat.

"Decker got me thinking," he muses.

"About what?"

"A lady and her throne." He chops a hand through the air. "Never mind. Will that be big enough for you?"

I take another glance at the wide section reserved for my butt. "I'm trying not to be offended by your question."

Crawford's scowl gains intensity. "We both know you have a fine ass. Don't go digging for reassurance. I just want you to be comfortable."

"Okay, that's better."

Crawford looms over me, his towering frame blocking out the sunlight. "Want me to worship your ass, Kee?"

I gulp as heat flares in my cheeks. "Uh, maybe later," I squeak. We're still in my freaking driveway, for crying out loud.

His dark chuckle snares me. "I'll circle round to that when we arrive at the landing."

"The what? You never told me where we're going."

"You'll see." He gestures to my seat. "Hop on."

As I get situated, Crawford digs through the saddlebags attached to both sides of his bike. He hands me an emerald green helmet and black leather jacket. "Hope those fit. If they don't, we can return them for the right size."

I take his proffered gifts with trembling fingers. When was the last time a man gave me a present? It's been years, and those came with conditions. I clear the lump of emotion from my throat. "Thank you. How much do I owe—"

"Don't even think about it. These are from me to you. End of."

"Okay." I nod while slipping on the jacket. "This is very thoughtful."

"And smart. Safety is important, Kee. Accidents happen too often."

I wince at the sting his reminder causes. The scar tissue throbs beneath layers of dense grief. Crawford isn't immune to the pain that tragedy delivers. He's all too aware of how fast circumstances change. I don't respond to the slash of caution in his voice. Words aren't necessary in this heavy moment.

He straddles the seat in front of me, leaning back to position my arms. "You can hold onto my waist or the bars at your sides. Sitting upright as a beginner can be an odd position, but you'll figure out what feels best for you. Just make sure you're following the flow of movements."

"Um, okay. Got it." I latch myself around his bulky

form, enjoying the feel of him against me a little too much. Barreling lust aside, this seems like the safest choice since he's responsible for steering.

"You'll see what I mean." Crawford's torso flexes beneath my flat palms. I try not to let his reaction, or nearness, affect me. The blast of heat under my skin can easily be blamed on the layers I'm wearing, but his muscles seem to quiver when I tighten my hold.

Before I can comment, he cranks the throttle and an explosive roar cracks into the silence. He revs the engine, and a plume of exhaust spits out behind us. The final warning I get is Crawford reversing onto the road. Then we're soaring, heading east out of town.

Within moments, a calm awareness hooks into me. There's already a natural buzz flooding my system, this state of utter relaxation that cradles me in a protective embrace. It's no wonder people escape the grind by cruising along the open road. I could be one of them after an experience like this. The rumbling growl of the pipes soothes me as signs of civilization thin out, leaving room for endless fields to get lost in. After about five minutes, a powerful floating sensation washes over me. The strong scent of gasoline and oil are carried away by the whipping wind. Out here, nothing can reach us.

We ride far enough that I lose track of direction. Crawford pulls off the highway and aims straight for a narrow gravel path. The bike slows to a crawl as we weave up a steady incline. An overgrown prairie with shallow dips and hills surrounds us on all sides. The climb crests at a flat plot to our right. The grass isn't quite as long on this random patch, allowing the motorcycle to navigate with minimal bumps. Crawford veers to one side and cuts the engine.

The silence is almost jarring after nearly an hour of booming noise. He yanks off his helmet and I do the same. Crawford dismounts, offering me a hand to get down. I wipe the dust off my clothes before attempting to tame the nest my hair has become. Once some semblance of normal settles in, I finally glance up to take in the scenery. The exhale in my chest stalls with a strangled hitch.

To the unsuspecting visitor, this section of field appears ordinary and blends in with the landscape. But I can hear the whispering breeze hinting at what's hidden below the surface. The view alone is enough to leave me motionless. From this perch, unobstructed miles of rolling meadows are visible. There's a stream cutting through a far end, and I wonder if that leads to the creek we swam in. A lone tree calls to me next. The weeping willow is a rarity to this part of the country; I assume someone planted it once upon a time. Strands of wispy branches wave at me, beckoning with a call I can feel in my bones.

I feel him approach from behind, his body a furnace engulfing me in flames without a single touch. "Another natural treasure," I breathe.

He spans an arm out in front of us. "It certainly is. This sight alone is worth the drive."

"This is quite a whimsical setting. Did you bring me here for a reason?"

"In all my years coming out here, I've never seen anyone else along this path." His raspy words brand the back of my neck.

I shiver despite trying my damndest not to. "You've got a lot of these secret gardens."

"Something like that."

"You do seem to enjoy isolation." I fiddle with a fraying rip in my jeans.

"I'm learning that it's better when shared with a chosen few."

Another wave of heat swirls in my lower belly. "Oh?"

He brushes against me. "That's why I'm showing you all of my hiding spots. They can be yours, too."

I let my eyelids flutter shut. "Be careful, Ford. You're bordering on being romantic."

"If it gets you naked faster, I'll be Prince fucking Charming."

"I thought you prefer being a beast?" But hell, for the record, I won't complain either way.

"People can change."

"Just part of the plan?"

"For now."

My pulse speeds up until the pounding feels like a marching beat. "If I didn't know better, I'd guess that you're trying to get lucky."

"What was your first hint?"

I motion to the vast beauty cocooning us. "Spelling it out isn't necessary."

"No?" Crawford presses his arousal into my ass, leaving very little to the imagination. "That works in my favor."

"Yes, you're all set. Very solid." Damn, my voice is one gasp away from labored.

"All for you, Kee."

That's a good enough commitment for me. I turn and grip the open edges of his jacket, tugging him into me. Crawford erases the remaining distance, slanting his mouth over mine. I sigh against his lips, melting a bit more on the inside. His arm circles my waist when I sway on unstable legs. Good grief, this man can kiss. I part for him, granting his tongue access to sweep along mine. Heat crawls up my inner thighs until the burning ache overtakes me. I need him with a fiery intensity that's setting me ablaze. If I don't release this pressure soon, my body is bound to burst.

"Want you so fucking bad," he mumbles against the corner of my mouth.

"I can tell." I rock my hips against the steely ridge prodding at me.

Crawford nips at me, delving back in for another taste.

My eyes nearly cross when he hauls me harder into him. "You do this to me. Only you."

I could call him out on that blatant fib, but my mind is fuzzy with desire. "Show me how crazy I make you."

He yanks his lips from mine and begins tugging the leather off my arms. After discarding the jacket into a crumpled heap, he gets to work on my shirt. The flimsy cotton doesn't stand a chance and gets tossed away with one upward yank. Crawford cups my lace-covered breasts, a sound of approval rolling out of him. His tongue licks a trail across the most sensitive skin of my throat. That sinful touch wanders down, drifting to my collarbone and lower. He sucks and nips at the valley of my cleavage. I arch into him, begging for more.

"Feels so good," I purr.

"Just getting started." He inhales, burying his nose in the dip of my bust. "Smell so fucking good."

I grapple at him, digging my fingers into his shirt. "Take this off."

Crawford jerks his head. "Not yet." He steps forward, taking me with him. The back of my legs tap his bike, and I reach out for stability. His chuckle tickles my already heightened sensitivity. "I got you."

A hum trips up my throat. "I like the sound of that."

He crouches in front of me, palms wrapping around my calves. "These boots are hot as fuck, but they need to go." His deft fingers lower the zippers, and he yanks the soles off my feet.

He attacks my jeans next, but grunts after getting the button open.

I quirk a brow. "Problem?"

"Your pants might be sexy, but they're clinging worse than glue."

"That's what you get for making me cover up when it's almost July."

Crawford snorts. "Biker attire does have its down side."

"Compared to what?"

"That glitter bomb you wore to the bar."

I shimmy and shove off the tight denim with some added force. The fabric gets thrown away with the rest. Only my bra and panties remain, but I have a feeling those will be stripped off soon enough. He lifts me up onto the seat, the sunbaked leather stinging my bare flesh.

"That's hot," I hiss.

His eyes flare with smoky embers. "I seem to recall you finding pleasure with a bite of pain."

"Thanks for the preview." After sprawling and reclining against the rear saddle, I grasp the bars for support. I bow my spine and edge closer to him. My lower half hangs in the balance, but not for long.

Crawford tears the thong from between my thighs, tucking it in his pocket. He crouches in front of me, hoisting one of my legs over his wide shoulder. I don't get a chance to protest before he's leaning in. "Remember, I want you spreading wide for me."

This position makes that more challenging, but I stretch until my muscles burn. "I'm definitely open for this."

"Exactly how I prefer you." He chuckles, a hot puff of air caressing my folds.

I open my mouth with a retort, but a whimpering moan escapes instead. Crawford licks along my slit, making two excruciatingly lazy passes from top to bottom. I spear my fingers into the length of his hair, gripping at the roots with a harsh pull. A wheezes tumbles from the depths of my lungs while I drag him harder into me.

He circles two fingers at my entrance, feeding those digits into me with a slow glide. I welcome him with a sigh as the coils in my lower belly twist. The teasing touch isn't nearly enough, and I buck my hips.

"So greedy for me," he whispers against my exposed center.

"It's your fault," I whimper.

"Then I better be the one to fix it."

Crawford laps at my clit with dizzying spirals. I'm panting, silent pleas dripping off my parting lips. What I want to beg for is beyond me.

I'm grinding against him, seeking the friction he readily gives. "More, please. I need you deeper."

He rams his fingers into me, crooking them up in search of my hidden detonator. The instant he finds that secret spot, my toes curl and everything goes still. For a split second, as I hover on that edge between pure pleasure and desperation, nothing exists except clawing need. I struggle to draw in enough air. All of my energy is centered on what this man's mouth is doing to me, sending me higher, further yet, until a burst of stars explodes across the blue sky.

With a final swipe, I'm shoved over the cliff and tumbling. Or gliding. I can't tell what's up and down, only able to ride out the quaking tremble radiating throughout every molecule inside of me. I'm suspended in a state of spine-numbing euphoria as seconds blend into minutes. The tide rolls over me, ripples of shockwaves tingling my hands.

When I regain control of my muscles, I prop up on a shaky elbow. My vision swims when I glance down at him still kneeling in front of me. His glistening mouth twitches with the beginnings of a smirk. He has every right to be cocky after that award-winning demonstration.

"Good?" Crawford straightens while wiping a sloppy palm over his lips.

I give him a crooked smile of my own. "Best yet."

"Careful, you might inflate my ego."

I hook my ankle around the bend of his knee, reeling him in. "Oh, I plan to do a lot more than that."

CHAPTER TWENTY-ONE

Crawford

Healing Hug #22: The instant before realization
strikes and all is calm.

TWO FANTASY-INDUCING WEEKS HAVE FLOWN BY SINCE I
brought Keegan to my landing in the prairie. Since
then, we've managed to crank the sexual creativity
scale to hotter than a July afternoon. My body is depleted,
yet wholly satisfied. The constant throbbing in my veins
is a welcome reprieve from the bitter dullness I'd grown
accustomed to. I can't stay away from her for more than a
couple of days. By some miracle, or rare stroke of luck, the
woman sitting on my left seems to share the same potent
desire for me.

This is how I find myself once again being chauffeured to
a secret location by the irresistible blonde behind the wheel.
Almost an hour has ticked by. My skin is starting to itch, but I
keep the pissy agitation on lockdown. It's not that I mind being a passenger in Keegan's ride, but there are far better ways
for us to pass the time.

A peek behind me reveals a sight that will soften the hardest man. Millie is snoozing in her seat with Elsa's head resting on her lap. The little girl's fingers are curled in the dog's
thick fur. Patch is sprawling out on the floorboards without a
care in the world. I can't even lie. A burst of warmth spreads
through my chest just considering I'm privy to witnessing

this moment. Fuck, these women are turning me into a sap. I wait for the gut-churning nausea to kick in, but there's nothing but the pleasant heat washing over me. I'm sinking into lost-cause territory with zero plans of return. Who would've thought? Definitely not me.

Keegan must notice me looking at the dozing trio. A toasty smile lifts her already rosy features. "It's been quite a while since she zonked out in the car, but she used to do it every time. She gets that from me. Fully alert one second, then bam. Zapped out like a blown fuse."

Her turns of phrase are a tad wonky, but I get the picture. More than that, a spark flickers in the back of my mind. What she said prods at my already burning curiosity. I swipe along the brim of my hat, collecting the fragments of courage to solve a gaping hole. "Can I ask you something?"

Keegan peeks at me from the corner of her eye. "Of course."

"You can tell me to screw off. It's not really any of my business."

She taps her thumb to a silent beat on the steering wheel. "I feel as though we're past the point of pussy-footing around one another. Don't you agree?"

"Uh, sure." She might change her tune once I pry into personal details.

"Just spit it out, Ford." Her green eyes roll faster than spinning tires.

"Where's Millie's dad?"

Her breathing falters, just for a moment. If I hadn't been paying close attention, her reaction would've been a mere blip. "That's a good question."

"Thank you?" I scratch my temple.

She hikes a single shoulder. "I honestly have no clue. Haven't seen that spineless sperm donor since I told him the news."

I almost swallow my tongue. "Uh, what?"

She waves off my evident shock. "Not literally. I didn't go to a bank and get knocked up at nineteen on purpose."

"That's good, I guess." My palms begin to sweat, along with the rest of me. I'm wading into very unfamiliar waters without any hope of staying afloat.

Keegan chomps on her bottom lip. "It's kinda an embarrassing story. I prefer to leave that part of my past in Cheyenne."

"It's all right. Forget I asked."

Her cheeks puff up with a lungful of air, blowing the stream out in one long exhale. "Just rip off the bandage, right? Gah, okay. So, Joel was such a cocky jerk. Big douchebag on campus. I can't for the life of me remember why we slept together. Too much alcohol, probably. The worst kind of peer pressure. That entire night is a blur. It was a piss-poor decision from all angles. Nonetheless, six weeks later, I was pregnant. I'm sick to my stomach just thinking about that day. He deserved to know, of course. Too bad he couldn't care less. The asshole even laughed at me."

Her grip on the wheel turns white-knuckle. "I paid for the paternity test for my own peace of mind. When Joel got the results, all hell broke loose. He threatened to take me to court for using a fake test. His posse of assholes ridiculed me. Only Josey took my side. Everyone else became a bully. It's crazy how much power popularity can give. At every turn, I was made to feel like the bad guy. I contemplated taking him to court, but money was already stretched thin. My parents had just died the year before. It was a really dark time for me. I could've stayed and held my ground, let their hate roll off me. But in the end, I didn't want them to ruin this beautiful experience for me. I was going to have a baby. A little miracle of my own. Eff Joel and his cronies for trying to drag me down to their level. All of them are cruel monsters."

A humming sigh escapes her pinched lips. "I transferred schools the following month. The university I chose had excellent financial support, especially for single parents. Their specialty programs made graduating with a degree possible. Even though it was a struggle, I managed alone. Joel knows about Millie, but wants nothing to do with her. Again, I could've forced him to be involved and pay child support. Maybe I should've, because she deserves every opportunity, and there are some I haven't been able to give. But him having any power over us made me queasy. He officially signed all parental rights away when she was eight months old. It's her choice if she ever wants to try contacting him. I'd rather forget about him, but Millie can make the decision when she's ready."

Blistering rage bubbles under my skin. A turbine of wind thrashes in my ears while I try to control the brewing hurricane inside of me. Keegan doesn't need me to act like a rabid bear at this moment. What she needs is support. "Does Millie know about him?"

"Yeah, somewhat. I've given her a very glossy version. She rarely mentions having a dad, especially in the last few years. It breaks my heart that she doesn't have everything a little girl deserves. I feel guilty, even though it's not my fault or what I wanted." She throws me a quick glance, a slight wince tightening her expression.

"You shouldn't, Kee. You did what was best for Millie." My heart is thundering too fast. Could I possibly find a permanent place in their puzzle?

"But am I being selfish? Or weak?"

If I ever cross paths with this Joel tool, he's not walking away unscathed. "I think you're brave, and a survivor. When faced with shitty circumstances, you made the best of it."

Keegan begins nibbling on her lips again. "What if Millie resents me when she's older?"

I slash through the space between us. "That's not possible. I bet she understands already that having one of you is better than two parents. She's better off without him, Kee. I can speak from experience."

"Oh?" The way her voice lifts is enough for me to delve into the shark-infested ocean of my past.

"My father isn't a kind man. I can count on one hand the decent memories we have together. He gets some sick satisfaction by cutting others down. My brother and I were his biggest targets. Now that Grant joined forces with him, I'm the lucky recipient of his spite."

I lift my hat and shove it back on. An edgy tremble starts in my fingers. "Growing up, I wished my dad was never around. I was practically raised by a single mom. When my father showed up, everything was tense and distant. I can only hope you never have the displeasure of meeting him."

"Well, okay then." Her throat works with a thick gulp. "We all have piles of our own stuff to deal with, huh?"

"No truer words."

"Are your parents still together?"

I bark out a brittle laugh. "Absolutely not. My mom made sure of that. Her methods were a tad unconventional, and most definitely frowned upon, but she escaped him."

"Good for her. I don't know the situation, but your dad sounds awful. Your mom was smart to get out of Dodge."

"That's exactly what I tell her, while continuing to rub it in my father's face. Not my finest moments, but he deserves worse."

Keegan grins at me. "Thanks for sharing that."

"To be fair, you started it."

"Only because you brought it up," she murmurs.

I skim a finger down the length of her bare arm. A trail of goosebumps rise in the wake of my touch. Millie's convenient nap allows me to take liberties with Keegan that I wouldn't allow myself. We've been resorting to stolen moments of heated passion when the moon is our only witness. Filthy whispers. Lingering glances. Teasing touches. "I'm really glad we're doing this."

She dips her chin, but there's no missing the flush racing up her neck. "So am I."

"You're still holding back."

"Aren't you?"

I suppose that's true, just for different reasons. Keegan is the one with a daughter and larger priorities. The stakes are higher for her, and it isn't fair for me to wedge my way in if she's not ready. I give her a slow nod. "I'm not sure what to expect."

"And that's fine. I don't need you to plan for our future or anything. We'll just see how things go."

I narrow my eyes at her. "I can give you more than that."

She lifts her chin, a slight tremble wobbling her jaw. "I can't do this again."

"Do what?"

"Fall for the wrong man."

"Who's to say I'm wrong?"

"Every single sign since we met."

Moisture collects on her lashes, webbing the long hairs into spears. The last thing I want is to make her cry. "How do I fix this?"

"We don't start in the first place."

I rub at the ache searing through my chest. "Anything but that, Kee. Ask anything else of me."

When she shakes her head, blonde hair fans out into the space between us. "That's all I can do to protect myself. And Millie. She doesn't need another reason to feel abandoned."

I narrow my eyes. "I would never hurt that little girl, accidentally or intentional. You have my word."

Keegan scoffs. "And how good is that? Until the next worthy conquest comes along?"

"Damn, babe. Cut me deep." But I can't blame her. She's been through more than enough shit when it comes to men. "You're still holding a grudge over that?"

She peers out the window, trying to avoid me even though it's impossible. "Maybe."

"Listen to me, Kee." I grab her hand and flatten our palms

together. "I'm not a relationship guy and never pretended to be. Hell, being around people in general is a challenge. Commitment hasn't been on my radar. I wouldn't know the first thing about being a good boyfriend. But what you've already given me surpasses any shallow encounter I've had by a long shot. If I just wanted sex, I'd go out and get some. I can't picture anything better than a day trip with you and Millie."

Keegan glances down at our entwined fingers. "I want to believe you, Ford. But my lack of faith and trust issues, combined with our track record, doesn't bode well for us."

Panic should be cramping my stomach. This is too much, way faster than we should be moving. I'm obliterating every line we've slapped down. But fuck it—those walls were built to topple. I lean toward her, crossing over the center console. "Let me prove it to you."

She squeezes my hand. "I'm not the only one you have to worry about."

"Millie likes having me around." A backward glance proves the little girl is lost in dreamland.

"She's seven. Her heart hasn't learned to protect itself yet. Not that I'm giving you permission to change that."

"Do you think so little of me?"

Her brief pause that follows shoves my heart into a vice. The clamp adds pressure until taking a breath is painful. Keegan finally shakes her head. "No, just the opposite. Not sure how foolish that makes me."

I loop a section of her blonde hair around my finger, giving the strands a gentle tug. Her gasp shoots straight south and I nearly groan. "I won't take you for granted. Ever."

"You better not."

When her gaze slams into mine, a brick of explosives detonates. The car almost shakes from the impact. Our conversation tapers off with a mutual sigh. This time, the silence between us is comfortable. I want to drag her onto my lap and prove our connection is solid. The conditions are not on our side. We're still on the freeway, but Keegan merges into the exit lane.

"Is it just me or do we spend a lot of time in the car together?"

"Are you complaining?"

"Just the opposite. I miss taking road trips."

Keegan winks. "Stick with me and we'll take all the adventures."

"Maybe I could take a turn driving." As if proving a point, I accidentally slam my knee into the dashboard. A string of expletives bursts out of me.

"Does it bother you to sit bitch?"

A silent grumble escapes me. "I'm man enough to handle it."

She gives me a lazy once-over. "You certainly are."

"Better watch yourself when the possibility of execution is zippo."

"Pretty sure that's in my benefit."

"For now. You'll pay extra later."

"Promises, promises."

Before I get myself into real trouble, I wrench my eyes off her. I catch sight of a billboard and whip my head back toward Keegan. "No way. You're taking me to Holiday Twin?"

She grins. "Maybe."

I might've noticed we were entering Fort Collins if I'd been paying closer attention. "Shit, I haven't been to a drive-in movie since…well, I can't even remember."

"They're pretty rare nowadays. Wyoming only has one left standing, but it's over six hours away. This drive isn't nearly as bad."

"Damn, Kee. This is a kickass choice."

"Well, thank you. I was inspired by National Drive-In Movie Day. We're just a month late."

"Eh, I've always preferred belated celebrations. Drags the festivities out longer."

"We should definitely be honoring these traditions more often."

We're interrupted by a drawn-out yawn coming from the backseat. When I turn, Millie is stretching as the dogs rouse from their slumbers.

"Hey, sleepyhead." Keegan smiles at her daughter in the rearview mirror.

"Did I miss the movies?" The pout in her drowsy voice is covered by another yawn.

Keegan turns into the gravel lot. Only a few other vehicles dot the open space. "Nope, you're awake just in time. We're here."

Millie flings upright, suddenly more alert than a caffeine junkie. "Yes! I can't wait to sit on the hood. Can I be pickle in the middle again?"

Keegan quirks a brow at me. "Do you mind?"

New traditions are forming, patterns and habits I didn't expect to be part of again. A reflexive grin tips my lips at the possibilities. I feel the hint of a dimple pop in my cheek. "I couldn't think of a better spot for you to be, Peep."

The little girl squeaks. "This is going to be awesome. Elsa and Patch can watch from the front seats."

"You've got it all planned out, baby girl." Keegan parks in the front row, dead center, with the best view of the enormous screen.

"Uh-huh, yep. I've been picturing this since we watched the fireworks on the Fourth of July."

I give Keegan a soft nudge. "I'm thinking we can have a repeat of the grand finale."

She scoffs, peering behind us to find Millie distracted with Elsa and Patch. "You better try harder than that to get a sleepover invite."

"Remember what happened last time you wanted me to—"

She claps a hand over my mouth. "A reminder isn't appropriate, or necessary."

I chuckle against her palm, adding a little tongue for fun.

"Are you two done flirting yet?"

We simultaneously turn toward Millie. Keegan is the one to speak. "Uh, we're just talking."

The little girl huffs, looking so much like her mother. "I'm seven, not blind."

Keegan blinks at her. A few beats pass before she busts into giggles. Millie follows close behind. "All right, diva princess. Cut the sass."

"I just want to watch the movies."

"And we will. Let's go." Keegan makes a shooing motion.

We pile out in a rush, getting the pups situated on the way. With our stacks of blankets and pillows, we get settled on the car. The metal creaks under our weight and cringe, ready to volunteer to sit on the ground. Keegan laughs as I attempt to prop myself up without causing any permanent damage.

"I'm getting this dinosaur replaced soon. Don't worry about a few dents."

And that's what I do, reclining until my back rests against the windshield. Millie snuggles between us with a noise that can only be described as content.

Keegan smiles at me over her daughter's head. "You all good over there?"

I manage to sink a little further for this woman. How screwed that makes me is still up for debate. "Never better."

CHAPTER TWENTY-TWO

Crawford

Healing Hug #23: When good intentions go sour.

THE AFTERNOON SUN GLINTS OFF MY AVIATORS AS I PULL into Keegan's driveway. Summer is in full swing, testing records in rare bouts of humidity and temperature on a daily basis. With the creek to cool off in, the heat doesn't bother me. Especially when I have the company of two blondes to lift my spirits in moments of need. Two months ago, I never would've thought this could be my normal. Now, I can't imagine ever returning to my self-imposed isolation.

I hop up Keegan's front stairs with a bounce in my gait. Millie's wrapped gift is clutched under my arm. The thrum of good fortune pings off my sternum with every breath. There's a zest floating on the breeze that reminds me of coming home after a weekend away. But that's way off base. All of the fresh air is going to my head.

I raise my fist to knock, adding a peppy beat that mixes with the jovial rhythm inside of me. Millie's face appears in the thin crack she creates. When she sees who's waiting on the other side, the door flings open wide.

"Hi, Ford!"

"Hey, Peep." I hold out my free palm and she gives me a high-five, followed by a pattern of slapping and twisting motions that form our exclusive code. Maybe it's odd to create a special handshake with a child, but Millie's giggle is worth any gawking sneers from onlookers.

"I love doing that so much. We're so cool."

"The coolest." I nod along with her.

"Are you here to see my mama?"

Keegan appears behind her daughter. Skepticism strains her expression. "Well, hello. Should we have been expecting you?"

"Can't a guy randomly drop by to visit his…friend?" The labels between us are still a bit fuzzy. Better to be safe than awkward.

"I guess so…" she trails off.

Prickles stab at my nape. "I was going to call, but decided to make this a secret visit."

Millie bounces in place. "Oh, I love surprises from you."

"That's exactly why I didn't mention stopping over."

"I see." Keegan squints at me. "All right, what's up?"

Millie tugs on her mom's shirt, pointing at the present I'm carrying. "Look, Mama. He got you something."

Such a cutie, this little girl. I wink down at her. "Actually, this is for you. I'm always taking your mom out, right? Your turn is overdue. If that's okay with the boss lady."

Keegan crosses her arms, popping out a hip for good measure. "If you're planning on walking. There's no way she's going anywhere on your bike."

I hike a thumb over my shoulder. "Good thing I have alternative transportation."

She peers around my shoulder, catching sight of the basic sedan in her driveway. "Whose car is that?"

"Mine. Just bought it yesterday." Did I just puff my chest out a bit? Absolutely.

"Why?"

"So I can take Millie out without having you worry. The same booster you have for her is already strapped in the backseat."

Keegan drops her jaw, a breathy exhale wheezing out

of her. "Wow, that's incredibly thoughtful. You've officially crossed over into the very sweet category."

I give a little shake to my shoulders and straighten a very imaginary tie. "That's what I was going for."

She purses her glossy lips. "Nicely done, Ford."

"Are you beginning to believe me?"

Her eyes flick over me from ball cap to boots. "Yeah, this definitely helps your case."

Millie must reach the end of her patience, hopping onto the porch beside me. "Where are we going?"

"That's up to you, Peep. Why don't you open this first?" I pass over the box with a massive bow on top.

She rips into the paper, scraps flying in every direction. A squeal bursts from her when she opens the lid. "Oh my gosh, this is amazing!"

Millie whips the pink leather jacket out of the confetti tissue, pressing it to her chest. The beaming smile she flashes at me could melt all of the snow in Antarctica.

"Do you like it? The lady at the store told me this should be your size."

"I love it!" She slips it on, revealing a perfect fit.

"Looks great on you, Peep. What do you think, Kee?" When I glance at Keegan for approval, she's pressing a palm over her mouth. My gut clenches when I catch sight of the moisture glistening in her emerald gaze. "Are you okay?"

She nods, far too fast. "Mh-hmm."

"You sure?"

"Yep." She chokes on a swallow. "This adorable display is kicking me straight in the feels."

"Uh, okay. Is that good?"

"Very. You won't have to put in extra effort to spend the night."

Fucking score. I almost pump my fist, except that would defeat the purpose. "That's not why I'm doing this. I wanna take Millie out."

"Oh, I believe you. And that makes me very…agreeable."

It's my turn to sputter down a rough gulp. "Great. That's really…exciting."

A soft sigh has me looking down at Millie. Her gaze is jumping between Keegan and me. "You're so in love."

Now my throat is clogging for real, nearly suffocating me. "Slow down, Peep. That's serious business you're talking about. We're just taking things slow. Building trust and all that."

Keegan rolls her eyes, but she's smiling. "He's right, baby girl. The love we share is for you."

I can get on board with that. "Yeah, what your smart mama said."

Millie frowns at us. "But I want us to be a family."

Pretty sure my eyes bug out. Are we nearing that stage in the game? Shit. I open and close my mouth in rapid succession before getting any words out. "Um, well, I dunno know about all that."

Keegan wraps an arm around her daughter, squeezing them together in a hug. "You're my family, sweetie. Anyone else we gain along the way is a bonus, okay?"

Millie nods against her mother's shoulder. "M'kay, Mama."

"Go have fun with Ford. I can't wait to hear all about your adventures."

That reminder prompts a flip in her attitude. Millie straightens and returns to my side. "Can we go to your shop?"

"That's where you wanna go?"

"Uh-huh, yep. I never got to go back after you told me I could. My mama kept making excuses."

Well, shit. Millie is welcome at my garage any day of the week. "All right, it's settled. You can bring Elsa. I'm sure Patch would love to play with her."

"Yay!" She thrusts a hand up into the air, and I give her another high-five.

Keegan steps outside with Elsa flanking her. She passes me the leash with a smile. "Thanks for thinking of doing this. You'll be her hero for life, if you weren't already."

I stroke a thumb along her soft jaw. "Just the first of many."

She sighs, leaning into my touch. "Be careful about being too sweet, Ford. I might catch feelings of the romantic variety, and they're contagious."

I bend to whisper in her ear. "Whatever it takes to get you naked faster."

Keegan shoves me away with a scoff. "Such a horn ball."

"Don't pretend to be offended. You like it." I let my voice drop to the low octave that makes her shiver.

"Okay, get outta here. Have fun and be safe."

Millie waves and blows her mom a kiss. "See you soon!"

"We'll only be gone a few hours. I'll have her back for dinner."

Keegan bites her lip. "Maybe you'll eat with us?"

I wink at her, tugging the brim of my hat down low. "Only a fool would turn down an offer like that."

In the next beat, Keegan rises onto her toes and loops her arms around my shoulders. I return her embrace, wrapping her up against me. She hums and erases any sliver of space remaining between us.

I press my lips to her hair, inhaling a shot of paradise. "What's this for?"

She nuzzles against my chest. "Just because."

"I've never hugged just for the sake of hugging."

"It's nice, right?"

I think about that for a moment, but not out of uncertainty. There's no need to consider my answer. My pause is necessary to rein in other impulses, like confessing a slew of feelings I have no right to be feeling. This thing with Keegan, whatever we're doing, is beginning to burrow under my skin. When we agreed to spend a few hours between the sheets whenever the mood strikes, I didn't anticipate wanting more. Now, in this moment, that's all I can imagine. I find that things are once again shifting for me.

But am I still just a fuck buddy to her? I'm trying to earn trust to prove myself as a worthy…what? Boyfriend? That's the next logical step. Is that where we're heading? There's only one answer to that. I can't picture myself with anyone besides the woman enveloped in my hold.

"Take care of my little girl," she whispers in my ear.

I press Keegan closer, reveling in the feel of her body aligning with mine. "Always," I vow.

We break apart with a sigh, sharing a secret smile. Promises for after dark spark in the air crackling between us. She blows me a kiss, and I send her a wink. Cheesy as fuck, but the bizarre flurry of warmth spreading through my chest approves.

Millie is already waiting by the car. Even in the heat, she's wearing her jacket and petting the pink sleeves. A surge of pride launches in my heart. It's damn good to know I can do a few things right.

After getting situated and buckled in, we hit the road. The drive takes less than fifteen minutes. Millie fills the miles with entertaining chatter about Elsa and Keegan. I'm content to coast along while listening to her soft voice. It still boggles my mind that this little girl refuses to speak with some people. Around me, she's nothing but outgoing and spirited. My lips lift on their own accord. Being good with kids, or rather one in particular, isn't a talent I thought I'd acquire.

I park alongside the concrete building and hop out. Millie follows suit, letting Elsa run free along the way. Her gaze zips from one corner of my property to another as if witnessing everything for the first time. I guess it's been over a month since she was here last. Damn, the days have flown.

"So, what should we do?" I open the main entrance and usher her inside.

"I get to choose again?"

"Of course, Peep. This is all about you."

She taps her lips. "Do you have any motorcycles that need fixing?"

"Always. There's never a shortage of broken bikes at my shop. That's how I stay in business."

Millie giggles. "Good thing you have me to help."

"You can say that again."

"We'll make a great team, Ford. I won't even make you pay me."

She earns a loud laugh for that one. Millie joins in, her twinkling tune painting the dingy walls with glitter. Another roll of humor barrels through my chest as I stride over to the row of waiting projects.

I get a chopper rigged up on a set of blocks and open the engine cap. With a quick crank, I fire up the bike to get the fluids pumping. Then I lay out a few essential tools and up grab a drain pan. Millie watches me silently, waiting for instructions. After I kill the pipes, I settle onto the ground beside her.

"We're going to start by changing the oil. Sound fun?"

"Uh-huh. What's the first thing we do?"

I explain the process as we go through the stages. This type of routine maintenance usually takes me less than half an hour. With Millie following along, I slow my pace so she can digest the steps. The steady flow of our work distracts me from the storm clouds rolling in.

Tires spitting up rocks is my only warning. When the red BMW comes into view, my gut plunges to the stained floor. A muted groan billows out of me. Talk about the worst fucking timing.

The little girl crouching beside me tracks the vehicle's approaching path. "Who's that?"

"My father." I attempt to keep the bubbling hate out of my tone. The efforts fail as a burning inferno rages up my esophagus.

"Oh." Millie visibly shrinks beside me. She's smart to be wary. He never comes just to chat.

A boulder the size of Wyoming drops in my gut. Talk about the worst possible timing.

My father steps out of his luxury coupe, and he's not alone. The passenger door opens and Grant appears. A growl strikes a match in my chest. The weasel brought reinforcements, of course.

I stand and move in front of Millie to block her from their view. Both men are imposing forces that I prefer not to wrestle with. If they stay out of my business, I'm more than happy to pretend neither of them exist. That's how we've carried on for years, other than these inconvenient visits my father likes to taunt me with.

They pause before crossing the threshold into my garage. Smart decision, considering I'm ramped higher than a cage fighter facing his opponent. This is my turf to defend, and they're about to cross the line. I flex my fingers, curling them into wrecking balls. Based on how they're studying me, narrow eyes and stiff posture, my fuck-off vibe is coming across. But my father has never been one to surrender or accept defeat.

"Hello, son." His tone is crisp, sending frost into the dehydrated air cloying at me.

The fire beneath my skin boils hotter. "What're you doing here?"

"Cutting pleasantries? How surprising."

I allow a sneer to curl my top lip. "Killing 'em with kindness isn't my style."

"Since my calls continue to go unanswered, I brought Grant along to talk some sense into you." His snort is clogged with phlegm. I gag on a mouthful of bile. My father seems to take great pleasure in making me nauseous, a cruel smirk cracking his thin lips. "But now I can see that you've been preoccupied."

"I'm a busy man. Feel free to leave the same way you came." I jut my chin toward the road.

He strokes his pointy chin. "Yet you're playing house. Who's this little princess? Did you forget to tell me that I'm a grandpa?"

Millie's gasp draws my attention down. Her wide gaze flings to mine, endless questions swirling in those green pools. I force a smile for her benefit, but the expression wobbles. Every particle inside of me winding tight, swirling into a tornado set on annihilation. I return my glare to our intruders. "No, you're most definitely not. I didn't suddenly become a father, not that you'd be on the list to receive an announcement. This little lady is Millie. I'm friends with her mom."

"Ah, that makes more sense. A woman is using you for free babysitting."

"Nah, nothing like that. Millie is my friend, too. Right, Peep?"

A shadow of a grin crosses her lips, and she gives me a slow nod. The glassy glimmer coating her eyes gives me pause. I furrow my brow, ready to address her emotion. A loud hoot of dry laughter interrupts me.

"Peep? What the hell kind of nickname is that?"

"None of your business, similar to anything else in my life." My voice is slicing damn close to bloody. I think Millie is stunned silent, more than usual around strangers. Her eyes are popped open as she stares between Grant and my father.

"So touchy. These ladies must mean a great deal to you. My loner son has found a soft spot. Isn't that charming?"

Putrid sludge laced with iron fills my stomach. The dread is so thick I could chew on a piece until my jaw cramps. "Leave my property or I'll call the cops."

My father tsks. "Ah, turning guard dog for another stray. How fitting."

I gnash my teeth at him, barely maintaining restraint.

"You know nothing about them and I intend to keep it that way."

"So, this is your plan? I'm almost disappointed, Crawford. Choosing some floozy and her bastard child over your own family?" Grant flinches at our father's tone and words, but he doesn't say anything. Still the same old ass-kisser.

Millie whimpers and clutches onto my leg. Her small form trembles against me. The fury triples and grows into a rabid, foaming beast. "You're scaring her," I snarl.

"As I should be. She's not wise enough to stay away from you on her own."

"I'm not the one she needs protecting from."

My father cackles, the sharp ruckus slashes into the distance separating us. "Maybe not tomorrow or the next day, but you're bound to screw up. I mean, look at you. Living in the damn woods like a hermit. You can barely take care of yourself, let alone a single mother and her spawn."

His words penetrate too deep, finding a gaping hole in my armor that I've left exposed. The sensitive parts of me, where I keep Keegan and Millie hidden, take the brunt of his sucker punch. Those fractures allow my father's poison to flood in, sabotaging any progress I've been foolish enough to attempt.

A wheezing exhale rasps past my panting lips. "Get the hell out of here. You've done enough damage for two lifetimes."

He tips an imaginary hat. "Then I've done my job. Ruining any semblance of happiness you're trying to achieve is always my goal, kid. Just returning the favor. Figured you'd know better by now."

And I do. I use my mother against him, and in turn, he tampers with the bubble I prefer to live in. This time, his damage is detrimental.

My father and Grant spin on their loafers without a

backward glance. I watch them leave, kicking up clouds of dust. If they ever come back, it'll be far too soon. My threat about calling the cops isn't idle. When I turn to face Millie, the fire in my lungs turns to ice.

Tears are tracking down her cheeks faster than she can wipe the drops away. "I-I wanna g-go home."

Clawing my way out of the hole he digs usually takes a day or two. I can find a faster route to haul my mind from the murky chaos. The filth my father spat at me is nothing new. There's no shocking twist of who I am, and that's never been an issue. But this instance isn't about me. Millie's misery is my undoing. She relied on me to shield her from his toxic influence and I failed.

I almost crash to my knees from the sight of her pain. The shattering of my soul goes unnoticed. "Of course, Millie. I'll take you right away."

The following moments are a jumble of thudding beats that ricochet off my ears. My surroundings blur as we get loaded into the car. What kicked off as a stellar day with groundbreaking potential has become a smoldering heap of ruin. Our outcome is bleak.

We're halfway to her house when she chisels into the aching silence. "You don't want to be my dad, Ford?"

I sputter over my tied tongue. "What? I never said that, Peep."

But I'm the last guy, aside from her biological father, who's fit for the job. Another fissure of my heart cracks.

"I'm just your friend. You don't want to suddenly become my father."

The steering wheel creaks under the pressure of my squeezing palms. How the fuck do I handle this? Jesus, I feel like water is rising all around me and drowning is inevitable. "I can't fill that role, Millie. And you shouldn't want me to."

Her forehead scrunches in the rearview mirror. "What do you mean?"

Having tough conversations is never pleasant. For me, this is worse than ripping off my fingernails. Pure fucking torture. The solution is simple, but that doesn't make following through any easier. I clear the grit from my throat and shoot through the pitch black. "That man, my father, isn't a good guy. He's more of a villain. In order to protect you from him, things need to change. I probably won't see you as often for a little bit. Just to be safe."

"But I like hanging out with you." Her whisper clangs into the quiet that's enveloping us.

"I know, Millie. I really enjoy spending time with you, too. But you deserve to have a better friend than me. Someone who won't expose you to bad stuff." I cringe while shoving out the necessary truths. The thought of another man swooping into their lives rubs acid into my festering wounds. Every inch of my body burns, but the agony grounds me. I can't subject them to a lifetime of this.

"You get it, remember? No one else does."

"Give other people a chance," I choke.

"No. I don't want anyone else to love my mama. You're supposed to do that."

I already do. More than I was prepared to recognize. Maybe that's why this hurts so fucking much. The weight is crushing, stealing any chance of taking a decent breath. There's no response to give that won't be a lie. I choose to be a coward and let the silence absorb any opportunity for confession. Millie's sniffles increase in volume and frequency until I'm suffocating in her sorrow.

Pulling into the driveway should offer some sense of relief, but all I feel is blistering loss. Millie grabs Elsa and scrambles away before I can say goodbye. That's probably for the best at the rate of this downward spiral.

Sharing a life with Keegan and Millie is a loftier illusion than the wildest pipe dream. I've been kidding myself this entire time. In the fantasy world I've been living in, we all ride off into the sunset on my cruiser with a sidecar. In the ruthless reality where we actually reside, I have to break two hearts in addition to my own.

That's the brutal ending to an equally doomed story. How fucking fitting.

CHAPTER TWENTY-THREE

Keegan

Healing Hug #24: Falling apart isn't as easy when
there's glue holding the pieces together.

THOSE PEACEFUL MOMENTS BEFORE DISASTER STRIKES ARE glorious, yet deceiving as hell. It's almost as if I can smell trouble brewing along with my mint tea in the kettle. The house is calm and quiet enough for me to sprawl out on the couch without disruption. I almost allow my eyes to flutter shut for a quick nap.

Then that shitty catastrophe presents itself.

The front door crashes open with a resounding bang. I leap upright as my pulse bangs into the ceiling, spinning in rapid circles with the fan. Millie races into the house sobbing, and my hackles rise with a deafening rattle. I follow her trail of wails and tears upstairs.

She's laying face down on her bed, skinny shoulders trembling with sorrow. My scrambling brain is already launching to conclusions. Forget the slowpoke jumping crap. That line of irrational thinking isn't going to solve problems any faster.

Against all of my impulsive instincts, I tiptoe into the room and sit on her mattress. With a soothing stroke along her back, I hum the opening lines of her favorite lullaby. She hiccups into her pillow, but the wailing quiets ever so slightly.

"What's wrong, baby girl?" The pounding in my temple throbs harder with each cry she releases.

"Ford d-doesn't wanna b-be our f-friend anymore." Between being muffled and garbled, her words are tough to comprehend. I get the gist.

It takes all of my frazzling control to remain parked in place. What I really want to be doing is storming outside to give that guy a verbal and possibly physical smackdown. My daughter has her dramatic moments, but going to this extreme over a potential misunderstanding is unheard of. But there's always a very far off chance she's changing her stripes. "Why do you think that, sweetie?"

"He told me so." Millie coughs until I fear she's going to hack up a lung.

I shush her, singing a bit more. The tune is meant to calm her, but I'm also in serious need of a pause button. That rat bastard is messing with the wrong mama bear. "Well, that doesn't sound very nice. Maybe he needs a timeout. What do you think?"

She turns onto her side to face me. Her bloodshot, red-rimmed eyes threaten to split my heart in two. "He's being a meanie."

"Sure seems like it, Mills. Where's Ford now?"

She wipes a line of gooey snot on her arm. I picture her doing that to Crawford's face instead. "Waiting by his car. I think he wants to talk with you."

He can bet his sorry ass I have a few choice words for him as well. I plaster a wide smile onto my face entirely for Millie's benefit. "Will you be all right if I go speak to him? I'll make sure to hurry."

She nods, inhaling a choppy breath. "He's not in a good mood, Mama. But don't be scared."

A fiery thwack of heat singes my chest. "Did he yell at you?"

Millie shakes her head in vehement fashion. "No, but his daddy isn't very nice."

I store that tidbit of information into the recesses of my hazy mind. "Okay, baby girl. Be right back."

"Love you, Mama."

I swipe a lock of blonde hair off her sticky forehead, pressing a soft kiss in the balmy center. "I love you very much, Mills." And it's high time I defend her honor.

My battle ax sharpens as I descend the steps, locking the offender in my sights. Crawford leans against the passenger side of his ridiculously responsible vehicle choice. I bet he could learn a thing or two from that standard sedan. When he notices me approaching, his broad shoulders tense. His gaze is guarded, solid walls slamming down, as if I'm the one stomping into enemy territory. My sandals slap against the pavement as I erase the remaining distance between us.

I pin him with an unyielding stare, regardless of the maracas shaking in my chest. "Care to tell me why Millie is sobbing uncontrollably after spending less than an hour with you?"

"Father dearest dropped in for an unannounced visit." His vacant tone gives me chills. From a single flat statement, it's obvious this isn't the Crawford I've grown to care for. I blink at him, silently pleading for more. He doesn't give me another utterance. In fact, his stare veers over my shoulder with blank disinterest. This shell of a man reminds me of the guy I met alongside the road that fateful day.

"And what happened?" I make a rolling motion with my hand to prod him along.

Crawford exhales in that bored sort of way, as if I'm wasting his time. "Listen, Keegan. This was fun and all, but I'm not a family man. Who are we kidding, right?"

I reel back, nearly stumbling on air from the blow of his words. "Excuse me?"

His hazel eyes flick to mine before skittering away again. "I can't pretend this situation is a good fit for me anymore."

This *situation*? He's referring to Millie and me as if we're a problem to be solved. Something to be tossed away when no longer convenient. I point a finger at him, silently scolding the digit for trembling. "This is your fault. You did this.

I was perfectly fine leaving things casual. Then you started spouting off lines about trust and wanting more. How about all that stuff you said on the way to Fort Collins? Was that bullshit?"

A muscle tics in his jaw. "Get your finger outta my face, Kee."

"Are you gonna make me? Does this"—I stab that finger into his chest—"upset you enough to have a genuine reaction?"

His nostrils flare and I can almost witness him prowling to the surface of this phony facade he's hiding behind. "What do you want from me?"

"The truth would be a great start."

"I already told you what's most important."

"You're ending things. Just like that." I snap my fingers so hard the knuckles ache.

Crawford's expression morphs into a mask of smug cockiness. "There's nothing to end, Keegan. We didn't slap on a label to begin with."

Is he joking with this shit? I comb through my hair, yanking on the ends. "There's more to the story. Why now? Spit it out."

"Did Millie tell you I made her cry?" His voice sounds far away, mutters through a wind tunnel.

I falter at his sudden change in direction. "No, but she called you a meanie."

Crawford snorts. "That's almost cute, and the least I deserve. She's terrified, and it's my fault. It was stupid to let me take her out by myself. It was even worse to believe I could change."

I reignite my glare. "Lay off the attitude pedal, Mister Nice Guy. I trust you with her. She wouldn't have gone with you if that wasn't the case."

"Yeah, well, I've incinerated that bridge. It was bound to happen eventually."

"Quit being vague. What did your dad do?" I cross my arms so tight the skin pulls.

"Just spewed some hateful shit, like always. Millie took it really hard. I should've done more to stop him."

"I'm sure he hurt her feelings. That's unfortunate, but it's bound to happen. Millie will get over that easily enough because he holds no significance. You, on the other hand, mean a helluva lot to that little girl. If you walk away and leave her, she won't forget that." I hate that my voice rises in pitch, nearly crumbling over the last words.

Crawford scrubs the back of his neck. "She will eventually."

"Don't you do this to her. You promised." My vision blurs, but I blink the moisture away before he can see the evidence.

"I shouldn't have."

"How can you blow off her feelings so carelessly? She won't get over this, Ford." A ball rises in my throat, but fuck that. I'm not crying in front of this jackass.

He shrugs, rocking on his heels. "Maybe it's better if she doesn't. We all go through tough lessons."

I toss my hands up in the air. "Fuck that. She's a little girl. Millie has at least a decade to enjoy before getting her heart shredded."

"As you've previously mentioned."

"Stop pretending Millie doesn't matter."

Crawford's flinch is small, but it's visible. "Not sure what you're expecting me to do about her feelings."

"Fix this! Go up there and talk to her." I flail a wild arm toward the house.

His cold indifference slips back into place. "Nah, it's better to have a clean break. You'll move on. She'll bond with your next boyfriend. I'll return to my isolated existence."

"Is that really what you want?"

"Yes."

I stab him in his freakishly firm pec, twice for good measure. "What's your problem?"

"This conversation is going nowhere," he drawls.

"No one is forcing you to stay."

"Are we done arguing?" If I didn't know better, a hint of a smile twitches the corner of his lips.

"Does it matter either way?"

Crawford rolls his eyes skyward. "Of course. I'm not that insensitive."

I'm getting dizzy from his emotional whiplash. "What a pile of garbage. If you gave half a shit, you'd stick around and fight for us."

He barks out a laugh sharp enough to cut iron. "You got it wrong, babe. It's because I care that I'm letting you go."

"Oh, that's very kind of you. I'd prefer it if you drop the noble act."

"Ah, but you wanted to believe I was decent. Guess we're all getting life lessons today. My father made a good point, tough as that is for me to admit. I'm meant to be alone."

A dull pang vibrates behind my ribs, making it difficult to breathe. "How can you think that after everything we've been through? Move forward, Ford. Don't go in reverse."

"Nah, I've always been more of a backroads kinda guy."

"Because of what your father did? You shouldn't let him win."

"This has nothing to do with him other than the harsh reminder. I make my own decisions."

"So, give me the truth. What's the real reason you're ditching out?" I grind my molars, begging him to wake up from his nightmarish funk.

"Because this," he motions between us, "isn't what I want long term."

A red fog filters into my vision. I feel a twinge in my belly, the snap that sets off a chain reaction. He's done with us, and I'm only spinning my wheels trying to make sense of stupid. "Right, okay. I'm just good for a quick fuck. That should've been obvious all along. But that little girl in there deserves better. Even from a piece of shit like you."

His eyes flash, more green than brown, and he lunges toward me. I'm boxed in between him and the piece of reliable metal he bought with Millie in mind. "Once more, in case you weren't listening. You're better off without me. That'll sink into your thick skull soon enough. Until then, comfort your daughter and forget about cursing me."

"Who the fuck do you—"

He slams his lips over mine, effectively cutting off my rant. The kiss isn't a gentle show of affection. It's a brand, possessive and meant to leave a mark. We bite and hiss and lash. Everything we can't say gets poured into the balloon of pressure expanding between us. Soon we'll implode and be left with nothing but a fuzzy memory. Crawford hauls me closer, his grip on my hip punishing. This feels far too familiar, yet I can't pull away.

I sizzle against him, a live wire sparking in a storm. His palm spans over the curves of my ass and presses me against his arousal. The move is fueled by testosterone and some bogus sense of claiming, but I'm warped just enough to let it go. Any point of contact we share is searing hot and frying me on the spot. I'm burning with a lethal fever after mere seconds.

Crawford wrenches his mouth away with a snarl. I seethe at him and smirk at the trickle of blood from his bottom lip. Serves him right for being a jackass. He wipes at the superficial wound.

I hide the tears streaking my cheeks by turning away. This jerk doesn't deserve my pain. "Stay away from us, Ford."

His chuckle is darker than the midnight sky. "If I recall correctly, you sought me out after our last fight."

"Well, I won't be making that mistake again. Fool me twice and I'm the idiot. Fingers crossed we never see you again." I hold up my hand in a mock wave.

When I glance over my shoulder, his smirk is hollow. "For your sake, I hope history doesn't repeat itself. You can only cut our ties so many times before this looks desperate."

"I'm not the one clinging to the past and allowing my fears to dictate my future."

He holds up his arms, the sign of surrender as worthless as him. "And on that note, take care of yourself. Tell Millie I say goodbye."

"Tell her yourself, Crawford." My laugh is frail enough for the wind to sweep the sound away. "A real man faces his own demons."

CHAPTER TWENTY-FOUR

Crawford

Healing Hug #25: There is no form of comfort strong enough
to fix a fool.

Tᴏᴏᴏ— THE POST-Kᴇᴇɢᴀɴ ᴠᴇʀsɪᴏɴ ᴏғ ᴍʏsᴇʟғ ɪs ʙʏ ғᴀʀ ᴛʜᴇ ᴡᴏʀsᴛ. I'm almost a week in, and my grasp on normalcy is skewed as fuck. Considering I've spent the majority of my years in solitude, returning to the grind should've been a cinch. I can attest to the opposite being true. My routine is out of whack and nothing makes sense. There's an oozing gash across my heart that will never heal.

So, yeah. That's the latest on me.

It's safe to confirm that adjusting to life without them hasn't been successful. By this point, even the oil-splatter writing on the chipping wall is legible. I'm utterly screwed.

Gasoline and dust clog my lungs, along with the desperation hanging heavy in the air. I imagine inhaling pineapples and ocean kisses and tropical paradise. This is tribulation of the most ruthless, self-destructive variety. Torturing myself with the memory of her scent is another cruel punishment. I'm on a narrow, icy slope without a pickaxe.

The shop is silent, yet I picture Millie racing around with Elsa and Patch. Her peal of giggling laughter wages a war on my echoing ears. Because in reality, I'm alone. A glance at my phone reveals no calls or texts. The damn device mocks me with silence. Nothing speaks to me, not even the wind. The sun doesn't shine on my piece of property. Those blinding rays are reserved for those who appreciate the warm comfort. Even Patch is ignoring me.

If I've learned anything, it's that Keegan and Millie are irreplaceable. Those two own my battered, black heart. Because of them, I had a future to strive for. More than that, I wanted to be ambitious and aim higher. That's all shot to shit now. Bold hues of vitality left with their vibrant influences. Now that they're gone, my surroundings have returned to stained concrete, gray and ugly.

Keegan's parting words are haunting me. I'm a coward for running away, especially for leaving Millie without saying goodbye, but my plans were set with them in mind. No matter what she thinks, I care about them. That's why I'm choosing to suffer, sentencing myself to an existence of strictly surviving. I scoff at my internal drama.

Such a pathetic fucking martyr.

The wrench I'm holding slips and drops onto the knuckles of my toes. Even through the thick leather of my boots, a blast of pain explodes instantly. "Son of a bitch damned to hell. Mother fucking piece of shit."

Another colorful rainbow of curses flings off my tongue as I hop on one foot. I can't even do my damn job without causing damage. The intense throbbing settles into a pulsing ache. That offensive tool gleams under the fluorescent spotlights and I whip it outside in a boomerang arch. I toss a handful of discarded clamps into the box, metal clanging against wood with a dull thud. The noise matches the listless beat inside of me. Each moment pumps slower than the last. I'm stuck in quicksand and only wasting energy by struggling. My injury is already forgotten as familiar regret seeps in. The words spin and spin until I can't ignore them.

Fuck, what did I do?

A similar version of the same question has been plaguing me for days. I could pull my head out of my ass. We can clean up this mess. There's a possibility they'll forgive me. I should've fought for them like Keegan begged me to. Instead, I limped away to lick my wounds in private. Some fucking good that's doing me.

Eating is a chore. Sleeping is worse. Visions of Millie crying and Keegan's fractured emerald stare keep me awake. Such a courageous move. Self-sacrifice. This is my penance for being a selfish prick. If only my father could see his hand-iwork. I'm sure he'd be so proud.

But the fallout is all on me. I'm to blame. This state of misery is entirely my fault. Am I going to admit defeat, tuck tail, and plead for a second (or third) chance? Absolutely not. It wasn't a lie when I told Keegan she deserves better. Saddling her to an asshole who carelessly casts aside happiness is a larger injustice than I'm willing to commit.

I glance over at the one companion who's forced to remain faithful. Patch has been shunning me, as if she somehow knows of the crimes I've committed. She's slumped in her bed and steadily avoiding all attempts at interaction from me. How bad is it when even my dog is mad at me? That almost causes a bump of humor to batter at the fog of sorrow. But the weak attempt falls flat.

Loud rumbling streaks through the suffocating silence. I turn to watch as the growl of an approaching motorcycle interrupts my sniveling pity party. A hum of déjà vu rattles against my skull as two vehicles come into view.

Delaney leads the duo in her red coupe with Decker following close behind on his Harley. Even from deep inside the garage, I can see the deep scratches cutting into the usually flawless paint on his tank. Well, that's definitely new.

Patch perks up at their arrival. She trots to Decker's side and lingers for a few scratches behind her ears. Guess she's not pissed at the entire male population. She's reserving all the ire for me.

I stride to the edge of the stall, waiting with my arms

crossed and a scowl firmly in place. Decker hops off his wrecked chopper with the grin he's known for. He walks toward me with a pep in his step. His fiancée is more hesitant, her shuffling gait exposing guilt. It doesn't take a rocket scientist to formulate an educated guess on how the damage occurred. Patch nudges Delaney's hand, earning a laugh and another rub to her furry head. It's good to know my dog is accepting affection from everyone but me.

When Decker is close enough to get a decent look at me, the simple ease falls from his features. He studies me, almost recoiling from the sight. "Dude, you look like shit."

I snort, narrowing my eyes into a glare. "Hilarious. Did Erik tell you to say that?"

Deep grooves carve the space between his brows. "Nah, I came up with that all on my own. What's up, Ford?"

"Same old shit." I nod toward his dinged ride. "I can see why you're here."

Decker waves off my words. "We'll get to that in a minute. Why does it look like someone took a dump in your Frosted Flakes?"

"Not sure what you mean." The lie is sticky on my tongue.

"Does this have anything to do with Keegan and Millie?"

"Nope." I rip my eyes from his, finding a particularly interesting grease spot to focus on.

Delaney seems to perk up, most likely due to the attention being cast over me instead of her misdeed. "Ah, come on. It's no secret you've been spending time with them. You can tell us, Ford."

I grind my bruised foot into the ground. The shot of pain zaps up my leg. "Nothing to say. We had some fun. Now it's over. End of."

"I highly doubt that," Decker chuckles.

"Nah, we're done. I made sure of that."

They exchange a look. If I was fluent in the secret language of couples, their silent exchange might make more sense. Delaney flicks her gaze to mine. "How bad is the wreckage?"

I peer around them into the gravel lot. "Are we talking about Decker's cruiser?"

He taps his temple. "No, your mental wellbeing."

"Think I'm crazy?"

His chest shakes with a chuckle. "Well, I wasn't planning to be so blunt."

"I'm fine. It wasn't anything serious to begin with. Ending things was for the best." The damn irony isn't lost on me. I wouldn't accept that bullshit answer from Keegan.

Delaney squints at me while nudging her fiancé. "Sure, I can see that."

"All right, fine. We'll quit sniffing at your personal business." He pauses, as if I'm going to suddenly change my mind about spilling the secrets wedged inside of me.

I lift my chin, staring him down. *Good luck, buddy.*

Decker sighs, glancing at his future wife. "She hurt my baby, Ford."

"Oh, please. The machine is fine." Delaney swipes at the air, as if batting away a gnat.

"You treated her poorly, Dell. She needs to be handled with care," he scolds.

She pops out her hip. "Well, I wasn't properly prepared for how complicated it is to downshift."

"Are you suggesting this is my fault?"

She twists her lips. "You were teaching me how to drive. I tipped us over. We can share the blame."

"That's not how things went down. Literally."

Delaney huffs and rolls her eyes. "Don't be so dramatic. It was an accident."

"I sure hope you wouldn't do this on purpose." He gives her a side-eye full of inquisition.

She quirks a brow. "Don't underestimate a jealous woman."

Decker reaches over and squeezes her waist. "Not funny, Dell."

"No?" She wiggles her fingers toward his torso. "Bet I can make you laugh."

"I wouldn't try it," he growls.

She doesn't heed to his warning. They tumble together in a mass of squirming limbs and lewd noises. Dammit, here we go again. A white-hot stake drives through my chest and I nearly hiss from the burn. My misery craves company and these two aren't cutting it.

I cough into my fist until their writhing ceases. "I can get started on your bike right away, Deck. You can pick it up at the end of this week."

He pulls away from Delaney with a labored exhale. Her cheeks are rosy. His shirt is rumpled. They need to get a damn room far away from me.

Decker drags a palm over his hair. "Uh, okay. You won't need more time?"

"That's plenty already. Nothing else to do around here except fix bikes."

Delaney frowns. "Want me to put in a good word for you?"

"Please don't," I mutter. The gaping sore spreads faster through my gut at the thought alone.

"Let's take a hint, Dell." He steers her toward the parked coupe. "Thanks again, Ford. I'll come by Friday and check on your progress."

I tip the brim of my hat at them. "See you then."

The handsy couple drives off in a cloud of lust-scented dust. I fan the sickly-sweet notion away from my face. Heaven forbid those fumes are contagious. That's the last damn thing I need. My sorry ass is already pining over a woman who I made untouchable.

Just as I'm about to resume wallowing in private, the roar of pipes cracks through the silence. Who the fuck else is paying me a social visit? The shadows of isolation break apart as my next guest nears closer. I let my jaw drop when no other than Grady Bowen crests the hill of my driveway.

The biker cuts his engine along the front of my shop. He's alone, which I hear is rare nowadays. Grady removes his helmet and comes over to stand beside me.

We're quiet for a moment, sizing one another up. I flick my gaze to his seemingly impeccable motorcycle. "Need some work done?"

"Nah, she's running solid. Just dropping by to say hello."

I stare at him, waiting for the punchline. He doesn't follow that up with a joke, though. "Huh, all right. Well, hey."

He scratches at his scruffy jaw. "You got any beer?"

A snort scrapes out of me. "It's gonna be that type of conversation?"

"Absolutely."

"I have a few in the cooler. Grab a seat." I motion to the chairs folded up against the wall.

Grady has an empty spot waiting for me when I return. He's taking advantage of the open space, legs spread wide while reclining deep and low. I drop my ass onto the canvas seat with a groan. The shitty craftsmanship creaks under my weight.

He takes the outstretched bottle from me. "Thanks, man."

"No problem." I take a swig, gulping down another for good measure. "So, what's up?"

"Did you know Keegan is close with Sutton's family?"

I almost reel back from the unexpected blindside. With a heavy exhale, I force my expression to go slack. "Kinda," I mumble. "She might've mentioned something along those lines once or twice."

"Then you're aware of the shitstorm I've been hearing about for nearly a week."

"Okay." The non-answer neither confirms nor denies my very dense involvement.

"I'm going to need more dedication from you, Ford."

This guy is nosy as fuck, considering I can count the number of prior conversations we've had on one hand. "Not sure what this has to do with you."

"Aren't you listening? Keegan is friends with Sutton. Therefore, I've been hearing all about how awful men are. Dude, you're making us all look bad."

I gape at him. "Uh, sorry?"

"Are you really?"

"No."

"What the fuck, Ford? Don't you have any pride for brotherhood?"

Not since my actual brother abandoned me. But Grady doesn't need to hear that sob story. "Do you?"

"Of course. I wouldn't be here otherwise."

That's news to me. Last I recall, this guy isn't a huge people person. If anyone can understand my reasoning, it should be him. "I live off the grid for a reason."

"I'll remember that next time you need a favor."

"Noted." Erik was wrong to point me in Grady's direction. Good thing I didn't follow through. He doesn't get it.

He grunts, tipping his face toward the sky. "So, I'm gonna need you to fix this."

"Not sure I'm following." I swallow another mouthful of the hoppy brew.

His eyes roll to mine. "You broke up with Keegan, right?"

"I mean, we weren't really dating."

"Yes, you certainly were."

Something dark twists inside of my stomach. I normally like this guy, but his invasive assumptions are rubbing at my raw nerves. "Not sure it really matters. We aren't seeing each other anymore."

"Right. That's the part I need you to repair." Grady points at me.

I sit there for a moment, completely caught off guard.

My sluggish mind scrambles to catch up and formulate a worthy retort. "Are you trying to convince me to patch things up with Keegan?"

A sharp jerk of his chin. "Yes."

"Listen, Grady. I appreciate the advice and all." That's a steaming pile of garbage. "But my relationship or whatever I had with Keegan is over."

"I think you should reconsider."

"Yeah, I'm getting that vibe from you."

Grady turns to the side, staring me down. "What's the issue?"

"Do you want a list? How about she deserves better than me and we don't belong together."

"Quit being an idiot, Ford. If I can win the girl, you sure as hell can."

I tug my hat down lower. "I highly doubt that."

"Stop arguing with me while you're at it."

Drinking a beer has never been so labor intensive. I'm almost out of hot air from this waste of an exchange. "Well, this has been…fun. I appreciate you coming by and all, but this is my choice to make."

"And how is that going for you?"

"Just great, thanks for asking. I'm capable of managing my problems, however fucked up you think those methods are."

He tosses me a look that reeks of suspicion. "I'm not the one moping around like a rotting sack of potatoes. We can smell your stench for miles, even hiding all the way out here in the woods."

I can't control the chuckle that tumbles from my straining throat. "Damn, dude. You're kind of a dick."

He smiles against the lip of his bottle. "Thanks for noticing."

"Did y'all plan this?"

"Who?"

"You and Deck, banding together to lecture me?"

"Hardly, Ford. We're not creative enough to plan a mutual intervention." It's his turn to laugh. The gritty notes sound horribly out of tune.

"Are you doing this outta some obligation?"

"Not exactly. But a happy wife motivates a man."

"I see."

Grady's brow rises. "Do you?"

"Not in that way."

"You've got a long road ahead if that's your attitude."

"I'm well aware."

"And you're really okay with this?" He motions around the quiet yard.

I scan the seemingly endless woods. No sign of civilization for miles. "There isn't much of a choice."

"Holy shit, dude. Yes, there is. Get off your high horse and apologize."

That sinking sensation of sludge in my veins drowns me in the glaring facts. Keegan and Millie are better off without me. "Not gonna happen, Grady."

He holds up his palms. "All right, man. Don't say I didn't try."

"Wouldn't dream of it."

Grady grunts again while brushing off his jeans. "You're more stubborn than me. I can appreciate that."

"I guess I'll take that as a compliment."

"Whatever makes you feel better. Good talk, Ford." He claps me on the back.

Was it? I'm feeling a tad coerced after the last two hours of judgments. Talk about putting a man on the spot. "That's all?"

"Nothing else to say." His sudden departure seems rushed as fuck.

"Okay, then. Have a good one, man."

Grady offers me a salute over his shoulder as he walks

away. "Oh, I will. I held up my end of the bargain. Sutton gets to return the favor when I get home. Sure is nice having the comfort of a good woman waiting for me. Wish I could say the same for you."

I flip off his retreating form. Such an asshole.

CHAPTER TWENTY-FIVE

Keegan

Healing Hug #26: When trying to forget about boys,
rely on extra doses of girl power.

MOVE TO ANOTHER RACK AND BEGIN AIMLESSLY SLIDING THE HANGERS from right to left. The chic collection of clothes all blend together in a blob of colors. My vision blurs to match these potential wardrobes. We've been at Meadow Kisses for under an hour, but it feels like an entire morning has been wasted. Retail therapy isn't helping. Similar to the epic failures of ice cream, cheesy movies, and triple my usual hazelnut coffee servings. With extra vanilla.

The flowery perfume they infuse in this small space is giving me a headache. I check the clock on my phone again. Only three minutes have passed. The seconds must be stuck in molasses. What are the chances we can leave soon? I glance over my shoulder to find Millie and Josey giggling near a heaping display of bathing suits. A twinge cramps my belly at the reminder of the last time we went swimming. I rub at the spasm, but the sensation only spreads.

In the wide scope of things, Crawford was barely around long enough to be considered a blip on the radar. But in the month we spent together, that man weaved himself deeply into our lives. He seems to have unraveled himself just as quickly. The holes he left behind can't be so easily repaired, though. I haven't heard a word, even for Millie's sake. It's official. That rat bastard doesn't have a heart.

"Are you having fun?"

I blink at my friend. How did she get in front of me so fast? "Um, sure?"

Josey crosses her arms. "Liar. You haven't picked a single thing to try on."

She's right, of course. I'm physically present, but my mind is miles away in the woods with a certain reclusive mechanic. Damn Crawford and all his irresistible hotness. I rub my temples, repeating a mantra to forget all about him.

He's just a guy. A careless asshat without feelings. Some lonely jerk who can't be bothered to say goodbye to his biggest fan. That little girl is who I need to focus on. That guy isn't worth my tears or thoughts or regrets.

A strong grip on my shoulders snaps me out of the trance. Josey is studying me with intense scrutiny. "Why do you look so weird?"

I plaster a fake-ass grin on my face. "You'll have to be more specific."

"There's something strange happening here." She traces an invisible circle around my facial features.

"Oh, this?" I point to my expression. "It's my brave face."

She quirks a brow. "No one is believing that."

"It's working so far." I shrug, flicking imaginary lint off my shirt.

"Well, not for me."

"Me either, Mama." Millie pops out of seemingly nowhere. Was she hiding in a rack?

I blow some stray hair off my forehead. "Awesome, you two. Thanks for ganging up on me."

Josey offers a lopsided smile. "It's okay to miss him, Keke. Breakups are tough."

"There was nothing to break up. He wasn't my boyfriend. We weren't dating. And I'm fine with that." I find myself once again very thankful that I don't have a Pinocchio tell.

"What kind of friend do you take me for?"

"The best?" When all else fails, try flattery.

"Well, that's obvious. And because of that, I'm well aware that you're lying. Which is *fine*, but not necessary or appreciated."

I drape an arm over her shoulder. "Okay, I'm sorry. You're right. There's a pretty good chance my spirit is crushed. But I'll rebound."

"Was that so hard?"

"Extremely."

Millie has been quietly watching us, waiting for an opportunity to pipe in. "I miss Ford, Mama."

I flinch at his name coming from her mouth. We've managed to dodge addressing him personally. That small avoidance felt like a victory in our column. My soul cries out at the reminder, but I shush that susceptible piece of me. I kneel to Millie's level, placing a kiss on her nose. "Well, I love you. Did you know that, sweetie?"

She scrunches her brows. "Love you, Mama. But is Ford going to call soon?"

The throbbing in my chest cracks me wide open, spilling all of that sensitive gibberish onto the flood. I press a palm to my sternum, attempting to trap the sentimental goo from escaping. The loss is too great, and my knees wobble in this crouched position. Falling onto my ass would be icing on the damn humble pie. I try to suck in my lips when the corners tremble. How could that stupid jerk do this to her?

I gulp at the thorns stabbing in my throat, brushing a thumb over Millie's slightly chubby cheek. "I don't think we're going to hear from him anymore, baby girl. We talked about that, remember?"

She frowns. "But Ford can't be on timeout forever. He'll come hang out with us again. I know he won't stay away too long."

Another quiver attacks my lower lip. I rub at the sting

expanding across the bridge of my nose. My vision clouds, a smoky film obscuring the exit route from this mess. How do I tell this innocent child that the man she idolizes doesn't plan to see her ever again?

Josey must notice that I'm two seconds away from crumbling. She claps her hands and ushers us toward the door. "How about we go to Springing Swirls for some ice cream?"

Millie's slouching shoulders perk upright. "Yay! Can I get extra sprinkles, Mama?"

"Of course, sweetie. Double the cherries, too." Whatever gets her mind off the man who I'm not going to name, even in my thoughts.

She cuddles into my side as we stroll along the sidewalk. "Can we take Elsa for a walk this afternoon?"

I comb my fingers through her silky hair. The sunshine makes her golden strands shimmer and glow. "Absolutely. We just have to steer clear of the woods. Auntie JoJo is scared of monsters."

My friend snorts, gaining the attention of a few older ladies passing us. She waves at them as if her obnoxious noises are a typical occurrence. In her case, they most certainly are. "Yeah, that doesn't sound farfetched. I mean, that Boogie Man is terrifying. If only some mighty knight could rescue us."

Millie gasps. "Ford could save us!"

I roll my eyes toward my so-called bestie. "Thanks a lot, Josephine."

She scoffs again. "Put a little sparkle on that drab tone. There's nothing wrong with a little hero worship. You're the one trying to avoid him on purpose."

"For good reason," I grumble.

A jingle announces our arrival when Josey guides us into the sweet shop. "A heaping helping of sugar will boost your mood."

"Fingers crossed." The idea of eating turns my stomach

with a somersault. My appetite has taken a serious blow since that incident with the culprit. Yeah, that's a good attitude to have. I roll the knot from my neck and stride toward the counter to order.

We settle into a booth along the far wall. Millie attacks her banana split with gusto. Josey is licking her twist cone with overt enthusiasm. Porn stars would be jealous of her tongue-curling technique. Damn, how is she single? And why am I still watching? I blame my voyeurism on our table being too silent. The murmuring din from other patrons is irritating, like the tag on a shirt. I'm antsy and aggravated, and it's all his fault. Heat builds behind my eyelids and the dam bursts beyond control.

I slam my untouched sundae onto the table. My spoon clatters against the ceramic edge. For a moment I worry the bowl will crack. "I gave him a hug. Like a real hug. And what did he do? Just toss us away."

Josey places her hand over mine, which is currently gripping the table with white knuckles. "Okay, Keke. Let's just take a breath."

A growl rips up my clogging throat. "I don't need air or more ice cream or sappy movies. I just want him to give Millie the goodbye she deserves. Then she can move on." I give my daughter a watery smile.

She tilts her head at me in return. "But he's coming back, Mama."

I sniffle while wiping at my leaking eyes. "No, sweetie. He's not."

"Why are you saying that?"

"Because he told me. He didn't want to hurt your feelings more, Mills. So, he just left instead." Such a selfish, sniveling coward. I should've bit him harder when I had the chance.

My daughter looks down at her mostly devoured dessert. "Why would he do that?"

I hiss as the crack in her voice pierces the softest section of my heart. After a rough swallow, I reach for her hand with trembling fingers. "He's the only one who knows the answer. Maybe he thinks that will protect you."

"But it's not. When Ford isn't around, I'm not as happy. Isn't he sad without us?"

I nod, forcing a crooked grin. "He's probably very upset."

"Then he probably misses us a lot. We should call him."

"Absolutely not," I blurt. After a much-needed pause, I exhale a stream of bitter juju. "I mean, he's probably busy, and we don't want to bother him. If we stay busy, things will get easier."

Millie's posture slumps with a thick sigh. "Okay, Mama. I'll try to stop missing him."

And I'm officially the worst mom ever. The fact I gave him a chance in the first place lands heavier than bricks on my shoulders. Regret shackles to my ankles and drags me lower. I blink the moisture from my lashes, giving her palm a squeeze for reassurance. "I'm so sorry, Millie. Please don't let him steal your smile."

"It's not your fault, Mama. Ford hurt your heart, too."

My little girl is wise beyond her years. "But it shouldn't have happened to you."

Josey lets a loud whistle loose. "All right, ladies. Enough of the wallowing. What's next on the agenda?"

"I dunno. Maybe a nap?" I could sure use one.

She makes the sound of a buzzer. "Wrong answer. How about we go dancing?"

"No." There's no hesitation from me.

Her brows leap upward. "Why not?"

"First and most important of all, that's not a public activity Millie should participate in until she's at least twenty-five. And second, remember what happened last time?"

Josey smacks her lips together. "You satisfied the wild beast inside of you with crazy animal humping?"

Millie giggles at her inappropriate, albeit accurate, description. "You're so silly, JoJo."

She winks. "That's why you keep me around, right?"

"Uh-huh. And you let me stay up way past my bedtime."

Josey claps a palm over my daughter's mouth. A dry laugh scrapes out of her. "She's totally joking. All that sugar is going straight to her head."

I scowl at her weak derailing attempts. "It's fine. Far better than your innuendos."

"Oh, please. She's seen it all at the zoo."

"Yeah, Mama. The gorillas *really* love each other." My daughter is vehemently bobbing her head.

A groan vibrates my ribcage. "Not sure why I even bother."

Josey nudges me. "Darn, you're worse off than I thought. Her response is freaking hilarious, Keke."

"She's seven, Joe. Why must I keep reminding you?" I glower at her.

"Millie is mature for her age."

"Thanks to you."

"It's part of my auntie duty to prepare her for the real world."

Millie giggles again. "You said doody."

Josey flings an arm her way. "See? She gets it."

I glance between, a weak bump of amusement jostling my shoulders. "At least your spirit isn't tarnished, baby girl. If silly jokes make you happy, go right ahead. We could all use the comedic relief."

"This is a team effort. We just need to stick by each other, like always. That's why you moved to Silo Springs. Best decision ever." My friend lifts her palm for a high-five.

Her gesture reminds me of the secret shake Millie shares with Crawford. Screw not saying his name. Ignoring him isn't doing the trick—maybe overexposure is the way to go.

"Other than a few detours. I have Ford to thank for any ill feelings." I let the edges of my lips curl.

"Eh, it wasn't all bad. By next week, you'll be able to look back on the better moments."

"He's history, Josey. Ford chose to go. I'm not moping over him for another second."

"Yeah, there you go. Don't take any blame, Keke. You couldn't predict he'd turn out to be a prickle bush." Josey wags her brows, and I brace for whatever bomb she's going to drop next. "So, dancing?"

"Why are you so desperate to shake your booty?"

"I think a better question would be why aren't you?"

I peek over at Millie. She's beaming at me, waiting for my verdict. "How about a compromise? We can bust all the moves in the privacy of my living room where there's zero potential of anyone else seeing me."

Josey stands from her chair and Millie leaps upright to follow suit. They exchange a smile, turning to me. "Do we get to choose the music?"

They earn a genuine laugh for that. "Sure. I won't protest."

The far younger of the two pumps her fist in the air. "All girls party at our house."

Josey presses a finger over Millie's mouth while trying to keep a straight face herself. "I wouldn't say that too loud or we might get some uninvited guests."

My daughter visibly shrinks when she realizes others might have heard her. "Let's leave before they follow us."

Josey is still on the verge of cackling. "Good plan, Mills. Lead the way."

And I follow along with a legit pep in my step as the memories of Crawford stay behind.

CHAPTER TWENTY-SIX

Crawford

Healing Hug #27: A warped hold for testing loyalty.

I LEAN INTO THE SHARP TURN, SLANT MY BIKE AT A DIAGONAL, and crank the throttle. A pulsing rush flows through my veins from the spike in adrenaline. I haven't been able to reach that high lately. The engine howls as I demand more speed. That constant roaring grounds me, tethering my body to the moment. I've managed to slice twenty minutes off my commute to Gulligan Haven. That might be a new record.

Rows of houses frame the street on both sides, but there's no one else on the road. This sleepy subdivision would be a perfect starting line for a drag race. I snort, the sound bouncing against my helmet. These rigid homeowners would call the cops faster than drivers could congregate. Hell, they barely tolerate me whizzing by on a bimonthly basis.

I whip into my mother's driveway with a loud screech from gears grinding and the stench of burning rubber. There's no reason to linger on the curb today. I already made one hell of an entrance into her neighborhood. A thick cloud of exhaust and reckless decisions forms behind me as I dismount. Repairing the damage to my Harley will give me something to focus on later.

With a cyclone swirling in my gut, I bound toward the house. All appears normal until my boots nearly smash through her rickety porch stairs. I glance down to notice the boards giving way. A few spots on the railing could use a fresh coat of paint. Her lawn looks a week overdue for a mow. My mother's friend must be preoccupied with other tasks. A shudder rolls through me while I raise my fist to knock. That's trouble for another day.

My mom opens the door, takes one look at me, and smiles wide. "Who is she? No bullshitting this time."

I smirk at her while stepping into the foyer. "What're the chances we could exchange a few pleasantries before diving into my lack of a love life?"

"Zilch. And don't pretend you've suddenly taken a liking to frivolous greetings." She crosses her arms, giving me that stern expression I can't contend with.

"All right, fine. Can we at least sit down while I face your interrogation?"

She rolls her eyes. "Just give me the highlights. That'll appease me for now."

I study her for a moment. "Because that's not suspicious as fuck, Ma. Are you in a hurry?"

Her gaze skitters to a spot over my shoulder. "Not necessarily."

"Did I catch you in the middle of something?" I follow her line of sight while trying not to assume the worst. Bile threatens to tickle my throat. If her fuck buddy is waiting naked upstairs, I might retch all over the carpet.

"Nope, everything is all good. A little sooner than we expected, but we've always been the impulsive sorts." She scratches her scalp, still avoiding eye contact. "Tell me about your girl, Ford."

"After I find out what you're hiding from me." My tone is sharp and demanding, leaving no room for argument. Not that she's ever been one to listen.

"Okay, but I don't want you to freak out. Promise me?" My mother holds up her palms. The placating gesture immediately rouses my guard with a deafening bellow.

Before I can agree to anything, a figure appears at the entrance to the kitchen. Recognition slams into me an instant later. I blink in rapid succession to be sure, but there's no mistaking him. *No fucking way.* Deception poisons the air, squeezing the oxygen from my lungs. The stench is more powerful than turpentine and acrylic paint combined. I almost stumble backward onto my ass from the blow of betrayal.

"Fuck. No." I jab a finger in his direction while glaring at the woman responsible for raising me. "Not happening. I've had it up to my ears with being ambushed. This is going too far. I never expected my own mother to stab me in the back." I wrench open the front door, set to storm out the way I came in mere moments ago.

"Don't go, Ford." The authority in her melodic voice halts my hasty retreat. It seems even as an adult, I can't disobey my mom. "Stay and hash shit out. Your brother is here to make peace."

I target my focus on Grant, shooting the sharpest daggers in my arsenal. "You're a damn traitor. And what the fuck? You've been lurking in the kitchen until I put my guard down?" I pin my mother with another glare. "How could you do this to me, Mom?"

Her lips twist to one side. "Well, to be fair, I didn't know you were stopping by. But he's your brother and my son, Ford. We'll always be family. For that biological fact alone, you should hear him out."

"This is complete bullshit," I spit.

"I was wary at first, too. No one blames you for calling him out. He deserves some razzing, no doubt. But he's here on good terms, Ford. Stow your rifle and give him a fighting chance."

"I have nothing to say to you," I growl in his general vicinity.

Grant shoves his hands deep into his front pockets. "That's all right. I have enough to say for both of us."

A snarl barrels out of me. "I can only imagine the messages our father sent along with you."

My mom scowls. "Quit being dramatic, Crawford. Your dad has nothing to do with this."

A stampede of elephants wreaks havoc on my eardrums. "I don't think either of you has any right to tell me how to feel in this situation."

Grant rubs a palm over his smooth jaw. "Do you want me to leave?"

"Yeah, you're good at that."

He spreads his arms out, opening himself up for attack. "Dammit, Ford. I know, okay? I fucked up, but that's why I'm here."

"Ten years too late."

"Yeah, well, there isn't a whole lot I can do to change that now. But I'm hoping to fix things between us. Can I have five minutes of your time?" My hesitation hangs heavy in the space between us. His throat bobs with a heavy gulp. "Please?"

"Fuck," I groan. "Fine. I'll listen to your sorry-ass excuses."

His mouth twitches with a smirk. "Thanks. I'll wait on the deck."

Grant's retreating footsteps echo down the hall to where I'm standing with my head ripped to the ceiling. My stomach is more knotted than a rope swing. Another moan slips past my pinching lips. "I can't believe this shit is happening."

My mom shuffles her feet beside me. "This is a great thing, Ford. You'll see. Go outside and talk to your brother before assuming the worst." A light laugh bounces through her. "I really should've gotten the dirt on your lady troubles before shit exploded."

I scoff. "That's your fault."

She nudges my side. "Give me her name and I'll leave you alone. At least until you're done talking to Grant."

"There's no one anymore. I had been seeing a woman casually." That word tastes worse than ash on my tongue.

"Who is she?"

"Why does it matter? We have far bigger issues to solve." Now that we're broaching the subject of Keegan, I realize she hasn't been plaguing my thoughts since Grant randomly appeared.

She pinches my cheeks as if I'm a toddler. I suppose the maturity level is comparable in certain respects. "I'm your mother and need to believe there's a chance for grandchildren someday."

I squint at her, searching for more signs of deception. But my mother has no connection to the blonde seductress. Although, there is one possibility. "She actually adopted a dog from Rover & Meow for her daughter not too long ago."

Her brows shoot up. "Is that so?"

"Sure is. They couldn't be happier with Elsa."

My mother hums, a smile dipped in pure glee curling her lips. "Keegan and Millie, right?"

I grunt and shake my head. "Figures you'd remember them."

"They're difficult to forget. I'm sure you're well aware of that."

"Unfortunately," I mutter.

She pats my shoulder. "One problem at a time, Ford. Maybe mending fences with Grant will open your eyes to other possibilities."

"Highly doubtful."

My mom pushes me toward the patio door. "Give it a whirl. Good luck."

I follow her orders, like a puppy. But what choice do I have? None when faced with my estranged brother who apparently wants to make amends.

Grant is sitting in one of the wooden Adirondack chairs when I step outside. He turns toward me, offering up a beer. "Peace offering?"

"I hope you have more than Coors planned for that." But I take the bottle and twist off the cap.

He guzzles liquid courage before spitting out, "Our dad is a dictator."

I exhale a dry chuckle. "No shit."

"Mom was smart to find a way out."

Another noncommittal noise dips off my lips. "I guess there's still something we can agree on."

"I quit," he blurts.

I startle from the force in his voice. "Already? Damn, that was easy."

Grant chuckles. "No, you asshole. I left the practice. That lofty corner office wasn't for me. Not sure it ever was. Dad's borderline insanity pushed me over the edge. I've been thinking about how he treated you and that little girl. It's been haunting me. Why didn't I stand up for you?"

"That's a good question. And who are you calling an asshole?"

He shrugs. "Eh, I deserve that. The reason I'm here is for you, Ford. All these years and we've barely spoken five words to each other."

"Whose fault is that?" I shoot him a glare severe enough to slice his skin.

His head bobs to a slow beat. "Mine. I'm well aware and take full responsibility. That's why it's also on me to restore what I broke."

I rip my gaze off of him. "You've got one helluva uphill battle to conquer."

"Dammit, Ford. Just give me a chance to explain."

"I was willing to in the beginning, but you fucking left me. My big brother. My idol. My best friend. I was alone and lost and crushed with disappointment. It's no wonder how I ended up hating most people. You can take credit for that, too."

He holds up a palm. "I will. That's all my fault. When

I should've been protecting you, I abandoned you instead. There's nothing I can say to take that pain away. But I wanna right my wrongs."

Disbelief forms a clump in my throat. I choke it down with a swig of beer. "Why now, Grant?"

His exhale seems to weigh two tons. "Because I'm tired of pretending to be happy. I don't want to be a sniveling coward who runs from his problems. The accident didn't just damage my body. When I left, my head was all fucked up. Nothing made sense. Leaving was the easiest solution, but I never should've stepped foot out of Silo Springs. I realized that after only a month. It already felt too late. With each year, the choice to return only got harder. I got stuck in a dead-end routine. Enough was eventually enough, though. We're brothers. You're my blood. Nothing is stronger than that."

"Not even your bond with father dearest?"

A deep scowl carves his features. "I was wrong about following him. It's my biggest regret and worst mistake. I'll be paying the price for it until I'm old and gray."

"You're fucking right about that."

Another forced breath claws out of him. "Am I too late, brother?"

"Fuck off," I mutter.

"That's not really an answer."

"Only because I can't give the one you truly deserve."

"How's Iron Throttle?"

His abrupt change in direction makes my brain swell. "Oh, are we moving on already?"

"I can talk in circles about my bullshit excuses for hours. Let me have a few moments of rest. Tell me about your work."

"Why are you taking a sudden interest in my business?"

"Always have, Ford. I'm so damn proud of you. Sure, I've done a shitty job showing it. That's another thing that needs fixing."

I scoff into the open air. "Yep, the list keeps growing."

"I miss cruising down the open highway. A suit and tie are no match for leather and wind."

"Cheers to that." I lift my bottle to his.

"Do you need a partner?"

The beer sprays out of my mouth in a wide arc. "Are you fucking with me?"

"Nah, not even a little bit. I haven't been this serious about something in a long damn time."

I turn toward him and get my first good look in who knows how long. He's older and broader, but appears worn down to his bones. The man could use a double shot of whiskey and a comfortable bed. Hell, I could go for the same. "You honestly think I'm just gonna agree to that? I'm barely tolerating this conversation."

He lifts a single shoulder. "It's worth a shot. What better way to show you how serious I am, right?"

"That's a big decision. One I won't make ten minutes after being reunited with you."

Grant nods. "I don't blame you there. Trust takes more than words to heal. I lost my way, brother. There's been something here always yanking me back. It's long overdue that I come home."

"No shit," I mutter.

He chooses to ignore my brooding mood. "Still have my bike?"

"I do."

"Does it run?"

I give him a limp shrug. "Not lately."

He scratches at his chin. "Guess I have my first project already lined up."

It feels like the floor disappears and I'm freefalling into the Twilight Zone. My thoughts spin faster than I can process. "You're for real? This isn't a prank?"

"I wouldn't joke about that, especially with you. People make mistakes, right? Some bigger than reasonable compassion allows for. That's what makes us human. It also means others have to offer second chances so we can prove ourselves."

Pressure builds in my gut as the vision of blonde hair and green eyes assaults me. "I've been hearing that more lately."

"And you can forgive me?"

I shouldn't, at least not so easily. When he left, my world was crushed in half. That loss still blazes bright inside of me. But he's here for a reason. "I'll work on it. You've given me a lot to consider."

"So, you'll actually think about it?"

"Sure, why not? You're my brother, after all." And Grant is the only one who can fill the void caused by him leaving. Getting my best friend back will be nice, too.

He gives a loud hoot. "I'll take being redeemable. And that means you are, too."

"This isn't about me."

His mouth twitches into a knowing grin. "I heard what you said earlier about the woman. What happened with the little girl's mom?"

"She wised up and dumped me." That's a better tale than the truth.

He waves a hand in front of his face. "I smell bullshit."

"That's probably your breath."

Grant punches me in the arm. "Good to know you're still a little punk."

"Only when you're asking for it."

The humor on his face droops at the edges. "Are you happy, Ford?"

I tip the beer to my lips, drinking what's left in the bottle. "Hanging in there."

"What're you gonna do to make it better?"

"For starters, not discussing our feelings like a bunch of chicks." I figured Grady was a fluke. It seems Grant is all about prying, too. The festering wound in my heart is for me to worry about. I rub over the blazing ache, for no other reason than to revel in the burn.

My brother polishes off what remains of his beer. "I've broken my fair share of hearts. Hoping to fix one in particular if she'll have me. The love of a good woman is the greatest gift, Ford."

I point at him with my empty bottle. "You're already on shaky ground. Don't push your probation."

"I'm older and wiser. You should listen to me."

"Nah, it's too complicated. I fucked up. She hates me. There's no future for us. And you've always been better with relationships, so there's no comparison."

Grant seems to consider that for a moment. "I bet she'd be willing to forgive you."

I shouldn't reward his invasive behavior with a response, but talking about Keegan is a weakness I'm not strong enough to resist. "And why, dare I ask, do you think that?"

"Because you're willing to forgive me. Or I'm assuming you will in the end. I know you well enough to see us working side by side soon enough."

I allow my gaze to bounce around the backyard, not focusing on anything in particular. "I see what you're doing."

"Is it working?"

"Kinda. I have unfinished business to deal with first. Then I can begin to compute the odds that I'll ever be worthy of her. I'm not a betting man, but I know the odds stacked against me."

"Dad?"

A smirk tilts my lips. "Yeah, you've always been good at reading my thoughts. It always rolls back to him. He's gonna be hearing from me real soon."

Grant kicks his legs up onto the railing, getting comfortable. "Let him know I'm still waiting on my investment payout."

"That's on you, brother. I got enough shit to say." And

the list continues to grow after sitting with the man beside me. My father's transgressions have no bounds.

"Want me to come with you?"

"Nah, this is something I gotta do by myself."

"I understand. Just remember that light will be waiting on the other side of the tunnel."

"That's a good reminder. I've been living in the dark." And without so much as a match to guide me. Maybe with Grant's advice, things can actually swing in the correct direction for a change. Look at me being all optimistic and shit.

"Well, lucky for you, I'm here to help."

"Ah, luck never graces me with any favors. That cranky bitch hates me."

"Only because you play too safe."

I chuckle, scrubbing over my mouth. "Not sure I've ever thought of it that way."

"You're welcome." He makes a gun out of his fingers, shooting at me.

A random thought occurs to me. "Just realized I have no clue where you're living these days. Damn, that's messed up."

"You miss keeping tabs on me?"

"That's what younger brothers are good for."

He peeks up at the puffy clouds dotting the blue sky. "I have a place near the office in Vicken Falls. Thinking of relocating, though."

"Makes sense."

"Shouldn't have left to begin with. I miss Silo Springs. Always have."

I chuckle at that. "No surprise there. I think the biggest shock of all is when you moved outta town."

"Yeah, that was a stupid decision for a lot of reasons."

I stand to leave, pausing for a moment. "For what it's worth, I'm glad you're back."

A dimple dents Grant's cheek when he grins at me. "So am I, brother. Life sucked without you."

"Maybe we'll do this again soon." I brush my words off with a shrug. There's no guarantee that he's actually sticking around. That possibility whispers at me, murmuring reminders from the last lonely decade.

He straightens and claps me on the back. "A horny harem won't keep me away. In the meantime, go slay the dragon so you can get your girl."

"You make it sound so regal."

"It's better for our egos. Being the hero is badass," he drawls.

Another rescue mission? Wasn't sure I had the first one in me, or the second for that matter. But I can buy into the idea when Grant puts that spin on it. "Yeah, I guess it is."

CHAPTER TWENTY-SEVEN

Keegan

Healing Hug #28: Sneak attack for the desperate hearts.

MELODIC CHIRPING SERENADES ME FROM A BRANCH ABOVE. A lone robin is providing a cheery tune to complement the warm yet comfortable weather. The oppressive dryness isn't suffocating us quite yet. That's probably one of the reasons so many people chose this early hour to stop here. A thrill zaps along the bare skin of my arms. Even with the sun beaming over me, goosebumps rise on my flesh.

I push the sunglasses up higher on the bridge of my nose. The large oval frames were picked on purpose this morning, as if I'm incognito. A huff escapes me as I glance around. My undercover skills could use some serious improvement. Millie is dashing across the space in front of me, squealing loudly as Elsa chases her. It's no secret who we are to anyone who has the slightest clue. But deep down, I can admit the truth.

Being at the dog park is a risk. The chance of bumping into Crawford is much higher at one of his preferred and approved locations. But this is my town, too. Just because he took a sledgehammer to our arrangement doesn't mean I have to slink away in the shadows. We have to co-exist in Silo Springs. That man has done enough damage. He won't stop me from taking Millie and Elsa out to enjoy the beautiful summer day.

I scan the congested grassy field with a watchful eye.

Choosing a peak traffic time isn't an accident. It's highly doubtful Crawford's aversion to people has suddenly vanished. I haven't seen the shadow of his outline along Main Street in over two weeks. Not that I've been looking. Another scoff escapes me. It's a surprise my shorts aren't on fire by this point.

"Mama?" Millie's voice breaks me out of my circular thoughts.

I blink off the remaining ashes. "Yes, sweetie?"

"Elsa is lonely. She told me. That's why her ears are so droopy." My daughter squishes her beloved pet's face between her small hands.

I look at the dog, finding her eyes peeking up at me in that heartbreaking way. "You two were just running around having a blast. What happened?"

"She misses her friend. I bet Patch is super sad, too."

A thick exhale deflates my stance. "Mill—"

She interjects before I can correct her. "I know we're not gonna talk to Ford ever again. Does that mean we won't see Patch either?"

"Yeah, baby girl. That's kinda how things have to be."

Millie's bottom lip sticks out. "But why?"

"Because," I state. No nonsense. I even tip my chin for a false sense of authority.

My daughter squints, having none of that from me. "You always tell me that's not a good reason."

"It only is when there's nothing else to say." When did she start questioning my methods?

"But there are other ways, Mama. Maybe Ford will let us take Patch out with us. She can have a doggy slumber party with Elsa."

But that would involve talking to him. I don't point out that minor conflict in her grand plan. "Maybe, sweetie."

"But that means no."

"I don't think it's a good idea," I murmur.

Her pout cranks up another notch, adding a tremble for added impact. "You want them to be all alone and unhappy?"

I almost double over from the harsh dose of mom guilt. If I survive Millie's frequent administrations, it will be a shock. "No, baby girl. That's the last thing I want."

Before Millie can inject another round of shame, a familiar face appears in the crowd of strangers. It's as if she heard my desperate calling for a diversion. I smile at Kellie as she approaches. Millie clams up when the woman is within speaking distance. She slinks off to play with Elsa before getting herself into an awkward social situation.

"Hello, Keegan. I thought that was you, but wasn't sure until Millie took off." Kellie waves in my daughter's direction, but only gets averted eye contact in response.

"Hey, Kellie. It's nice to see you. Sorry about Millie. She's very shy."

She waves off my concern. "I totally understand. My son was the same way until he was a teenager. He's still very particular about who's worthy of his words."

That sounds familiar. I shove the comparison away before anything can take root. "I'm hoping Millie will expand her circle of trust as she gets older. She allowed a new person in recently." But he's gone now. The dark cloud rests above my head regardless of my attempts to shove the gloom away. "Anyway, do you live around here? I haven't seen you around before."

Kellie shakes her head, dark hair fanning around her shoulders. "No, I'm from Gulligan Haven. I meet foster families here frequently for puppy exchanges."

"Oh, that's convenient."

"It is. I also get the chance to check up on adopted favorites." She smiles warmly at Elsa chasing after a ball with Millie hot on her heels.

"Well, this is a nice surprise visit. Millie couldn't be more pleased with her. She's been the perfect addition to our family."

The older woman smiles at me. "That's so wonderful to hear. And speaking of coincidences, I believe we have a common thread aside from Elsa."

I lift my brows at her "Oh?"

"My son is Crawford Doxe."

"Oh." The bagel I ate for breakfast forms a ball of acid in my stomach.

She laughs at my flat tone. "I was expecting that reaction from you."

Dear Lord, what has he told her? This is a freaking nightmare. I discreetly press on my temple, wishing the pounding to cease. Did she come here to reprimand me? The only answer I give is a tight pinch of my lips.

"Don't look so petrified, dear. He didn't tell me much beyond your names." She nods to Millie playing with Elsa in front of us.

That revelation eases the pressure dumping on my chest. "Uh, okay. Crawford is a very, um, talented mechanic."

"Did he get a glimpse under your hood? Or maybe he focused on getting your motor running really smooth?"

I choke on my tongue. "W-what?"

She tips her head back and laughs. "Oh, just a little humor. It's quite all right if that's the case. I have no room to judge. Trust me, I'm not looking to stir the pot."

Heat infuses my cheeks to the point that I'm sweating. I fan my face, blowing out a billow of steam. "This is very uncomfortable for me," I admit with a whisper.

Kellie clucks her tongue. "Well, shoot. I don't mean for it to be."

"That's okay." A breeze kicks up, blowing loose curls around my face. I tuck the strands behind my ear, appreciating the moment of reprieve. Another layer of strain chips off my rattled frame. "Do you recognize other dogs here?"

Without hesitation, she plows through my weak attempt at changing the subject. "My son is a complicated man, Keegan."

No duh, lady. What was your first clue? Instead of spewing my honest opinion, I plaster on a wide, fake grin. "Really? How so?"

"He's always been abrasive and misunderstood. Most people think he's rude, but that's just one of his defensive mechanisms. Underneath the surly crap, Ford is a softie."

I hum low in my throat. "That's interesting. I didn't notice those broody qualities."

Kellie barks out a cackle. "It's all right, Keegan. You don't have to bullshit with me. That's kind of you to defend him, though. I can see why Ford is so taken by you."

A brittle laugh scrapes out of me. "Oh, I think you're mistaken. We were just friends."

"Past tense?"

Is she trying to dig for dirt? I study her gentle expression with a wary gaze. There's nothing waiting for me except kind eyes and a trusting smile. "Yeah, I suppose that's correct. We haven't spoken recently."

"Pity. He seems to be rather infatuated still." She turns to give me a slow once-over. "Remember what I said at the shelter?"

The options scroll through my mind on a twisted loop. "Can I get a hint?"

Her features manage to brighten another degree. "I was certain that my son would remain single for all of eternity. Heck, he never showed much interest in the opposite sex, from what I could tell. But that went along with his disinterest of people in general. I'd said you two would hit it off. Seems my predictions were accurate."

Where is she getting the information to justify these wild claims? "I thought Ford only told you our names."

"That's right, but one look at him was enough to know he's met his match. Like your daughter and Elsa, some connections really click. You know what I mean?"

I try not to gape at her, but my jaw seems to have a brain

of its own. Is this type of invasive behavior normal for parents? I might need to step up my helicoptering, if that's the case. It's hard for me to imagine my mother in this situation. Would she corner Crawford and pry answers out of him? I can't see her doing that, but my mom wasn't around to experience me dating anyone of significance. Maybe she'd be a fierce mama bear. That's a nice vision to imagine. I place a palm over my stomach when the roiling begins. Crying in front of Kellie would be a grave mistake.

"Um, ah." The garbled noises stumble out of my mouth. What am I about to admit? Vague for the win. "I guess that's true."

She beams at me, patting my arm. "Then my job here is done."

"Good?" Yeah, it's official. I've been bamboozled. To be fair, I stood still and let it happen. I should've known. I almost snap my fingers at the sneaky wit of this lady.

"I'll be seeing you, Keegan. Take care until next time." She's about to vanish faster than she appeared.

Before she takes two steps, I halt her retreat. "Hey, Kellie?"

She glances at me over her shoulder. "Yes, dear?"

I lick my lips, allowing courage to brew inside of me. "Can you do me a favor?"

"Of course." Her eyes crinkle in the corners with a genuine smile.

"If you see Ford, tell him we say hello. And, maybe, that I hope he's doing well." Holding a grudge will only allow bitterness to eat away at me. I don't need another reason to fester over the past. We can be civil adults and move forward in very separate directions.

Kellie laughs, the sound more of a titter. "Oh, that won't be necessary."

Ouch. I guess being cordial is off the table. Just to test my newfound conviction, I ask, "Why not?"

Her full smile returns. "I have a feeling the opportunity to tell him yourself will arise very soon."

That prediction has me whipping a glance behind me and across both sides. Of course there's no sign of him. I ignore the sinking sensation in my belly. "I'm not so sure about that," I murmur.

"Never doubt a mother's intuition, right?"

"If you say so." I'm sure the stare she's getting from me is blank.

Kellie winks at me. "I'll accept you eating those words when I'm proven to be correct."

I can see where Crawford gets his confidence and snarky attitude. "And if you're wrong?"

She shakes a finger at me, the scold already clear. "I'm sorry if I led you to believe that was an option. It's not, dear. What's happening between you two is just a simple misunderstanding."

Once again, I find myself questioning how much she knows. "He wasn't exactly ambiguous."

Kellie leans forward to squeeze my hand. The motherly gestures jumpstarts my stunned heart. "You might assume things are over, but I'm willing to bet Ford is far from done with you."

I almost shiver from certainty vibrating in her words. A powerful surge floods my veins a moment later. On a scale of one to being a lost cause, where I do fall if I'm hoping she's right?

CHAPTER TWENTY-EIGHT

Crawford

Healing Hug #29: A shot of pure relief.

CONCRETE PUMPS UNDER MY SKIN WITH EACH CITY BLOCK I pass. I'll be a solid mass ready for battle once I arrive. The miles tick on, erasing more distance between salvation and freedom. Comforting sunshine and my slice of paradise fade in the rearview mirror. All that looms ahead is thundering darkness and soul-sucking shadows. After taking a final left, the steel fortress comes into view. My muscles seize, threatening a lockdown on their own accord. But this is something I must do. Fear doesn't exist in my vocabulary since he disgraced me for the final time.

The parking lot is decorated with luxury vehicles in all shapes and colors. My bike stands out like a bolt of chrome lightning in the midnight sky. Seems fitting, since I've always been an inky stain on my father's manufactured prestige. I speed toward the front and snag a guest spot. Security will realize I don't belong when my tires are burning rubber on the way out. I've always excelled at making an exit.

After dismounting the only worthy ride in plain sight, I stride to the arching metal entrance someone paid way too much for. The thick soles of my boots pound into the pavement. That steady beat conducts the rhythm attempting to go wild in my chest. I'm finally taking Keegan's advice and facing my largest demon. Slaying him to the ground would be my preference, but saying my piece will have to suffice.

I swing open the set of frosty glass doors, revealing a disturbing amount of stark white. Dressed in all black and leather, I'm the instant target for anyone with decent eyesight. Lucky for me, this is the last place where I want to belong. The lobby smells heavily of plastic, rotting dreams, and fitting into a mold. One whiff of the artificial odor singes my nostrils. I couldn't survive a day trapped within these pristine walls.

The receptionist tilts her chin up at me, the angle sharp and haughty as fuck. If she thinks that bullshit display is making anybody feel inferior, I can give her a few pointers. I pay her zero mind and stride by without a second glance. A stunned squeak puffs from her injected lips, but I'm already too far gone.

A small jolt shoots through me when I notice the tracks of mud trailing behind me. So much for his spotless floors. That's the first jab of happiness anything related to my dad has brought me. I even let a crooked smirk tip my lips. A bit of payback after years of torture.

The massive corner suite beckons me. A wrought iron distressed door isn't hard to find against the muted background. Father dearest might appreciate order and uniform simplicity, but his demand to stand out from the pack rules higher.

His secretary leaps from her seat when she catches me approaching. "You can't go in there. He's in the middle of—"

I throw a hand up, cutting her off. "This will only take a minute of his precious time."

With that, I barrel into his office as if the devil himself is chasing me. A loud crack of wood against drywall announces my entrance. My father looks up from a stack of paperwork without any sign of distress. His beady brown eyes narrow on me.

"You might be my son, but barging in unannounced is unacceptable. Nice fucking stunt you're pulling in front of my staff."

"Figured I'd return the favor for once. Am I disturbing your precious routine?" I begin picking the dirt from under my fingernails.

A joint pops in his wrinkled cheek. "Who the hell do you think you are?"

"A man pushed far enough to quit caring about wounded pride. What's a little more?"

He taps his pen to an agitated beat. "Temper tantrums at your age aren't attractive, Crawford. It's no wonder you're single."

"Just like it's no secret why mom cheated on you. She wasn't willing to waste more years. I've finally come to that point myself."

A ruddy tint bursts across his cheeks. I almost expect flames to erupt from his eye sockets. The glare he's shooting at me is meant to detonate and destroy. He grips his armrests with white knuckles, leaning back in the chair until the springs creak for mercy. "I'd ask what you're doing here, but I have a feeling you have an agenda. Why don't you get on with this desperate act for attention so I can return to what's truly important?"

"You're a piece of shit," I spit. "Because of you, I almost threw away the greatest thing that's ever happened to me. You've always cut me down, but those days are over. I never want to see your smarmy face at my shop again. Forget where I live."

His face screws up in a distorted grimace. "Is this about that whore—"

I stomp toward him until my broad frame towers over his hunched position. "Stop talking or I'll rip all of those words out of your mouth."

"Threatening your old man?" He might have a set of brass balls, but I catch the way his gaze skitters off mine.

"Seems only fair after the hell you've put me through." I cross my arms, leaning further into his space.

His expression is deranged, shifty and unstable. I widen my stance to brace for impact. He catches my slight movement, narrowing his eyes into barely visible slits. "Oh, poor little Crawford. My son can't handle strong guidance or the truth. But you've always been weak."

I dig my toe into his beige carpet, smearing grime into the plush beige fibers. "That might be true, but I'm done being a spineless wimp. This toxic association between us ends today if you refuse to change. You'll be dead to me, but maybe that's what you'd prefer."

My father is quiet for a moment, staring me down without so much as blinking. "I'd threaten to cut you off, but you've never taken my money. Your brother, on the other hand, has lost his damn mind. I assume you have everything to do with that."

"Grant is his own person. I'll admit to being fucking giddy that he finally wised up and came to his senses. But how he chooses to run his life is all on him, and he has his own amends to make with me. I refuse to be your verbal punching bag for another second. If you need to feel better about yourself, go see a therapist."

A chuckle that lacks any ounce of humor jostles his paunchy gut. "Thanks for the advice, Ford. I'm of sound mind and go to bed each night without a single worry. You, on the other hand, are one fatal disaster after the next."

"That's where you're wrong, pops. I'm finally seeing things clearly. This is for Keegan and Millie and the happiness I almost let you destroy. Just because you're miserable doesn't mean I have to be. You're a miserable schmuck. I have every intention of redeeming myself." I deserve some damn closure to smooth over this shit cannon.

"Good luck with that, boy. You're antisocial. Always was, always will be." His putrid breath contaminates the sterile air pumping through the vents. It takes all of my control not to gag.

A tight smile bends my mouth. "Only because I've been letting your opinion define me. I'm ready to move on."

"With a single mother and her mute child? They'll never stick around. You're being a naive fool, which is no surprise."

He might be right about that, but it's a risk I'm willing to take. Fear will no longer dictate my decisions. I won't stand silent and ruin the potential of finding love. Hell, if luck is lenient enough to grant me a favor, I've already found it.

"Well, that's on me." I straighten, separating us with some much-needed space.

"It most certainly is. It makes me almost proud that you can accept defeat." He juts his jaw, resembling a bulldog. The image is fitting in this situation.

"I can tell you're not ready to accept our differences, but guess what? I can be the bigger man." I slap my chest, the strength within gaining momentum. "Holding grudges has caused enough damage. I'm not interested in loose ends and unanswered questions. If you truly want to be a family again, fucking prove it. When you're ready to make peace, come find me. Grant will be waiting, too."

His sneer shows off the pearly whites he spent a fortune on. "How fucking cute. My sons are finally a team again."

"Isn't that nice? You lost a partner, but I gained one."

He sputters on his inflated ego. "Grant is working at that filthy garage with you?"

"Damn straight. I'd say it's long overdue. Maybe we'll send you a flyer once the logo is updated."

"Gloating does nothing to impress me."

"No? Could've sworn you tried teaching me the opposite."

"Being a grease monkey is never going to get you a decent woman."

"And the days of me tolerating your disrespect are over. Keep that in mind before dropping by."

"I'm not listening to this from you." My father swats the air, dismissing me with a flick of his wrist.

My patience snaps faster than a fraying piece of twine. I lunge forward and grip his collar. "You better hear me. If I see you again with this shitty attitude, prepare for a restraining order."

"Is that supposed to scare me?"

I pat his cheek in the same patronizing manner he's always done to me. "Nah, it's just some friendly words of advice. Take it or leave it, pops."

He struggles out of my hold, forcing me backward. "Get out of my sight, you ungrateful little shit."

"With pleasure." I slam out of his office the same way I came in, taking great satisfaction when the wood splinters further.

The slaying is done. Not an ounce of remorse or regret weighs me down. All I feel is relief whisking the ache away. The iron walls constantly holding me back vanish and I'm free to move forward.

There are two girls waiting on me, whether they realize it or not. My pulse thumps faster with each rushed stomp out of this prison. Hopefully I'm not too late and they're still willing to be mine.

Only one way to find out.

CHAPTER TWENTY-NINE

Crawford

Healing Hug #30: For chances not necessarily
earned, but given regardless.

WALK ALONG THE COBBLED PATH WITH TOO MANY THOUGHTS fighting for control. The words blur and stick together, forming a clusterfuck of epic proportions. Prickles of doubt battle with stony resolve. Where do I even begin? How will I fix this? Why didn't I come sooner? Is this going to be a massive failure? Do they even want me to try? My arms are loaded up with tokens of apology. The need to grovel has never struck me until I let Keegan and Millie slip away. I'm ready to crash down onto my knees and beg for their forgiveness.

The door swings open before I can knock. Keegan stands just beyond the threshold, wearing a grimace to match the threadbare tee that's one stitch away from ripping apart. Her shirt would pair well with the tatters of my heart. I almost smile at the sight. Just having her within reach has relief pumping into my deprived veins.

Keegan quirks a skeptical brow, but she doesn't appear surprised to see me. Her visible irritation makes it seem as though she's been expecting me. "Can I help you?"

"I'm an idiot," I blurt. That's what I open with? I truly am an idiot.

That slim brow arches higher. "Newsflash, Ford. That's not a secret."

I thrust the flowers at her. "These are for you. I have some for Millie, too."

Keegan accepts the heaping bunch, but barely glances at the colorful assortment. "Thanks."

I try not to let her terse tone discourage me, but the clamp around my ribs cranks tighter. A shallow exhale breezes through my frown. I peer around Keegan's steely blockade. Millie hovers on the last stair, gripping onto the banister with both arms. She's hesitant, keeping a safe distance, and I don't blame her.

I swallow the thick lump clogging my throat. "Hey, Peep. I'm really sorry for leaving when you were upset. And for not saying goodbye. There's so much I need to apologize for. Maybe you'll be able to forgive me one day."

My peace offering for her now feels insignificant and small. Millie's bundle is also full of vibrant blooms, much like the arrangement I brought for Keegan. Her variety has a few special additions. Instead of leafy green accents, the florist used gumdrops and jellybeans. I thought it was a nice touch for the little candy addict.

Keegan snatches the second bouquet out of my hands. "You can't just swoop in and expect us to instantly forget what happened. I'm not going to collapse into your arms, grateful that you showed up."

I hold up my empty palms, the weight of nothing has never been heavier. "I don't think that. Not at all. I let the past get to me. That's over with now. I confronted my demons, like you so eloquently suggested."

"Good to hear you took my advice." She crosses her arms, crushing the stems without flinching. She isn't making this easy on me, that's for sure. A swell of pride simmers inside of me. My stubborn girl hasn't lost her fight.

"I appreciate you giving it to me straight. That was needed. I'm a sad, lonely, pitiful, stupid—"

She slices through the foot of space separating us. "Stop reciting the list I've already created."

My gut clenches. "That doesn't sound good."

"What do you expect, Ford? A warm welcome after you tore apart the flimsy trust we'd managed to restore? You know the crap I've been through. I don't need empty promises or meaningless words. After two weeks of nothing, I figure there's nothing left to say."

I'm shaking my head halfway through her speech. "No, Kee. That's not true. There's plenty left for us. Everything. Please don't give up on me. I screwed up. I know. Dammit, please."

The tension radiating from her thin frame hasn't eased. She stands strong and proud, lifting her chin to pin a fiery glare at me. "You blasted me with so much shade that there's permanent damage. All that callous indifference thrown at me, without hesitating. How do you think I feel, huh? You laid the explosives, set the detonator, lit the fuse, blew up the bridge, and walked away unscathed."

The truthful lash is brutal enough to make my legs quake. "I'll agree to the first two, but I've been living in hell without you. I can't go on like this. Please tell me what I can do to fix us. I'll do anything."

Keegan sniffs, dropping her gaze to the crushed bouquet I foolishly thought would help. "Maybe you should've considered that before setting fire to everything we built. There's a hole in my chest, and you put it there. You pulled the trigger. That's on you, Ford."

"You can't forgive me." It's a statement without question. I hang my head as any lingering hope fizzles in my queasy stomach. Grant was wrong. I'm not the hero. Keegan and Millie don't need me.

"I don't think so, Ford. There's too much damage." Her choppy exhale is almost my undoing. But I'm already fading regardless.

"Okay, I understand." I glance from Keegan to Millie and back again. Their solemn expressions brand me, leaving a stamp on my crushed soul. The shattering in my chest is painful enough to steal my breath. I drag in a labored pull, my lungs protesting the forced motion. "For what it's worth, I'm really sorry."

She wipes at her already wet cheek. "So am I."

I turn away, properly chastised and punished. Millie's quick footsteps pound into my ears. Her whispered protests crash into me, cracking what's already broken. I deserve worse. My boots drag against the pebbles littering her walkway. I don't bother lifting my feet to avoid the minor bumps. This isn't the end I wanted, but the choice wasn't mine to make.

"Ford," Keegan calls.

When I glance over my shoulder, Millie is yanking on her mother's shirt. A slew of desperate pleading falls from her lips faster than I can track. I force myself to remain rooted in place. What I imagine, and want with clawing desperation, is to eliminate the frigid wasteland separating us. "Yeah?"

"Don't go."

I freeze with my gaze locked on her. How cruel is my brain to plant such a tempting trap? There's no chance in this warped reality that my ears are being honest. In this suspended moment, I can only assume my mind is playing nasty tricks. Or I'm really losing my grasp. I blink and she's still standing there, waiting for me. "What?"

"Maybe we can start fresh. From the beginning." She bites her lip while thinking something over. "We got off on the wrong foot from day one. What do you think?"

All of the air rushes out of me with a loud whoosh. "Really?"

She shrugs. "Yeah. Watching you walk away again is a bit more than we can handle. Willpower only stretches so far on its own. We've all been pretty mopey without you. That's gotta count for something, right?"

With three long strides, I eat the distance keeping us apart. "You won't regret this."

Keegan peeks up at me from beneath her damp lashes. "That's what I'm banking on."

"Does this mean we can be friends again?" Millie's soft voice chimes in, the sweetest sound I've heard in two weeks.

"Maybe, if your mom says that's okay." Uncertainty continues to prod at me. I can't be sure until Keegan tells me.

The little girl smiles at me and just like that, my spirits soar to the clouds. "We missed you, Ford."

Keegan huffs, rolling her tear-stained eyes. "Don't let him off the hook so easily, Mills."

"But he's sorry, Mama. Look how sad he is without us."

"She's right. I'm barely breathing."

"I expect a lot more groveling."

"And I plan to give it. For many years to come, if you'll have me."

"Let's not get too serious. I thought this wasn't about dating?" She twirls some blonde strands around her finger.

"That was part of my idiotic front. The one you punched gouges in after a simple glance. I think we both know exactly where this is heading."

"You just want to have adult sleepovers with me again." She states that as if it's a crime against her.

"I can't say that hasn't crossed my mind. Let's be honest, I'd be blind or batting for the other team if that wasn't the case. But this is about far more than S-E-X."

Keegan scowls at me. "Millie can spell."

I wince. "Oh, sorry."

Millie giggles, covering the sound with a tiny palm. "You're so in love. I can't wait for the wedding. Can I wear a pink dress with silky sleeves?"

Keegan pats her daughter on the head. "We haven't officially started dating yet. Let's start there and see where things go."

"I'm gonna learn that secret language for couples and knock your socks off."

A gape parts her ruby lips. "What?"

I allow a lopsided smirk to tilt my lips. "Never mind. Just remember that I'm prime boyfriend material. You'll see. I'm gonna earn all of your trust again."

Keegan's eyebrows leap toward her hairline. "Pump the brakes, Mister Swoony. I've been disappointed enough for a lifetime, Ford. My little girl has already experienced more emotional warfare than any grown adult ever should. How is this going to be any different? What's to stop you from leaving again?"

I shuffle forward, putting me that much closer to paradise and a future worth striving toward. "You have every right to question me. I can't guarantee a day won't arrive where my gut instinct is to flee. But I promise to reach out and let you reel me in. No more leaving unless you make me go. But I won't go without trying to tough it out first. I wanna be grounded here, to you and Millie. Being reliable and dependable is who I hope to become. Both of you have left a permanent mark on my lonely soul. There's no moving on without you."

She nibbles on that plump bottom lip again. "You'd let us do the saving for once?"

A low rumble rises out of me. "I would love nothing more."

With her next breath, Keegan shifts and sidles up against me. Her arms loop around my waist in a gentle embrace. I'm stunned for a moment and don't move. When her cheek rests over my left pec, all of the pressure releases from inside of me. I reach out, scooping Millie in the process, and hold them both against me. We all share a mutual sigh that sinks straight to my wounded soul. What's left of my guard and misplaced reservations dissolve into dust at our feet. I'm laid bare and splitting open. Nothing has felt so…good.

Keegan nuzzles closer, erasing any possibility of separation. The notion she wants to be plastered against me warms the coldest sections of my mending heart. "Hugs are the best medicine."

"I'm pretty sure it's laughter." Her head bumps into me when I chuckle.

She clucks her tongue. "There's more than one prescription."

"I'll have them all, so long as you're passing out the doses." I press my lips to her forehead.

"Thank you for the flowers. They're beautiful."

"You're welcome, babe."

"I'm sorry if the stems got a bit broken. An unfortunate casualty."

"Don't worry too much. There's plenty more where those came from."

A muffled squeak of protest interrupts the intense voltage sparking between us. Wriggling for an escape shortly follows. "You're squishing me," Millie complains.

She separates from our huddle with a huff. Her hair is a mess of rumpled blonde braids. She looks so much like her mother, which sends a powerful surge of protectiveness through me. Beating punk-ass boys with a spiked club is in my very near future. I wonder where Keegan stands on the rules for letting Millie date. It's far too soon for concern, right? A weak exhale trickles out of me. Jesus, this could be my life. Maybe that should freak me out, but all I can do is smile.

"Get used to it, Peep. There are gonna be a lot of group hugs in our future."

"Really?" Her gasp, that lingering doubt, gives me something to prove. "You're really gonna stay this time?"

I drag Millie back into the fold, and she collapses against us without making a fuss. "There's no place I'd rather be."

"Turning into quite the charmer," Keegan murmurs.

"I'm just getting warmed up. Twenty-six years of lonely solitude will do that to a man. Especially after he's found the right motivation."

"Be careful. You're beginning to trigger those pesky romantic feelings."

"In that case, I hope they're contagious." I tip her chin up with a finger, sealing our mouths together for a chaste kiss. That single touch is enough to ignite a blazing inferno in my gut. "I already have them."

Keegan's sharp inhale zaps off her lips. I feel that static down to my toes. "Oh, my."

Before our public display can border on indecent, I straighten and force a foot of distance between us. "Do you have plans tonight?"

"We were just about to settle in for a movie."

"Does the couch have room for one more?"

She steps back and opens the door in what I can only hope is a permanent invitation. "Come see for yourself."

CHAPTER THIRTY

Keegan

Healing Hug #31: Giving voice to possibility and
the potential for more.

I SWIRL ANOTHER FORKFUL OF PESTO NOODLES, THE CREAMY
sauce dripping off my utensil. A burst of herbs and
spices greets my mouth with the culinary equivalent of
cymbals crashing. I let my lashes flutter shut to simply enjoy
the flavorful morsel. An indecent moan slips past my lips as
I swallow the linguini. There's not a single speck of shame
flushing my cheeks.

Once my foodgasm has subsided, the restaurant comes
back into focus. Tonight might be our first visit to Donte
Louie, but one taste will never be enough. After this meal, it's
safe to say I'll be returning soon and often. It's a little romantic getaway not far from town, with dim lighting and a lot
of ambience. Staging a calm and soothing mood. It's a very
appropriate setting for our first official date.

The large dining room is speckled with couples or multiple sets of pairs. Our threesome seems to be a rarity. Perhaps
most choose to leave their children at home, given the white
tablecloths and crystal oil lamps. Crawford made sure that
Millie was invited. Heaven forbid she gets left out of this special occasion.

"Do you like my choice?"

Crawford's question makes me smile, mouth stuffed and

all. I dap at my lips, but there's probably leftover evidence in my teeth. "Very much so."

"This would be a great spot for another new tradition, if you approve."

"I certainly do. Monthly dinners would suffice. Or maybe weekly."

"It's so pretty and nice," Millie chimes in. "My spaghetti is so yummy. I even ate both meatballs."

"I'm glad my girls are happy," he coos. The man devoured his steak in record time, proving we're not the only ones with satisfied tummies.

"And really full," I add. I take a final bite of the decadent pasta, humming when the rich basil hits my tongue. "Oh, this is too delicious. I'm past my limit, but want to keep eating. Where do I get a doggy bag? I'll make myself sick."

Or I could lick the plate clean. Decisions, decisions.

Crawford traces a finger along my splayed hand. "You have to save room for dessert."

Millie giggles, tipping her chin to hide a wide grin. "Yeah, Mama. The fun isn't over yet."

I pat my protruding belly. The food baby is ready to start kicking. "Nothing else is fitting in here at the moment."

"We can sit and relax for a bit. There's no rush." He glances over his shoulder, maybe searching for the server.

"Well," I toss my napkin onto the table. "This calls for a quick restroom run. Please order me another glass of that fabulous champagne if our lady swings by."

Crawford's hazel eyes carve a path along my curves when I stand. "Will do."

I blow a kiss at him before tugging on Millie's pigtail. "Do you have to go potty, sweetie?"

She frowns at me. Cute as she is, the expression is almost thunderous. "No, I'm staying with Ford. Have fun, Mama. I love you."

I furrow my brow at her stern tone mixing with sugary

words. "Um, okay. Someone's touchy. Maybe you need an extra-large slice of chocolate cake. Love you, baby girl."

The bathroom is a short walk and down a hallway bathed in blue. My stiletto-clad toes are thankful for the easy trek. I strut into the overly perfumed space and do my business. When I get in front of the mirror, a hive of honey-starved bees wakes in my belly. The buzzing travels through my veins, giving me a zing from scalp to sole. I press a palm flat to my stomach and inhale until my lungs strain.

This is just a date. One of many, according to the man who planned it. Just a regular evening out with a guy who happens to be crazy about me. His words, not mine. Crawford hasn't been shy about his feelings. Quite the opposite, really.

Since our impromptu movie night where Millie conked out halfway through the animated film, he's been taking advantage of every second we spend alone. Getting reacquainted has made our near-parting almost worth it. During these heated moments, Crawford has hedged around the L-word. He gets close and veers off, saying everything except the one I've been secretly waiting for. Maybe I should spill my guts before he does. Lord knows I'm close to bursting at this point.

I shake off the heady sensation and focus on reapplying my lipstick. Why am I nervous? There's no reason to be. Plus, Millie is with us. There won't be any deep and heavy confessions until the moon kisses the stars. I walk back to the table on my teetering heels with that solid fact in mind. When I get within a few strides of my seat, I stumble to a stop. Crawford is smiling at me, appearing as if everything is normal. My daughter, on the other hand, is very noticeably absent.

"Where's Millie?"

My newly solo date widens his grin. "Josey picked her up."

I'm sure my eyes are near bulging. "What? Why? Is she sick?"

Crawford chuckles and pats my empty seat. "It's all been planned, Kee. The rest of tonight belongs to us."

"Oh." I peer around the bustling section we're cornered in. "Did you order dessert?"

"We'll be savoring it at my place." He reaches for my hand, placing soft kisses along my knuckles.

"Okay." How can I argue with that?

"Ready to go, love?"

A shudder rolls through me at his choice of endearment. So close, yet not quite right. I don't need to exchange verbal sentiments. He's showing me in more ways than those three little words ever could. His actions have been shouting from the rooftops for the past week. I mean, one fast glance at the guy shows a changed man. And that's just on the surface. A fancy shirt and tie don't impress me, though. The way he listens and lavishes us with attention and strives to be the best for himself means so much more than any fancy meal. But I'm not complaining about the combo platter of goodness he's spoiling me with.

"Keegan?"

I shake off those wayward thoughts. "Oh, sorry. You have me a bit dazed."

"Is that a good thing?"

"Very much so." A ripple of heat spreads from my lower belly.

A satisfied noise tumbles off his succulent lips. "I'm about to make it even better."

"How is that even possible?" My voice is breathy and wanton. There's no use trying to mask my desire at this point.

"You'll see."

And he does, in quite a hurry. We make the drive to his house in under fifteen minutes. The woods are pitch black, but there's a soft glow coming from his loft windows. Someone has definitely been planning something.

Before I can take a single step, Crawford scoops me into

his arms. A startled yelp escapes me while I wiggle in his hold. "What're you doing?"

"I don't want you to trip in the dark wearing those sexy as fuck shoes."

With a purring exhale, I press kisses along the base of his throat. "That's very thoughtful of you."

After climbing the winding staircase, Crawford unlocks the door. He sets me down in the foyer with gentle care. It takes me a moment to gather my bearings, but all the air leaves me an instant later. His studio space flickers with flameless light from numerous electric candles arranged across every surface. A blend of loose and bundled wild flowers decorate the floor and his bed.

"Ford, what is all of this?" I cover my gaping mouth with a shaky hand.

He presses into me from behind. "I picked all of those for you. Figured it was overdue."

"That's very sweet of you." I peek at him over my shoulder and suck in a rasp. While I was distracted by the display, Crawford started stripping. Lust rolls off him in rapid waves. I allow the current to sweep me away without hesitation. Appreciating his sense of urgency, I turn to get a better view.

He's already ditched the fancy button-up and silk tie. Only a plain undershirt conceals his upper body from my starving gaze. The white cotton stretches across his wide chest, each subtle shift pulling at the seams. His pants are unfastened at the waist, falling to pool around his ankles with a single tug. Crawford steps forward, a hunter tracking his next meal. Dessert might be the last course, but I plan to come first. Based on the blatant hunger in his light eyes, he couldn't agree more.

Crawford traces the thin straps crossing over my shoulders. "I want to make love to my girlfriend. All. Night. Long."

"Oh, you're smooth, with all of these surprises." Tingles break across my chest, tightening my nipples into stiff peaks.

His finger lifts a string and snaps the stretchy fabric against my skin. "Is it working?"

"Absolutely." I tilt my head to the side, granting him better access to the dip at my neck. He takes advantage and draws a path along that sensitive area with his nose. A sighing wheeze curls off my tongue. "And I might have a little secret of my own."

He growls against my ear, nipping at the lobe. "Tell me."

"I'm not wearing any panties."

He grips the elegant draping at my hips, bunching the slinky material in his fists. "Even at dinner?"

I shake my head. "It's very freeing, and a bit naughty."

He nibbles along my jaw. "Fuck, I love you."

I freeze in his grip. "What?"

Hazel eyes crash with green. There's no looking away, even if Millie burst into the room. "I love you, Kee. Isn't it obvious?"

The rigid knot in my throat makes it difficult to swallow. "Well, um, I guess. You've been doing a good job showing me."

"Just the words were missing." His mouth meets the corner of my lips.

It's as if he's reading my thoughts from earlier. "I was convinced I didn't need them, but it's nice to hear. I love you, too. Do you know that?"

"I could've been an ass and assumed, but wasn't positive."

"Well consider all your suspicions confirmed." I untie the knot at my nape. With a hiss of silk, my dress becomes a puddle on the floor. "Enough talking."

Crawford feasts on my bare form, giving me the slowest once-over in the history of ogling. My skin pebbles further under his watchful gaze. Heat swirls around me, pooling in my lower belly and fanning out to my limbs. I twitch my fingers, desperate to touch him. His Adam's apple bobs with a thick gulp as he tilts my face up.

"This mouth." His kiss is delicate, yet I shiver against him. Crawford's palms drift from the flare of my hips to the ridges of my ribs. He cups my breasts in his big palms, the pillowy flesh almost spilling over. "These tits." A slow drag of his tongue along my cleavage follows that choppy statement. "So perfect. Every inch."

I press myself into him. "Aren't you dishing out all the compliments tonight?"

He groans into the crook of my neck. "I still have a lot of making up to do."

"Where will you begin?"

His fingers dip between my folds, zeroing in on that needy bud. "Here?"

After a few swipes, I'm already nearing the edge. My body is primed and ready for the taking, building and spinning higher. I rock my hips into his hand. The relentless circles against my clit make me dizzy. My muscles clench on nothing, demanding more. He speeds up, and I grab his arm as an anchor.

"Oh, yes. There."

Crawford pulls away just as the edge of my vision is beginning to blur. The suggestion of an orgasm fades faster than I can protest. "Not yet, Kee. I wanna be inside you. We're gonna find release together."

I'm nodding along, on board and raring to go. "Yes, I need you."

With a harsh jerk, the T-shirt gets whipped over his head. He holds his arms out. "Take me, babe."

No further encouragement necessary. I shuck his briefs with a single downward swoop. He palms my ass and hoists me up. I cinch my legs around him as he carries me to the bed. A second later, I'm falling against the mattress with an exhaled *oomph*. Crawford settles over me, aligning us just right. His hardness prods at my entrance, and I spread wider for easy access.

He brushes his lips over mine. "I love you, Keegan."

I slay the sliver of distance, sealing our mouths in a hot, wet embrace. "And I love you."

Crawford enters me with a smooth glide, my slick core welcoming him with ease. I'm seconds away from drooling from the burst of molten smoke curling around my center that he's stoking. His biceps strain as he holds himself still. I lift my hips, urging him on.

He presses a kiss to my flushing cheek. "There's no hurry, babe. Let me enjoy you for a minute."

Well, when he puts it that way. I dance my fingers along the sinewy muscles bulging in his back. My touch wanders lower, landing on the firm globes of his ass. He flexes against my hold until I smooth my palms upward to settle on his shoulders. Tan pecs stacked with muscles nab my concentration next. I suck and nip and lick along his collarbone until he quakes.

After another moment of my teasing, a groan vibrates off Crawford's chest. "That's not gonna help me last longer, Kee."

"We have all night. Make love to me. Again and again."

He shudders again, giving in with a forward thrust. I jolt upward on the bed from the force. We set an easy rhythm that makes my mouth water.

I grip onto him harder. "Yes, yes. Show me who I belong to."

"With pleasure, babe."

His strokes are languid, a slow roll of hips colliding and receding. I gasp and Crawford swallows the sound, sipping at my pleasure from an endless tap. We're joining in the most intimate place, sharing private whispers with each seamless push. He buries his face against the base of my throat while grinding us tighter than a screw. The staccato of slapping skin ricochets off the walls, matching our laboring exhales. I arch off the mattress until his skin sizzles along mine. Everywhere.

The temperature spikes and plunges our passion to a heightened level.

He trails his mouth along the slope of my bust, latching onto one taut point and flicking the other.

"Ford," I moan.

He releases me with a wet pop. "So fucking hot, babe. I love your body."

"Good thing I'm yours." I squeal when he tweaks my nipple.

"And I'm yours, Kee."

I let my eyelids grow heavy and hooded as he gives me another lazy stroke. We're not in a rush. The love we expressed moments ago is now being shared between our bodies. The words cycle on a wheel, gaining strength with each burning coil of our connection. When he slams into me, we're one being. I spear my fingers in his hair to drag him that closer. The tang of sweat hits my nostrils, and I inhale our devotion with a ragged breath.

He kisses the affection curling on my mouth. "Ready?

"Always." I press my damp forehead to his, nodding against him.

Crawford's motions speed up, striking me in the place I need him most. The tingles tickle at the base of my spine, and I chase the rising flames. He punches deeper and harder and faster. I writhe beneath him, begging for more. His palm slips under my ass and tilts for a better angle. A burst of white flashes across the ceiling as I revel in the new position. He pins me against him, sending a skittering shock through my veins. My mobility is lost, but that doesn't matter. I climb until being hurdled over the edge with an electric explosion. With a scream, I surrender to the spasms and convulsions cramping my core. Crawford's flowing movements falter and seize as he follows me over.

His name is a chant spilling off my lips until I'm hoarse. He blasts me out of the atmosphere, until I'm no longer suspended to this earth. I have chills, but my skin is on fire. He's sending me to another universe—hell, another realm—where orgasms shatter everything I've once known.

Crawford collapses beside me, but we're still a tangle of entwined limbs and rushes of toe-curling pleasure. When we finally catch our breath and float down to reality, he threads his fingers through mine.

"Damn, Kee." He raises my hand, raining sloppy kisses on my wrist. "If that's what love is, we're fucking soulmates."

I giggle while snuggling closer. "Fated by simultaneous climaxes and destined for a mutually satisfied forever."

CHAPTER THIRTY-ONE

Keegan

Healing Hug #32: The only one that truly matters is when you're free to love with open arms.

PLUMES OF CHARCOAL-RICH SMOKE WAFT OVER TO MY SPOT ON the patio. I slouch lower in my lounge chair, sipping on the fruity cocktail our resident and borrowed bartender blended for me. Decker sure knows how to mix a lot of booze together and make the end result taste delish. With another pull off my straw, the liquor sends a warm buzz through me. A nap is very likely to drag me under if I remain seated. I force myself to stand, stretching once I'm upright.

Groups of friends and family form chatting clumps across our backyard. All of our guests are smiling and sharing laughs. Elsa and Patch are partaking in the festivities, chasing each other all about. Mother Nature has been kind enough to grace us with a cloudless yet balmy afternoon. I allow a grin of my own to curve my glossy lips. This tradition in the making is long overdue.

Crawford appears out of seemingly nowhere, wrapping an arm around my waist. "What're you thinking about?"

"Nothing much. Just enjoying the view. I never thought to gather everyone together like this. Thanks for the suggestion." I bump my hip into his.

"Didn't expect that coming from me, huh?"

"I do now. Social events seem to be growing on you." I

lean against his side, savoring the woodsy musk floating off him. The alcohol in my system takes a backseat as his addictive scent goes straight to my head.

A low rumble drums in his chest. "That's not the only thing expanding for me. I happen to be rising to the occasion, just for you."

He turns into me and a noticeable bulge presses against my ass. If the semi in his jeans is any indication, this man is always ready to romp. Not that I'm complaining one little bit. The path of love bites and hickeys hidden by his shirt are proof of just how much I appreciate that insatiable need. His nose and mouth carve a hot path along my jaw.

"Not the time, Ford." Yet I tilt my chin, granting him access to explore.

"That's not what you said this morning." His tongue joins the party, trailing fire down my neck.

"I wasn't serious about sneaking off for a nooner." A squeak escapes me when he nips at my exposed nape.

"Never tease a man with that," he murmurs. Rather than force me to reconsider, Crawford straightens and resumes a more publicly appropriate pose.

I allow my thoughts to wander as his thumb draws circles around my hip bone. "Have you heard from him again?"

His smile dims at the edges at the mention of his father. "He called yesterday. The tone in his voicemail is slightly less scathing. I think he's coming around very slowly."

"How do you feel about that?"

Crawford shrugs, tipping a beer to his lips. "Pretty good. I said my piece. The next step is up to him."

"And Grant? Is he adjusting to the new grind well?" I scan the crowd, finding his brother. The man in question is currently trying to flirt with my bestie. Based on the scowl pinching Josey's features, she's not impressed with his attempts.

He follows my gaze with a chuckle. "I'd say he's doing just fine."

"Maybe I should rescue her," I muse.

"Ah, he's harmless. They're probably just reminiscing over the past."

I furrow my brow. "Do they have history?"

"Barely."

"Vague much?"

Crawford nods at them. "We'll see how this plays out first. I don't wanna give you a reason to dissuade her."

I squint at him. "That's ominous, and interesting."

"Life in a small town, babe."

A familiar figure appears in my periphery. "Speaking of, did I ever tell you that I bumped into your mother when we were…fighting?"

He stares at me from under the curved brim of his ball cap.

"I was not aware of that. Did she tell you a bunch of embarrassing stories?"

An unladylike snort stings my nose. "I wish."

His hum is soothing. "She's probably saving those for our wedding."

I almost swallow my tongue on a garbled choke. "Oh?"

Crawford bends to whisper in my ear. "Don't pretend you haven't pictured it."

"Maybe," I murmur.

"Close your eyes and imagine with me." His warm exhale prompts me to follow instructions, my lashes fluttering shut. "You're wearing a lacy white gown, heading down the aisle sprinkled with wild flowers. I'm waiting at the altar in a black suit, ready to promise you forever. Millie has our rings fastened on a pillow, our lives merging as one."

I blow out a stream of hot air at the vivid dream he paints. "You've given this a lot of thought."

He nods against me. "I'm a man with a plan."

"Well, this is me getting on board." I press closer to his chest.

"That's good to hear because I plan to begin carrying it out very soon." His hold on me tightens for a moment.

"Okay," I agree.

The sizzle of meat being flipped makes my stomach growl. I press a hand against the noise, but Crawford notices.

"But first, it sounds like my woman needs to eat. Hungry?"

"The scent is such a tease. Erik needs to grill faster."

He presses a kiss to my temple. "I'll get you a burger. Do you think Millie wants one?"

I search for my daughter among the sea of joy. She's off to the side near her jungle gym, with Alice and Barry. Her blonde braids shimmer under the sun as she gabs openly about who knows what. "She looks well taken care of. I'll check on her in a bit."

Once he strides off toward the buffet table, Kellie takes his place by my side. It's as if the older woman's ears were burning. "Hello, Keegan. Quite the shindig you have here."

I greet her with a grin. "Hey, Kellie. I'm glad you could make it."

"Wouldn't miss this for anything. Seeing my son settled and smiling is a gift I never thought would be delivered. Thank you for that."

"He can take most of the credit." And that's not me being humble. Crawford has outdone himself at every turn.

"Isn't it great to see, dear? I told you everything would work out for the best."

"You certainly did. We're all doing very well."

"A happy family." Kellie sighs, the sound of finding peace.

I peek at her from the corner of my eye. "He's been a true blessing for us. Blends right into our fold."

"Are you thinking of expanding?"

"On the house? I glance over my shoulder, studying the two-story rambler. "There's plenty of room for us."

"I meant your family, but it's good to know the home can accommodate."

It feels like my brain isn't processing her meaning quite right. She can't be referring to what I'm assuming. "Okay, sure."

"This seems oddly familiar, yeah?"

If she's referring to the invasive topic of conversation, I couldn't agree more. Regardless of the flutters attacking my stomach, I give her a warm smile. "It does."

"I'm not actually going to make you eat those doubtful words. As my reward for being right, I'd like to request more grandchildren."

Oh, she certainly meant what I hoped was a wild misunderstanding. I drop my mouth with an audible pop. "Uh, well…"

"Not immediately. But I'm not getting any younger." She pauses for a moment while I try to regain normal functioning of my voice. "Something to think about."

Crawford struts over at that moment, saving me from further interrogation. Both hands are full of plates piled high with food. He passes me one with a wink, but my appetite has been replaced with too many thoughts. His gaze moves to his mother and presses a loud smooch on her cheek. "Hi, Ma."

Kellie titters under his open display of affection. She pats his scruffy jaw in return. "Such a good boy. I was just talking to your lovely girlfriend about babies. Your future ones, to be specific."

A blush stains the tan skin of his throat. "Jeez, mom. Thanks for putting on the pressure. All in good time. Right, babe?"

I lock my wide eyes on his. We just discussed our imaginary wedding. There's more to that fantasy, apparently. "You want kids?"

"Yeah, of course. All part of my grand plan, if you're willing. Plus, Millie would be a great big sister." His beaming smile is my undoing. I'll agree to anything if he keeps looking at me like I hung the moon and stars just for him.

His mother wags her brows at me while edging out of our circle. "Well, I'm sure this gives you two a lot to consider. I'll leave you alone to discuss."

I lift a single brow at my boyfriend, who's intending on being my husband and baby daddy. Soon. "Not sure what to say after all that. You're a bit of a surprise, Ford."

He winks, the expression a newfound favorite. A tiny thrill zips through me with each one. "I prefer hopelessly optimistic. It's my new outlook."

I gaze up at him, lost in the possibilities of our love. "I'm beginning to believe we're living out our very own happily ever after."

Crawford seals my vow between us with a kiss. "And that's how we will always stay."

EPILOGUE

Crawford

Healing Hug #33: The one meant to carry on through it all.

SWEAT COATS MY PALMS AGAINST THE STEERING WHEEL, AND I almost swerve from the slippery grip. My nerves bathe the air with a pungent tang that anyone with a nose can scent. If that isn't suspicious, I don't know what is. I try to be discreet while wiping the dewy evidence away. Crashing Keegan's new ride will not bode well for me.

There's no squeak of outrage from my right so I'm probably in the clear. For now. This is probably a stupid plan that I'll pay for later. But those consequences could really end up being rewards if I play my ace in the hole right. The rapid beat pounding against my ribs is a warning I should listen to.

This doesn't need to be rushed. I can wait longer. Hell, maybe I should. Keegan probably won't take too kindly to this idea. But the grand finale should be enough to smooth things over. I allow a smirk to tilt my lips at the mere idea of her reaction. One glance at her sitting so prim and proper in the passenger seat cements the decision into my gut.

The timing is ideal, and all the details are settled. I've enlisted the assistance of a certain almost eight-year-old. Speaking of, Millie is practically vibrating in the backseat. There's no telling how long before she bursts. This morning, she assured me the secret is still safe. Only one way to find out.

We're halfway home, cruising along a very familiar stretch of interstate. I pull over onto the shoulder at the precise location, kicking up dust and killing the engine. Once the cloud of chalky gravel clears, I get a good look at our surroundings. Just right.

Keegan turns in her seat to face me. "Why did you stop?"

"Recognize this spot?" I lift a brow, the pressure on my chest settling deeper. Her memory is an important factor at this moment. To any bystander, this strip of highway is nothing more than a basic road splitting the rolling prairie in half. Wyoming wilderness at its finest.

A smile spreads across her lips. "How could I ever forget the place where we met?"

"That's what I want to hear." I lean across the console, threading our fingers together. "What else?"

With a nibble to her bottom lip, she humors my request. "My knight in chrome armor rescued me with his impressive tire-changing skills."

A groan rises off my chest. "Yeah, Kee. And do you know what today is?"

Her patience with me wanes with a thick huff. "Um, Tuesday?"

"Exactly four months later." I nuzzle her nose with mine. "I figure what better way to celebrate than having a re-do."

"You've lost me." She drops a peck on my lips before pulling back.

"I'm gonna teach you how to change a tire."

"But it isn't flat."

"Doesn't have to be for practice." I glide a palm up her silky thigh. The smooth skin is bare and mine for endless enjoyment. *Thank you, late summer.*

Keegan flicks her gaze outside. "Can't we do this in the garage?"

"Then we lose the sentimental value. Where's the fun in that?"

Her narrowed eyes swing back to mine. "Your idea of a good time is concerning."

"Not what you said last night." I let my eyebrows wag.

Keegan shoots a look toward Millie, who hasn't released so much as a peep. "Seriously, Ford?"

I grip her knee, stroking more satin temptation. "Some habits are much harder to break than others."

"For the sake of my daughter's innocent mind, please put more effort in being clean."

I lean forward until only an inch separates our lips. "But I like getting you—"

She presses a finger over my mouth. "No."

I nip at her and she pulls away. "You didn't even know what I was gonna say."

"It wasn't anything appropriate, I'm sure."

I squint out the windshield, trying to come up with an alternative to prove her wrong. My mind is too busy doing a backstroke in the gutter. "Yeah, you're right."

Keegan is quiet for a moment, and I wonder if her thoughts are swimming in the filthy depths with mine. "Are you really going to make me change a tire?"

"It's a vital skill to learn."

"Don't you like coming to my rescue?" She bats her long eyelashes at me.

"I love being your hero, Kee. But this is important to me."

I give her a responsible-male-adult look. "Millie and I will be your assistants." I pop open my door and motion for the little girl to exit on the passenger side. "I'll grab the tools."

With a languid stretch, Keegan unfolds from the confining front seat. "Okay, fine. I'm doing this in the name of independent women."

"That's the spirit." I jam wheel wedges under the rear tires.

Both girls stand close to watch. Millie squats and points at the orange block. "What're those for?"

"They stop the car from rolling backward. Right, Kee?" I feel the corners of my eyes crinkle with a smile aimed at her.

She nods while waving a hand at me. "Yeah, of course."

I get the front set locked in and beckon her forward. "We'll use the right side since it's not facing the road. Safety first."

"This also happens to be the one that blew on my old car," Keegan points out.

I snap my fingers. "See? You're buying into this."

She flattens her lips. "Something like that."

I don't allow her less-than-enthusiastic attitude to dissuade me. "Use this wrench to loosen the lug nuts."

"Um, okay." Keegan crouches beside me and grabs the tool.

I let her huff and struggle for all of ten seconds before stepping in. While covering her hand with mine, I guide our movements until the first bolt drops to the gravel. We repeat the motions for the remaining four and opportunity begins knocking. Booming crashes in my ears as I release my hold on her.

"Can you get the jack?" I nod toward the collapsed metal a few feet to her left.

Keegan stands and brushes off her palms. With a slight breeze, the skirt of her dress billows like a signaling flag. The current position we're in makes this the optimal proposal setup. Do I dare? She's my girlfriend, and we're committed, but the need to get my ring on her finger is bordering on desperate. Call me barbaric or possessive—I'll be quick to agree with you.

Similar to twenty minutes ago, resolve settles deep into my bones. This is the moment. I'm already conveniently down on one knee, crouching in front of her. The velvet box is ready to burn a hole in my pocket. That small square might as well weigh a ton as I dig it out. Keegan catches sight of the baby blue object, her gasp zinging between us.

"Oh my gosh. What're you doing?" She slaps a palm over her gaping mouth.

I ignore the rhetorical question, reaching for her left hand. "You mean everything to me, Kee."

That's all I manage to spit out before she's blubbering, fat tears rolling down her cheeks. I squeeze her fingers, pressing gentle kisses to each one. "I love you so much, babe. Between fighting against you and myself, I fell so damn fast and hard. And I wouldn't take a moment back, because it led me here, to this moment with you and Millie."

Her muffled sob breaks apart my words. She's trembling in my grip and appears to be barely hanging on. I gulp at the tightness in my throat, pushing forward through the strain. "Because of you, I'm no longer alone. You fill my days with vibrant laughter and happiness that can never be replaced. It would be my greatest honor to spend forever by your side. I can only hope you'll grant me the privilege of walking this life with me." I snap open the lid, showing off the solitaire diamond encrusted with emeralds. "Will you marry me, Keegan Quinn Daniels?"

She's nodding so fast her face is a blur. "Yes! Yes, yes, yes."

I slide the diamond on her finger and stand, wrapping us in a tight embrace. This is the first hug of our new beginning, the life we'll cherish together. I crash my lips against hers to cement our words with an unbreakable unity.

After thoroughly kissing my fiancée and wiping away her tears, I turn to Millie. The little girl is beaming at us, tiny palms clasped against her chest. She's been included in most of my plans, except for this. I reach for her left hand and return the smile she's directing at me.

With a slow exhale, I dig in my other pocket to retrieve the small box reserved for her. Millie's mouth drops open when she notices the bright pink bow. "This isn't just about your mama, right?"

She blinks at me, moisture shining in her green eyes. "I dunno."

"I'm not just asking to spend my life with her, Peep. You need to agree, too."

"Really?"

"Yep, sure do. Amelia Marie, you're my little warrior, standing up for me when I wasn't strong enough to do the same. Because of you, I've found understanding and compassion. You're incredibly precious and important to me. None of this," I gesture between the three of us, "would be possible without you. So, I have a question to ask."

"Okay, I'm ready." Her voice is barely more than a squeak.

"Will you allow me to stick around permanently? Agree to be my little girl?"

"Like you'll be my dad?"

My heart has never pounded so hard. Any moment, I expect the organ to fly out of my chest. "If that's okay with you and your mama."

She doesn't hesitate, launching into my arms. "Yes! I accept."

"This is for you, Peep." I hand her the gift with a shaking palm.

With wide eyes, Millie rips open the wrapping. A gasp tumbles from her as she stares at what's waiting inside. Her tiny fingers remove the silver bracelet, holding it up so the diamond ring charm sparkles in the sun. "I love my bling. It's so pretty."

I open the clasp and motion to her wrist. "May I?"

"Uh-huh." She thrusts her arm at me while wearing the biggest smile known to little girls.

Keegan is releasing a fresh round of tears when she joins our huddle. She presses her wet cheek against mine. "Was this your plan all along, Prince Charming?"

I kiss the corner of her lips. "Are you impressed?"

"Very. You never cease to amaze me, Ford."

"And you just agreed to forever. Here's hoping I continue to deliver."

Her lips brush along my jaw. "Without a doubt."

That's the end for *Loner*, but I wrote a short story for Josey. Will she get her dream happily ever after? Download *Charmer* for FREE here! (https://dl.bookfunnel.com/4v2eg8xpkm)

WHAT TO READ NEXT

**Did you know Decker and Delaney have a story?
They're from my standalone romance, *Keeper*. Read
this excerpt for more of them!**

MY NEWFOUND FOCUS WAVERS WHEN TWO NURSES RUSH BY ME and turn down another hallway. The burst of activity is familiar in an almost comforting way. But the racking sobs following close behind is a bucket of ice water.

Almost on autopilot, my body pivots toward the weeping sounds. This isn't my mother's room. I shouldn't be stopping. A doctor, or hefty medication, will soothe this audible pain soon enough. Just as I'm about to move along, another gut-wrenching whimper cracks through the air. But the tone is feminine and delicate, and I'm drawn closer on instinct alone.

The door is open, but that doesn't mean I'm free to enter. A woman is practically folded in half on the bed. Her small frame trembles with a fresh cry of grief. The halo of red hair surrounding her is a fire I can't ignore. Call me a damn moth, but suddenly I'm a single step from crossing the threshold. I falter when I realize where I am. *What the hell am I doing?*

The sole of my boot catches on the linoleum and releases a loud squeak. I cringe and freeze in place. The woman snaps upright and faces me. Everything around us tunnels until she's all that remains. *No fucking way.*

An eerie tremor ripples down my limbs, and I almost drop the bouquet. I blink, rubbing my eyes for good measure. She's still sitting there.

Hot damn. Delaney Wallace is back in Silo Springs. The years have been very good to her. Most of her body is hidden underneath a hospital gown, but that's not what I'm gawking at. A silky cascade of red waves frame her porcelain face. There's a small smattering of freckles dotting her button nose. Pink splotches decorate her skin, revealing a roadmap of misery, but rather than grief-stricken, Delaney appears cleansed. I've heard a good cry can be cathartic.

Mile-long lashes flutter at me, concealing those stunning baby blues from view. Delaney was the beauty queen without a crown, the girl with brains to spare. Varsity athlete. Way out of my league. That didn't stop me from lusting after her. I was a cocky little shit, but she never fell for my crap. Like I said, smart girl.

But now? She's staring at me with zero recognition. This girl from my not-that-distant past eyes me with the scrutiny of a detective. The expression on her face makes me believe she's actually peering through me. Doesn't she recognize me? It hasn't been that long. I lift a hand to the thick beard covering my jaw. The facial hair is new since high school. It's possible she doesn't know who I am.

Our silent stare down continues. Maybe I look like a different guy. I'm the one to break, cracking under the intensity of her piercing gaze. "Dell?"

Her forehead dents with a deep furrow. I can almost hear the cogs in her mind working overtime. After a few tense moments, she appears to shake herself out of the stupor. Her gaze slides down my body with a slow assessment before lifting to retrace the same path.

I clear the gravel from my throat and try again. "Do you remember me, Dell?"

Those bottomless baby blues brighten when catching sight of the flowers in my shaky grip. "Are you my husband?"

Pressure squeezes my lungs and a strangled wheeze escapes me. "W–what? No! No, no, no."

The fuck? Husband? We never went on a single date. I take stock of her state again. What are they pumping into her veins? Other than the confusion clouding her gaze and some fading bruises, Delaney appears right as rain. But for her to assume I'm her significant other is absurd. I'm definitely not the marrying type, even to this stunner. She should recall that well enough. On the other hand, it doesn't seem as though she remembers anything about me.

I wipe the shock off my face. Where's a reset button when I need one? I flash her the panty-melting smirk that keeps my pockets padded at Howlers. The rundown bar isn't known for attracting ladies, but we do all right. "No, Dell. We went to high school together. That's all."

Her features collapse lower. "Oh. I didn't know that."

Is she for real? Damn. My ego staggers back with the hit. "Well, it's been close to five years. People change." I scrub the back of my neck.

"The doctors say my name is Delaney. Why are you calling me Dell?"

I squint at her, brushing away the dust collecting in my memories. Another reminder of how long it's been since we've seen each other rattles through me. "It was a nickname in school. Not many used it. Just the kids who knew you best."

Her expression crumples. "Oh. That makes sense. I'm sorry, I probably sound stupid. I, um, have amnesia."

Are you curious about Sutton and Grady?
They're from my standalone romance, *Breaker.* Enjoy this
excerpt from the prologue!

"I WANT YOU TO TAKE MY VIRGINITY."

Grady is silent for a few beats. I peel my lids
open, watching the stacks of muscle in his shoulders
flex with harsh breaths. The knot in my chest pulls tighter.
My offering dangles in the few feet separating us. He just
needs to reach out and grab me. But his lips pull into a sneer.

"Are you fucking joking?"

I cringe at his foul language. Grady's tongue has always
been sharp. Even more so lately, especially with me. "No," I
whisper. "I'm very serious."

"Go home, Sutt. We're not discussing this."

"Why?"

A tic of strain pops in his jaw. "Because I say so."

"Doesn't it matter what I want?"

"Has it ever?"

The answer is no. A loud, resounding boom meant to deter. But I don't hear it. I've been waiting all of my teenage
years for this moment. I'm not letting it slip away.

"Just once. No one has to know."

His eyes flash with a streak of lightning. "How fucking
nice. I can be your shameful secret. No fucking thanks. Find
someone else to slum it with."

I almost smack my forehead. How could I be so dense?
"That's not what I meant, Gray." This is not going according
to plan. I lick my lips and search for a different route. "I want
you, and always have. I've saved myself for *you.* My first time
is meant to be with *you.*"

Grady flops onto his bed with a groan. "People accuse
me of doing a lot of bad shit, but I've never been a thief. I'm
not stealing your fucking cherry, Sutton."

I'm shaking my head before he's done talking. Heat

crawls up my chest and neck, but I'm already buried too far. "But I want to do this with you. It has to be you."

He scrubs a palm over his face. "Don't do this desperate act. Give yourself to a man who's deserving."

"I'm looking at him." This wall between us needs to crumble. I step out of my soggy flip-flops and instantly feel more at home. If I reach forward, my hand will skim his blankets. It's been years since I've felt the comfort—albeit platonic—of his arms. I curl my toes into the carpet at being this close again.

Grady glares at the ceiling. "Seriously. I shouldn't have to repeat myself, but I will. Go home, Sutt."

"Please, Gray." The two words trickle off my trembling lips.

His scoff echoes around the dark room. "Begging is far beneath you, Sutt. Keep that silver spoon in your mouth."

That has me clacking my teeth together. "Don't be an asshole."

"Then don't force my hand. Go back to your side of the fence. You don't belong in these bunks."

Something dark flips inside of me. "This is my property. I have every right to be here."

He grunts into a clenched fist. "Don't need another reminder of who reigns."

The strength that brought me here is beginning to crack under his pressure. But a lingering spark ignites when I catch him staring at me. Grady rarely looks my way for longer than a casual glance. But the privacy of his bedroom is proving to make a difference. He doesn't conceal the way his eyes skitter across my exposed skin. There's unmasked hunger waiting for me there. That gives me a much-needed confidence boost.

It's not an accident that I'm wearing a daringly low-cut shirt. The hem of my skirt is a few inches too short. Am I acting desperate like he claims? No doubt. Do I care about being the one pursuing this? Not in the slightest. Am I worried about being rejected? More than I care to admit. But that fear doesn't hinder me.

"Did you know that I'm leaving tomorrow?" I catch a brief glimmer of shock register across Grady's features. A twitch snags his eyebrow. His throat bobs with a heavy swallow. He rolls his gaze off mine, avoiding the truth. If I hadn't been standing so close, watching his every move, the reaction would be missed.

"And your point?" It appears he's choosing to address the wall.

"I'll be gone. We won't see each other anymore." I hold my breath while waiting for more honesty to show.

Grady's lips tighten. "So, you came for a farewell fuck?"

I wrinkle my nose. "Must you be so crass?"

"Don't act like this is a new development." His tone is flat and stiff.

I rub my temples. I'm beginning to see the massive error in my ways. But my heart is stubborn. "I always wanted things to be different between us."

"Sorry to disappoint." His tone reveals he's anything but.

I'm already waist-deep. Why not wade a bit further? "It's not too late, Gray. I'm here now. This is what I've been waiting for."

"Wait longer. You're still a fucking kid, Sutt."

"I'm eighteen. Only two years younger than you."

He waves off my words. "Age is just a number. You're sheltered as fuck. Get out and experience the world before shackling yourself to the gutter. Get outta here before Jace finds you missing."

Rather than retreat, I erase the remaining distance to his bed. "I don't care about my brother."

Grady's snort resembles a bull. "I sure as shit do."

Of course he does. They might as well be related by blood, not just sentiment. Defeat appears in two large boulders weighing my shoulders down. He won't budge, no matter how hard I push. A seed of nostalgia plants itself in my mind. I find myself changing tactics as a last-ditch effort. "Tell me a happy something, Gray."

His chuckle is empty. "Nah, we're too old for that shit. But nice try. Don't have any spare joy to share."

I blink at the unshed tears slowly building momentum. I want to scream at him. Demand that he forgets the pain and anger for one second to see what's standing right in front of him. But I force the fire down. "Want me to tell you one?"

"Won't change my mind."

I glance away to hide my wobbling lip and wet lashes. "Will you at least hold me for a bit? Like you used to during storms?"

"Sutt—"

"Please, Grady. I never ask for anything from you." I scoot forward until my legs bump the mattress.

With a resigned sigh, he opens his arms. "All right, fine. Five minutes, then you're going home. C'mere."

I nod and quickly cuddle into his side. He smells of a hardworking man, that familiar mix of motor oil and fresh hay. I snuggle deeper while inhaling the scent of my dreams. "Remember the first happy something I gave you?"

Grady nods, his chin ghosting across my forehead. He doesn't protest while I tug us along some pleasant highlights. I fill the chilly silence with sunny chatter. Grady doesn't add to the conversation, keeping it one-sided. It's probably for the best. Nothing he shares lately is good.

My five minutes loop several times before I run out of steam. We're stuck at a fork in the road. Sad as it might be, I find myself turning in the direction that leads away from him. "I'll miss you, Gray."

A rumble rises off his chest. "Yeah? Try forgetting me while you're at it. You'll be better off."

I don't bother responding. With that final blow, a gate

slams shut between us. The clang ripples through me, solidifying what I've been trying to deny. This is the end of us. But this has always been the story of a girl desperately in love with a boy. Irrevocably and unrequited.

I'm ready to leave these well-worn pages behind.

MORE TITLES FROM HARLOE RAE

Ask Me Why

One deep breath. Two slow blinks. Three hollow beats.
I'm still here.
After three years, that reminder isn't as necessary. But everyone has their bad days. This is definitely one of them. Until an adorable little boy dashes into my store. His zest for life makes me smile in a way that's been long lost. Then I meet his father.
Well, confront is more like it.

Brance Stone is volatile.
Offensive.
Harsh.
And can't be bothered to care.
Not that I want him to. I get frostbite just looking into Brance's glacial stare. But there's something undeniable about him.

My misery suddenly craves company. The suffocating numbness lifts whenever Brance is near. That alone should have me running in the opposite direction. Try as I might, there's no avoiding him. If only I could understand why. As if he'd let me.

I don't ask. He doesn't tell. A silent, bitter truce settles between us.
That was our first mistake.
It's certainly not the last.

GENT: **An enemies to lovers standalone**

Raven Elliot blasts into town like a wrecking ball—striking
and devastating.
With a few simple words, my reliable routine crumbles to
dust.

"Is this seat taken?"

I could close my eyes and let her voice wrap around me like
a lover's caress.
But this isn't that type of story.
And I'm sure as hell not that kind of man.

She hovers in my space, batting her lashes and smiling shyly.
The glimmer in her sapphire eyes is a promise of peace.
But I'm not falling for it.
And Raven doesn't take the hint.

What starts as a battle of wills, explodes into a turf war.
She stands directly in my path everywhere I turn.
No matter how hard I shove, she won't budge.
Raven seems dead set on driving me insane.
But I was here first.
And I'm not going down easy.

After all, no one ever taught me how to treat a lady.

LASS: A friends to lovers standalone

She's the one I've been saving myself for.

Addison Walker is every fantasy I never dared to believe in.
Moving to this town was already monumental.
Finding her removes any lingering doubt.
She's bold and vibrant.
Beautiful and confident.
Far too good for the likes of me.
Luckily, I'm not good at avoiding temptation.
But is she?

My desire is growing beyond control.
I'm done watching on the sidelines.
When opportunity strikes, I eagerly take advantage.
Signing on the dotted line before thinking twice.
The repercussions cross my mind far too late.
When she swiftly sticks me in the friend-zone, there's not a damn thing I can do about it.

Addison is just down the hall—might as well be miles away.
Every lingering glance drives me to the edge of sanity.
She speaks to my deepest cravings like a siren.
Our chemistry blurs every line.
This battle seems impossible to win.
Yet my determination doesn't wane.
It only takes one night to change everything.

After all, I didn't wait all this time to settle for less.

MISS: A second chance standalone romance

The boy she loved is gone. The man I've become doesn't deserve her.

Delilah Sage was the first girl I loved, my first for many things, but that's only the beginning. She was a warm embrace after especially hard nights, offering comfort where there was only pain. Delilah kept me from sinking and I promised her forever. I should have known better.

I ruined the only good in my life. Now all I have is regret, constant and relentless. My need for Delilah hasn't faded after all these years. She's the only woman who understood me. There's no moving on from that. I've accepted my fate of being alone. This is what I deserve.

Until I'm handed a second chance—whether I want it or not. A job brings me back to the small town I swore would stay in my past. The memories and mistakes are waiting to greet me. I try to keep my distance, but Delilah has always been my weakness. One look won't hurt. How quickly I forget she's impossible to resist.

After all, letting her go was never my intention.

Redefining Us

A standalone friends to lovers, military romance.

In order to truly save him, I need to redefine us.

Xander Dixon was my best friend.
Loyal and dependable.
A brave warrior.
A permanent presence in my life until that fateful day he
boarded a plane headed overseas.

Xander's unwelcome silence haunted me for three years…
Until he suddenly resurfaces.
Blinded by misplaced fury.
Trapped in a pool of darkness.
Unable to escape the perpetual pain.

Though it would be easy to walk away, I refuse to give up on
him.
I want to know his misery and torment, so I can rescue him.
Then Xander will finally be mine.

Forget You Not

A standalone sweet second chance, military romance.

I didn't believe in love at first sight until Lark stood before
me.

Pretty sure I would have married her on the spot.
Too bad fate had other plans.
Duty called and I had to answer—no matter the
consequences.
There wasn't a chance for goodbye, but I'd never forget her.

Time has a way of creating change—but only on the surface.
Even after all these years, I know Lark is mine.
I belong to her just the same.
The moment I see her again, it's a done deal.
All I've got to do is convince her this is forever.
She can push but I'll only pull harder.

I'm not letting our second chance slip away.

Watch Me Follow

A stalker, double virgin romance.

Creep. Freak. Crazy Eyes.
I've heard it all.
Over the years, they've slammed me with every demeaning
name in the book.
Their taunts warped me like a steady stream of poison.
Anger replaced anxiety as I started believing the cruelty spat
my way.
Until she showed up and changed everything.

Lennon Bennett is pure innocence—warm sunshine
breaking apart my stormy existence.
She's everything good and maybe I can be too.
For her. With her. Because of her.
Lennon doesn't know I'm beckoned closer with each breath.
She isn't aware that I'm completely consumed with her.
It's become my sole purpose to protect her, by any means
necessary.
But if she discovers the depth of my obsession, it will be the
end of me.
So, I remain in the shadows,
Waiting. Watching. Wanting.
She'll be my first. My last. My only.

ACKNOWLEDGEMENTS

If you've made it to this point, hopefully there's a smile on your face. I loved writing Crawford, Keegan, and little Millie. Thank you so much for taking the time to read their story. Did you know that Loner is my tenth published novel? That still takes a moment to sink in. This journey over the years has been nothing short of incredible and I'm eternally gratefully to each one of you for taking the ride with me.

First, I'd like to send you all a virtual hug full of warmth and hope. These last few months haven't been easy. I'm very happy you're out there and persevering. The fact you picked up Loner during these challenging days means more than I can ever shout from the rooftops. You're incredible. Thank you, thank you.

I have to give endless credit to my husband for his patience and kindness. When I'm deep in the cave or lost in my thoughts, he picks up all the slack for me. Not only is he the greatest husband, but also an exceptional father. I couldn't do this without him.

If it wasn't for Renee and Jacquelyn, I'd be wandering around without a clue what day it was. These ladies keep me motivated and moving when I'd rather be napping. They also keep my life on track when I tend to forget the details. Thank you both so very much for making the days brighter for me.

I am incredibly fortunate and eternally grateful to have Talia constantly by my side. We've been making beautiful magic together since this author life started for me. I can't imagine spending endless hours working with anyone else. Her talent is bottomless. So much love to you, friend!

Heather and K.k. are my beeches from another mister. These two are ridiculously impressive authors and always winning at life. I'll take you two to the trash room any day of the week. Hopefully there's a beach nearby that will lead us to Jamaica for another baptism. Just let me know where and when. I'll bring the fruity shandy and floaties.

Kate might pretend to be salty, but she's honestly one of the sweetest ladies I know. She spins circles around me on the daily. How she gets so much done with a full house is beyond me. Thank you for always being there for me when I need to whine or complain or just send a random GIF. You're not only a very talented author, but your graphics make me so very happy. All the hugs to you!

Parker, Ava, and Leigh are a trio of awesomeness that I probably rely on too much. These ladies are truly incredible. Not only are they crazy talented and skilled in many avenues, but also have genuine and kind hearts. Thank you for always having my back, and front. So much love to you!

It's because of people like Keri and Katherine that the book community is such a positive space. These two are so encouraging and sweet and supportive. I'm very fortunate to have them in my life as friends. Let's hope we'll be together again next year!

I need to give Ace a massive shoutout for being totally kickass. Not only is she an amazing friend, but she was vital in helping me make Loner even better. We'll share a Sipping Pretty one day soon!

A big thank you to Lauren for always stepping up to assist me with the multitude of tasks I pile on her lap. Partying with you is always wild. Hopefully we'll be belly up at the bar together this time next year.

I'm so thankful for Tijuana and MPP. You two are such bright spots in this community. My gratitude will never spread far enough so hopefully endless hugs will do. I'm lucky to call you both friends.

Anne, Nicole, Tia, Ella, Suzie, Michelle, Jane, Meghan, and many more—thank you for the endless support each of you give me. You're inspiring and encouraging and simply wonderful. I've lost count of all the ways you guys lift me up and push me forward. I couldn't survive the grind without your doses of sweetness. Thank you, thank you!

For my Hotties, you're the bestest bunch of beautiful support an author could ask for. I'm so thankful each day that I have such a positive group to hang out in. Your cheering and encouragement is priceless. Thank you for always being there.

Harloe's Review Crew is full of the greatest readers I could ever ask for. The excitement you give me means everything. Thank you for wanting to continue reading my books. I'll keep writing so long as you want to be on the receiving end.

Candi and Candi Kane PR are the best in the publicist business. This team of professionals works tirelessly to provide the best possible services for their authors. I'm lucky to be one of them! You're such an incredible lady boss and I love you. Thank you so very much for all you do!

Thank you to all the ladies of Give Me Books. I've been working with you guys for almost three years and you always provide amazing release services. Thank you, thank you, thank you!

Book Cover Kingdom gets another shoutout for the GORGEOUS Loner cover. As always, you never cease to amaze me.

Thanks to Rafa G Catala, the very talented photographer who shot the very scrumptious image of Christian. Thank you for giving me the perfect cover photo for this story.

A huge thank you to Kiezha with Librum Artis Editorial Services for editing Loner until the pages were polished. You're amazing at what you do and I'm thankful to have you in my corner!

Stacey from Champagne Book Design once again created the most gorgeous interior for my book baby. I cannot recommend her formatting services enough!

One last thing? If you enjoyed Loner and want to do me a huge favor, please consider leaving a review. It really helps other readers find my books. Thank you for reading!

ABOUT THE AUTHOR

Harloe Rae is a *USA Today* & Amazon Top 10 best-selling author. Her passion for writing and reading has taken on a whole new meaning. Each day is an unforgettable adventure.

Harloe is a Minnesota gal with a serious addiction to romance. She's always chasing an epic happily ever after. When she's not buried in the writing cave, Harloe can be found hanging with her hubby and son. If the weather permits, she loves being lakeside or out in the country with her horses.

Harloe is the author of the Reclusive series, Watch Me Follow, and #BitterSweetHeat series, *Ask Me Why*, *Breaker*, *Keeper,* and *Loner*. These titles are available on Amazon.

Find all the latest on her site www.harloe-rae.blog

Subscribe to her newsletter at bit.ly/HarloesList

Join her reader group, Harloe's Hotties, at www.facebook.com/harloehotties

Follow her on:

BookBub: bit.ly/HarloeBB

Amazon: bit.ly/HarloeOnAmazon

Goodreads: bit.ly/HarloeOnGR

Facebook Page: Facebook.com/authorharloerae

Instagram: www.instagram.com/harloerae

Book & Main: bookandmainbites.com/harloerae